The
Wishing
Tree

The Wishing Tree

Sandra Paretti

translated from the German by
Ruth Hein

St. Martin's Press
New York

Library of Congress Catalog Number 76-62786
Manufactured in the United States of America
Designed by Riva Danzig

Library of Congress Cataloging in Publication Data

Paretti, Sandra.
    The wishing tree.

    Translation of Der Wunschbaum.
    I. Title.
PZ4.P2315Wi3   [PT2676.A67]   833'.9'14   76-62786
ISBN 0-312-88418-4

The
Wishing
Tree

One

1

It was still very early, and she wondered how it could be so light. There was a faint glow behind the yellow cretonne curtains, not vivid enough to suffuse the room but nevertheless too bright for this hour of the morning, for it was winter and not yet six o'clock.

Her room faced east; it was what she had asked for. Early morning was her special time of day—the brief span when the world awoke from sleep, when everything was created anew. She always spent this time out of doors, winter and summer, in the spacious grounds surrounding the house. No one heard her leave, no one saw her return; but some of the glow of dawn clung to her and radiated from her. Why don't I get up? she wondered. What am I afraid of? Could it be that I'm not really here anymore, in my room? Had she already been cast out?

Which wall held the portrait of her grandmother, the one with the straw hat, the one where the resemblance between them was so striking? What corner harbored the desk where yesterday she had made so many attempts to write a letter, finishing none of them? Where was the dress she was to wear that night? The room gave up none of its secrets; impenetrable twilight enfolded her, pressed on her like a nightmare, hampered her breathing. She forced herself to raise her head, feeling the weight of the long, dark hair which she normally wore in two thick braids while she slept. She began to

3

loosen the plaits, but she still lacked the energy to get out of bed; it was almost like the terrible dream she had had in the night.

She did not often recall dreams on waking, and even more rarely did she lie awake during the night. She enjoyed the sound sleep of any seventeen-year-old. Last night she had gone to bed early and fallen asleep at once, anxious to be fresh for this day, the last one of the year 1900, that was to be so important in her life. When it came right down to it, everything was already settled; she had promised her father. There was no going back, and no savior would rush in at the last moment. She would see the day through, and if she felt like crying, she would know how to hide her tears from the others.

Again her thoughs returned to her dream. Without warning, her bedroom door had opened. Rothe had entered, had approached her bed—boldly, as if he already had that right—had leaned over her and reached out for her. His hand had been so close that she could see the black hair growing up to the second joint of his fingers. . . . She had started up in terror, and even the memory constricted her throat.

For the rest of the night she had heard the clocks strike every hour. The church bells in Steglitz, the clocks in the house—the grandfather clock in the hall, the decorated clock in the library, with its peculiarly light, carrying tone. Sounds had crept from the most remote corners of the house to invade her room. All at once the thick brick walls seemed porous; heating ducts, water pipes, and fireplace flues sent their messages. Shortly before midnight a carriage drove up to the front entrance—the doctor her mother had called. At three her father had come home. The lateness of the hour told her that he had spent the night at the card tables. As always when it was so late, he used the back drive to the stables, and as always he did not go to bed at once but spent some time in his den, using a fresh deck of cards to replay the more interesting hands, especially the ones he had lost. She had thought about going to him in the middle of the night and telling him that she must take back her promise, regardless of the consequences. But in fact she could not be indifferent to the consequences, most of all the loss of this house. And besides—how could she refuse her father anything face to face when she had not even been able to write out her denial. . . ?

Slowly dawn began to overtake the darkness. The first outlines her eyes could discern were those of the dress, hanging against the armoire placed across from her bed. It had taken two maids to carry it

4

up from the pressing room, to make certain that the fragile silk would not be crushed. Tonight, at the New Year's Eve party, she would appear in it before her family and the assembled guests. How was she to endure the long hours until midnight, until Papa tapped his knife against his glass, raised a toast to the new year, and ended by announcing the engagement of his youngest daughter, Camilla, to Alexander Rothe? Were all of them really as unsuspecting as Papa claimed? Even Keith? She could only hope that at this very moment he was already outside in the gardens, making the final arrangements for the fireworks.

What a wonderful day December 31, 1900, might have been! What a good end the old year might have made, and what a good beginning for the new one. Even when she bought the material for the ball-gown, how happy and carefree she had been! Nine yards of the finest silk, nine yards of spun gold—but now, in the dawn light, the color was a pale, spectral gray.

She had chosen the fabric with her father, in Paris, as a reward for her work during the Exposition, where the Hofmann Company had had a stand in the pavilion of German perfume manufacturers. Now she wondered if even then Papa had had his reasons. After all, it could hardly be that from one day to the next the money had run out and the situation had become so critical that Papa—of all people —could see only one way out: giving her in marriage to Alexander Rothe, in exchange for a capital investment in the business.

Alexander Rothe. If she at least understood why Rothe had taken a fancy to her. She tried to recall their few meetings: some general remarks about the play in a theater lobby; meaningless banter at the charity bazaar, where she had helped out in the "Soul Store," one of the most popular booths, which made a fantastic amount of money with its Lovesickness Serum and Anti-Jealousine; and a single dance at a carnival ball. No personal word had ever been spoken between Rothe and herself; never had he sent her a note or made any attempt to arrange a tryst. She had never given him a thought except that even in their brief meetings his peculiar hair tonic had struck her as unpleasant. His way of breathing noisily through parted lips was still more disagreeable. Even these traits she recollected only after her father had revealed to her that Alexander Rothe had asked for her hand in marriage.

Her first reaction had been amusement at the situation—her father

5

as marriage broker, playing the role that was surely tailor-made for Mama but never for him. But gradually he had admitted the true state of affairs—not directly, of course, for that was not his way. It would have been easy to believe that it was not he who was strapped but some other person, as if he were viewing the imminent disaster with the curiosity of an uninvolved bystander, unable to suppress a certain amount of glee at someone else's misfortune. Finally, he had explained this much: he was up to his ears in debt, and only an alliance between her and Rothe could save him. . . .

The day of their discussion, three weeks ago, everything still seemed far in the future. Besides, Camilla had grown up with three sisters, each of whom had married the man Mama and Papa had chosen for her. During the last seven years some alliance had always been in the works; since her daughters had reached marriageable age, Mama had made it her life's work to find husbands for them. She had scouted everywhere for good prospects, had sent out feelers, indefatigable and with a cunning worthy of a criminal. The daughters had never challenged their mother's authority in these matters. A veto from her was enough to nip a romantic inclination in the bud, and when at last she had made her choice, everything else was a formality. Oddly enough, when it came to Camilla, her youngest daughter, Mama had taken no steps, and looking back, Camilla concluded that Mama too had long since seen financial ruin approaching and had known that the dowry of a hundred thousand marks—an absolute requirement for any match she considered suitable—was no longer available.

What a comedy had been played out before Maxi, Alice, and Lou were safely ensconced in the harbor of matrimony. Camilla had found the spectacle entertaining, but most of all she thought it natural that where marriage was concerned, love was hardly the thing that mattered; the prospective husband's name, his social position, and his property were factors of much greater significance. A marriage without love—perhaps that was quite normal, perhaps there was nothing terrible about it, at least not as terrible as she imagined. . . .

The light behind the curtains grew brighter and brighter. Gradually the room took on shape. The delicate green stripes of the wallpaper became discernible, as did the outlines of the walnut furniture and the pattern of the Smyrna carpet, the last and most handsome rug Grandmama had knotted. Nevertheless the light remained odd, and the sounds coming from the garden had a different ring. Hampered by her long nightgown, Camilla ran barefoot to the window. As she pulled aside the curtain, she discovered a perfectly natural explanation for the unusual brightness that had bothered her so much. Snow had fallen in the night, not just a thin layer that would not last the day, but masses and mountains of snow, with the sky holding still more in readiness. Yes, the sky itself seemed to have disappeared, leaving only a boundless white waste, lightly sketched with lines where paths had once been and hummocky with tiny hills that might be bushes. Only the tree at the center of the broad clearing stood as it always had, the thick black trunk surmounted by the powerful dome of the crown.

True, it was too late now for her to have the park to herself; already a path had been shoveled clear to the gardener's cottage and a second one to the hothouses that would furnish the palms, the laurels, and the many bouquets of flowers for tonight's party. The path to the servants' entrance was also partially shoveled; she could not see anyone, but when she opened the window, she could hear the shovel scraping against the walk and the dull thud as each load fell on the full wheelbarrow. The sounds told her that the snow was firm and would not melt too soon.

She had wished for snow, in spite of the predictions of the gardener and of Aunt Lenka, who had sworn that there would be no more snow in the old year—and she should know, coming from Russia as she did. She had been right after all, and now Keith, who had never seen snow in his life, would get to see the house and the grounds cloaked in white before he left.

She stood at the open window, breathing deeply of the snowy air, thirstily, as if it might allay her feverish restlessness. It would not be much longer before broad daylight. When she closed the window and turned toward the room that was now filled with cool, wintry light, the yellow ballgown gleamed before her, threatening and unavoidable. Suddenly she could stand it no longer. She had to get away, out of the house.

The clock struck seven as she left her room wearing her coat, heavy boots, and a fur cap from which her long dark hair streamed out. She could hear a carriage drive up to the main gate—the barber, coming to shave her father. He arrived every day at the same hour, punctual to the minute. A trifle, but at this moment Camilla found it significant. Everything is still as it's always been, she thought as she marched down the broad staircase with the carved wooden banister. Nothing has changed yet.

In the hall a maid was whisking a feather duster over the gold frames of the Rembrandt copies; the lounge would serve as the dance floor tonight. The gardener's basket now stood on the parquet, already half filled with the wilted flowers he was collecting from the rooms before bringing in fresh ones. Another maid, carrying a basket of linens, was on her way to the guest rooms in the west wing. In the course of the day Camilla's three married sisters and their husbands would be arriving to take part in the New Year's Eve celebration, and as in every other year, they would stay until Twelfth Night.

Soon Aunt Lenka would be leaving the house to attend early Mass. Papa would be closeted with the barber, discussing the New Year's Day trotting races. And later, perhaps in half an hour, a bell would ring in the kitchen as the number 15 lit up on the board, and Mademoiselle Schröter would begin to prepare Mama's breakfast—the bitter, medicinal tea and the rusks which the doctor was sure to have ordered in the middle of the night. Mama would send it all back and demand her coffee, a special blend that had to be sent by express from Hamburg. With it she would want something "hearty"—perhaps a few crabs, some boned quail with Cumberland sauce—not leftovers from Sunday's dinner but something prepared especially for her, that very moment. Mama was convinced that warmed-over food was poison.

The downstairs door opened, and the barber came through the draft-catcher, a heavy red felt curtain that was always installed during the winter. He stamped the snow from his feet, hung up his coat with its triple cape, and carrying his leather satchel, disappeared down the hall that led to the library, the smoking room, and Papa's den.

Camilla listened to the steps slowly fading into the distance. She waited until she could hear a door open and close and her father's voice ring out, "Good morning, Schütte. Well, what do you think of the snow? That's going to give a pretty advantage to the Russian nags, don't you think?" Camilla smiled. It was good to hear Papa's voice, to find confirmation on all sides of the established routines of the house, the ticking of all the clocks, the servants' quick steps, the feeling of subdued activity that came from the housekeeping rooms.

No, it could not be, it could never be that all this was coming to an end.

2

There was something curious about Camilla's love for the house. Papa had built it, and Mama ruled in it, but Camilla felt herself to be the sole proprietor. The house was six years old, having been built between 1893 and 1894. At that time Steglitz was still a sleepy suburb, and compared with the farms and small one-family homes, the house erected by Herr Hofmann, well-known soap merchant, looked like a palace: a long, low structure with a two-story center section and two single-story wings, dressed in pale gray stucco, with a slate roof, white shutters, and many windows—just as Camilla had pictured "her house" ever since Aunt Lenka had read her a story from an old book printed in Cyrillic. From that day on Camilla had clamored for the story over and over, just to hear one passage, when Aunt Lenka raised her eyes and said, "And the house had three hundred and sixty-five windows." Pausing, she added, "One for each day of the year."

At that time Camilla's family was still living in Neukölln, between the two canals just before the place they merged, where there were no more chestnut trees and the banks were bare. During the summer the water was always overlaid with an iridescent layer of oily scum, and during the winter it did not freeze solid because of the wastes deposited in it. The factory, an old building long in the possession of the Hofmann family, was still impressive enough, but the rear house, where the family lived, was extremely plain. Besides, it was permanently dark and damp. From her narrow room on the third floor Camilla had a view of the factory yard. It abutted directly on the canal, so that the raw materials could be unloaded and the finished goods shipped off easily.

It was only to make money that her father had taken up the manufacture of soap—only later had he added perfumes—and it was impossible to open a window without letting in the stench of the boiling fats. The odor seeped through closed windows, the whole house was drenched in it, even their clothing reeked of it. Camilla felt this drawback most acutely when she was little; even in school she was surrounded by the smell of blubber.

In the mornings she was awakened by the noise of the cast-iron kettles being fired. Year by year there were more of them, and the stench grew more penetrating still. She was constantly embarrassed at the outdoor market when vendors in their stalls cried out the name of Hofmann's laundry soap, or on the street when she encountered the wagons that made deliveries to the firm's Berlin clients. The carts were emblazoned with the advertising figure known throughout the city: the laughing laundress, standing behind a washtub full of suds. The same figure, enlarged to giant proportions, decorated the walls of the adjoining houses, a sight Camilla could not avoid whenever she looked out the window.

But all of that had ceased to be important from one day to the next. It happened on that special Sunday when her father took her along for what he said was to be a visit to the zoo. But instead of taking the horsecars as they usually did, Papa had summoned a cab and taken her, a nine-year-old girl, to the other side of the city, into a neighborhood where she had never been before. Finally her father had asked the cabbie to stop, and they had continued on foot.

It was a hot day. They walked across fallow grazing land, then into a section bordered by pines and firs. The tall reedy grasses rustled softly in the wind; plovers shrilled in the hedges. Papa seemed to have lost his bearings; twice he uncovered a boundary stone and checked the direction in which they were moving. Finally they stepped out into the clearing with the huge linden tree at its center. From then on they had not spoken another word. Papa no longer called Camilla's attention to the various plants and birds. He had taken her hand, and they had walked toward the great tree. Under its widespread crown her father, spreading out both his arms as if to embrace the whole clearing, announced, "This is where our house will stand."

That was how he came to share his secret with her—the first important secret anyone had ever entrusted to the little girl, for he pledged her to absolute silence. Only many years later did she understand that her father had needed an ally in his daring plan, and that there had been no one else—only she, a child. Poor Papa!

The pact between them withstood the test. She had guarded the secret, and he had taken her into his confidence about everything that followed. He had spread out the architect's first sketches before her eyes; together they had stood at the edge of the excavated foundation. It had been terrible when she came down with the measles, so that the excursions to the "observatory" had to be stopped. But every evening Papa came to her bedroom to report on the progress of the construction, speaking in a muffled voice even though the door was bolted.

The outside was finished, the roof beam was in place, the workmen were busy on the interiors—and still they preserved their silence with all the other family members. Even when the house was fully furnished and Papa was already walking around with the latchkey in his pocket, he hesitated to initiate the others. Camilla almost burst with impatience to take possession of the house. Finally he gave in to her urging, and one day at dinner he announced that on the same afternoon the whole family would take a "picnic in the country." It was August 22, 1894; the date became forever etched in Camilla's memory. Shortly after three o'clock, after Mama's nap, the horses were hitched to the coach. To make sure that they would be quite alone, Papa took the reins himself. Time and again he stopped the carriage to point out the beauties of the landscape, but gradually he fell silent, as if he were afraid of letting the secret slip out too soon. Or so it seemed to Camilla, sitting next to him on the box and barely able to wait for Mama and the others to catch sight of the wonderful structure. To Camilla the house was a miracle. If it did not have a window for every day of the year, it had at least as many as there were weeks in the year, if you were generous in the counting. Her heart was beating in her throat when they arrived in Steglitz, drove past the church, left the last house behind them, and turned off the road. A few more yards, a last bend in the road, and the row of trees would part, the wrought-iron gate would come into view, the house behind it. And then . . . how often she had pictured the coming moment!

But the whole excursion ended in disaster. The "surprise" was not joyfully received but harshly rejected. To this day Camilla had not forgotten Mama's expression, first incredulous, then stony. Papa could barely persuade her to walk through the rooms. Perhaps he had hoped that once inside, her attitude would change; not once during her tour of inspection did Mama utter a word. Even during the drive home—and she had insisted they leave at once—she cloaked herself in chilly silence. Not until they were back home did the storm between her parents break out. They argued behind closed doors, but their voices were loud enough for Camilla, listening in the hall, to understand every word. Mama refused to allow herself to be banished "to the ends of the earth." A flood of accusations showered on Papa's head. One sentence in particular, repeated over and over, impressed itself on Camilla's mind: "So there's enough money for that sort of thing, is there!"

In the days and weeks that followed, the quarrel flared up anew at every opportunity; Mama waged war for six months. In fact the house in Steglitz stayed empty throughout that first winter. It was not until spring that Papa got his way by arguing that their present house was needed to expand the factory. But the battle between Camilla's parents did not end. It had continued to the present day, no longer noisy, without dramatic scenes, but unremitting and implacable. Even the doctor who had been called to attend her mother last night was a pawn in the struggle.

These thoughts were going through Camilla's mind as she left the house and, passing the hothouses, turned into the grounds. With every step, memories rose in her mind—the way her parents had bickered for years over how the grounds were to be laid out. At the back of the house, where Camilla walked at this very moment, Papa had wanted to preserve as much as possible the original appearance of the land. Mama simply waited until he went on an extended business trip. During his absence her workmen put in an artificial pond, erected a wooden pagoda, installed an aviary, and planted exotic conifers. Mama's luck did not hold; the trees perished, the birds did not manage to survive the first winter. By no means discouraged, Mama took a trip the following year to the North Italian lakes and brought back a cartload of palms, magnolias, and orange trees. These too were no match for the northern climate. After this second failure Mama had taken no further steps to give the grounds a "cultivated" appearance. She consoled herself with a pleasure garden in the French style at the front of the house as well as the two hothouses, where the gardener grew not only the acres of flowers required to fill the rooms daily, but also serried ranks of ornamental trees, such as the lemon trees that would decorate the dining room tonight.

Camilla had never connected all these things with money—as now she did. How much could all this have cost? The land, the house, the stables, the carriages and horses, the hothouses, the army of servants. . . .

She had come outside to get away from such thoughts, but she could not shake them. They followed her wherever she went.

The high wrought-iron gate had just opened; the closed carriage of the caterers drove up to the service entrance. The cook and the footman came to the door, boxes and baskets were carried into the house. The parade would continue all morning long: the pastry chef, the fishmonger, the butcher, the decorator who came to hang the garlands in the hall, and finally, though not until late afternoon, the additional servants that had been engaged and the musicians who would play for the ball. The routine was the same for every big reception. An intimate celebration within the family, without guests and without a certain amount of glitter and pomp—that would not have been a party, as far as Mama was concerned. This, too, Camilla had always accepted as a matter of course, but now she was compelled to think about the cost of it, of the many bills that would pile up on Papa's desk after such a night. She had seen the large leather folder where he kept them; during their talk about her alliance with Rothe, Papa had shown her the folder, already filled to bursting. She remembered the gesture with which he had pushed it back under the racing newspapers, and she remembered his remark, "They'll wait till the first of the year. But after that?"

Camilla had long since strayed from the freshly shoveled walks. It was not as cold as she had expected. Animal tracks were lightly traced in the snow; there were a few squirrels on the grounds and many birds. The cloud curtain still hung low, but Camilla was not certain whether this meant more snow or whether it portended rain. She had walked aimlessly, just to keep moving, to breathe fresh air and somehow to deal with her thoughts. Not quite conscious of her movements she had turned onto the path to the old linden tree standing alone at the center of the clearing. There was a rise in the ground near the tree, as if its roots were lifting the soil.

She stood still for a moment to gaze at the tree. She had seen it in every season, and in each it had its special beauty. The crown was so high and so dense that in summer sunlight trickled through in patches of gold. Not even in the fall, when the tree cast off its leaves, did it grow bare like the other trees; seen from a distance, the crown remained full and thick even then. Now each branch, down to the tiniest shoot, was outlined with snow as with a silver pencil, and the sky was suspended above the filigree, seeming to rest on it.

The snow lay less thickly under the broad circle formed by the crown; immediately at the trunk, mosses pushed through. The snow falling from the ends of the branches had created a line below, reinforcing the impression that the tree stood in a magic ring.

From the first day, long before she had learned what powers were attributed to it, she had been drawn to this tree. Visible from a great distance, it rose above the flat plain, solitary and commanding, and its scent—it was blooming at the time—had filled the whole neighborhood. Each year in the spring, when the windows were wide open in the house, the strong odor of its blossoms spread through the rooms.

The tree was very tall for a linden, and it took three men to span its trunk. There was disagreement about its age; some said it was two hundred years old, others said four hundred. It really was surprising that it had grown so old, for it stood in a region where wood was in short supply. Perhaps it had been allowed to go on growing because of the shade it gave during the summer, or perhaps because it was so handsome, large and symmetrical, with the commanding dome of branches and leaves.

The local people—the farmers, the fishermen, and the hunters—always called it the wishing tree. How the name and the legend connected with it arose—there were as many opinions about that as there were about the tree's age. But everyone believed in its wondrous powers: if you stood under it and spoke your wish, you could be sure that it would come true.

The legend was current not only among a few oldsters. Time and again strangers asked permission to visit the tree. But most pilgrims secretly stole into the grounds under cover of darkness, and the gardeners were kept busy mending the damaged fence.

Now Camilla stood under the tree, her back against the broad, smooth trunk. The firs on the other side of the clearing swayed softly in the breeze, but here the air was still. How long was it since this tree had bent to the wind? How many summers and winters had to pass, how deep did its roots have to burrow into the earth before it became so strong?

She had though a lot about the legend, and during the early years she had been tempted more than once to test the tree's magic. Something had always held her back. Sometimes she thought that it was not right to call on magic for a trifle; sometimes she was restrained by a kind of common sense that told her simple waiting and hoping were not the way to make wishes come true. But now, at this moment, when she stood there alone, the trunk warm against her back, looking across to the house, she was tempted to close her eyes and make a wish. Don't let it happen, let me stay in this house!

But she noticed the barber's carriage driving away, and her thoughts took another direction: I must ask Papa whether he has already begun to take steps to have the house signed over to me. No matter that Papa's marriage arrangement had taken her by surprise. She had recovered her wits quickly enough to make a deal with him that included the promise of the house.

The horse pulling the barber's two-wheeler broke into a trot. All she could see of the barber himself under the black roof was his hands holding the reins. Now the right hand rose to the brim of the black hat as he greeted a tall, slender woman wearing a fur coat down to her ankles: Aunt Lenka, returning from early Mass. As if she had only been waiting for this moment, Camilla quickly stepped out of the tree's protective circle and ran across the clearing, back to the house.

3

Aunt Lenka's official title in the household was the Major's Lady, or Madame Major. Camilla's mother, who set great store by anyone's name and rank, had introduced this form of address. She felt that "Madame Major" sounded attractive and turned the widow, her sister-in-law by marriage, into a person of standing.

The young woman's fate—Lenka was nineteen and had been married scarcely a year in 1870, when her husband was killed at Metz during one of the first skirmishes of the war—had given Emmi Hofmann no rest. Magnanimously overlooking the fact that she herself had been born into the von Weskow family while Lenka was only the daughter of a caviar merchant in St. Petersburg, she was determined to arrange an advantageous second marriage for the young widow. She pulled strings at court, but Lenka gave no sign of wanting to marry again. Emmi Hofmann had to stand by and watch the girl trample her good fortune underfoot. She refused the best offers—an officer, a titled banker, men on the court list. The two women would surely have quarreled openly if Lenka had been nothing more than a poor relation. But Lenka had money of her own, and in expectation of an inheritance—either for herself or for Camilla, who was Lenka's goddaughter—Emmi would overlook much worse character flaws. Money, lots of money, was the only thing that could compare favorably with nobility. So the Major's Lady was a member of the household, a part of the seasons like summer and winter. She herself was something of a season. She arrived without announcement, every year on November 10, one day before Camilla's birthday, and in early March she returned to Warnemünde, where she owned a house. Each year she left with the family's promise that they would come to visit her at the shore, but when summer came, Mama always ended by taking her three older daughters with her to Bad Ems or Bad Homburg. Of the resorts on the Baltic the only one she might have considered was Heiligendamm, and that only recently, since the Crown Prince had begun to frequent it. Never under any circumstances would she honor Warnemünde with her presence. By Emmi Hofmann's standards Warnemünde was hopelessly petit bourgeois. So only Camilla and her father spent their summers there, and in her aunt Camilla found the warmth, love, and understanding that she had always missed in her mother.

Camilla reached the hall just in time to help Lenka take off her coat. Aunt Lenka picked up the little whisk broom to clean her high-buttoned black boots a second time.

"Well, what do you say now? We've got snow after all!" Camilla looked at her aunt. Lenka was fifty, and although her dark, old-fashioned clothes and the way she wore her hair seemed designed to make her look older, there was something youthful and vivacious about her.

"Snow! That's what you call snow? Feel my hands, child, do they seem cold to you? And I didn't even wear gloves. A winter in St. Petersburg—you can't talk about snow until you've lived through that. All you have to do is step outside the front door, and your petticoats are frozen stiff as boards."

"But you said it wouldn't snow at all."

"Oh, you Berliners and your obsession with snow—powdered sugar!" Lenka's voice was dusky, and her laugh was darker still.

The sliding doors to the dining room stood wide open. The footman and a maid were busy stretching the white damask cloth across the long table. Another maid came from the kitchen, holding a silver salver containing a pile of cards. Aunt Lenka motioned to the girl and took one of the printed menus on which each guest's name was added by hand. "New Year's Eve, nineteen one," she read half-aloud. "Consommé double, brook trout, baron of lamb garni; Kiedricher Auslese eighteen eighty-three; truffled goose liver on toast points, Roederer . . . champagne so early in the meal"—the words slipped out—"poularde lyonnaise, salad, artichoke hearts with marrow, Chateau Cru-Yquem eighteen seventy-eight; hazelnut bombe, cheese straws, Cliquot; demitasse; midnight buffet." She placed the card back on the tray. "That's fine," she said to the maid, who smiled and curtseyed. "You may go." Lenka waited until the girl had disappeared into the dining room. "Someone's breaking her own record!" She shook her head. "Is something afoot?"

"What could be. . . ?" Camilla, who had gone to the wardrobe to hang up her own coat and hat, gave a brief look into the mirror. No, you couldn't tell that she had hardly slept. As always when she came in from outdoors, her color was fresh and healthy and without a trace of the pallor that was almost obligatory for young girls of her class. No, she thought, I don't exactly look like someone who's unhappy, and that's good.

"Chateau Cru-Yquem seventy-eight—that's a vintage I haven't seen served for a long time: your father hoards his last bottles. . . ." Aunt Lenka was not averse to a good wine.

"Don't forget, Mama's sons-in-law will be there."

Aunt Lenka did not seem to want to question Camilla further. She turned toward the stairs. "How is your mother feeling this morning? I heard the doctor come in the night."

"You mustn't take it too seriously. I don't think she does either. And she has a marvelous way of running things from her bed."

The stairs, covered with a scarlet runner, were broad enough for them to climb the steps side by side. Aunt Lenka's rooms were on the second floor. She had been given a large parlor and a smaller bedroom. Lenka had furnished the rooms herself. After her husband's death she had given up her Berlin apartment, had sent some of the furniture to Warnemünde, and had stored the rest in Berlin for more than twenty years, until her brother-in-law and his wife had permanently ceded her two rooms here, in the new house in Steglitz. Not even then had she been able to part with a single object. She had crammed everything into these two rooms, so that they were filled with too many pieces of furniture. The armoires and cupboards themselves were too heavy, and almost burst at the seams with commemorative cups, colored miniatures, friendship albums, daguerreotypes, silhouettes, music boxes, and more unusual objects about which Camilla never dared ask, such as a pair of evening slippers with paper-thin soles and a buckle of fake stones. The old painted grand piano took up the greater part of the room.

Once in the parlor, Lenka placed her black velvet drawstring bag on top of the piano. Camilla could not suppress a smile at the thought of what the purse contained. Together with the slim missal—perhaps even between the pages, marking today's lesson—there was sure to be a thin cardboard printed with today's horoscope. In Warnemünde a woman came daily to bring Lenka the message from the stars; here in Steglitz, Aunt Lenka went to the railroad station every day to get her own card from a monstrous red and green Automatic Astrologer. When you dropped a coin in the slot, a mechanical figure ran its hand over a crystal ball, suddenly stopping as the machine spit out its green card.

Camilla could not have said how seriously Aunt Lenka took the whole thing, and she did not think it was important. Even Mama's claim that Aunt Lenka took part in spiritualist seances did not rouse Camilla's curiosity. Even now she did not comment as Aunt Lenka went to the table where a pack of cards was laid out—most of them face down—and picked up one.

"The ace of spades, of all cards. I guess I'm in for something or other. I'd better be prepared." Looking at Camilla, she smiled. "Be glad that I'm not your mother, or you'd surely have inherited the trait. I got it from my mother, too, and she had it from her mother. That sort of thing runs in families, like red hair. We're too eager to know everything that's hidden from humanity, all the secrets between heaven and earth. . . ." She put back the ace of spades and turned to the sideboard, where the samovar gleamed. "I'll make us some tea." She lit the flame under the samovar, fetched two crocheted doilies from a drawer, and set out two cups. Again her glance studied Camilla, and only now she noticed that Camilla's hair had not yet been done. "Sit here." She pointed to the footstool which like all the other upholstered furniture, was covered with a crocheted throw. Aunt Lenka made these antimacassars herself, from the most delicate natural-colored silk yarn. Camilla watched her aunt as she went into the bedroom to fetch brush and comb. The bed that came into view when she opened the door was surely the most remarkable object among all of Aunt Lenka's possessions: a sort of gothic shrine of ebony, with red damask drapery and a pointed canopy, it stood on a two-step pedestal covered with a faded tapestry. Since the day she had watched it emerge from the furniture van to be carried through the house and installed in her aunt's bedroom, Camilla's curiosity was focused on this bed. She would have liked to know what the world looked like behind the red damask drapes, in the dusk of the canopy, and yet she avoided going anywhere near the bed.

Aunt Lenka had spread Camilla's loosened hair over her shoulders and began to comb it out. "What lovely hair you have," she said.

"I think I'll cut it."

"Cut it? Whatever can you be thinking of?"

"It bothers me, it gets in my way."

"I can't imagine what you would want to do that you can't do with long hair."

Camilla did not reply but asked instead, "Do you think I'm pretty?"

"What's the matter with you today?"

"Am I?"

Aunt Lenka laid the comb aside and picked up the brush. "Have you fallen in love?"

"Just because I asked if I'm pretty?"

"Is it that American, Keith?"

"No."

"How much longer is he staying?"

"A couple of days, as far as I know."

"It seems a little improper to me to have him staying here in the house, even if he is the son of good friends. What's he doing in Berlin anyway?"

"I'm not sure. Looking over some breweries. . . ."

"I don't imagine he can learn a lot that way. After all, they do things differently in America."

"He's never seen snow in his whole life."

"Then he should have traveled farther than Berlin. But that place he's from—California?—is that so far south? I'll have to look it up on your father's globe." Aunt Lenka clasped Camilla's head with both her hands. "A little more forward. And hold still . . . tell me, you're not up to anything foolish, are you?"

"What do you mean, foolish?"

"Falling in love with someone who doesn't know anything about it and whom you'll never see again as long as you live. Hold still,

21

I told you." She pushed the long pins into the chignon she had woven from five strands of hair. "It's not exactly a masterpiece, you were too restless. Well, we'll make up for it tonight."

Lenka went to the sideboard, where the samovar was humming. As she filled the cups, Camilla caught sight of the two wedding rings on her aunt's right hand; years of wearing them had worn them very thin, so that they almost looked like one ring.

"Did Mama marry Papa for love?" Camilla asked. Her aunt looked up briefly, then she took her cup and sat down in her usual place at the window.

"I asked you a question," Camilla insisted.

"Look, your mother—"

"Why does everyone treat me like a child? Did she love him? And if she did, what became of it? Who else can I ask?"

"Of course we can talk about it, although . . . my own experiences in that area are not very extensive. You'd be better off talking to your mother."

"Talk to Mama! What can you be thinking of? And that kind of question!" Camilla's glance wandered through the half-open door into her aunt's bedroom, ineluctably drawn to the bed; she had to make an effort to articulate her next words. "Since we've been living in this house, Mama and Papa have separate bedrooms. . . ." She could feel herself blush. "Is a woman old at the age of forty? Once I heard Mama say she was glad she wasn't troubled with *that* any more. . . . She put it more bluntly, you know?"

"When did you start listening at keyholes?"

"I wasn't listening. I would have been much happier if I hadn't heard, but she makes no secret of it. She talks about it with Lou, and with Mademoiselle Schröter, quite hatefully, as if Papa . . . I can't repeat what she really said. And yet she couldn't wait to find husbands for her daughters. How she watched us, how she whispered with the doctor who had to examine us . . . and she herself lives like a stranger with her own husband. Why does she hate him?"

"Does she?"

"Why does she hate this house?"

"That's easier to answer, at least some of it. She had something different in mind, you know. She had even made her choice already—a house close by the Imperial Palace. She'd been a visitor to the house for years because one of her friends lived there, you know the one I mean, the lady in waiting, I can't think of her name. But finally the house came on the market, and your mother had her heart set on it. You know how she feels about the court. That house would have allowed her to watch all the comings and goings—every royal carriage, the sentries. With a telescope she could even have seen precisely who was asked to Imperial receptions and the two big balls. She had something more in mind, too; whenever there was an official celebration, she could have rented out the window places for good money. Once she took me along and showed me everything and explained it all. . . . And then your father goes and spends a hundred thousand good gold marks for a house in the country."

"A hundred thousand?" Camilla was surprised. "Are you sure?"

But Lenka only nodded without elaborating further and took her crocheting from the basket. "Your mother never forgave him. You know she never passes up an opportunity to allude to her aristocratic ancestry and to her connections at court. An At Home day with a choice guest list, that was always her dream. The house near the palace would have been the ideal setting. At heart she has never come to terms with the fact that she married beneath her. Your father is only a merchant, not a military man, not a high official, not even a scholar who, decked out with the proper titles and decorations, might in a pinch pass for a member of Berlin society."

"Then why did she marry him?"

"How should I know? Perhaps she thought that her ambition and her connections would suffice to bring him all those things in time. Except that your father didn't go along. It's true that he's been given the title of Counselor of Commerce, but he doesn't use it. He has an order, but he never wears it. He has no feeling for such things. 'Buttonhole Day' is what he calls Honors Day—and he says so in front of your mother! And finally the money, that's what really drove them apart."

"I always thought we were rich. I mean, I never thought about it at all."

"Not rich enough. Your father is only a chemical dealer, my child. No chemist is poor. But rich, as your mother understands the term? He is a good pharmacist, an excellent chemist, almost a genius. But he is not a manufacturer. The soaps, the perfumes—those were your mother's idea. Probably she already had visions of him as a newly

23

ennobled purveyor to the court; in any case, she could see a lot of money in it. She put him up to it; she didn't give him a moment's peace. The fact is that both of them needed more money all the time, more and more. No matter how much he made, it was never enough."

Camilla stared at the ball of yarn in her aunt's knitting basket. So it's true, she thought, and an idea came to her. "You think Papa is in trouble?"

"I'd say he's always been in trouble. He simply doesn't know how to handle money. No matter how much he has, and no matter how cleverly he plans to invest it, as soon as he gets his hands on it, it turns to water and flows through his fingers."

"If he were in serious trouble, would you help him?"

Aunt Lenka's hands holding the crocheting dropped to her lap. She gave Camilla a searching look. "What's the matter, child? Are you keeping something from me?"

"I just meant, would you help him . . . it might be necessary someday. . . ."

"No, child, I would not help your father. First of all because I know him. And then, all of you think I'm rich, but that was a long time ago. Your father knows the true situation—it was he who lost my money for me. No offense, you can see it doesn't trouble me any more. But you ought to see your father as he is."

"He did you out of your money?"

"Not all of it. I still own the house in Warnemünde, and I've got enough to get along. But most of my estate is long gone. Of course it all began with a grand scheme, as does everything he gets into. He thought only of my happiness, and I was stupid enough in those days—I was nineteen—to fall for it like a ton of bricks. There's no harm in talking about it just this once, now that we've started on the subject. I had a considerable fortune. I inherited it from my parents. But I didn't understand the first thing about money. Your father offered to invest it for me; as my brother-in-law, he felt responsible for me, I suppose, and I was grateful. Unfortunately he bought railroad shares—in Russia, in the Balkans, in the Orient, I don't know where all. Your father had it worked out that in a few years I'd be a millionairess. Three years later, in eighteen seventy-three, the dream was all over. The man who was supposed to be financing and planning the railroads turned out to be a swindler—and all my beautiful shares and bonds weren't worth the paper they were printed on.

24

Perhaps now you'll understand why I'd never trust your father with money again. Nothing has changed, he hasn't learned a thing. He's incorrigible. Excuse the expression—but he's a gambler. He never stops having grandiose ideas—'a few irons in the fire,' as he calls it. He's a hopeless optimist. He sees only what he wants to see, and he will never change. As long as you understand how it is, all is well. But you have to understand, then you can like him for what he is."

Camilla wished she had never started, for now Aunt Lenka rose, took Camilla by the chin, and raised her head so that Camilla's gaze had to meet her aunt's eyes. "What's the matter? There *is* something. Why so many questions all of a sudden? What is happening? Are they planning to marry you off?"

"No, no." Camilla withstood Lenka's sharp look, but she was not certain whether she had succeeded in deceiving her aunt.

"Camilla, I'm not such an innocent! Consommé double, brook trout, truffled goose liver, baron of lamb—that's what I read. I studied the seating plan for the New Year's Eve dinner, too. A Herr Rothe to your mother's right, his wife next to your father, and one Alexander Rothe at your side!"

What could Camilla say without betraying her father? She could not lie, but she could not tell the truth either and give her father away. And yet her aunt had made it so easy for her, and she so much wanted to pour out her heart. Everything good that had ever happened to her was connected with Papa: the visits to the observatory, the circus performances, the trips, the wonderful weeks in Paris during the World Exposition—and of course the house, which Camilla felt he had built solely for her.

"Are you supposed to bring in the money now? Is that your mother's idea?"

"No, no, she has nothing to do with it." For a moment Camilla was relieved that her aunt's suspicions were directed at the wrong quarter. But then she thought, money—always money, that hateful stuff! As long as we've lived in this house, everything hinges on it, the good as well as the bad. Not a conversation that does not inevitably get around to it; no quarrel that does not break out over it. Sometimes the house is divided into two enemy camps for days on end, Papa on one side, Mama on the other, and Mama stays out of sight until she has her way and Papa comes across with the cash.

Having grown used to the situation at an early age, Camilla tended to behave as she did in bad weather; she avoided it as best she could but she did not take it too tragically. Her aunt's final question suddenly made her take a different view. Love, marriage—these were financial arrangements, nothing more. Girls could only get husbands if they had dowries. Husbands were loved only if they brought in a tidy sum. A family was respected only if it was rich. Money—money—money—nothing else mattered. Always only the one thing: money. . . .

Camilla turned her eyes on her aunt. She forgot that Lenka had once been married. It was easy to forget: she seemed more youthful than Mama—yes, even than Camilla's sisters. It was as if the fifty-year-old woman were only a shell hiding a very young, untouched girl. "I'll never marry! Never, no, no, I don't want to get married!"

"But child! What is it now?"

"I'm going to live like you."

"Oh, don't say that." Lenka's face took on the faraway expression it sometimes wore when Camilla unexpectedly entered the room to find her sitting at her sewing table.

"But you're happier than all the others."

"Happier?"

"Aren't you?"

"Let's say I'm not unhappy, at least not any more. But it took me a long time to get there. And not to be unhappy is still a long way from being happy."

She rose to refill the teacups. "More for you too?" She returned to her seat at the window. "Between seventeen and nineteen, those were the two years in my life when I was happy. That's a lot, you know, two years of happiness."

Her voice grew softer, the words were barely audible. It was as if she were speaking to herself and had forgotten that another person was present, so that Camilla felt she should quietly leave the room. But Aunt Lenka quickly glanced over her shoulder and made a brief gesture that told Camilla she was fully aware to whom she was directing her words.

"I've lived and yet I haven't lived at all—is that what you want me to want for you? I want you to really live, not in dreams that never come true, not in fantasies about what might have been. To really live, you have to be able to forget. You have to remain curious, and you mustn't be too fearful. I lack all those traits." She shook her

26

head vehemently. "No, you mustn't take me as a model. I can't even give you good advice about how you should arrange your life, much as I'd like to. I can only hope that you'll be happy and that you'll hold on to your happiness with both hands. Come here." She rose and opened the window. The snow had begun to fall again.

Aunt Lenka pointed outside with her right hand, the one on which she wore the two intertwined gold rings. "In St. Petersburg," she began and laughed in her warm, dark voice. She began again, "Memories . . . but that's not happiness. Happiness is the present."

4

She was sitting up in the pink double bed, several pillows piled at her back, chewing, holding a napkin to her mouth as if no amount of food counted as long as it was squirreled under the cloth. Her pink face still glowed from the night cream and her blonde hair was still tousled, held up only by a few carelessly inserted combs. She leaned against the pink pillows, looking like a pink female Buddha except for her eyes—light blue eyes that missed nothing.

As soon as Mademoiselle Schröter approached the curtains Emmi Hofmann said sharply, "Don't. There's enough light. Do you want my headache to come back?"

To either side of the bed two white china lamps with pink shades made pink the dominant hue of the whole room: they tinged the silken wall covering threaded with gold, and the mirrored doors of the wardrobe that took up the long side of the room seemed to be made of rose quartz. Only the Chinese carpet was able to assert its deep amber tone.

Paying no attention to her mistress' protest, Mademoiselle Schröter parted the curtains. "How can I straighten up in here if I can't see what I'm doing?" She was a short, somewhat stocky woman; not even the high heels of her low boots or the white cap on her head made her seem more attractive. She pushed the heavy armchair back into place, bent over to pick some object off the rug, and regarded with

28

deep disapproval the two empty candy boxes that formed part of the wild disarray on the table next to the chair. "One of these days you're going to need two armchairs to sit down in."

Emmi Hofmann laughed. Schröter was the only person who felt free to make such remarks. Emmi Hofmann would probably have enjoyed her gluttony only half as much without these constant reproaches that made her feel she was engaging in some forbidden action. The reproaches had begun long ago, when she was a young girl. She wiped her lips and let the napkin flutter from her fingers, to land among the clutter in and next to her bed: books, magazines, fashion journals, and the inevitable court calendar tucked within reach under the pillow.

Mademoiselle Schröter had stepped to the side of the bed. "How about it? If you want me to make the bed, you'll have to get up." She spoke a cultivated German; only occasionally, and only when she was addressing her mistress, did her original Posnanian intonation break through. She had started out in Emmi Hofmann's father's service; he was an ennobled agrarian, as she was wont to put it, who owned large estates in Poznan, and Emmi had brought her along when she got married. "At least let me plump up the pillows."

"That can wait. There are a few things we have to talk over."

"As you wish." Schröter was happy to put up with the daily skirmishes with her mistress; they served to reinforce her preeminent position in the household. Even under ordinary circumstances Emmi Hofmann had never been known to leave her bedroom before eleven o'clock; some days she never left it at all, and there were periods when the days turned into weeks. This was one of those times. No one in the house had laid eyes on Emmi Hofmann since the day after Christmas except for her doctor and, of course, Schröter. They were all used to it; no one worried about her, since they all knew that one of these days the patient would reappear, glowing, almost aggressively healthy.

Making sure that even during her seclusion Emmi Hofmann remained omnipresent and that the household regime in no way became lax—that was Mademoiselle's job. Should mistress and the servant tangle like cats and dogs here in the bedroom, as soon as Schröter left these four walls, not a single word against her mistress crossed her lips. No gossip, no remark about the state of the lady's health; the mistress' private sphere was sacrosanct. Only her orders traveled beyond the four walls—the commands to the kitchen, the servants, the gardener, the delivery people, the repair men. And that was how the preparations for the important New Year's Eve dinner had been made.

"Everything's going like clockwork," Mademoiselle said. "The rooms are ready. And they've started fixing up the table."

"Oh, I'm glad you reminded me. This time no bowls of flowers and green stuff on the table! And no garlands at the windows and around the chandeliers! That's one of those fads. The warmer it gets, the more the stuff stinks. I don't want that. And what about glasses? One pattern only, I insist. At Christmas the table looked like the inventory of a crystal shop."

"Then we'll have to buy some more."

Emmi Hofmann made a gesture that said she did not wish to be bothered with such trifles. "And now the champagne." A glass stood ready on the table next to her bed. Even as she spoke, she stretched out her pink arm, picked up the glass by the stem, and put it to her lips. In contrast to her smooth face and smooth arms, her neck was ringed with deep folds, and these now moved up and down as she sipped greedily. Only when the glass was empty did she put it down. "Too sweet."

"Perhaps it's not chilled enough."

"I tell you it's too sweet."

"Most people like it sweet."

"I suppose it doesn't matter what I like. I tell you, Roederer, Cliquot, all those are out. Ladies' drinks, not fit for a meal. Here . . ." she poked around in the sheaf of magazines but then gave up. "Sweet sparkling wines are old-fashioned. Take my word for it. A good champagne must be dry, really dry. So let's serve Pommery brut. Wait. . . ." Once more she began to search, and this time she had better luck. She pulled a clipping from between two glossy journals and pointed to an underlined passage. "Pommery brut eighteen eighty-four, that's a famous vintage."

"I'm sure we don't have any."

"Then we'll order some."

"But Roederer and Cliquot are already printed on the menus."

"Then we'll change the menus."

"You mean, have them printed all over again? Before tonight?"

Emmi Hofmann's remarkably small hands, lying pink and peaceful

30

on the openwork cover of the down quilt, suddenly began to drum soundlessly. Schröter responded at once by changing the subject. "We were going to go through the clothes." She fetched the baskets she had put down by the door. "Where shall we start?"

"With the evening gowns, they take up the most room. Those in the left-hand armoire, the ones that have been put aside, you don't even have to show me." She sat up a little straighter to keep Schröter in view.

Schröter moved a footstool to the wardrobe and climbed on it. She took four long robes from their hangers, folded them, and threw them in the basket.

"If there's anything there you can use for your family, please. . . ."

"They wouldn't know what to do with this kind of clothes." She took down the next dress and held it up. "You've never worn this one."

"Yellow isn't my color."

"When a dress becomes too tight, it's always the wrong color. And what about this one?"

"The navy blue? Out! It always reminds me of our dress uniforms at school. Do you remember how I used to cry when vacations were over and I had to go back? How cold I was there! But my father, that skinflint . . . why is it that all my life I've been at the mercy of stingy men?"

"What about the black one with the cape?"

"If we have to have a discussion about every single gown, we'll never finish. Let's not forget the shoes, either. I need the room."

For a few minutes there was no sound but the clatter of the hangers and the rustling of materials, the sound of drawers opening and closing. There was no need of words; the two women could understand each other better through looks and gestures. They had just begun to sort the purses when there was a knock at the door.

Within seconds Emmi Hofmann was transformed; her bearing became rigid, her expression strained. The room had three doors—one to the bathroom, one to the hall, and the third to a room that had originally been intended to serve as her husband's bedroom but which she had claimed as a private sitting room for herself. A second knock now sounded at this door.

"One moment," Emmi Hofmann called out, and her voice took on a note of suffering. She and Schröter exchanged a look while Emmi pointed to the bedside table. Schröter understood at once; quickly she carried the tray with the remnants of a lavish breakfast and the split of champagne into the bathroom and brought in another tray holding a variety of medicine bottles, vials, and a glass with a thermometer. Then, already turned toward the door, she gestured questioningly at the full baskets. What about the dresses? Her mistress' hand answered, Leave them! It was a kind of deaf-and-dumb language the two women practiced on other occasions as well—at an evening meal, for example—and which both had mastered perfectly.

"Come in." Emmi Hofmann sank back into the pillows and the pink ruffles of her nightdress.

The incredible actually happened: her husband stood in the doorway, he walked toward the bed. With a simple knock on the door he had gained entry without, as usual, first asking Mademoiselle Schröter if his visit would be agreeable. Emmi stared at him with the expression of a martyr, mustering his slender, tall figure with rising ire. No one would have guessed that he was fifty-six years old. His closely fitted jacket showed not a single fold. If she could at least have consoled herself with the thought that he owed his waistline to a corset! There were men who resorted to such aids, but he did not need to; nor did he ever require the services of a doctor, much less any medication.

"Would you be so good as to draw the curtains," she whispered, as if each word sapped her last reserves of strength.

Silently Fritz Hofmann fulfilled his wife's request, only too grateful for the short delay and also glad of the dimmed light, which unfortunately was still bright enough to let him see at once the baskets full of discarded clothing as well as the new wall coverings. At his last visit to this room, during the summer, blue moiré had been the prevailing note; the walls, the bed covers, the upholstered furniture, the rug, all had been blue. On the morning of her birthday he had come upstairs, alerted by Schröter, to deliver his good wishes and his present along with a bouquet of orchids. What a young girl's fantasy, he thought as he looked around the pink room. So that accounted for the hefty decorator's bill; though he had not been able to explain it, he had not dared ask his wife about it.

"Thank you," she said. "The light exhausts me so terribly."

Fritz Hofmann looked briefly at the collection of medicines at his wife's bedside. He pulled the thermometer from the glass, looked at

32

the register, allowing her to note with a certain amount of satisfaction that he had to hold it at a great distance before he could read it. He stepped closer to the bed. "Permit me." He took her wrist and felt her pulse.

She let him do it but remarked, "Don't tell me that I'm not running a fever and that my pulse is normal—I feel awful just the same."

She had closed her eyes, and so he could observe her undisturbed. Once he had loved her, but now he sometimes wished that they had never met. The distance between the two emotions hardly seemed twenty-eight years long. He remembered only too well how she had stood next to him before the altar, the only woman on earth made just for him. Of course, it was a law of nature that love in marriage diminished with the years, the attraction weakened—but did it have to go as far as it had with them? There were still resemblances between the girl he had loved and the woman here in this bed. She had grown stout, he could see that even under the coverlet. When she was dressed, the tight lacing produced a provocative contrast between her slender waist and the voluptuous curves above and below. But her hair, though uncombed and mussed—did it not still have a beautiful honey tint? All in all, time seemed unable to attack her face; it was still beautiful. Her skin was still smooth and rosy, her features cleanly chiseled. Her beauty had withstood the years well, though her love had not.

"Are you using a different toilet water?" she asked, her eyes persistently closed. "It smells awful."

"Always the same, for twenty-eight years." As he released her wrist and stepped away from the bed, his foot bumped into one of the books strewn over the carpet. He did not pick it up—it belonged here. He fought against the memory the sight aroused: a white deck chair in a garden, the blonde head of a girl, books all around her in the grass. Even in those days she had devoured everything she could get her hands on—novels, biographies, travelogues—indiscriminately and voraciously, with the same greed she later developed for tidbits and sweets which she indulged at any time of the day or night, as if confronted with the specter of famine.

She sat up straight, pulled up a robe hanging half out of the bed, and drew it around her shoulders. "What can be important enough to bring you here?"

He tried to listen to the voice: no harshness, no undertone of im-

33

patience, but no warmth either—really only another form of her silence. The matter he had come to discuss with her was delicate. He knew how quick she was to bridle and how hard it was to calm her again. "I hope you'll be feeling better by tonight."

"No one cares how I feel."

"Surely you won't leave us in the lurch? With fifty-two guests. By the way, did we have to invite quite so many?"

She raised her eyebrows, a warning that he had ventured onto dangerous ground. "What do you think a New Year's Eve party is? A few gentlemen whose money you can help yourself to at a game of cards, provided they're drunk enough? Bad enough that I have to hire additional help for such an occasion; what a middle-class impression that makes. . . ."

He was tempted to rattle off the full staff, though it was unlikely that he could come up with a complete list—Schröter, a cook, two kitchen helpers, a laundress, someone to do the ironing, two housemaids—or was it three by now?—the coachman, the footman, the gardener and his wife. Was that really all? But he had no illusions; when the discussion dealt with expenditures, he always got the worst of it.

"I've had a list sent to you," she said. "Did you get everything?"

The list concerned favors for tonight's guests, devised by Emmi Hofmann—silver flacons filled with perfume for the ladies, and for the gentlemen cigarette cases, all engraved. He had figured out what these "trifles" would cost and then ordered them resignedly, merely to avoid a confrontation. "It seems to me exaggerated to give presents to our guests, but I've got all the things downstairs. How I'm going to pay the bill, on the other hand—"

"Spare me, I beg you."

He summoned up all his courage. "I'm afraid I can't do that."

"And last night? Oh, I heard you come in. You can always find the money to gamble. I'm cutting corners wherever I can."

"I'll send you the decorator's last bill to show you how you're cutting corners! And these things?" He pointed to the overflowing baskets. "One of your economy measures? Do you know what all these clothes cost? Do you ever bother to find out? I know, you're not interested in bills, bills are my affair, but I tell you, my darling—"

"Tell me, go ahead. Get it over with. I'm used to your year's-end

34

laments. If you really must know, I'm selling these old clothes for a worthy cause."

"Who's going to take them off your hands?"

"A dealer in the East."

"Lang? He won't give you twenty marks for a gown, and the cheapest of them cost six hundred."

"Give me a check for our committee, then."

"I can give you one, but it won't be covered."

"When did you ever write any other kind?"

She spoke scornfully, putting on the bored expression that ordinarily forced him to retreat. This form of understanding was still functioning between them; the realization made her triumphant rather than resigned, for it was she who always remained in the right through these maneuvers. But for once the habitual reaction did not set in. He made no move to leave her alone; he remained rooted to the spot and seemed both uncertain and determined, so that she wondered irritably what the true reason for his visit might be. Only one topic remained. Until now she had stubbornly refused to assign any significance to the matter. "Are you really serious about the engagement?"

"And what if I am? Surely you aren't going to start to worry about Camilla at this late date?"

"I only meant to remind you of your responsibilities." She swallowed a remark that was on the tip of her tongue. After all, she had not protested when he had presented the guest list to her and the name of Alexander Rothe had been mentioned for the first time; she had had her reasons. "Is he really one of the richest men in Berlin?"

Though he was delighted that for her part she viewed the matter from this angle, he still hesitated to express what was on his mind.

"Did you really check him out properly, or does his fortune lie only in your fertile imagination?" She had been more deeply troubled by his increasing complaints about money, about unpaid bills and pressing creditors than she had let on, and she was especially worried since he had dropped the first hints about a possible union between Camilla and Alexander Rothe. A pawnbroker—even now she had not come to terms with the idea. "How can you make that much money with a hockshop?"

Through women like you among other ways, Hofmann almost

answered but prudently kept the observation to himself. It was time to get to the heart of the matter. "Rothe does have one condition." To interpret Camilla's desire as a demand by Rothe—it had not occurred to him until this moment, and he saw it as a masterstroke.

"Conditions?" Emmi Hofmann forgot about her intention to play the long-suffering patient. She sat bolt upright, heedless of her robe, which slid from her shoulders. "Rothe has conditions?" She laughed out loud. "A pawnbroker under my roof! And he sets conditions! Perhaps he wants a dowry, the fine gentleman!"

"And were your other sons-in-law willing to do without? They were certainly after the money! A lord of the manor, up to his eyeballs in debt, with a pack of kids from his first marriage. An ambitious lawyer who uses his wife as bait for his titled clients. And a lieutenant of the guard looking for someone to foot his tailor's bills. Those are the sons-in-law you chose."

Was she smiling? The tiny, contemptuous smile between closed lips that she had adopted during the years of their marriage and that had by now become a standard expression. She wore it only in his presence; it was like a chemical reaction that set in whenever he was with her and disappeared when he left.

"Don't worry," she said. "I've seen to my daughters' security. They alone have power of attorney over their own money. You see?"

"I thought all of them married for love."

"They all imagined they did. That's enough."

He had no idea where the piece of candy had come from. It suddenly appeared between her fingers, and she was wholly absorbed in undoing the gold-colored foil; her rapt face bent over the tiny hands with pink, buffed nails. Again he was overcome with the memory of the young girl she had once been. Why had that girl loved him? And why did the woman in the bed no longer love him?

"Well, spit it out. What kind of condition?"

"The condition . . ." he repeated absently. "Oh, yes, right. It's a kind of a dowry. Yes, for Camilla. Surely you wouldn't like to see her at a disadvantage compared to her sisters."

"I thought the money was all gone?"

He stared at the carpet. "That's why I thought we should compensate her in some other way, with something that might correspond to the value of a dowry."

36

"And what would that be?"

He had not expected her to make it easy for him. "Well, it occurred to me that this house—"

"This house?" She pretended to be utterly taken aback, but she knew at once what he had in mind, and she congratulated herself on having anticipated him when, six months ago, she had had the house transferred into her name. Dr. Kannenberg, the administrator of her estate, had advised her to take the step, for reasons she did not want to hear in detail. She had resisted simply because of her old prejudice against the house; but finally her highly developed pragmatism had triumphed. Building in a far from fashionable suburb might have seemed ridiculous eleven years ago, but it had turned out to be a farsighted speculation. The area had developed since the municipal railroad was run out in this direction, and other elegant mansions soon rose in the neighborhood; these had considerably increased the value of the land.

". . . corresponds to a dowry of about a hundred thousand marks. That's why I would consider it only fair. . . ."

She did not interrupt. She did not protest. She merely listened. Things must be in a bad way if he dared demand this of her.

"In short, I want the house transferred into Camilla's name. I don't want to run the risk of losing the match over this. . . ."

"It doesn't have to be decided today, does it?"

"I have an appointment with the notary for this afternoon."

"Today. It seems to me you're expecting too much of me." She did not betray her real thoughts. Why should she object openly when she had more effective means to deflect the matter? Then at some later time she could turn him down flat. She let herself sink back down into her pillows; sighing deeply, she picked up the thermometer, shook it, and stuck it in her mouth. A final, faint hint of a smile, and he knew that, no matter what he might do or say, he would not receive an answer. He threw a final look at her smooth face, tinged pink by the light of the lamps, and left the room.

5

Perhaps the many generations of pharmacists the Hofmann family had produced had gradually exhausted their enthusiasm for the drug trade. In any case, Fritz Hofmann's father looked after the business with his left hand only. The real focus of his life was mountains, especially the Swiss Alps. He had been the first to conquer more than a dozen summits, and to honor his achievements, one peak had been named after him. His apothecary duties were taken care of by a walk through the shops and offices every morning and evening. The rest of the time he spent in a studio he had set up next to the laboratory, surrounded by relief maps, books on geography and geology, telescopes, mineral samples, and an extensive collection of such mountain-climbing apparatus as crampons, pickaxes, hammers, and ropes. He reacted to any interruption about tiresome business details with the bitter complaint, "Is there no end to it!"

His son, too, had fallen prey to interests that had nothing to do with business. The den, where he retired after the audience with his wife, attested to this fact, as well as to the difference between him and his father—the ephemeral and erratic nature of his hobbies.

Glass cases were built into the walls, and the objects they contained proved that he rarely kept his enthusiasm for a subject for very long. There were objects from Egyptian and Greek archaeological excavations, an extensive collection of votive gifts—arms, legs, hearts, lungs made of wood, wax, glass, semiprecious stones, or silver; seals and signets in every conceivable design; and finally his clocks and watches. He had remained true to this one passion all his life. He had been loyal to a second one as well: horses. The walls were covered with numerous etchings, the desk held photographs of famous steeds. It was as if he wished to be surrounded by his darlings the way a father wishes to have his children's likenesses around him. Racing journals from every country in the world were scattered over the large rosewood table in the middle of the room. They were arranged in a way comprehensible only to him, and no one was allowed to touch them. The days when major races were run—the Kentucky Derby, the Queens Plate in Toronto, the British Derby and Grand National, the Irish Derby in Curragh, and the Grand Prix de Paris —were important days in his life.

Even now, after returning to his realm, he immediately began to busy himself with several of these journals and with the notes he had made after his morning's conversation with the barber. December and January were profitable months for his passion, since the trotters had been running in the Moscow Hippodrome since Christmas day and would continue for the next two months. When he looked over the balance of his daily bets to date he could be quite pleased with himself.

But soon he realized that he was unable to concentrate; the conversation with his wife kept breaking into his thoughts and interfering with his calculations about the New Year's Day races. Actually he ought to have been reflecting on matters other than horses and jockeys. His desk held books and files with long columns of figures, with balances waiting to be restored to health, for the debit and credit to be equal once again. There was still time for everything to turn out well. It all depended on his flair. The course was set. Just a little more patience, and a grain of luck. . . .

He reached into his vest pocket, but his favorite watch was not there. This pocket watch, a precision instrument made in Switzerland, had a maximum deviation of about thirty seconds a month; but that was so important to him that on the last day of each month he drove to the observatory to have the correction made. In addition, in December of each year he sent the watch to be repaired and checked in Geneva. The few weeks without his watch put a considerable strain on his nerves. When had he sent it off? Rummaging around for the post-office receipt, his hands came up with the letter Herr Rothe had sent him yesterday, asking for a meeting today. Why? Hadn't they discussed everything already?

Old Man Rothe—suppose he had somehow found out the information Hofmann had so tenaciously kept from him? He had been asking himself this question ever since he received the letter. It was possible that Rothe only wanted to show him the engagement present for Camilla. That was an obvious explanation, but it did not reassure Hofmann.

There was no point in trying to concentrate any longer. He picked up one of the packs of cards lying in the desk drawer. He shuffled them with the dexterity of a professional croupier, an activity that had an almost magical effect on his nerves. That was why he always carried a pack of cards with him. Driving into the city in his carriage, he passed his time this way; in the middle of a conversation, too, he might pull out his cards and let them slide in and out of the pack with a clever motion of his hands. Shuffling, dealing, picking up one, calculating the odds—that was his way of philosophizing. Everything was a gamble, everything was chance, everything was luck. If you weren't willing to lose, you couldn't win.

Suddenly he laughed aloud at his thoughts. Without his wife he would never have discovered the importance of money, and if he had not learned that, he never would have understood about gambling. The soap factory—compared with it, a hand of blackjack was innocent child's play. He had warned her more than once: I'm a pharmacist, not an industrialist; but she had talked him out of his scruples, had pointed out how rich he could become. Looked at this way, he owed his rise to her alone.

Gradually his optimism regained the upper hand. He was just going through a streak of bad luck, that was all. How often in roulette he had put everything on a number—preferably zero or Camilla's age at the time—and been lucky. Wasn't he doing the same thing now? He wagered everything he still owned on one thing: his name, Camilla. . . .

Quickly he put the cards away as he heard steps approaching his room. Camilla? How could he possibly tell her? But it was Mademoiselle Schröter who stood at the door he now opened. "May I come in for a moment?"

He did not like her particularly. His conversations with her were generally limited to one topic: his white linen suits, which were never pressed well enough to satisfy him.

"May I?" she repeated. "For just a moment. It's personal."

His intuition told him that it could only be something disagreeable. "Well, come in then. And close the door."

She fingered her stiffly starched apron, which she wore like armor over the cotton dress spotted with little purple flowers. "You remember my niece," she began. "The girl's married now. A good man really. Both of them work in the laundry, and they've got a chance to buy into the business." She hesitated, somewhat breathless after her running start.

Now Fritz Hofmann understood why she had come. Could she have listened at the door upstairs and become worried for her own money? Once that sort of thing started, they'd all come; it would be like an avalanche, burying him.

"It's . . ." she groped for words. "You invested some money for me. . . ."

"Well, let's have a look." With the nonchalance of a man familiar with the ups and downs of the game, Fritz Hofmann pulled out the side drawer of his desk and took out a fat ledger. "Come over here, let's look at it together. Eight years ago you made the first deposit."

"It's been nine years. . . ."

"You remember exactly, do you? Here it is, five hundred marks in December eighteen ninety-two. And since then you've deposited, yes, that's it, three thousand marks altogether." He looked straight at her. "What do you think happened to it?"

"It's the laundry, we have to help each other out. . . ."

"Six thousand! Now what do you have to say? It's doubled—well, not quite, but almost. There, you can see for yourself."

Schröter stared at the ledger he held out toward her as if it were a sacred text. She seemed more overcome than overjoyed. "Can I have the money?" she finally asked.

"It's been a long time since you paid in anything. Nothing for a whole year."

"If the two of them don't jump at the chance . . . there's another buyer, you know."

"You've got six thousand! Your savings have doubled! Doesn't that please you at all?"

"All I need is three thousand."

41

"The money has been invested in stocks."

"You don't have it?"

"I'd have to sell the stocks."

"But I told them for sure I'd get them the money."

Fritz Hofmann understood that it was no use trying to talk her out of it. "Just don't get excited. How much do you want? All of it? Six thousand?"

The sum confused her. Of course she had eavesdropped on the Hofmanns' conversation and become fearful for her meager savings. That was why she was here. All she wanted was the three thousand marks she had given Fritz Hofmann over the years to administer for her. And he was talking about six thousand. She had made up the story about the laundry out of whole cloth, just to have a reason for approaching him. She had thought she was being very clever, but now she was ashamed of her suspicions.

"I don't need all of it," she said. "I'd like to leave some of it. Two thousand will be enough."

"And you need the money today?"

"Yes, please, because I promised it, you know."

Three thousand or two thousand—Fritz Hofmann had no idea where he would get it, but he said, "I'll bring the cash back from the city. You'll have it tonight. Is that all right with you?"

"Oh, thank you, thank you. I never thought it would be such a lot."

Fritz Hofmann locked the ledger away. At least he had gained a few hours' time. His conscience should be bothering him at the thought that he had squandered the life savings of an old woman and trusted employee. The stocks existed only in the ledger—but what did that matter? For the moment he had brushed her off, and the necessity of having to conjure up two thousand marks by tonight did not trouble him. He saw it as a challenge. Suddenly he was hungry for his breakfast.

"Have you seen Miss Camilla?" he asked Mademoiselle Schröter as she was about to leave.

"As far as I know, she's upstairs with the Major's Lady. Before that, she was walking in the grounds."

"Then tell her that I expect her. And have them bring breakfast in here, for myself and for my daughter."

While she was still in the hall, Camilla heard her father laughing at one of his own remarks; the words were indistinguishable, but the tone of infectious good nature was typical of him. Higher-pitched laughter answered him, and the maid, carrying the empty tray, stepped out into the hall, still beaming broadly.

Fritz Hofmann greeted Camilla with open arms. He led her to the window where the table which was normally used for card games was set for breakfast. "What a day this is! And snow, too. You've been outside already, I hear. I bet you've worked up quite an appetite. Let's see what we have for you."

She watched him as he peered under the silver cover. His happy mood seemed genuine. He had an innate gift of cheerfulness, of enlivening others, making them laugh. This quality was a welcome relief in a house presided over by her serious and stern mother. But Camilla was no longer deceived by it as she had once been. The three months she had spent with Papa in Paris had taught her how quickly his mood could change.

He held a chair for her, then sat down himself, urged her to help herself, and now asked, "Who's the little girl who brought in breakfast? Is she new?"

"I think so. I never saw her before. Mama has had a lot of new staff lately."

"A pretty one for a change! Usually your mother hires flowers of ugliness. One more horrible than the last. Do you think she really took me for one of those men who fool around?" He cut himself off with a laugh but fell silent when she did not join in. "What about your hair? You're wearing it differently today."

"I don't know, Aunt Lenka did it for me." He was a man who noticed such things. She liked that in her father, as she liked so many things—the way he looked, the way he dressed, his courtesy and consideration; how he had held her chair just now, how he would never fail to notice when her cup was empty. When they were in Paris, staying at the small hotel near the Bois de Boulogne, they had always begun the day as they were doing now, by breakfasting together. Some of her memories of Paris were less pleasant, but she wanted to be like her father and have only good thoughts. "Maybe I'll cut off my hair."

"What an idea!"

"Why shouldn't I?" Hard as she tried, she simply could not fall in with her father's light tone; she would have had to forget every-

43

thing Aunt Lenka had just told her about him. She let her eyes rove around the room, hoping to find something to take her mind off the topic. And in fact she spied on a shelf a sample of the new laundry soap. "Is that the final packaging?"

"What do you mean. . . ." His eyes followed her glance. "Oh, the soap, no, there's something not quite right about it yet."

"Are you really going to stick to the name—Laundry Soap?"

"It says exactly what it is. Laundry soap gets bought by housewives. They don't care about fancy names."

"You're probably right. It's not a name you forget easily. And it sounds honest."

"Exactly, and that's why the wrapping is right too."

"The lettering shouldn't be so fancy. Very simple letters would be better."

He nodded. When they were in Paris, he had sometimes been astonished to find how serious an interest she took in business matters. She spent all day at the Hofmann booth in the German pavillion, and on her breaks she studied the products of the other exhibitors. Many of them were from Berlin, respected firms. Fritz Hofmann had tried to picture what it would be like if Camilla were to marry one of the heirs. . . .

"Are you listening? When will you put the soap on the market? It could be very successful."

Oh my child, he thought in a sudden onslaught of despair; you have no idea how many cakes of soap I'd have to sell to get myself out of the hole. A couple of pfennigs, that's the profit from each cake; fifty thousand wouldn't even be enough to pay off Schröter. How cold such figures were, how depressing. "Success . . ." he said, and his glance wandered out the window. "Oh Camilla, if you knew. . . ."

"If I knew what, Papa?"

He had had a thought just now, but when he tried to express it, it vanished; he reached for the next best thing that came to mind. "We shouldn't have gone to Paris to the Exposition. The price of the booth alone! Not to mention the other expenses. I let myself be tempted by the idea of international connections, export, all that. But it was a mistake—like so many things I've done in the last few years."

"You were very proud of your medals. Two gold and one silver. It was written up in all the papers, and you said yourself if you'd had to pay for that kind of publicity. . . ."

All he wanted to do was bend across the table, take her hand, and say, you know exactly why I wanted to go to Paris. You know how little I cared what happened at the booth. You know that all I thought about was the races and how I could arrange a game of faro in the evening, or at least some three-handed whist. You heard me sneak out every night, you heard me come back near dawn. You saw how quickly I cashed the checks that were given to us as down payments for orders.

But why put into words what they both knew? It wouldn't help; besides, his moments of self-judgment never lasted long. In a voice that no longer gave any sign of the depression that had overcome him, he said, "Let's talk about something else. What are you going to do today?"

"I'm going shopping with Aunt Lenka. We need some things for the fortune telling, you know that's what she likes best about New Year's Eve. And later I've got a date with Keith. . . . He's looking over a factory in Charlottenburg. He wants to order some machinery. . . ."

"Yes, Kammer. Now that's the kind of man your mother could have appreciated. He always knew what he wanted. We were in school together, Keith's father and I. But he didn't go on to the university. Instead he bought into a small rural brewery. By the time I finished my studies, he'd already made a fortune. He wanted me to go overseas with him, but I had just met your mother. Sometimes I think I'd like to take a trip over there and visit all of it, especially his stud farm. That's what I envy him the most. Race horses! Kentucky is the land of horses, you know."

"I thought the family had breweries."

"The breweries bring in the money, but Keith told me his father's only real interest is his horses. He can afford it. Yes, Kammer's lucky in everything he does. His colors won the Derby five times, three in a row. You know, to own a stud farm and race your own horses, that must be marvelous. . . ." He would have liked to pursue the thought, but somehow it seemed improper to reveal his intimate desires to Camilla on this particular day. "Keith is buying machinery? Since when is he interested in brewery equipment?"

"I simply promised to go with him."

"You like him?"

"I like being with him," she said and quickly added, "I suppose because I never had a brother."

"Yes, a son. Maybe that would have changed things. Imagine if I had a clever son with a good head for business; I might have retired long ago and lived like Keith's father. I'd care about nothing but horses. Just think, maybe I'd have some of my own to enter in races and. . . ."

Once more he came to a halt. Suddenly his appointment with Herr Rothe came to his mind. Then he thought of the two thousand marks he must find for Mademoiselle Schröter before the day was out. He placed his teaspoon alongside the cup and reached into his vest pocket; two fingers slid into the narrow slot and remained there when they did not encounter the watch.

"I think it's time I left. The coachman is about to bring the carriage around. How about meeting in the city, the three of us, Keith, you, and me, for a snack?"

Camilla did not raise her eyes from her plate. "I thought we had an appointment with the notary. You didn't forget?"

Hofmann had certainly not forgotten. But what was the use of making an appointment with the notary when he had not obtained Emmi's agreement to transfer ownership rights in the house to Camilla? What kept him from coming clean with Camilla? Why was he hiding from her the fact that he alone no longer had the right to dispose of the house, that everything depended on her mother? Did he really believe there was still a chance? He tried to make himself believe it, as he tried to make himself believe that by tonight he would have found the two thousand marks for Schröter.

"Did you speak with Herr Dr. Berger?"

He heard the carriage come around the drive and stop at the front door. He folded his napkin—carefully, precisely, fold on fold. "Unfortunately I couldn't get an appointment for today. He's away over the holiday, he won't be in his chambers until after January sixth." He pushed back his chair, went over to Camilla, and kissed her forehead. "Why don't you change your mind and come with me?"

"You promised me," she said with sudden determination. "I want the house! Maxi, Alice, and Lou—"

"And you shall have it. On January seventh we'll see Berger and take care of the whole business. A promise is a promise. I'd be happier too if we could have taken care of it today, you know that. But

46

now something else. I'd like to round off your bank account; we've always done that at the end of the year, and today is our last chance."

"Nothing is stopping you."

"How much do you have in your account, exactly?"

Camilla pointed to the chest behind the desk which contained a built-in safe. "We can look it up. After all, you keep the account book. It should be somewhere near ten thousand marks. Five hundred marks a year from Aunt Lenka, that alone comes to eight thousand five hundred. Then what I've saved out of my allowance, and whatever you added each year. And the interest."

She was only putting into words what he himself knew perfectly well. He knew the state of her account to the penny. More than once he had been tempted to withdraw the money. Nothing could have been simpler; he had full power of attorney. But something had stopped him, and even now he felt restrained. A short, painful struggle, and then he knew that this was the day he would close out the account. He had no other choice. It was his only salvation. Camilla would know nothing; the very first chance he got, he'd put it all back. When and with what—he would not ask himself that now, it remained to be seen. He kissed Camilla again, with almost too much feeling. Only a few minutes ago he had thought it would be impossible to come up with the money for Mademoiselle Schröter, and now he had it. The solution had fallen into his lap.

The first sign that everything would turn out all right after all? Hadn't he had a premonition? A streak of bad luck was tough, but not to notice when your luck turned, that could be fatal. Perhaps today was a particularly lucky day for him? Nothing for a long time and then, all at once—he knew the rhythm all too well from the gaming tables. His optimism swelled like a sail in the wind. Perhaps he should put some of the money on the New Year's Day races in the Hippodrome?

He gathered up the notes he had made at his desk about horses and jockeys. "You'll see," he said cheerfully to Camilla, "everything will turn out fine."

But then, as he was forced to unlock the safe and she watched him take out the bank book, his mood changed again. The discouragement that had seized him when Camilla talked about the possible success of the new laundry soap returned. Success, achievement, money—how he hated all of it! A galley slave was better off. A slave

47

was in chains—as he was himself—but he bore no responsibility. That was what turned life into a hell. And it did not help to amass riches. "Don't you ever get attached to money, my child," he said.

Her reaction took him by surprise. She laughed. There she sat at the table and laughed at the words he had meant so seriously. "You'll never change," she said. "Never, as long as you live." She knew him better than he knew himself. To have money without a thought about where it came from or how it was earned. Aunt Lenka was right; he would always see only what he wanted to see. And for a fleeting second she wished that she too possessed this convenient trait.

6

The huge dining room, more like a banquet hall, was one of the
rooms Camilla had loved dearly from the beginning. A large
family gathered around the table for a meal—that was one of the
most wonderful things she could imagine. Perhaps this feeling explained why she had learned sooner than most children to behave properly at the table, so that even her mother had praised her time and
again and held her up as a model to her older sisters.

The room was made for celebrations. The walnut paneling lent
it warmth, the four tall French doors leading to the terrace gave it
spaciousness, the light-green taffeta draperies imparted color, and
the four-branched wall sconces bathed it in a golden shimmer. Tonight
an accent of luxurious frivolity was added by the dwarf lemon trees
with artificial fruit twined in their glossy leaves and yellow taffeta ribbons wound around the slender trunks. The room had another special
quality: its dimensions seemed always to adapt exactly to the number
of people it contained. Whether the center table was set for twelve,
thirty-six, or as it was today, for fifty-two, it always seemed the right
size, so that the diners never felt lost or crowded. It would not even
have been noticeable that four places remained unoccupied if one
of them had not been the host's and the other three assigned to the
Rothe family.

A critical moment came when the dinner, planned for seven thirty, was delayed because of the absentees. But Mama had mastered the situation. To avoid any embarrassment, she had arranged for the hors d'oeuvres to be passed in the lounge and the conservatory. Maids, dressed in black taffeta with white pleated silk aprons, and hired waiters in tailcoats had appeared with large platters heaped high with delicacies; the glasses were filled a second time with sherry; and in answer to a wave of her mother's hand, Alice had sat down at the grand piano and played a medley of operatic tunes. After an hour of waiting in vain, Mama had led her guests into the dining room and had begun the meal.

Camilla could not help but admire the style and presence of mind her mother was demonstrating tonight. She had not lost control for one moment. Instead she remained the beaming, relaxed hostess. Even now, during the dinner, she saw to it that no lull arose in the conversation, and she displayed every trick known to a lady of high society to make everyone at the table forget the absence of the host and three guests. Watching her during the meal, it was impossible to believe that anything might be worrying her; the idea was absurd. Some women are at their most beautiful when they are silent; others, when they smile; Mama, Camilla was thinking, is without a doubt at her most beautiful when she is eating. She watched across the table while her mother slowly, carefully separated a piece of fowl from the bone and trickled a little sauce over it. The motions of her hands, the lowered eyes, all expressed a voluptuous concentration. When she looked up, she nodded at Camilla with a soft, contented smile. Was Mama trying to convey praise, to tell Camilla that she was playing her part well? In any case she tried as hard as she could to match her mother's cheerful spirits. She took an active part in the conversations of the people sitting near her. Like her mother, she formed the center of the general conversation. The words flew at her, she caught them and returned them like balls—yet her thoughts were elsewhere.

Time and again her eyes wandered to the great sliding doors, but always it was only the maids and the waiters who entered. It became increasingly less likely that the Rothe family would attend this New Year's Eve dinner. Did that mean the engagement would not take place, not tonight, perhaps never? She still did not dare entertain the hope.

50

She leaned back in her chair as the girls carried away the last entrée and brought in clean plates for the hazelnut bombe. The mood in the room was noisy, almost boisterous; the excellent meal and superb wines had succeeded in melting even the stiffest and most taciturn diners. The guests could be divided into three groups: the top layer was made up of Mama's friends, all of them aristocrats of course, some even holding positions at court. The next level consisted of officers. The rest were bachelors whom Mama was in the habit of calling "dancing civilians." She had recruited just enough of them from the ranks of junior partners in law firms, minor judges, and legation secretaries, to match the number of unattached ladies present. It was not exactly the selection Mama would have hoped for in an ideal situation, but it was impressive considering her middle-class household. And then one could not overlook the three married daughters, Maxi and Alice with their husbands and Lou alone, since her husband, a lieutenant of the emperor's bodyguard, had been summoned to the court to perform as a leader of the dancing.

Camilla had never had a particularly close relationship with her older sisters. As far as she was able to judge, Maxi, Alice, and Lou were not particularly close to each other either. Camilla had realized early on that this distance basically emanated from Mama and was encouraged by her—by playing the sisters off against each other, the better to dominate them all. Because she realized this, Mama's tactics had not succeeded with her. Her mother held that very much against her, especially after the older two daughters had already left home and Lou, influenced by Camilla, developed a kind of independence that did not suit Mama at all. Of course Camilla saw it from the opposite side; she felt that she could learn a lot from Lou. She thought Lou exceptionally pretty, much prettier and more interesting than herself with her red hair, her alabaster skin, provocatively full lips and innate flirtatiousness that could drive any man mad. There was something about Lou that sparkled; she wore clothes that were either high-necked as a nun's or cut so low that hardly anyone else would dare to wear them. Tonight she wore one of her off-the-shoulder gowns. Keith sat next to her, and the two were absorbed in an animated conversation. They caught Camilla's glance, smiled, raised their glasses to her across the table, and put their heads together again. Did Lou know about the engagement that had been

51

planned? Presumably; like Mama, Lou had a sixth sense for such matters. Was that what she and Keith were whispering about at this very moment, was that why they were laughing?

The slice of hazelnut bombe still lay untouched on Camilla's plate when the servants came around again to offer second helpings; they were followed by girls bringing champagne. Camilla's dinner partner, who had been eager all evening to shower special attention on her, wanted to pour her drink for her, but as he did, he knocked over his own glass. While Camilla helped him stem the flood, she missed her father's entrance. She only became aware of it as he was greeting some of the guests at the table. He was alone, and clearly he had just returned, for he still wore the clothes he had had on when he left the house that morning—gray narrow trousers and a double-breasted jacket with a nipped-in waist. He uttered excuses, inquired about whether the dinner had been good. Camilla waited for a glance from him, a sign, but he avoided her eyes. Despite the nonchalance with which he shook hands with the men and said nice things to the ladies, his manner gave signs of tension and nervousness. He seemed in a hurry to reach the head of the table, where his wife presided. When he stood by her chair at last and Emmi Hofmann made no move to interrupt her conversation with a friend, Camilla thought for a split second that he was about to lose control. He had to step still closer and speak to her before she would take notice of him.

Whatever he whispered in her ear, she kept her composure. She arose, imperturbable, and stood waiting at her place calmly until all eyes turned to her and the voices died away. Then she announced in her clear, high voice that dinner was finished, that coffee would be served to the gentlemen in the smoking salon and to the ladies in the conservatory, and that dancing would begin in half an hour at the most. She responded to the applause that greeted her words with a modest gesture. Then, on her husband's arm, she left the dining room.

Camilla remained seated until all had risen to their feet and the general conversation had been resumed. Then she followed the stream of guests into the hall.

It was almost eleven o'clock. The meal had lasted for more than two hours, and only now did she realize how tense she had been; all her muscles ached. The subdued light in the hall felt good, as did the fresh air coming from the conservatory, where the skylights were open. The music stands and instrument cases were ready on the platform that had been set up next to the stairs. The gardener and some of the hired footmen were already busy putting up tall screens that cut the lounge off from the corridors and the front door and gave it the appearance of a ballroom. Everything ran its accustomed course, as it had at earlier parties. A few young men—Keith was not among them—came up to Camilla and entered their names on her dance card.

There was no sign of Papa or Mama. They must have retired to the library or to his den. Aunt Lenka stood at the foot of the staircase and tried to brush off the retired chamberlain who had been her dinner partner on New Year's Eve for many years; Camilla knew that her aunt would now disappear, not to return until midnight, to join the party for the ritual fortune telling. Camilla wondered if she should join her aunt, but then she heard something—wasn't that Mama's voice? Clear and cutting, in the unmistakable pitch that indicated a quarrel. . . .

Camilla left the lounge and hurried down the corridor that led to Papa's den, where the voice was coming from. Suddenly silence set in. The door burst open and Mama stormed out, white-faced. As she caught sight of her younger daughter, she froze, her eyes shooting hatred at Camilla. Seconds passed; then, as though she could stand it no longer and had to let off steam, she slammed the door at her back as hard as she could. For a moment it seemed that she would rush past Camilla without a word, but then she said, "Go, go in there with him. The two of you, you're a pair. But don't think that I'll put up with everything. You'll have to face the music alone, you two, nobody else. Go to him and . . ." she fell silent. One last icy look, and she turned to go, head thrown back, her right hand snatching up the train of her gown. The only remaining sounds were her short, energetic steps and the rustling of her dress. Camilla no longer understood what was happening. She reached for the doorknob and was suddenly overcome with the fear that if she entered Papa's den, she would find the entire Rothe family there. She felt her mouth go dry. She was close to running away. But when she opened the door, she saw to her enormous relief that Papa was alone.

He stood at the window, staring into the night. He did not turn around, and even when she spoke, he did not respond except that his shoulders seemed to grow even narrower and more drawn, like those of someone who is cold. "What is it now? Do what you have to, but don't ask me to. . . ." He seemed to think that Emmi had returned. He looked over his shoulder. "It's you, Camilla?" He walked toward her, and the two or three steps were enough to remove the tormented expression from his face. "How beautiful you look! That's our material, isn't it, the stuff we bought together in Paris? Let me look at you. And your hair, yes, that's a beautiful style for you. . . . But tell me, how was the dinner? Did you enjoy yourself?"

Perhaps he was a coward, but surely only because he was reluctant to hurt her. Perhaps it took more strength to play out this comedy than simply to tell the truth. Camilla thought at this minute she understood her father better than ever. Perhaps life was much simpler if you postponed whatever was unpleasant and hoped it would go away by itself. But she could not live this way.

"Papa . . . what's happened?"

He let the opportunity pass. "I have to change. You won't want to dance with me looking like this. You did save the first waltz for me?"

What would she have to say to get an answer from him? If her parents' quarrel had been about the Rothe family's absence, surely that could only bode well for her. . . .

Neither of them heard the knock at the door. It was Mademoiselle Schröter; she stood in the open door but did not get a chance to say what she had come to say, for Papa sent her away impatiently. "Not now, please. You see that I must speak with my daughter. Please come back later, surely you can do that, can't you? You can see that you're interrupting. Please."

Camilla was so involved with herself that she noticed neither Mademoiselle Schröter's odd behavior nor her father's unusual curtness. When they were alone again, she said, "Aren't the Rothes coming? Is it over?"

"I must go and change, my child. I can't join our guests looking like this."

"Tell me, Papa! Is it over?"

He stood before her, his eyes still glued to the door, as if he were expecting Mademoiselle to return at any moment. He had to tell Camilla the truth, there was no help for it. She must know everything. If anyone had a right, it was she. But after a long struggle with himself he said only, "There will be no engagement."

"No engagement? Is that true? Is that why Mama was so beside herself?"

"Wait, my child. Your mother had another reason to be angry, and I'm afraid it concerns you also—"

He got no further before Camilla threw her arms around him. He wanted to fend her off, but she paid no attention. It was not until she was about to reach for his hands to kiss them that he was able to withdraw, with a gesture of shock.

"So it's true. No engagement! That's what you said, isn't it?"

"Yes, it's over."

"Over! Over! Over!" She twirled around with pleasure. "Over! Over! Over! And Mama is almost bursting with rage! Marvelous!" She stopped short. "It's really true?"

"I'll explain it to you—"

"No. Just tell me that it's true."

"It's true. They won't be coming. Not tonight, not tomorrow, not ever."

"I'll never forget you for this, never."

Until now he had looked at the alliance with the Rothe family almost exclusively from his egotistical standpoint. He had never seriously considered what such a marriage would mean to Camilla. Only now, faced with her outburst of joy, did he measure the sacrifice that she had been ready to make for him.

"Was it very difficult for you?"

"Not too bad. To tell you the truth, he made the decision for me, sort of." He commanded himself to tell her the rest of the truth now—but should he really burden her with it at this moment, when she was so happy? He would only spoil the dance for her without making anything better. One way or another, nothing could be changed now. From now on everything would run its course, inevitably. And the strange thing was that he felt something like relief, as if a heavy burden had been lifted from him. "Really, it's high time for me to go and change. . . ."

"And you'll have the first waltz," she said. "The first, the second, as many as you want. . . . Now it's begun to be a real party!"

7

"What's the meaning of all this? You can't just abandon your guests. Come on, Mama, speak up. What happened?"

Unimpressed by the questions that pelted her from every side, Emmi Hofmann paced the bare space between the Christmas tree and the quince-yellow sofa. Now she came to a stop and asked for silence by raising both her hands. "Are we all here?" Her glance traveled over Maxi, Alice, and Lou, as well as the two sons-in-law; they were all gathered around her in the sitting room with the ornate furniture. "You"—she pointed to Maxi's husband—"stay near the door and make sure no one interrupts us."

Emmi Hofmann sank down into the sofa. The reaction to this family council, called so suddenly, was exactly as she had expected; besides uneasiness and curiosity, the chief emotion reflected in the faces of her daughters and sons-in-law was reserve. Emmi Hofmann promised herself to remain on guard. What luck that she'd had time to adjust to the situation. Where would she be if she hadn't roused herself this afternoon and driven into town to consult Herr Doktor Kannenberg, the man who administered her estate? An inner voice had propelled her, almost a premonition of the coming catastrophe. It was too bad the premonition had turned out to be true, but it was better that she had found out from Kannenberg. At least that way she had been prepared; she had been able to plan ahead. True, she had still had one glimmer of hope—Camilla's marriage to the Rothe boy. That was all over now too.

After the confrontation with her husband she had been on the point of calling off the rest of the party and sending the guests away —especially considering that everything nibbled and sipped from now on, every broken dish or glass, all the fireworks shot into thin air would be coming out of her own money. . . . But she had overcome the momentary panic, just as she had received Kannenberg's report without batting an eyelash; and she would withstand this family council as well.

"Are you finally going to tell us what's going on here?" As usual in family gatherings, it was Alice who spoke for all of them.

Emmi Hofmann glanced at the grandfather clock. "Don't worry, you'll be back in time for the first dance. I'll make it brief." In almost the same breath, and with the same calm, even voice she had been using, she added, "Your father is bankrupt."

"What! That's impossible. Bankrupt—who says so?"

Once again the voices buzzed. Then there was silence. Lou, standing next to the Christmas tree, poked her fingertips at one of the transparent globes, making it sway; Maxi, the oldest, threw a beseeching look at her husband, who was watching the door; Alice paced back and forth restlessly, her steps typical of a woman whose shoes are too tight. Her husband tugged at his mustache. "I can't believe that. The factory has been going steadily upward."

"That's what I always thought. You don't think I would have herded you together here if it weren't serious. This afternoon I went to see Kannenberg." And then, in a very calm, factual tone, she began to repeat the gist of the interview she had had with her administrator.

She could not, however, maintain her composure for long, for even as she spoke, she relived the whole event. How she had sat across from Kannenberg in his office and he had said, "God knows I'd have preferred telling you something more pleasant, my dear lady." This careful dose of human sympathy had helped Kannenberg rise quickly in Berlin, until he became one of the most sought-after administrators. "But unfortunately your husband's financial situation . . . I have the figures here, you can see for yourself. . . . Dismal, very dismal. . . . I can't compare it to anything, there are no standards. . . . Of course, if Rothe should actually decide to infuse some capital. . . . At least it would gain time, at least six months . . . possibly. . . ." Incomplete sentences and a sure instinct for how much optimism would be effective: these were some of Kannenberg's other gifts. "Yes, my dear lady, that's how the matter stands. . . . But what is it they say, we must face facts, and you. . . ."

Later Emmi Hofmann could not remember leaving the office building and emerging into the street. Only behind drawn curtains, during the drive home in the closed carriage, did she succeed in ordering her thoughts and making a campaign plan for the immediate future. She set up the following ground rules for herself: don't rush matters, remain level-headed, arouse no suspicion, save face. In short, don't fumble and remain on guard, even if the engagement with Rothe should come off after all and the immediate danger be averted.

How she hated her husband! Not him alone either—she hated all men. Once before in her life there had been a similar moment, just as horrible, just as degrading. That time it had been her father.

His property lay in Poznan—he was one of those eastern estate owners whose lands were said to be rooted in air, since the soil was more sand than fertile loam. There had never been any money. She had come in touch with it only twice a year—on her birthday and on her name day—when her father handed her a gift, a gold coin. And each time he immediately took it back again—"for safekeeping," as he put it.

The household was run with Spartan simplicity. There were no parties, no outings; the only entertainment were the walks to and from church and to visit her mother's grave. Aside from her beauty and her noble name, Emmi owned nothing. From the time she was a little girl, her father drummed into her head that she could not expect a dowry. She had to be grateful when Herr Hofmann, a pharmacist, asked for her hand. He was only a merchant, but he married her without a penny's worth of dowry, without a trousseau; he even had to pay for the wedding. And then, one month after their marriage, it turned out that her father was as rich as Croesus!

The sixty-year-old landowner had sold his estates and run off to the Italian Riviera with a young Polish woman of doubtful reputation. Word came back that he had bought a castle and a yacht; he had installed a private zoo and thrown his money about in other lavish ways. Emmi Hofmann had tried to establish rights to her paternal inheritance, but she had been unable to make the claim stick. When she renewed her efforts after her father's death, she had learned there was nothing left to inherit. Everything had been squandered. To add insult to injury, the Pole had had the impudence to turn up in Berlin and ask for assistance; she had even insisted on calling Emmi her stepdaughter. Emmi had been young and inexperienced then; this time, however, she would not be such a fool. She promised herself that.

"Yes," she closed the report of her conversation with Herr Dr. Kannenberg. She had carefully left out any mention of the possible salvation through Rothe. "This is where it stands—total bankruptcy." She looked again at the grandfather clock and noted that five minutes had passed; five minutes had been enough to list the balance sheet of a life, a family. . . .

Her speech was met with silence. Alice checked her restless wandering. "Did this have to happen tonight? With a houseful of guests? Surely it could have waited until tomorrow." Her hands toyed with the long rope of pearls around her neck. In the course of the evening the necklace had been admired repeatedly, and Alice had always answered simply, "A Christmas present from my father." But now she began to wonder whether the strand had really been paid for, whether they could take it away from her. . . . She turned to her husband. "Could we be drawn into it, Tassilo? I mean gifts, and my dowry. . . ."

Tassilo von Faber tugged at his mustache before he spoke in the exaggeratedly distinct and arrogant way he had adopted for the courtroom. "I do not believe your mother intended to imply anything of the sort. Did you, Emmi?"

Emmi Hofmann stared at her daughter Alice—or rather, at the pearl necklace. "If you want to offer me your help, please. . . ."

But Alice took care not to seize the opportunity offered her. "Not all of us are even here. Lou's husband is absent. It concerns him as much as the rest of us."

"And Camilla?" Maxi gingerly interjected. But no one paid any attention to her.

Lou tugged at the neckline of her gown. "I can't say I understand what we're supposed to decide, but I'm sure you needn't put it off because of my husband. You can hear his opinions from me just as well." She was glad that her husband had been called to court; it would be better if she broke the news to him herself at a suitable moment—gently, and in a slightly cleaned-up version. "All right, then, what is it we have to decide?"

"I've only put you in the picture. Now you know your father's financial position. I expected you . . . the least you can do is tell me how you feel about it."

Otto von Donath, Maxi's husband, left his post at the door; with one hand he grasped one of the massive chairs and placed it near the sofa. He was a tall man, weighing more than two hundred pounds, and the chair gave a resounding groan when he sat down. His behavior corresponded to his foursquare appearance. As a Conservative Party representative in the national assembly he liked to play the country squire. "What are you expecting, Emmi? That we help with money?"

"I can only answer with another question. Would you?"

"If the situation is as you've described it, there doesn't seem to be much left to salvage." He tried to loosen the trousers that tightly gripped his knees and thighs. "As I see it, the situation is a bottomless pit. There's no choice but to accept the consequences. Broke is broke. A hundred thousand marks owed the bank, did you say?"

Emmi Hofmann nodded.

"And roughly the same in unpaid bills. No outstanding assets, no inventory worth mentioning—that's it, isn't it? Correct me if I'm mistaken on any point."

Emmi Hofmann nodded once more.

"Salesmen's demands of twenty-five thousand marks, a mortgaged factory, and as sole active asset, the two old buildings and the grounds they stand on."

With a glance at her husband Alice gave him to understand that he should terminate this fruitless conversation; he obliged by intervening with an energetic "Hopeless. Hopeless and completely bungled."

Emmi Hofmann's expression betrayed neither her feelings nor her thoughts. "I did forget one thing when I was telling you the story. There was one interested party who might have been prepared to invest some capital."

"You're talking about the mysterious engagement?" asked Lou, suddenly interested.

"Yes. One of your father's grand schemes. I don't know how he brought it off, the matter was as good as settled. And this ominous pawnbroker was ready to help your father out with two hundred thousand marks."

"Two hundred thousand? For Camilla!" The exclamation escaped Lou, but she was only expressing what all the others were thinking.

"That would have altered the situation considerably, though Kannenberg saw it as no more than a reprieve. But this has all become theoretical—the deal has fallen through at the last minute. I suppose your father's view of things was too rosy as usual—or else he represented them in too rosy a light to this Rothe. When he finally saw the figures, he backed out." She turned her gaze on Donath. "All the same, with two hundred thousand marks—Kannenberg confirmed as much—we'd be able to avert the bankruptcy . . . if you want to help your father—"

" 'Your father, your father' !" Alice lost her patience. "You keep on saying, 'Your father.' And you, Mama, aren't you involved as well? Have you ever cared where the money came from? For thirty years he gave you the best possible life. Do you have the slightest idea how much a party like the one you're throwing tonight costs? You don't care about such tawdry details, I know. You refuse to listen to the talk of tradesmen. Penny-pinching, that's what you call it. No, no, you're not blameless in this disaster. How do you think we live? I can't spend money like water." She looked around the room. "None of us can."

The room grew still—so still that you could hear the sound of the instruments tuning up in the lounge. Emmi Hofmann could be pleased with herself, for even now she managed to preserve her calm—a bitter consolation. But when she answered, her voice contained an undertone of sharpness for the first time. "May I remind you that it was I who saw to it that each of you received a dowry of one hundred thousand marks?"

Maxi, the only daughter who had inherited her mother's tendency to plumpness, now pulled a chair up closer to her mother's. "Of course we'll have to pitch in. We're talking about Papa, after all, not some stranger. If we each chip in . . . I mean . . ." she corrected herself after a warning glance from her husband. "It would be a kind of loan, that's all. Isn't that right, Mama, that's what you meant, a loan against collateral?"

"Listen to her!" Alice's tone was irritated. "Big sister telling us what we're supposed to do again."

Otto von Donath made a motion to indicate that he was about to speak. He leaned forward slightly, fixing his mother-in-law with a probing look. "You didn't seriously think we should put our money into what can only be called a lost cause, did you? To be honest . . . forgive me, I don't think you're that simple. On the contrary, I always thought of you as a very realistic person. If this pawnbroker pulls out, that must mean—to use a metaphor—that it's a sinking ship. In six months our money would be down the drain. Sentiments are all very fine, but they won't solve financial problems. That takes a cool head. We would not be doing Papa Hofmann any favor by throwing our own money after his. One must learn to cut one's losses, to finish the matter off as quickly and painlessly as possible. I assume we are agreed on that point. Fine. The fact that the central person—Papa Hofmann—is absent and that you called only the five of us here together—surely I may interpret that to mean that you are no longer counting on him. Correct? Fine. So that matter is cleared up as well. Why waste our time beating around the bush?"

"I wanted to see your reactions, especially my daughters'. . . ." For all her calm and composure, a trace of bitterness had gradually etched its way around her lips; it grew deeper as she said, "You're quite right, I'm no longer counting on him. Your father is a—" She groped for a word that would express all her hatred and contempt, but it eluded her. "He's a gambler, a gambler by nature, not only at the card table; he thinks life is a game. No, I don't intend to spare him in any way. I brought you here so that we, the family, can get out as easily as possible, so that he won't draw us in any further and so that not too much trouble is stirred up." Her eyes traveled over the assembled company before returning to Donath. "With all due faith in Kannenberg—no man can serve two masters. We must remember that he is your father's administrator as well. So I'd prefer you to handle my affairs in the future. As I said, there are one or two active assets— the old pharmacy, the back house, and the land on which they stand; I can't tell yet what it's all worth, or how it can be sold. Under the circumstances we won't be able to get the maximum, but I'm sure it will be enough to cover some of the debts."

"Sell the pharmacy!" Maxi was outraged. "It's been in the family for three hundred years!"

A motion of Donath's hand urged her to be less emotional. "Of course I'll be glad to look after your affairs," he said to his mother-in-law. "There's only one thing; I'd need to be authorized by *him*."

Emmi Hofmann laughed. *"His* authorization! You've got it. I took care of that. He'll agree to everything. Can you imagine? And as long as we're on the subject, I want you to know this, too: as far as I'm concerned, the man is dead, once and for all. I don't want anything more to do with him."

"You want a divorce?" Maxi was beside herself.

"A divorce causes too much of a stir. A separation serves the same purpose. Please, save your breath. My mind is made up. I just hope he'll have enough decency left to disappear from my life of his own accord."

"But what's to become of you?" This time, too, Maxi found no support among the others, and she no longer expected it. "What are you going to live on?"

Her final words, however, fell on willing ears. All turned to face Emmi Hofmann, and Lou expressed what was going through all their minds. "Most important, *where* do you plan to live?"

Emmi Hofmann wiped an invisible crease from her blue velvet dress. She had thought about that too, without arriving at a satisfactory solution. Living with Lou would be the most amusing, but they would be very crowded in the small city apartment. Alice ran a large household, but she was moody and domineering. Maxi was hardly worth considering, since the thought of spending most of the year on an estate in the provinces was in no way tempting to Emmi Hofmann. She had counted on all three spontaneously declaring themselves eager to take her in. But she saw only sheepish faces: Alice, Lou, even Maxi—only a moment ago they had been animated, now they seemed turned to stone. It was no different with the two men. She could hardly believe it. Was this really her favorite son-in-law, Donath, who always sat next to her at the table to spare her any embarassment when she ate too much? None of them had a word, not even a glance for her. They surrounded her as before, and yet they seemed to have drawn away. Her own daughters! That was the thanks she got! The first time she asked anything of them, they stood there like stuffed dummies. It was just as well she'd held back her last trump card—the house. She forced herself to smile. "Well, any suggestions?"

The tip of Alice's shoe peeped out from under the hem of her gown and bored into the carpet. Donath got to his feet and, taking a deep breath, stretched to his full height.

Lou dropped the pine needles she had been plucking off the tree. "You know my doll's house of an apartment," she said. "There's not even room for a canary. You're used to a large house, to servants. You'd be better off with Alice."

Emmi Hofmann's back was straight as a ramrod. She turned to Alice. "And what do you think?"

"It's all so sudden. Of course we have the space. But I should remind you that every time you stayed with us, you said you couldn't stand the noise from the street. Anyway, do we have to decide right this minute?"

"Of course you can come and live with us," Maxi put in. "Can't she, Otto?"

"Thank you, Maxi, but I've had all I can take of the country. Wild horses couldn't drag me to your lonely paradise. I shall stay in Berlin. Lou and Alice may settle it between them. At their leisure." Thinking of the two women at each other's throats, Emmi Hofmann involuntarily smiled. "Yes, talk it over and let me know. You can go now. Look after our guests. . . . No, not you, Otto, just one more minute, there's a little matter. . . ."

Lou was the first to reach the door. The others followed. Music could be heard, and the voice of Rozanski, a distant relative, who was calling the couples together to take their places for the first waltz.

"You don't mind staying a moment longer, do you?" Emmi Hofmann indicated a spot on the sofa next to her.

"I don't like dancing anyway. Especially not after a good dinner. A noble wine, your Chateau Cru-Yquem, and a good vintage, seventy-eight. I rather doubt you'll get anything like that living with Lou or Alice. I can only second Maxi; you're always welcome at our home in Pillkallen."

"I can't even stand the name."

"You'd probably bring your own furniture; your own servants, too. Of course they'd have to come out of your own pocket."

Emmi Hofmann laughed. Donath was one of those men who began by adoring the mother before marrying the daughter. A second aspect that had won Emmi over was the shrewdness he had shown in negotiating the marriage settlement.

"At least with you a person knows where he stands. Don't worry."

64

She made a well-calculated pause before continuing. "Fortunately I own this house."

"This house? You own it?"

Of course that is another liquid asset, Kannenberg had said. The remark had taken root in her, sustaining her. The house meant nothing in itself. She had moved in against her will and had always considered the years she spent there as a kind of banishment. But "liquid asset"—what a marvelous phrase! "Yes, it belongs to me. At least one liquid asset."

"Free and clear? No mortgage?" And when she confirmed that fact, he smiled contentedly to himself. "My congratulations. That changes your situation by a hundred and eighty degrees. I know you never had a good word to say for the house, but as a capital asset. . . . Well, if I had to make an estimate. . . ." But he thought it advisable not to fix a sum. "Are you planning to buy something in the city?"

"What makes you ask?" However much she liked Donath, she was not about to drop her guard. He had almost guessed her plans: to live in the city again, as close as possible to the palace. Perhaps she could move in with Frau von Schack, a friend of long standing who had a post as lady-in-waiting at court. Why shouldn't her old wish still come true? An apartment on a level, as it were, with the Emperor; daily news of the court right from the source. If, after officially separating from her husband, she were to resume her maiden name, perhaps it might still appear on the court calendar some day.

Donath had mentally calculated the commission to be realized on the sale of the house. Now he asked, "Surely you don't intend to hold on to it. I don't have to tell you how much it would cost for the servants alone."

"No, no, I intend to sell it, the sooner the better. But perhaps we should wait until the bankruptcy proceedings are finished. Once grass has grown over the affair, we're sure to get a much better price."

"Is there any other catch?"

"Not as far as I know. No, nothing can go wrong. Actually, Camilla was meant to have it, as a dowry you know, instead of cash."

"Wait a minute. Is there an actual notarized transfer of the house to you?"

"What do you take me for? Of course. I have it in writing."

"Title and usufruct? No restrictions? No clauses protecting Camilla's rights?"

"No. This afternoon in Kannenberg's office I looked the document over very carefully once more. She could hire ten lawyers . . . not to mention that she'd never do anything of the sort."

After brooding a moment, he announced, "I'll take the job. I'll get your husband to give me whatever signatures and authorizations I'll need tomorrow. I won't charge you for settling the bankruptcy proceedings, but I do want a commission on the sale of the house. Shall we say—fifteen percent?"

They looked at each other candidly, two accomplices who had found one another. Emmi Hofmann smiled slyly. "I don't imagine it will be very difficult to sell the house, provided we're not in too much of a hurry. Kannenberg though it would be easy to find a buyer. He offered—"

"All right, let's agree on ten percent." As so many times before, in other situations, he was glad Maxi took after her mother only in looks. "You're a hard woman," he said. "I can't imagine what kind of man would have suited you. Certainly not the one you got." He examined her smooth, contented face. "Or would you rather be taken for an unhappy woman?"

Emmi Hofmann had been listening with only half an ear. The sounds of the opening waltz seeped through the closed door; as at court dances, here too they were playing the "Blue Danube." You could rely on Rozanski in such matters. She was already thinking of her move to the center of the city. It couldn't have come at a better time if she'd picked it herself. All the important court festivities took place in January. The celebration of the anniversary of the Imperial Proclamation, Honors Day, the Emperor's own birthday, the parade. And then February! With its major costume balls that took place in the palace of the Crown Prince, the charity bazaar in the ice palace, and all the other balls and parties. Every evening at seven the parade of carriages could be so comfortably observed from the windows of the von Schack apartment. . . .

She rose to her feet and took Donath's arm. "Take me to my guests."

8

Victor Rozanski—Count Rozanski, though the title was subject to doubt—kept the dancers swaying. He had been an expert master of ceremonies for more than thirty years. Sometimes he asked himself how he could possibly make a living, considering the wear and tear on tailcoats; not to mention the countless dickeys, lost buttons, and patent-leather slippers with soles worn through from dancing. Perhaps Rozanski did not mind if the job cost him money, as long as it satisfied his insatiable drive for sociability. "Choose your partners," his voice trumpeted through the hall. "Now gentlemen, gentlemen. No hanging back! Where's your spirit? Come now, a little more spirit, if you please. That's what pleases the ladies. Now a waltz in double time—with spirit, let's go. . . ." He signaled to the band leader to start the music. "O-o-one, two, three." He accompanied his calls with a clapping of hands. "A little faster now. O-o-ne, two, three! O-o-ne, two, three."

"That's enough. A waltz in double time: I'm not up to that any more." Fritz Hofmann led Camilla from the dance floor. "Leave it to the youngsters; stick to them. As for me. . . ." He gravitated toward a group of three men who stood a little aside, waiting for him with undisguised impatience.

"Go ahead." Camilla knew the type, men who usually became restless before dinner was finished. "You really ought to be lucky tonight."

She was not annoyed with him for leaving her to join his friends in the smoking room for a game of cards. She stopped at the edge of the dance floor and looked around for Keith. He was not easy to miss, not for Camilla, but she could not find him anywhere. All the rest of the family were dancing: Maxi, Alice, and of course Mama, who, in spite of her plumpness, was as light as a feather when she danced. True, to get Otto von Donath moving took quite a bit of doing, and even then he remained a clumsy dancing bear.

The waltz was over, and Rozanski announced a cooling-off round for the ladies. A lively to and fro ensued on the dance floor, but there was still no sign of Keith; the same held for Lou, but Camilla refused to see a connection. There was still a half-hour to midnight. Camilla walked off in the direction of the dining room. The table had already been cleared and reduced to half its former size. New damask cloths had been laid, and the hired waiters were busy setting up the midnight buffet. The center was resplendent with a five-tiered cake. Camilla crossed the room, opened one of the French doors, and stepped out on the terrace. She was sure that she would find Keith here, busy with the final preparations for the fireworks, but only the gardener greeted her. "Have you seen Keith, Willeke?" she called to him.

Willeke, kneeling next to a wooden block to attach a Catherine wheel, raised his head. "He was going to help me, but I guess he decided to duck out. Don't catch cold."

Disappointed, she returned to the house. In the meantime the maids had stacked plates along the sideboard and set out the baskets with silver. A selection of false noses, paper hats, streamers, bags full of confetti, and other joke items were spread out on a console.

Camilla was trying to figure out where Keith might be—maybe in the conservatory, or the smoking room—when Schröter, who was supervising the arrangement of the midnight buffet, stopped her. The white cap, which usually seemed deeply anchored in her gray hair, rode crookedly atop her head; her face was flushed a deep red. "I must ask a favor of you, Miss." The low tone of her voice only emphasized the excitement gripping her. "After all, you have influence with Herr Hofmann. . . ."

"Not now." Camilla tried to step past the woman, but Schröter quickly placed her hand on the girl's arm. "Please, it will just take a minute."

"Later, really—"

"It can't wait. He promised me early this morning, he gave me his solemn word, after all, it's not asking too much if I give him a day's grace. It's my life savings. Later—what does that mean? He said he'd bring the money from the city. Could you talk to him? Please!"

Without clearly knowing why, Camilla shared her father's dislike of Schröter. "Now, in the middle of the party!" she answered, annoyed. "Surely it isn't the right moment, you have to admit that yourself. Come and see me tomorrow, we'll take care of the whole matter then." She turned to go, leaving Schröter standing on the spot.

A glance at the dance floor told her that Keith had still not returned; instead, she was approached by several young men who wanted to dance with her. She put them all off until later and headed toward the conservatory. The light in that room was subdued. A couple was half-hidden among the palm trees and the blooming bougainvillea shrubs: Mama and Frau von Schack were sitting in the niche, on the wicker bench by the fountain, so engrossed in their conversation that they had eyes and ears for nothing else.

Where else should she look for Keith? Irresolute, Camilla left the conservatory and walked along the corridor. The party was approaching its climax, and the whole house hummed and vibrated—an atmosphere Camilla loved. After a short rest the music started up again. Rozanski's trumpet call, the clapping of his hands, rose above it. How much she would have liked to dance, but not with just anybody, only with Keith. Aimlessly she walked on, not noticing that she had already arrived at the housekeeping rooms. A door opened at the end of the corridor and Keith emerged. It really was him! Camilla was so happy to see him that she did not stop to wonder what he might have been doing in the pressing room. She ran toward him. "So there you are! I've been looking all over for you! I don't want to dance with the others, I put them all off, come. . . ."

Hastily he pulled his tie into place and ran his fingers through his hair. In the joy of finally finding him she would certainly not have noticed these movements if his scent had not confused her. Keith, who did not even use hair tonic! It was a sweet, cloying smell of hyacinths. Camilla knew only one woman who used such a perfume. Keith had taken her hand and was trying to pull her along with him. "Let's go then, we have to make up for lost time. Come on. . . ."

Camilla looked back at the door, which was closed tight again. It had closed by itself. "Where is she?"

"Who? What's the matter with you? Come along. I'll have to show you that we know how to waltz in America too. If not, it's high time you taught me."

His German was flawless, but since his father had taught him, he spoke it with an unusual accent, half Berlin and half American. His voice, unusually deep for his age and build, had had an especially strong effect on Camilla from the first moment, and even now she was tempted to do exactly what he asked her, to dance with him, to be happy. . . . But then the heady scent rose to her nostrils again. She pulled away from him and hurried toward the door through which he had come. He caught up with her and tried to hold her back, but the only effect was to make her all the more determined to get through the door.

"What's the matter? Let's go dance. Come with me. I'll explain everything, don't be childish. . . ."

He could not have said anything worse. She snatched her arm out of his grasp, and he could do nothing but watch her disappear into the pressing room.

The room was almost dark. A gas cylinder was burning with a low flame, and the window was lit with the glow of the bright winter night. Smoothly ironed sheets were piled on the pressing table. She could not find Lou at once, but then her sister called attention to herself. "Don't just stand there! As long as you're here, help me. You know your way around here, where's the sewing box?"

The room contained a sofa, covered only in white muslin, where the pressing woman sometimes rested. Lou stood there, one foot on the seat pad, fixing her stockings. Her reddish-blonde curls had fallen forward, covering her forehead; one shoulder was bare, the strap of her gown seemed torn. When she had adjusted the stocking, she slipped back into her sequined evening slipper and turned around. When her lips formed an innocent pout as they did now, she had a face exactly like a doll: a round forehead, round eyes, long lashes, full cheeks, and, as if pasted on, two thin strokes for eyebrows. "A tempestuous young man, I must say." It sounded very unselfconscious. "Come, help me. I've got to fix this thing somehow."

Camilla stood still and searched for words that would not give

70

away any of her feelings. "The door has a bolt. You could at least have locked it."

"But baby, who says I *didn't*. Surely you don't mean to give me lessons—not in *this* subject." She pulled open a drawer, rummaged around in it. "I can't find the damn sewing box." She giggled softly. "Remember what Mama always said, 'Swearing is the first step on the path of sin.'"

"I don't know if your husband would laugh." Camilla was angry at herself. Why didn't she leave? Why did she allow Lou to engage her in chatter?

Lou heaved a deep sigh. "My husband—how horrible the word sounds on your lips. Do you think I know what he's up to this very minute? An officer of the guard, a leader of the dance, *and* good-looking! Do I ask him what he does? Do I lie awake tormenting myself with jealous fantasies? My dear child, you've got a lot to learn." She came toward Camilla, holding her dress at the neckline. "Are you planning to run to him and tattle on me? You can save yourself the trouble. He wouldn't believe a word you say; he'd just think you were a jealous kitten. Are you jealous?"

"Have you deceived him before?"

"Deceived!" She shook her head. "I cultivate my secret little garden, I enjoy my youth. That isn't forbidden, is it? If you're just the least bit clever, it's quite practical to be married. It's true; you should take lessons from me. But start by changing your expression."

"You've only seen him twice, at Christmas and tonight." Camilla was reminded of the dinner. She had not thought anything of it when she saw Lou's animated flirting with Keith; that was Lou's way. It was part of any conversation she carried on with a man—an essential part, like salt in the soup.

Lou laughed again, a deep, throaty laugh, like a doll's. "Nothing better! No long preparations, no aftermath. Once you start with those. . . . But you really are jealous. What do you know, our little Camilla. You're really busting out all over." She loved salty, slightly vulgar expressions; she thought them spicy, and at the proper moments they helped her achieve her "colossal success" with men, as she was wont to put it. "Here at home she hangs on to the impetuous young man, at the same time setting her cap for Mr. Moneybags!" The fact that Rothe would contribute two hundred thousand marks to have Camilla marry his son still haunted her. In the whole conversation about her father's bankruptcy that was the only item that had captured her interest. "Two hundred thousand! However did you manage it?" She came a step closer, and with her came a whiff of perfume. "Two hundred thousand—he must have regretted it after all, all that lovely money! Left you in the lurch! At the last minute." She snapped her fingers, and her eyes glittered with malicious pleasure. "Just like that! Well, calm down, you're not the first. And as for the young man, you can have him. It's true that he's impetuous, but he's pretty clumsy as well."

"Nobody left me in the lurch."

"Well, well. It gets more interesting by the minute. So you're the one who turned down the two hundred thousand?"

"Papa did that. For me. I didn't want to marry Rothe."

"Papa did that! What a good man! Your dear Papa, so pure and noble. What a touching story!"

"I don't know what you're talking about. I don't know anything about . . . two hundred thousand marks. Papa needs money, that's true. Just the same, he chose to do without it because he knew that I—"

Rising from deep within her body, Lou's characteristic laugh interrupted the girl. "Tell me, are you really that dumb or are you just pretending? You're not trying to tell me you bought Papa's fairy tale? He called off the engagement for your sake! Baby, have you got a lot to learn about men! Now I'll tell you what really happened. Your father would have licked his fingers if he could have brought it off. He's in hot water up to his eyeballs. He has more debts than he has hairs on his head. He's broke, don't you understand? The end. *Finit*. This party is the last act. Tomorrow the fire curtain comes down. The comedy is over. London Bridge is falling down. The pharmacy, the factory—all done for. Even this house will probably come under the hammer. Your marriage was the last straw he could grasp at. That's how it was. But the Rothes—they're a cautious lot. I suppose they made inquiries at the bank. They got cold feet and called off the engagement. Open your eyes at last to your adorable, selfless Papa! Men! Ah . . ." and without transition she went on, "Ruined my dress. . . . Dammit, where's the sewing box?"

Camilla stood at the door, her hand on the latch. It was cowardly to run away. She had to contradict Lou, she had to defend Papa. But by the time she understood what she had to do, she had already left the room.

In the hall the mood had become even more exuberant. Carried along by Rozanski's irresistible temperament, even the older ladies and gentlemen were dancing now. Some were already decked out to see in the new year, wearing cardboard noses and those ridiculous little hats. Confetti was strewn over the floor, and the chandeliers and sconces were garlanded with colorful streamers. In barely fifteen minutes it would be midnight, and the servants were ready to hand a full glass of champagne to every guest on the stroke of midnight.

A few men momentarily without ladies greeted Camilla boisterously; they blew noisemakers in her face and threw handsful of confetti over her.

The smoking room was empty except for the four men at the green-covered card table. The lamp with the pearl tassels was pulled low over the felt surface. The circle of light it shed lit only the white-cuffed hands of the four players clutching sheaves of cards. Smoke from an ashtray rose into the lamp.

Now one hand left the circle of light, dipped into the dusk, and motioned to Camilla to come closer. "Come, sit with me. You don't mind, do you? She won't say a word, I guarantee it." Fritz Hofmann leaned back in his chair. "Well then, come over here. You're sure to bring me luck."

His voice expressed cheerfulness, comfort, but what else had she expected? Camilla stepped closer hesitantly, acknowledged the men's greeting with a silent nod, and leaned over her father. "I have to talk to you."

"Now?"

She was reminded of Mademoiselle Schröter. Would he put her off the same way? "It can't be helped," she said. "Please."

The urgency in her voice must have persuaded him. Whatever it was, he pushed his cards together into a neat little pile and said to the group, "Excuse me a moment. A father's duties! And don't forget, Aschenbach raised." He held on to his cards as he got to his feet. He led her toward the window embrasure farthest from the table, determined not to leave the room. "Well, my child, what can be so important?"

"Can't you finally stop calling me that?"

Though he had given in to her request, his thoughts were still

73

occupied with estimating the strength of his hand. What was it she had just said? Irritated, he looked at her.

"I can see you're eager to get back to your game," Camilla resumed. "Just tell me one thing: why did you have to lie to me? You! I always thought that would never be necessary between the two of us." It was preposterous that the words, which she wanted to shout out loud, had to be said softly, almost in a whisper. But somehow it fitted—it was like the deep, peculiar sorrow she felt. She stood there stiffly, her arms at her sides; she was aware of the breeze coming in through the window. The window doesn't close properly, I'll have to have it seen to. For an instant she was totally possessed by the irrelevant thought.

"If you'll tell me what you're talking about—"

"About my engagement. About Rothe. You didn't really stop it, you didn't want to stop it."

"But it was stopped, isn't that true? Isn't that what matters?"

"But I thought—"

"Please lower your voice. Look, you didn't give me a chance. The thing fell apart. How and why—does it matter? Be glad, have a good time, dance, enjoy tonight."

Why was he determined not to understand her? Didn't he know that for her he was more than a father, that she was losing more than her faith in him? She was losing the belief that people were reliable, that they could be trusted. Her thoughts were not clear, only deeply tormenting. And once more she was reminded of Schröter, of her strange behavior in the dining room. "What about Schröter? What about her savings? Did she want her money back and you didn't have it to give her?"

"I administered three thousand marks for her, and I doubled the sum."

Anyone who did not know him would have been content with his answer. Just an hour ago even Camilla would have been satisfied. But now she was filled with suspicions. "Then why didn't you give it to her?"

"I meant to give it to her."

He avoided her eyes; suddenly his assurance was gone, and Camilla saw it all clearly. He had closed out her account. Of course he had intended to pay Schröter with it, but then he had gambled it away in the city, in a last desperate attempt to change his luck. She had

74

always been on his side. He had been the measure of everything. It had not always been easy, but she had turned and twisted facts until it was he who was in the right. But now she could no longer do it, and probably she would never be able to do it again. The pain he had caused 'her was too great. She would never be able to forget it, never quite get over it.

What was she still waiting for? Was she secretly hoping that there was, after all, a justification for him?

"So you gambled it away?" Why didn't he say no? Why did he not give her an honorable explanation, whether it was true or invented? But he was silent, his head bowed. And this mute admission of guilt made everything worse.

"Yes," he finally said. Since he did not himself know exactly how it had happened, how could he explain it to Camilla? The short interview with Rothe who had canceled everything on the basis of information received at the bank, both the business and the personal partnership; the shock he felt leaving Rothe's office, which soon after turned to a feeling of exhilaration, a conviction that nothing more could happen to him; his fixed idea that with Camilla's money in his pocket he would win, that he would return home a rich man. . . . "I'm sorry."

There was another silence before Camilla spoke. "The sad thing is, I'll never be able to trust you again."

"Camilla. . . ."

She turned away before he could grasp her hand. She had had one more question, more important than all the rest, but she could no longer think clearly. The card players' eyes bored into her back, and the way to the door seemed endless. How was it possible to walk without feeling one's feet? Where could she go in this house, so filled with joyous revelers? Where could she be alone?

She tried the library, and when she saw that it was empty, she pulled the door closed behind her. On a small table, lit by a single lamp, stood some demitasse cups and a tray of pastries. Camilla extinguished the lamp, so that the room was illuminated only by the fire in the grate. She had spent many an evening on the leather sofa facing the mantel, alone with a book or simply with her thoughts, and sometimes she had fallen asleep here until the cold and the uncomfortable position had awakened her.

Over the mantel, inlaid in the paneling, hung a painting; now it was in the dark, for the glow of the fire did not reach that far up-ward. It was the tree from the estate, the old linden tree, the wishing tree. Papa had commissioned the picture shortly after they had moved into the house.

Her legs tucked under her, arms and head leaning against the rounded armrest, she stared at the painting and listened to the crackling of the fire and the noises of the house. She had not put the most important question to her father: what would become of the house? But how could she go back to him, once more interrupt the game? The thought of him turning his look on her, the look that begged her not to begrudge him this one pleasure, was enough to discourage her. If what Lou had said was true . . . that the phar-macy and the factory were to be auctioned off, and probably the house as well. . . .

"Please," she whispered to herself. "Please." She had nothing specific in mind, she was simply hoping that everything would turn out all right after all. She closed her eyes. Not to think any more, not to brood. To forget, to sleep.

She heard the door behind her opening and then Keith's voice. "Camilla, are you in here?"

She kept still; she knew he could not see her over the high-backed couch. The tangle of voices from the hall trickled through the open door.

He must have discovered her nevertheless. His steps came closer. "Hurry! It's almost midnight. You'll miss the best part!"

She kept her eyes closed, and yet she knew that he was standing in front of her, for the warmth of the fire diminished. She opened her eyes and screamed in fright, unprepared for the large paper nose he was wearing, which seemed even more disfiguring in the flickering light. "Take that thing off!" she shouted, and when he did not comply at once, she jumped up and snatched it from his nose. But that only made matters worse; now the nose hung from its elastic around his neck, dangling large and red on his chest. "Go away," she said. "Go, leave me alone."

When he had gone to look for her, he had had a different fantasy of the moment when he would find her. When it came to women and taking advantage of favorable circumstances, he could usually rely on his instincts. "Don't you want to come along," he pleaded, "and drink a toast with me to—to a happy new year?"

76

"It's too late," she said.

"How can it be too late?" He no longer understood anything about her.

"Everything . . ." she glanced at the painting over the mantel. "How can people believe nonsense like that—wishes that come true. . . ."

A clock began to strike; the noise in the house began to swell, and then, outside on the terrace, the fireworks began to explode. Camilla's eyes remained fixed on the painting; the tree changed colors with the red, green, and white lights.

Two

1

Suddenly she felt the cold, and she broke off her search for fossils. Since her eyes were fixed on the sandy beach, the changing light must have told her that a cloud had drifted in front of the sun; but now she saw that the entire sky was covered with clouds. They drifted thickly across the water, the lower layers more swiftly than the upper ones. In spite of the many summers she had spent at the seaside in her childhood, she was still not used to these abrupt weather changes. The sea—that was another world and another life. It was like her hair, which had now been cut short for six months and which sometimes she still tried to smooth down her back.

She gazed out over the ocean to the dark cloud banks, and at first she thought the wedge of birds was another cloud, it approached her in such a dense formation and so silently. Carried only by the wind, without any beating of wings or cries, the flock headed toward the shore, sank downward, and came to rest on the small strip of sand that formed the shoreline. The only sound was the rustle of plumage, like a waning wind. Only then did she recognize the birds as petrels by their glowing yellow webs.

It was a lonely piece of shore, hidden behind steep dunes that were about forty yards high. Many shells and crabs had been washed up at high tide. But the scrawny birds with the white wing markings paid no attention to them; instead they remained lying on the sand, exhausted. There must be more than a hundred of them, Camilla thought, reminded of what the fishermen in Warnemünde often said: that summer was over when the first petrels came in from the north.

A cold wind came off the outgoing tide. She was most aware of the cold on her bare feet and on the nape of her neck, no longer covered by hair. She looked for a place close up against the dune, where the sand was still warm from the sun. She had discovered this stretch of beach in the spring, when she had been looking for gulls' eggs; since then she had come here often. It took half an hour by bicycle from Aunt Lenka's house, which was situated at the western end of town. At first the road was even, hemmed in by pines and furze; farther on, the vegetation grew more sparse, and the road rose steadily up a high dune. To get from there to the water was simple enough, you just allowed yourself to slide down the sand. The return was more difficult, but with time Camilla had beaten a path that led her to the top in a zigzag route.

Little by little the petrels revived. They shook their feathers, picked up bits of food, dug sleeping holes in the sand with rapid beats of their blunt tails. The wind was driving more clouds inland, still in two layers. The upper ones were great white pillows; the clouds below, rushing along at almost twice the speed, were small and dark and threw restless shadows on the water. Camilla never carried a watch when she went roaming; time meant nothing to her, and she could always use the excursion steamers that plied their trade between Warnemünde and Heiligendamm as points of reference. This afternoon she had not noticed any of the boats, and even now only a couple of fishing skiffs were out to collect their nets. Camilla had often watched the night train being loaded—it carried away the catch, packed in ice chests. Camilla imagined that all of it must go to Berlin.

Between the buoys that marked the lane to Warnemünde's harbor she now discovered a freighter, then a second and a third, heading for the estuary of the Warnow River. All she could see of the town itself was the jetty, reaching far out into the sea, and the tall lighthouse.

The cold breeze had now managed to penetrate even her sheltered spot; reluctantly she started home and climbed the zigzag path up the dune. Her bicycle was leaning against a twisted pine. She brushed the sand from her feet, pulled on her stockings and her shoes, and fastened the trousers of her bloomer costume with clips at the ankles. It was the first time she had worn trousers. Mama had never allowed her to wear them; she found it scandalous enough that any of her daughters would ride such a "poor people's vehicle." That was another thing that had changed in her life: there was no longer any "no" from her mother.

On the downhill path, with its white cover of crushed seashells, the wind at her back, the bicycle moved by itself. She even applied the brake, so as not to get home too soon, but it did not help much. After one last curve the resort town emerged; the long promenade bordered with locust trees, to the left the broad bathing beach and to the right the row of hotels and boarding houses, first the little ones and then, closer to the jetty, the bigger and fancier ones. Aunt Lenka's house was right at the entrance to the town, where only locals lived: fishermen, and captains' wives whose husbands were still at sea or dead—one never knew.

Except for the slight hum of her bicycle and the monotonous rhythm of the surf there was no sound. The voices of playing children that normally rang from the beach were gone; the sand castles sported no colorful banners. The blue-checkered tent where rowboats could be rented was no longer in its place and the boats themselves were beached, keel uppermost, showing their tarred bottoms. A few men were picking up litter at the water's edge, and at the place where the shell path turned into a paved street she encountered a wagon loaded with beach baskets.

Camilla knew the heavy-set man on the box. He was Kleinhans, Aunt Lenka's neighbor. As he brought his wagon to a halt, Camilla too stopped her bicycle and got down. Kleinhans touched his black, faded cap and in his laconic way asked, "Been out there?"

"Yes, I was out there." Camilla had noted with a single glance that Aunt Lenka's company had not left yet; her aunt was standing in the front yard, near the bed of savory, talking with Witte. He was already wearing his hat and coat, and Camilla hoped that she might be spared having to talk to him. She stepped a little closer to the cart to continue her conversation with Kleinhans. "I saw some petrels, a whole swarm of them."

83

"That right? Early in the season. Early petrels, early winter." He stared at Camilla's trousers and her flimsy shirtwaist. "Dress more warmly."

"Winter?" she asked. "What about autumn? Don't you have autumn here?"

"We don't know anything about autumn. Only long winters. You're staying this year, I hear?"

"Yes, we're staying." Her eyes wandered to the deserted beach, and she tried to imagine what it would be like in the winter, but she could not picture it. Until now she had always managed to push away the thought that this year she would also be spending the winter here, as she had managed to put off so many other thoughts that had to do with her future.

Kleinhans scratched the back of his neck, pushing his cap forward. "Boring for a young lady like you. Nothing goes on." Like many locals, Kleinhans had adapted to the new era, to the transformation of Warnemünde from a fishing village to a seaside resort. He had packed in his fishing business, and for the last few years he had worked for the resort administration, taking care of tennis courts and repairing beach chairs. During the winter he took little wooden plaques— preferably birch trunks cut into ovals—and painted them with quatrains, with the lighthouse or the town coat of arms. During the summer these were sold in the souvenir shops. He picked up the reins. "Got to get on. Two more trips. Witte—I bet he's waiting for you."

Camilla followed the man's glance to her aunt's house. Lenka and Witte, the local pharmacist, were standing at the gate, and there was no way she could avoid an encounter now. "Decent man," she heard Kleinhans say, "not poor. . . ." She almost had to laugh at the sight of him trying so hard to praise Witte. Aunt Lenka must have put him up to it.

She pushed her bicycle to the house. Somehow you could tell that at one time the one-story brick building had belonged to a sea captain; in the narrow front yard typical of the houses hereabouts not much grew, because the soil was always being swallowed by sand.

Hermann Witte, who owned a pharmacy on the town's best street, opened the garden gate for Camilla. She had known him since coming to Warnemünde for the first time as a child. She could never pass the windows of his shop without staring at the large round glass with the leeches; the figure of the pharmacist himself, with his side-burns, had always been in the background.

"You're late. We've been waiting for you. Herr Witte was de-termined to see you."

Hermann Witte was unable to shake hands with Camilla because she was still holding the bicycle. He did not speak at once either. Instead he reached into the pocket of his buttoned-up, three-quarter-length dark-gray jacket and held out a silver box. "You can't be too careful in this weather," he said. "It's healthful, but you have to be used to it and dress accordingly." Perhaps he was afraid that she would take his remark as a criticism, for he hastened to add, "At your age one is not aware of the weather, isn't that right? It's going to blow a lot more, too. It's coming from the north, toward us. Rain. The whole sky is full of rain, but we need it."

She took one of the small brown lozenges the druggist made up himself. This too was part of life at the seaside—the enormous im-portance accorded to the weather. The weather determined conversa-tions, determined everyone's well-being, memories, and future.

It was clear Aunt Lenka considered Witte's attempt to get the conversation going exceedingly clumsy. "It won't be all that bad with the weather," she interjected. "September is the most beautiful month here, and October. . . ."

"Yes," Witte echoed. "They're often the best months in the year."

"Herr Witte came to invite you to the Feast of the Ships."

Once again the pharmacist gratefully took the hint. "Of course, that's why I'm here, the Feast. The resort commission has dug deep into its pockets. The *Queen Christina* will be anchored at the estuary and decked out for the celebration, to close the season. There will be dancing, fireworks—"

"I'm so very sorry," Camilla interrupted. "But I promised I would not go dancing, not this year." She said it off the top of her head, simply to have an excuse. No other reason occurred to her for turn-ing down his invitation.

"I didn't know." Witte sounded irritated. "A death in the family? I'd be sorry if my invitation. . . ." He made such a ceremony of pull-ing on his gray gloves—stroking down each finger separately, closing the two snaps meticulously—that the process expressed all his em-barrassment. Camilla felt sorry for him and almost more sorry for her aunt, who seemed equally confused. Then she remembered the fossil she had found. She asked Witte to hold her bicycle and brought out the piece of rock in which a sea urchin was clearly marked. "You understand something about these, don't you?"

"May I?" He took the rock from her and turned it in the light. "A spatangoid urchin. And in excellent condition. They're quite rare in this form. Do you have more?"

He was going to give the fossil back to her, but she shook her head. "It's yours. You're the collector."

"You don't collect?"

"No." And in truth she had picked up the fossil only because the impression was particularly sharp. One of her saddest memories was of the moment when Papa had had to say goodbye to all his collections, especially the clocks and watches. At that time she had made a resolution never to collect anything. What good was it to get attached to things that you were bound to lose one day? "No," she repeated. "I'm not a collector. There are enough collectors. Even Kleinhans has his collection."

"Kleinhans? That's news to me."

"He collects cigar bands. Paper bands from cigars from all over the world, sorted by countries. He has a box full of them."

Witte cleared his throat. "Anyway, many thanks. A splendid specimen, really, a rarity . . . it will remind me of you." And then he quickly took his leave. He went out through the garden gate and walked along the locust-lined road in his jacket, knickerbockers, and puttees, all of a uniform gray.

Aunt Lenka shook her head as she and Camilla walked into the house. "Why do you always have to treat him like that? He doesn't know what to make of you."

"Is he supposed to?"

"Don't be foolish. Where have you been all day?"

"At the beach . . . it will soon be over. Kleinhans says that the winters here are very long."

"Is it true that he collects cigar bands?"

"It's true. He showed them to me just the other day, hundreds and hundreds of them. You can pore over the whole genealogy of different royal houses. . . ."

"Your shoes!" They had entered the tiny vestibule, a kind of porch in front of the hall proper. The baseboard was lined with a row of shoes; Lenka insisted that all shoes be changed here. Nothing annoyed her more than someone dragging sand into the house. In previous years, during her short summer vacations, Camilla had not paid much attention to this fussiness in her aunt, but now she felt put off by it.

The two women had entered the large parlor with all the heavy pieces of furniture—a Renaissance sideboard, a sofa in the eighteenth-century style, upholstered armchairs, and paintings thickly framed in gold. They were not suited to the proportions of the house, to the small windows and low ceilings. It was as if a fishing scow had been furnished with the leftovers from a luxury liner—at least that was how it struck Camilla. In the glassed-in veranda, which gave a view of the sea, stood the table on which Aunt Lenka's tarot cards were spread out; the card representing The Master lay to one side, separate; obviously her aunt had been doing a reading for the pharmacist.

"By the way, it was thoughtful of you to make him a present of the fossil. You gave him great pleasure." Aunt Lenka had begun to pile the tea service on a tray. It was not the onion pattern she ordi- narily used but the thin, almost transparent china that really came from China, with a reddish-gold dragon pattern.

Camilla took the tray from her aunt to carry it to the kitchen. "Tell me, Aunt Lenka, you're not seriously planning a match between me and the pharmacist? That would be a whole new side of you."

Her aunt did not answer at once. She sat down in one of the overstuffed chairs and picked up her crocheting. "I'm just a little more farsighted than you, that's all. Or can you tell me what your plans are? Go on now, you'd better change your clothes."

Besides the kitchen and the parlor, the ground floor consisted only of Aunt Lenka's bedroom. The next floor consisted of a bathroom and two other rooms, now occupied by Camilla and her father. In all the years they had spent their summer vacations here, Camilla had never been bothered by the smallness of the house; instead it had struck her as cozy. But now she sometimes felt as if the roof were about to fall in on her. Not even in her room was she truly alone. She could hear every step taken by anyone else in the house, and she knew that everyone could hear her.

Even without her aunt's admonition—despite her tolerant ways, Lenka would still rather see her niece in a skirt than in bloomers— Camilla would have changed, for she had grown chilly in the flimsy things. Back in the living room Camilla sat down by her aunt and picked up a book, but she was unable to concentrate. Plans? Indeed, what plans did she have except to get through each day, each exactly like the one before? In an hour her father would come home. The table would be set; he would sit down to dinner, pass on the day's news from Warnemünde, retire to his room, change into evening clothes, and disappear again. Or would that be over now that more and more of the summer visitors were leaving the resort? Would he go back to spending the whole day sitting around the house, as he had done during the early months of the year, after they had left Berlin? The memory had faded with the onset of summer, but now, as she thought back, she realized that she had forgotten none of it: the rain, which seemed unending; the sky, which did not clear for weeks on end; the cold, the wind that never ceased blowing; her father locking himself in his room all day long; and the moment when he reappeared, in his dressing gown, unshaven. He had never shaved himself as long as he lived—"not even during my travels in Africa"—and he refused to do so even now. Never had Camilla seen him like this; never had he worn a shirt for more than a day. But she had noticed changes in herself as well. She had always been waited on; one of the upstairs maids had straightened up her room and made her bed, a lady's maid had buttoned her shoes and tied on her veil—and now she stood in Aunt Lenka's kitchen washing dishes, she swept the hall, she aired the bedding. . . .

"What are you thinking about?"

"Papa," she answered, because she did not want to talk about herself. "The first months here."

The situation had improved as spring came, for her father as well as for herself. She had been able to go outside on long walks. Her father had found a barber—true, not one who would come to the house, but he set some time aside every morning for Hofmann. Papa had discovered the reading room in the seaside pavilion, where all the Berlin newspapers were available. Besides, there was the bandstand, there were the hotel terraces where he could spend hours, the billiards room in the Palace Hotel, and finally a gaming parlor, although Camilla never understood where her father found the money needed to enter it.

"Do you know where he gets the money for his card games?"

"First of all he bets more cautiously, and second, the people he plays with around here—they aren't up to his skill."

88

It was not an upsetting thought—a father who did harmless summer visitors out of their money and seemed content with the way of life. "You mean he wins?"

"I assume so. At least he hasn't tried to borrow money from me recently." She laid her crocheting aside. "Camilla, I'm sorry, but make your peace with it once and for all—that's how he is. Basically he's very pleased with this life. He doesn't want more than to live for his pleasure—maybe he never wanted more. He's delighted to be rid of all responsibility."

"He talks about having plans—friends who'd advance him the capital for a new factory. Maybe when winter comes, we'll be in Berlin—"

"No, no, no—don't ever believe him when he talks that way. He only says these things to please you. Maybe he believes them at the moment he says them, but only for the moment! Really, he's happy like this. Believe me, I know what I'm talking about. My father had a friend who was a gambler. He won thirty thousand rubles at cards every year, just as someone else might collect his civil-service salary. Your father reminds me of him; he would prefer to live like that too, win his thirty thousand rubles so casually. . . . Have you forgotten so soon? You can't count on your father, you have to take your life into your own hands."

"Witte?" She could not even have described how he looked, only his gray jacket and the gray gloves.

"Why so sarcastic? You'd do better to ask yourself what you want. Do you want a family? Do you want children? For that you need a husband, that's the way it is. The—"

"I know, I know . . . the time goes quickly, and if I don't watch out . . . please, Aunt Lenka, how often do you think I've heard that? Whenever Mama preached at us. Is there no other choice for a girl? Witte—he could be my father."

"Don't be so touchy. He's forty-two years old, so what? A man of that age—"

"Decent man. Not poor."

"What are you saying?"

"Nothing." Again she wondered what he looked like. She could more easily have described anything in the world than his face—the big glass globe with the leeches, for example, or the brown throat lozenges which he had been offering her as far back as she could remember. Oh yes, and the beetle collections he sold in glass boxes.

She had discovered one of his advertisements in a Berlin newspaper: "German beetles, assorted by species, the ideal gift for boys. Also excellently suited for visual instruction in schools."

Had her aunt been speaking? ". . . who waits until he is able to offer a woman something—doesn't that tell you that a woman will be well cared for in his keeping? He owns a good deal of property. Two pharmacies, the one here and another in Rostock, and both buildings belong to him. That's in addition to the concession in the Warnemünde mineral-water pavilion. He told me, but I forget, how many thousands of bottles he sells each month. And then there's his quinine tonic, Witte's Quinine Tonic. . . ."

There was a knock at the window. Kleinhans' head appeared, this time with the cap pushed back on his neck. A shock of brown hair curled on his forehead. "Barometer falling fast," he said after Camilla had thrown the window open. "About the storm windows. Tomorrow? Tomorrow I've got time."

Aunt Lenka nodded. "Fine, let's put up the storm windows. That means we'll have to clean them today."

Kleinhans was so large that he filled almost the entire window frame. "Better that way. Barometer falling fast. Water's gray all over. Summer's over for this year."

"How late it is." Aunt Lenka stared dreamily into space. "How quickly the time passes."

Camilla was reminded what it was like in Berlin when the storm windows were cleaned, a procedure that took two full days. Her thoughts often wandered to the empty house in Steglitz; she pictured herself running all alone through the rooms lit only by the weak rays that peeped through closed blinds. The daydream held a peculiar fascination for her, almost displacing the tormented memories of moving.

It had happened right after the new year. Mama had been the first to leave the sinking ship; the servants had followed, all except the gardener, Willeke, and his wife, who stayed to take care of the house and the grounds. She herself, together with her father, had moved to a hotel for the last few days, and they had driven out to Steglitz one more time. But by then the rugs had already been rolled up, the furniture hidden under sheets, the heavy curtains taken down and put in mothballs. Not one of the many clocks was still in its place. Her father had handed them over for auction, along with his other collections and the entire contents of the wine cellars—a hundred and fifty bottles of Chateau Gruaud, two hundred bottles of Les Clos Grand Cru, three hundred bottles of Kiedricher Auslese, five hundred bottles of champagne of every kind and vintage. In spite of all that, she was convinced that the leavetaking was only temporary, that she would soon return. She had never had a moment's doubt. "Do you know what I dream sometimes?" she said. "That I'm wandering through the grounds of our house but the paths are all gone. Everything is overgrown, and I no longer know my way around. I get lost."

"Camilla! How often must I tell you—stop thinking about it."

"But it's important for me to think about it." She stepped out on the glassed-in veranda. Kleinhans had been right, the sea had lost its blue color and was a dirty gray. A dory was rocking on the waves; it did not seem to make any headway, though the man in it was rowing with all his might. "When do you want to start on the windows?"

"We'll do them in the morning."

"Maybe I'll go for another walk, then. Just for half an hour."

"To see the train leave for Berlin? Come over here instead. Sit down. Listen to me. Somebody has to tell you, and since your father can't gather the courage to do it. . . . The house. . . ."

"What about the house?"

"I'm about to tell you! The house doesn't belong to you any more. Did you hear me? You will never return there; most likely other people are already living in it. It's been sold. Well," she sighed deeply, "now you know."

Camilla stood very still, then she made the motion with which she used to toss her long braids over her shoulders. "How can it be sold?" she asked. Of course she had learned at the time that Papa had not assigned the house to her at all, that it belonged to Mama. She had consoled herself with the idea that in that case it was exempt from the general bankruptcy. That fact had been more important to her than anything else. The house was not subject to the same fate as the factory: the men who came and tore out the machines, the auction of the inventory, the vehicles, the rest of the stock. The house was not threatened with any of that, and that was what she concentrated on— that and the idea that one day they would return. "When did you find out?"

"A week ago. They wrote for the house key. They knew there were six of them, and two were missing. They wanted to get hold of them because otherwise they would have had to change the lock."

"You sent the keys?"

"What right did I have to refuse?"

"Even mine?"

"Yes. Won't you listen to reason at last? Consider yourself lucky that your mother had the house conveyed to her—now at least *she* has the money. That way your father no longer has to see to her upkeep. She is his wife, after all. Sometimes a body could think you'd built the house. . . . Stop! You can't run away now and lock yourself in your room. You can't run away from everything in life."

"I didn't intend to," Camilla said in a cool, brittle voice.

"Where were you going, then?"

"I'm going to clean the windows. Stay there, I'll do it by myself. I'd rather do it now. Maybe tomorrow it will be nice again after all, and I'll be able to go to the beach."

She left by the back door. The wind had risen. As soon as she left the shelter of the house, she had to fight for equilibrium to withstand the strong gusts.

During the summer the storm windows were stored in an abandoned arbor. Camilla brought them into the house one by one, washed them, polished the panes with old newspapers, and put them in order. All Kleinhans need do was insert them in the window frames tomorrow morning. The work calmed her; it was better than sitting around idly with a book, which she would not have read anyway.

Gradually she succeeded in ordering her thoughts. The house was sold. Other people were living in it now. Would they make any changes? Put up new wallpaper, redesign the gardens. . . . By then she had used up her common sense. No, she would never accept the idea that the house was lost forever. It was in the hands of strangers now, fine. Still it continued to be her house and would always be her house. Some day she would return, but how? She could not count on her father, not even on Aunt Lenka. She was the only one who could help herself!

But what could she do? She had learned languages—French and English, and a little Russian from Aunt Lenka; she played the piano passably well; she could draw quite prettily. That meant that she could take the road so many girls from good families without a dowry were compelled to take, and seek a position as a governess. But how could she earn enough that way to buy back the house? What else could she do? A position in an office or a shop was no better paid. She knew a few manufacturers in the perfume industry, but that would not bring her any closer to her goal. Looking at it soberly, a young girl had only once chance: to marry a rich man. And she'd had that chance already; what an irony that at the time she had done everything in her power to escape the trap, and now the same trap was opening for her all over again.

She threw a woolen scarf around her shoulders and went outside, around the house, through the front yard, crossing the promenade, struggling against sand and wind. It felt good to let her thoughts be blown out of her head. The boat she had observed earlier was still on the water. It disappeared in the troughs of the waves, then turned up again. She even thought she could see the water running off the rower's oilskins. He had not made much progress, but he struggled on, unflagging, pulling the oars through the water with long, energetic strokes. For a moment she wished she were in his place, in the boat. She was sure that he was not harboring a single superfluous thought, such as wondering whether he should turn back or simply give up. He could not allow himself a moment of weakness. He knew that he simply had to keep on rowing. . . .

She stood still and waited until the boat grew smaller and finally disappeared behind the jetty. The gray waves smashed high against the stone walls. But behind them, she knew, the waters were calm.

2

In the eyes of the residents of Warnemünde, Am Strom was the best possible address. The Bismark Promenade might be good for hotels and boarding houses and for the summer people as it ran parallel to the beach, but Am Strom—the stream was the Old Warnow —was where a native felt at home. One could take walks along the shore path next to the slightly lower riverbed and rest on the green benches along the embankment, where the grass always remained sparse in spite of loving care. The houses were on the other side of the avenue, their elegance in no way diminished by the fact that the ground floors of many were occupied by shops. The house number was all that counted—the higher the better. Herman Witte's house was number 93.

After three stormy days of damp cold, the weather had changed overnight and again become clear, calm, and sunny. Now, in the early afternoon, the thermometer stood at a warm 22° C, as if especially ordered for the Festival of Ships, which was to take place that night. The two ships designated for the festival were already lying at anchor in the estuary. Spectators watched with fascination as the decorations were installed on board. Camilla too had stopped to stare for a while, but when the last chain of colored lanterns was attached above the railing, she gave herself a push and started to walk toward the pharmacy.

94

As always, one of the two display windows was filled with Witte's own products: his quinine tonic, Dr. Witte's Diet Pills, Wiocitin—a nutritive and restorative for thin blood—and a regiment of table and health waters, "which in a few short years have achieved world renown."

Camilla had never studied all these items as thoroughly as she did now. The other window had been newly and somewhat hastily decorated; the ointments against sunburn, chapped lips, inflamed eyes, and mosquito bites had disappeared, making way for medication to combat sore throats, coughs, rheumatism, and lumbago. The most conspicuous object was no longer the red-and-white beach ball but a glittering vaporizer. The sight of this paraphernalia, familiar to her since childhood, almost caused Camilla to turn back; she particularly feared the pharmaceutic smell. She thought it would make her ill as soon as she crossed the threshold. But she also knew that it was only her imagination, and at last she walked through the door. She had come at a propitious moment, for there were only a few customers in the store. Two old women sat on the black oilcloth-covered sofa on the left, waiting for a prescription. A younger woman, holding a child by the hand, stood at the counter and was being waited on by one of the clerks. There was no sign of Witte himself. The familiar large globe with the leeches, solemn as a work of art, now crowned a black laquered shelf. The wall behind it was covered to the ceiling with the glass boxes holding the beetle collections. There was also a weighing machine and a small fountain with a blue marble dancing on its jet.

"May I help you?" A second clerk had appeared. "Oh, it's Fräulein Hofmann! How are you? And Herr Hofmann? He's given up his factory, I hear. Is that true? But why? Have you any idea how much Hofmann's Hand Soap we sold? It was a real hit I tell you, people continue to ask for it. . . . Oh, I'm sure you'd like to speak with Herr Witte. I'll tell him you're here."

The customer at the counter had become alert; she looked Camilla up and down, then leaned over to the clerk and whispered. Camilla stepped to one side; she was not anxious to overhear the conversation. She could guess only too easily what they were talking about. A rich man like Hermann Witte, back on the market after his first marriage, was a constant source of conversation for the people of Warnemünde, especially for families with marriageable daughters. Camilla was relieved when the clerk returned and asked her to follow him. He led her to the archway in the paneled back wall. "Straight ahead. At the end of the hall."

The pharmacy smell grew stronger when she opened the door at the end. All four walls of the rectangular room were lined with built-in shelves and cabinets. In the center of the room stood a long prescription table with four work places separated by carved wooden strips. Witte had just taken off his white smock and was about to slip into his gray jacket. He came toward her, still occupied with doing up the long row of buttons; he got muddled and had to do it a second time.

"Well, this is my realm," he said, "some of it at any rate. I've been hoping for a long time that you'd come visit me."

White, milky light filled the room; at the back an iron circular staircase led to the next floor. If it connected with the living quarters, then the same smell must pervade the private apartment too—just as in Papa's old factory the smell of boiling fat rose even into the attics.

"I hope you've come to tell me that you'll attend the festival with me after all."

Camilla nodded and forced herself to look at him carefully, as if she were seeing a stranger for the first time. He wore rimless glasses and muttonchop whiskers. Often those very features gave a man distinction; the man in the portrait on the wall next to the door was like that. Hermann Witte, who had a different interpretation for Camilla's interest in the painting, explained, "My father."

Camilla tried to imagine how Witte would look clean-shaven. "The resemblance is startling," she said, comparing father and son. "But perhaps that's only because of the whiskers, they make you look older."

"Do you think so?"

"Yes, much older." Suddenly she was overcome by a conviction that if she could only bring Witte to shave off his muttonchops, she could not fail at anything. Actually the whiskers did not bother her at all, for they were cut short and his hair was very light, perhaps already graying a little. It was clear that Witte took great care of them. Perhaps the whiskers were his pride and joy. Perhaps it would be like betraying his father for him to shave, but in that case it was a particularly good test case. "I'm sure they're a lot of trouble, those whiskers."

"Yes, I guess they are."

"You've always worn them, haven't you?"

Witte seemed to be looking around for a mirror, but since there was none in the room, he fingered his whiskers, almost as if to protect them. "How about it, would you like to go for a walk? I mean, if you can spare the time." He picked up his hat, gloves, and walking stick, then added, "You don't like them. Be honest, you dislike my whiskers."

"I only mean that you'd look younger if you were clean-shaven, that's all. Much younger. And you know, my father never grew any kind of beard."

"True, true." Witte was embarrassed by the turn the conversation had taken, yet at the same time he was flattered by her interest. "You're probably right. Probably I would look younger, probably. . . . It's worth a try. Nobody ever sees himself clearly, I mean nobody really notices. It's just a habit, that's all; you start it, and you just go on. All of life consists of such habits." He seemed to have regained his composure. He was energetic as he buttoned his gloves, once more reached for his cane, and taking long steps, moved ahead of her. "It really is stupid, the way people cling to their habits," he said, and it sounded like a promise.

As soon as they had left the pharmacy, he took her elbow. "The weather is doing its part." He pointed at the festive ships. "It will grow cooler as its gets dark, but it will still be warm enough. I told you before, September often brings such surprises. You'll see, it's a prejudice to believe that only the summer is pleasant at the seaside. As time goes by, more and more people will visit here in fall and winter as well." He stood still and pointed across to the building site between the two rivers. "Over there, that's going to be the new ferry slip; to the right, the station for the trains. The basin they're dredging right now will be where the ships will dock. It will be in use no later than two years from now; the two ferries are already being constructed in Rostock. A seven-million-mark propect all in all. Do you realize what that means? Already we have excellent transportation; but by then Warnemünde will have the best of all the Baltic ports—six hours to Copenhagen, four hours to Hamburg, four hours to Berlin. We already have the lead with barely ten thousand summer visitors a year, but as soon as we have the ferry connection, the number will double."

"Four hours to Berlin?" she asked.

"Yes, not quite four hours."

They walked on, past the empty bandstand and the lighthouse, before starting on the path to the jetty. Witte repeatedly greeted passers-by, and the curious looks cast at them could not be ignored. When they had passed, people stopped to stare at their retreating backs.

"Are you aware that you are under constant scrutiny?" she asked.

"I'm used to it."

Witte was thought to be a widower; according to the official version his wife had died ten years ago, childless, after a brief marriage. At the same time a rumor persisted that she had left him and that a quiet divorce had subsequently been obtained.

"They all want to know whom Herr Witte will marry one day, isn't that it?"

"You become suspect, that's true. Every woman becomes suspect as soon as I single her out in any way or visit her frequently. Even your aunt has come under suspicion. A walk to the jetty, however, is the most daring deed I have allowed myself. Does it bother you?"

"It wouldn't be this way in Berlin."

The increasing breeze made it difficult to talk, and they headed for the glassed-in cabin at the end of the jetty. No one else was there, and they had the circular bench to themselves. The bathing beach lay deserted. A few solitary beach chairs were scattered in the sand. Far away, near the men's bathhouse, recognizable only by their bright caps, two undaunted swimmers bobbed in the surf.

"It's lonesome here during the winter, isn't it?" she said.

"It's all in the way you look at it. For me fall and winter are the best times. Fewer visitors, less bustle. You have time for things you have to neglect in the summer. During the summer, for example, I can't even begin to think of classifying my collections. You've never spent a winter here, but you'll like it, I'm certain."

"To tell you the truth, I'm a little afraid of it. Recently whenever I go to the train station to get the newspapers for my father and see the train leaving for Berlin . . . it's all I can do not to jump on at the last minute."

They were sitting on the bench. The wind could not penetrate into the glass cabin, and it was warm. Even the smack of the waves against the stone foundation was dulled. "This is the time we always used to go back to Berlin. It must be homesickness that I'm feeling, simply homesickness." She had quite forgotten that there was no home left to which she could return. "I like being here in the summer. But to live here all the time?"

Once again Witte's features took on the troubled expression she had seen in the pharmacy, when she had talked about his whiskers. "Wait and see."

Camilla shook her head. "Winter. Six months of cold and solitude. I wouldn't be able to stand it."

Visibly upset, he raised his hands. "Wait, wait. You're forgetting about Rostock." He looked straight at her. "You've got it all there—theaters, concerts, shops. My parents always spent the winter in Rostock. Many of the people from here do. . . . I mean, when you've lived alone as long as I have, you lose your standards. You're right, my mother would not have been able to stand the winter here either." As he spoke, he worked up a fine passion. "You'd be astonished at what Rostock has to offer. It's a Hanseatic city, so they not only understand how to make money but also how to live. Marvelous restaurants, I tell you. And Rostock is not the end of the world. Really it's just a jump away: fifty minutes by train, eighteen trains a day."

"You have a house there?"

"Yes, my parents' home. At the center of town, the best commercial location. I have a manager to run the pharmacy, but I could change that any time. It's just a question of arrangements. For example, he could take over the pharmacy here for the winter, the idea already occurred to me. . . ."

"No, no, I didn't mean it that way, you shouldn't think about that. The place a person grows up—that's where he's at home. For you it's Warnemünde, for me it's Berlin." She was tempted to talk about the house in Steglitz; at heart that was what she had been doing all along. Her going to see Witte, her sitting here on the bench with him now—it was all for the sake of the house. The fact that it was sold would not give her any peace. It was as if she had been robbed of her roots. She had no choice, she must find a way to undo what had been done. "You've never been to Berlin."

"Berlin?"

"Yes. It's a wonderful place to live."

"I can't claim to know it, really." Witte laid both hands on the silver knob of his cane. "The railroad station, a hotel, the building where the pharmaceutical congress was held, that's all I've seen of it. I don't mean to say anything against Berlin, really I don't."

"And the exhibitions?"

"I told you—railway station, hotel, congress."

She looked at him and smiled. "Not even the emperor? Everyone who comes to Berlin wants to see the emperor, at least."

"Really, I . . . I mean, once I tried, at the Spring Parade, but there was no way to get through. I was jammed in by a mass of people and was shoved this way and that, that was all."

She laughed. "That's not really what I meant. I don't mean the court receptions, the balls. Not the opera, theaters, concerts. I don't even mean the shops. It's none of those things. I mean the city as a whole, the air, the whole atmosphere. I feel good when I'm there, I can breathe more freely when I'm there. Here . . . here I'd feel I was living in a fishbowl. When I think about how they watched us! And I bet they're keeping track of exactly how long we're staying here. . . . I think we'd better go back."

"Wait." He followed her hastily. "I think I know what you mean. . . ."

She felt strange in this role. It was an altogether new experience to hear herself speaking in a language she knew only from her mother and sisters. She would never have thought herself capable of it, but now it was not even difficult. "Would it be out of the question for you to live in Berlin? I know that here I'd feel like a prisoner."

She quickened her steps. She could not put it any more plainly. She had made demands that he surely had not expected in his wildest dreams; yes, suddenly she herself felt the whole thing was an awkward, transparent maneuver.

Witte had adapted his steps to hers. They walked side by side silently until he spoke. "If I understood you correctly, that is your condition . . . forgive the expression. I did not misunderstand you, really I didn't. Frankly, I value your honesty. I mean, you have examined yourself and you let me know the outcome before—" He got no further, made a new start, and then said resolutely, "As a rule, women come out with these things only after the wedding. Isn't that right? You knew that I was married once before?"

"Yes, I knew."

"But there are no children, and no longer any obligations."

"Please," she said. "Please don't." Suddenly he seemed to grow taller at her side, his bearing more self-assured. Briskly he tucked his walking stick under his left arm, pulled off his gloves, undid the top buttons of his overcoat. "Berlin," he said with an entirely new emphasis. "Berlin. Scientific exhibits, you said?"

"And the oceanography museum."

"Oceanography! Do you know what I wanted to do after I qualified for my licence? I wanted to go to sea. Yes, I looked for a position on one of the big ocean liners. As a ship's pharmacist, you know. I signed a three-year contract. I thought I would see something of the world. . . . And then my father died suddenly, and I had to take over the business. That was the end of my dream. I don't want to make myself out as anything other than I am. I'm cautious, I avoid risks, but I wasn't always that way. And with you—" He came to a stop, reached for her hand.

She had planned it that way. What other choice did she have if she wanted to attain the goal she had set for herself? She had learned a great deal these last six months; she had gained a distance from things and people. Aunt Lenka—no, she could not live so much in the past as her aunt. And she did not have her father's easygoing nature. She loved both of them, but they were no longer models. Both escaped from reality; at heart they were both too soft for this world. They did not protest, they let things happen. They had not even tried to save the house. To marry for common sense—it sounded cold, almost bitter. But what other way out did she have?

"If you will allow me, I would like to speak with your father."

"Of course," she answered, glad to have gained a little more time. Not much, however, for as they approached the Hotel Berringer she spied Hofmann on the terrace, and he saw them as well. He took his leave of two men and came to meet them.

"I'll be expecting you this evening," Witte said to Camilla. "I've reserved a table on the *Queen Christina*." He bowed a little stiffly to Fritz Hofmann, who was wearing a white linen suit with lapels and pockets piped in brown. "We were just speaking of tonight," Witte said. "About the festival. May I count on you as well?"

"You're very kind, but I don't really know. Dancing is for young people like yourself." Hofmann kneaded his hands the way pianists do who want to keep the joints flexible. But his only concern was to preserve his hands for shuffling and dealing.

"I would like a word with you," Witte added.

Hofmann glanced at his daughter but made no remark. There seemed to be something more important to him, for he pulled an envelope out of his pocket and handed it to Camilla. "Would you take care of this for me before the last post?" He laid his arm across

Witte's shoulders. "All right then, let's go. Shall we go to the Berringer? You've never been there? My good man! You don't care for a little friendly game? Diversion, I always say. Man needs diversion. The secret, Witte, lies in diversion, and a friendly little game. . . ." He countered Camilla's warning glance with a smile. "Leave the menfolk alone! Men have to be by themselves now and again, isn't that right, Witte?" And he led the pharmacist away, his arm still around the man's shoulders.

Camilla watched them as they went up the stairs and disappeared through the hotel door. She opened the envelope and found the text of a telegram to a large betting office in London. It read, "Fifth race, British Derby, First Place Fairy Queen, thirty guineas." Shaking her head, she put the paper back in its envelope and walked quickly away. Fairy Queen—that was Papa, that was all that was on his mind.

3

After going to the post office, she had started home. She wandered through the municipal park, taking her time. There was no hurry—there would be plenty of time to answer Aunt Lenka's many questions. The winding paths between the clumps of trees and rosebeds were strewn with white gravel, but as happened every year toward the end of the season, sand seeped through everywhere. She met few summer visitors, only some local people who were in the habit of coming to the park every day at this hour: the woman in the shabby sealskin coat who was feeding the ducks in the pond, and the man in the wheelchair whose attendant rolled him to the croquet ground. The benches had been removed from around the band shell, and hillocks of raked leaves lay ready to be carted away. It was so still from the tennis courts she could hear the sound of rackets striking the balls, a sound she especially loved. Whenever she heard it, she speculated about the best place to build her own tennis court on the grounds of the house in Steglitz.

Even as she turned the corner into Aunt Lenka's street, she noticed the man circling the house. He tried the back door before returning to the front entrance. As she opened the garden gate, he was standing at the windows of the veranda, trying to peer inside. Obviously Aunt Lenka was not at home, and he had rung the bell in vain. As he heard her approaching, he turned and walked toward her, holding a white straw hat with a colorful ribbon. "Fräulein Hofmann! At last! I was about to think I'd come all this way for nothing."

She did not recognize him, and the last six months had taught her that strange male visitors did not bode well. Usually they asked to speak to Papa and acted very friendly until it turned out they were bill collectors. They all resembled each other somehow—inconspicuous faces, inconspicuous behavior. They even wore similar clothes. This man, too, wore a gray pin-striped suit that had been out of fashion for several years, with three buttons and narrow lapels. Only the straw hat in his hands was out of place; it was brand new, apparently never worn. It was almost like a ticket of admission to the seaside resort.

"Have we met?" She was reserved and determined to bar him from the house.

"Have we met?" Without laughing, his whole face beamed. "How long ago did we meet? Many years ago, you always wore your hair long, but short hair is also becoming to you! You have a lovely place here. And your father—how is he?"

"You wished to see my father?"

"He retired here? Somehow I can't picture it. How ever does he stand it? Berlin and Warnemünde, two different worlds. Wait, I'll help you, give me the key. . . . No, you go first, it's your home. . . . No, no, I don't want to sit down. I'm just wondering where I can find your father. There's something I'd like to discuss with him. . . ."

It was as if these last words restored her to her senses. They were standing in the parlor, he still holding the straw hat in his left hand. She offered him a chair, and yet she had no idea how he had gotten inside, quite against her will. She had taken the key out of her pocket, and suddenly it had been in his hand, he had turned it in the lock, and now he was here in the parlor, moving as if he were a close friend of the family's and everything were familiar to him. Yet she was not even certain that they had met before. Suddenly she found herself laughing. When he looked at her, she said, "Can you tell me how we got into the house? I had no intention of letting you in, you know."

"Look at me. What do you notice about me?"

"I don't know what you mean. Nothing, really."

"You don't notice anything basically. That's just it. I'm not too elegant and not too plain. I'm not too tall and not too short. I'm just serious enough for you to trust me, but not so earnest that my long face would intimidate anyone. In short, it's my job to get into houses where they hadn't meant to let me in."

"My father owes you money?"

"No, no. I'm a salesman, you know. I used to travel for your father, for many years, in Mecklenburg-Strelitz. My name is Senger, Carl Senger. That's how I know you, from Neukölln, when I came to pick up my samples."

When he said the word "salesman," Camilla automatically recalled the large maps in her father's office that showed the territories of the various travelers, and their sample cases, which seemed to weigh a ton in spite of their compact shape.

"You really don't want anything from my father?"

"Certainly not. On the contrary, I want to make him a proposition. The whole thing . . . the bankruptcy . . . grieved me deeply. We always got along well, your father and I. And I made good money working for him. The bankruptcy could have been avoided in my opinion. There are many possibilities in that particular business. I've traveled in other goods in my time, but to go bankrupt with soap products, that's like . . . but I don't want to bore you. Can you tell me when your father will be returning home or where I can find him?"

"You'll find him at the Hotel Berringer. But wait. . . ." He was the first one to say that the bankruptcy could have been avoided, the first who had a good word to say about her father. "May I offer you something?"

"Thank you, no. I want to get it over with. Hotel Berringer, you said?"

"What kind of proposition is it?"

"Well . . . but I'd better discuss it with your father. Anyway, thanks a lot."

She did not like his sudden eagerness to get away. Looking at him, she had to agree that there was nothing conspicuous about him. He had a somewhat broad, almost peasant, face, and light hair that would probably recede from his forehead at an early age. There was nothing about him that would inspire romantic notions in a girl, but he compensated for that lack by something else, a radiance that Camilla could not define exactly. "It's the big hotel right next to the lighthouse," she said.

"Yes, I know. Warnemünde was part of my territory."

Camilla was reminded of the remark the clerk in Witte's pharmacy had made. "Was the hand soap really such a hit?"

Carl Senger, already at the door, turned around. "Well, I'll be—you know about that!" But he gave no further explanation, and she accompanied him to the front gate. With quick, sure steps he walked down the street; even now he had not put on the straw hat but still held it in his left hand. Probably he never wore it because that would have made him conspicuous. Holding it, however, made it an effective prop. It aroused attention without being irritating.

Supposing he had some claim on Papa after all? Supposing he had hoodwinked her in a particularly clever maneuver? The thought should have been disquieting. Strangely enough, it did not really trouble her.

For the festival she had dressed in her navy-blue jacket costume with the pencil-slim skirt. As she stood before the mirror, however, she focused neither on her wardrobe nor her hairdo but on herself. The six months in Warnemünde had turned her into an entirely different person, as she was only too well aware. Externally none of it was noticeable, however. She looked no older—on the contrary, the short hair made her seem younger, if anything—no more unhappy, not even more mature. Was that the reason why a man such as Carl Senger would not speak to her as an adult? She stood still before the mirror as if her perseverance could bring forth an answer, could reveal even in her appearance the changes that had befallen her. Then she heard her father come up the stairs. As he put down his hat and cane and walked toward his room, across the hall from hers, he was humming to himself. Usually she was relieved when he came home in a good mood, but now she was bothered by his good cheer. He had probably succeeded in bringing off the miracle of seducing Witte into a game of cards or, worse yet, borrowed money from the pharmacist. She took the receipt the postal employee had given her and thought bitterly of the embarrassing scene she had had to endure at the post office.

As always when she entered her father's room—a dormer room with two small windows in the sharply slanting niches—her anger at him evaporated. It was so different from his roomy, luxurious den in the house in Steglitz. At the sight of this visible punishment, how could she reproach him? And so she now simply held out the receipt. "I paid it all."

"Fine, fine, it got sent off all right then. Put it down on the night-stand, please." He was standing at the cupboard, where his books were kept on a shelf, looking for something.

Softly he began to hum again, and although she tried to ward it off, her anger surged up anew. "I've spent almost a hundred marks for you—for all the telegrams you sent in the last two weeks."

"I'm looking for a black notebook, black linen cover with a leather spine, long and narrow, and then—"

"At least you could listen to what I'm saying."

He turned around, glanced at the receipt, but did not seem affected. "Fairy Queen, that's a sure thing. If I were in Berlin, I'd know the outcome by now."

"And do you think that in Berlin you could find a postal clerk who could be persuaded to take telegrams you can't pay for?" She felt as if she still saw the clerk's embarrassed face as he shuffled, hemmed and hawed, and finally came out with the truth as if it were all *his* fault. "How could you do such a thing? The poor fellow—you filled his head with stories. You were going to let him share in your winnings! But it takes time for the money to get here, so for two weeks he reached into his own pocket for you, more than he earns in a whole month! He'd have done it again, too, if he'd had the cash. How could you take money from such a little pipsqueak? And he begged my pardon a thousand times for having to ask to have his expenses repaid."

"He always got his money before—as well as his share of the winnings. This time I'm having a run of bad luck, that's all."

"That's why you sent me. You knew that he'd ask for his money back. You were too much of a coward to go yourself. But you were willing to subject me to it. What I should have done is refuse to send the telegram, and especially to pay off your debts. If you've come to that, to putting the bite on little postal clerks, what else can you be up to?"

Her father took a cigarette from the box on the table and lit it. As long as she could remember, he had always smoked only one brand: English Three Castles, available at only one shop in all of Berlin and sold only in packets of fifty; each cigarette carried his monogram in gold. Now he smoked anything he could lay his hands on, and Camilla knew they were always the cheapest brands. She appreciated the fact that he never complained. In fact, he claimed that the new cigarettes were much better for his digestion. He no longer rode in a carriage because it was better for his health to walk; the menus in expensive restaurants were much too rich; the behavior of expensive tailors too arrogant—there was no end to his rosy view. But now this same trait turned Camilla against him. "And how do you plan to pay off your debts? Is it starting all over again, as it was in Berlin? Little things yes, trifles—a hundred marks here, a hundred marks there, until it becomes an avalanche."

He shook his head. "Of course not. I may have some good news, in fact. I haven't been idle, you know. I have several irons in the fire—"

"Please stop pretending to yourself."

"Come over here," he said. "Sit down." And then he added, "Tell me, do you really want to marry him, that druggist?"

"Do you have a better suggestion? You ought to be glad. Your daughter taken care of, without a dowry, and you gain a son-in-law who can slip you a little cash now and then."

He watched the smoke of his cigarette curling upward. "What would you say about going back to Berlin at the end of the month? First to a hotel, then we'll find a small apartment."

She had to force herself to keep calm. "Please, Papa, that's all over. Not that I wouldn't like to believe you. It would be so wonderful. But I can't, not anymore. Nothing can change between us, but that I should go on believing your pipe dreams—no, that's over, for good. I can't change you, but I've changed."

"Oh yes," he said in an attempt at levity. "You've become a beauty."

"If my thoughts had anything to do with it, I'd look as ugly as a witch."

"The things you say! Now you've finally succeeded in spoiling my good mood. No, no, I didn't mean it that way, stay. Perhaps it's true that I'll never change. I should never have had a family, to tell the truth. I always lived as if I were alone in the world. But let's stop talking about it. And I meant it, the business about Berlin. We just have to hit a gold mine. Come on now, help me look. Tall, thin, black with a leather spine." He began again to rummage through the books and resumed his humming.

She would have liked to leave, but just then she saw him pull an armful of books off the shelf and throw them into an empty chair. From the hole he had created he pulled a black ledger. "My gold mine!" He opened the book and let it fall closed again. "Here it is, my gold mine! Do you know, I made one grave error. The wide selection we built up over the years—another perfume, one more kind of bath salts, nail buffers, more powder and rouge, and then new bottles, and perfume in solid form for Her Royal Highness, the Crown Princess Marie of Romania—my salesmen had to lug three bags, and in a market that was already more than adequately supplied. My soaps, my soap powders—I should have stuck to those. A handful of products, and push those until they're used in every single household. . . . Ah, here's the other one. Always the last place you look for it." He pulled out a broad black linen notebook and blew the dust off it. He stuck both ledgers under his arm. "I have to go out for a little while. Perhaps we'll meet on the *Queen Christina,* and perhaps I'll have some good news."

"Wait." It was altogether new for her father to give serious thought to the reasons that had led to his commercial ruin. The words he had just said sounded as if someone else had put them into his mouth. Perhaps that traveling salesman, that Carl Senger. "May I have a look?" She took the two volumes from him and opened each. Both were filled with his precise handwriting, page after page. One contained chemical formulas and pharmaceutical prescriptions, the other a long list of names and addresses.

"They hold a fortune, even if you think I'm exaggerating."

"What are they?"

"The formula book and my complete customer list. I've finally found what I've always been lacking—a good partner. You know, I understand chemistry. But selling, that was never my line. Now I have the man I need. Give me the books. I don't want to be late."

"Someone who used to be on the road for you?"

Her father did not seem surprised at her question. "I should have recognized his talent sooner."

"What did he offer you? What does your partnership look like? Are you planning just to hand over both"—and she pointed to the books. Simply the fact that her father had saved both notebooks and brought them along to Warnemünde told her that they must be of value.

"That, as it were, is the capital I am contributing." He took a fresh handkerchief from the drawer and with a practiced gesture thrust it into the breast pocket of his jacket.

"And he? What does he have to offer?"

"He's a sales genius. Mecklenburg-Strelitz was always at the top as far as percentages went, and it was his territory. He knows the market inside and out, he's even memorized the prices of raw materials. He's old enough not to be foolish, and young enough to be able to build up something. And the most important thing—he has a sense of what people will buy. I may be wrong about a lot of things, but I've got an instinct for a winner."

"You're not answering my question. You're willing to hand over your customer list and your formula book without any security? So he was one of your travelers, the best even—what does that signify except that he's clever? He was here, I saw him and talked to him. . . ." She was reminded of the way he had managed to gain entry to the house. No wonder he knew how to handle her father as well, knew how gullible Hofmann was, how simple it was to influence him and kindle his enthusiasm. "He may be everything you say, but what were the practical terms you decided on?"

"You see, he has to invest first. He has to buy a site, raw materials. He has to have a finished product before he can enter the market, then he has to engage salesmen, advertise. . . ."

"He's already explained all that to you. And on that basis alone. . . ."

"We settled on ten percent."

"'Settled! Ten percent? Ten percent of what?"

He gave her a long look before speaking. "You really have changed. There's a . . . hard core to you that one wouldn't have suspected. He promised me ten percent of the profits."

"Profits—and on that you're ready to move to Berlin! Profit—you know what that means? Nothing. There won't be any profit. He'll invest, buy a site, raw materials, advertising. Everything will go along very properly, you can check the books, I'm sure he told you that. You can check the books and find out that the firm has no profit."

"You say you talked with him. You think he's capable of that?"

"It's not a matter of what I think. In any case, it's possible. Have you forgotten what people are like—or at any rate can be like? Did the bank grant you a delay? Did your sons-in-law come to your rescue? Have you forgotten what we lost—the house!"

He sat down. Head bent, he scrutinized the backs of his hands. "I'm sorry. I simply could not talk about it. I thought it better not to poke at the wound. Let me say it just this once—I wasn't honest with you about the house, I know that, and I'm never going to forget it. I always thought some day I'd be able to make it up to you. But you're right, that's all wishful thinking, good intentions, hollow—you can't count on me."

"Look, I wasn't trying to take the wind out of your sails. Probably you're right, these two books are a gold mine. Otherwise a man like Senger wouldn't want to get hold of them."

"Do you really think so?" He raised his head, immediately prepared to hear only the pleasant part of what she was saying.

"I'd like it as much as you if something were to come of this business. But I don't tell myself, now we're already in Berlin, now we move to a hotel, now we look for an apartment. To spend money I don't have yet, that I may never have—I can't do that. As long as I live I'll never forget that we had to give up the house. I'll never forget the voice of the auctioneer in the plant. I'll never forget how Schröter wanted her money back, and I'll never forget the creditors who followed you here. *You* wouldn't see them, you were never home when they arrived. We were here, Aunt Lenka and I, and Aunt Lenka paid. You owe her more than six thousand marks, did you know that? She's the first one you have to think of if there's money coming in." She picked up the two books. "Where are you planning to meet Senger?"

"At the Strand Hotel. It's the first cross street. But wait a minute, what's going on? What are you up to?"

"It's very simple. I will keep the appointment. I will talk with him." The thought had come to her suddenly, brought on only by her father's question. And now she waited for him to object, to laugh at her, but neither thing happened. He sat still, hands on his knees, and then he made a gesture of resignation. "Don't you want me to come along at least?"

"It's better if I go alone. I'll listen to what he has to say, then we'll see." If she had fully realized what she was doing, she might not have had the courage to act as she did. Only afterward did she understand that for the first time she had asserted herself against her father, almost effortlessly. It did not make her feel triumphant, not even glad. Instead, she felt astonishment and a certain sadness, as if she had a premonition that the price of the independence she had just gained would be her youth.

4

The Strand Hotel was an old frame building. Its location close to the railroad station and on the road to Rostock determined its regular clientele. The Strand was one of the few hostelries open the year round, for its guests were not resort visitors but businessmen, engineers working at the ferry installations, and commercial travelers. It was a solid, plain structure, and somehow it seemed typical of Senger that he had chosen it.

The entrance was blocked by a black-and-white spotted dog; the huge animal rose to its feet and trotted forward to lead the way. In the entrance hall the lamps were already lit. A municipal electric plant had been providing the town with current for several years, but in this hotel the sconces were still fed with oil. They must have been lit only minutes ago, for the air was still redolent with the odor of sulfur lucifers and oil-soaked wicks.

The hotel was very silent, the only noise being the dog's paws on the tiles. The man in the chair behind the desk seemed to have dozed off. Only when Camilla rang the bell did he slowly sit up, wiping his hands on his green apron. "May I help you?"

"I'm looking for Herr Senger. Carl Senger."

The porter pointed to a glass door, its lead-encased panes etched with ship motifs. "Dinner is being served. You may go in, though."

The dining room was a mixture of parlor and sailors' bar. The tall tiled stove was hung with old copper pots, the floor was covered with narrow druggets, and a stuffed swordfish hung over the bar. Little oil lamps with green glass cylinders burned on the tables. There were only a few people: two men, each alone in a corner, and one couple, Carl Senger and a woman. Senger still wore the same gray pin-striped suit, but the woman's get-up could hardly be called unobtrusive. Her white organdy dress was printed all over with bright red poppies, and the little hat pulled down over her blonde curls was also decorated with poppies. Camilla, who had been prepared to find Carl Senger alone, stopped in the doorway. The two single men, each of them working on some notes, looked up; a waiter materialized behind the bar. But in the meantime Senger had noticed her. As he stood up, the napkin slid from his lap; he caught it as it fell, laid it aside, and walked toward her "You! I was expecting your father."

"Would you have preferred that?" She did not know what made her continue, "It probably would have been easier for you to do business with him."

"You're here in his place?"

"If you don't mind."

"Of course not. I hope you've decided to believe that I have no claims on your father."

"I don't know that what you plan instead is much better."

"Well, we can talk about that. Come, sit down. We've just finished dinner, but perhaps you'll allow me to order something for you." He preceded her to the table, cleared a chair for her, and performed the introductions: "Frau Gilchowski, Fräulein Hofmann. . . . She is the daughter."

"I thought he was going to come himself. Isn't that what you said, Carl?"

Camilla felt herself being scrutinized by a pair of bright eyes peering out from under the brim of the little hat. Up close the woman looked older than Camilla had thought at first; the round-cheeked face with the heart-shaped mouth betrayed her liberal use of rouge and powder. The glass in front of her and the napkin next to her plate showed clear signs of lip rouge. "Tell me, that festival—which ship has the better band?"

"I'm afraid I have no idea. . . ."

The waiter was at their table. "Are you sure you wouldn't like a little something?" Senger was asking. "The cakes and tarts are first-rate."

"Danish apple pastry, red-currant kisses, nut cake," the waiter claimed in.

"Nothing, thank you."

"But you can fill my glass again." The woman held her goblet out to the waiter. "I hope they play something besides that boring stuff," she said. "What I like—"

"How would it be," Senger interrupted, "if you'd leave us alone for a moment? We have something to discuss, and I know it would bore you."

"Oh yes, it certainly would." She rolled her eyes heavenward and made a face. "So-o-a-a-p! Well, make it short. You'll see, he's repulsive when he starts talking business. He never stops. Business, business—as if it was the only thing in all the world. And you understand something about it? About soap?" She rose and, standing, emptied her glass. "I'll give you a quarter of an hour, not a minute more." She picked up her purse, gave her hat a little tilt, and left.

"So you think my offer isn't genuine?"

"What? Oh . . . well, if you know my father at all, you must know how easy it is to get him excited about anything." She had not expected Senger to come to the point so quickly—while she was still staring at the woman's departing back and speculating about the relationship between the two. He did not offer an explanation, he simply passed it over. He was a traveling salesman; presumably he had several such women in his life, in different towns. "What concrete proposals did you make to my father?"

"To avoid any misunderstanding—I don't intend to talk him into something that is not in his best interests."

"Don't worry about his interests. Tell me instead where your interests lie. What exactly is it you want?" She watched his hands folding the napkin. He had astonishingly well-cared-for hands, with nails that seemed to be manicured; they were cut short except for the nail on the little finger of the left hand, which appeared a little extravagant, like the white straw hat he had carried in the afternoon. He wore no rings.

"I have to talk about soap." He leaned back in his chair.

"Go right ahead. Assume that I'm interested."

"I tend to think that I understand the business very well. I'm not talking about the manufacture now, but the selling. Making soap is a relatively simple matter. Boiling soap—that's the most primitive industrial process there is. A couple of kettles, packaging machines. Anybody can start, and there are enough of them who try, though with little success. I know a number of small manufacturers. There's not much difference between their products. They control a small local market, but they can't get beyond it, and so they creep along. Your father was launched on a higher road. First of all, his products were first-class. Second, he had the huge Berlin market. His mistake, I think, was wanting to gather laurels with luxury items. Toilet soaps, bath salts, perfumes—the market in those fields is already glutted by a few well-established firms. Large profits on each unit, but limited sales. Hardly any chance for increasing the market. All the manu-facturers so far have overlooked one thing, and that's the market for mass products. Are you sure I'm not boring you?"

"You're talking about products like Hofmann's hand soap."

"I mean still simpler ones. Laundry soap, soap powders—that's the market! The fine lady—she's not an interesting customer. She never finds her way to the laundry room, she doesn't even know what they use there. The simple people, especially the families of workmen— they do the most washing because they live with the most dirt. Those are the people you have to sell your goods to. It's an enormous group, and it's going to get larger, and they'll earn more. And believe me, soap products are the first thing additional earnings go to, especially for Germans. Cleanliness is the luxury of the poor. That's the market I can see, and—"

He interrupted himself, and when Camilla followed his glance, she saw his companion standing by the glass doors. Senger stood up. "Excuse me a moment."

He led the woman from the dining room. Her clear voice could be heard through the door. Though she could not make out the words, Camilla understood well enough from the intonation. She recognized it from her parents' quarrels. Whenever Mama took this tone, Papa always gave in. Silence fell, and Senger returned almost immediately. Camilla wondered whether she should suggest that they postpone the rest of the discussion until the next day, but to her astonishment he sat back down as though nothing had happened. Perhaps he was a little paler than before, perhaps he seemed a little absent, but other-wise he gave no sign of being upset. He had complete control, and again he saw no need to give any kind of explanation. "Wouldn't you like something to drink after all?"

"Perhaps a cup of tea?"

"You wouldn't rather have mulled wine?"

"All right, mulled wine, if it's made with cinnamon."

"That's the only kind they serve here."

"You've given this project a lot of thought," she continued. "I have a feeling that it's all fixed in your head. Where does my father come in? Does he come in at all?"

"I need his name—yes, most of all his name. Do you know how laundry soap is generally sold? Not in drugstores or pharmacies. In ordinary grocery stores. Often it's cut from the slab, without packaging, without a name. The customer asks for a certain amount, a pound or three pounds, and that's cut off the bar and weighed. The customer has no idea who made the soap or where it comes from. She asks for laundry soap, that's all. It's the same way with soap flakes. That's the normal way. Your father started by packaging hard soap in individual pieces, first without any label, then with a signature, then with a trademark, and finally we added the coupons. That was five years ago, and every year we were able to increase the turnover considerably. The customers suddenly knew what they had to ask for —Hofmann's bar soap and Hofmann's soap powder, the ones with the laughing laundress on the label. I bought up everything I could get my hands on from the bankruptcy estate. I can tell you, I could have used ten times as much."

"The bankruptcy estate!" He had touched a raw nerve. The scene was still vivid in her mind's eye—the factory yard, the dense rows of buyers, the voice of the official auctioneer ringing across the courtyard, the triple thud of his hammer when an item had found a taker. How she had hated the auctioneer! And the buyers, who appropriated Papa's possessions simply by raising a hand. Carl Senger had been one of them! "So that's what gave you the starting capital you needed?"

"That too, yes, and I'm not ashamed to admit it. I acquired goods and a number of machines for a ridiculous price."

"Why didn't you speak to my father sooner about your plans?"

"Don't forget who I am. A small commercial traveler, that's all."

"Now then. . . ."

116

He looked at her, surprise in his eyes. She came from a world that had remained closed to him until now. Her hands had practiced piano sonatas, sketched flowers with delicate pencils sharpened for her by others; she had learned languages. Everything about her never ceased to ·remind him of the class difference between them, though she did not make much of it and though she listened to him attentively.

"You really want me to go on talking about soap?"

She laughed. "Go ahead, do it. Do you know that when I was a child the worst thing I knew was the smell of boiling soap? I never, never wanted to have any part of it. When I looked out my window, I could see the laughing laundress on the opposite wall; I could have scraped it off with my fingernails."

"And yet that was the best idea your father ever had. That is the second crucial point besides the quality of the product—advertising. Most manufacturers begrudge the expense, and besides they think it's frivolous, vulgar, and so they're stuck with their tiny circle of customers. What I have in mind is establishing something like a monopoly with a single product, and I can do that only with advertising, widespread advertising, in newspapers, on pillars, in railroad stations, in trains, on every commuter railroad ticket and even on walls—anywhere where millions will see it every day. And that with one product, at most two—and when we've conquered the market, then we can think again."

"And you told my father all that?"

"Not in so much detail."

"You mean, he didn't really want to know. No, you don't have to protect him, you'd better tell me why you want him for a partner. That's the part I still don't understand."

"First of all there's the clientele. Second, the established goods, the name, as I told you. That already gives me a certain territory I can count on. To start from absolute scratch—I don't have the means for that." Again he looked at her searchingly. "You're pretty clever. You let *me* say how much your father's partnership is worth to me."

"Ten percent of the profits that don't exist. That's what you call a partnership?"

"It was his suggestion. I tried to make it clear to him that in the first few years the profits would remain low. The money will have to be put back into the business right away. Establishing a business means investing."

"But surely you must be offering my father some kind of security."

"The only security I can offer him is my person, that I'm the right man and that my plan is a good one. And that's exactly what I told him. Of course I could guarantee him some definite amount, but then I'd be forced to look for still another partner, and I don't want to do that, I want to remain alone. Quite honestly: I've saved up twenty thousand marks, I have some of the machinery and the chance of a site. I'll need every penny of my capital for raw materials and wages, even if at first I don't hire any travelers and do the selling myself—"

"When do you mean to start?"

"Right away. Autumn is a good time, and besides, with each day that passes Hofmann products are less well remembered."

"And where?"

"In Neustrelitz."

"Why there?" Somehow she had expected him to say Berlin. Neustrelitz—the name aroused visions of a small, sleepy county capital. But it was halfway to Berlin.

"I thought about Berlin for a long time," he said, as if guessing her thoughts. "Berlin would offer many advantages, but I figured that I'd need three times as much capital there. Berlin is above my means. Rents, wages—in Neustrelitz they're a fraction of what they are in Berlin. I can buy up a bankrupt barrel factory, a good site with electrical current and direct access to a rail line and an option on additional land. I've carefully calculated the whole first year, every position. If you're interested. . . ."

At the beginning, when he had spoken of the day when people all over Germany would be buying only one brand of soap, Senger had reminded her of her father, a visionary feeding on illusion. Now that he was speaking of money, wages, raw materials, electrical current, he revealed himself as a sober realist. Perhaps he was both, a dreamer and a pragmatist; perhaps anyone who intended to go far would have to be a combination of the two. The only question was which side was stronger in Senger. What would happen at the crucial moment? She was suspicious, not so much of him as of the trust he inspired in her. She had been trusting once before.

He had stopped talking. They were alone in the hotel dining room. The two solitary guests had left, and even the waiter was no longer in sight. There was no clock in the room, and the hotel was silent. Silence had also fallen between the two of them, but Camilla was not disquieted by it; it was as if both were testing whether they could communicate without words.

"I think we should try it together," she said at last without planning her words.

"That means you'll encourage your father?"

"If you want, we can go see him together."

"Now?"

His question reminded her that someone was waiting for him, and also of Witte, who was sure to be on board the *Queen Christina* already, looking for her. "Of course I wouldn't want you to miss the festival."

"Would we be missing anything?"

The avenue along the river was a thicket of lanterns. It did not matter that some of the vacationers had already left; to make up for it, half of Rostock seemed to have come to Warnemünde. Merrymakers were streaming along the booths on the shore and onto the two festival ships. Music resounded across the water, a polka from one of the ships, a country waltz from the other. They were taking the long way around to get to her father, yet they had chosen it in wordless agreement. They made their way through the throng. Camilla ran into some of the ladies who had turned around to watch her that afternoon on her walk with Witte. The same pantomime was repeated now, though their curiosity was no longer veiled and no longer so kindly. Near the gangway leading to the *Queen Christina* they came to a stop. The dance floor was at the stern, and Camilla recognized the blonde among the mass of dancers. She was whirling past the rail in the arms of a sailor. Certain that Senger had noticed too, Camilla said, "You can still join the party."

Senger did not answer; a motion of his head indicated the foot of the gangplank. "I think someone is looking for you," he said.

Even before Camilla saw him, she heard Witte's voice calling her name. Perhaps he had waited there, perhaps he had repeatedly left his table and run to shore to look for her. In any case he came toward her, calling and waving. When he realized that she was not

119

alone, he stopped abruptly. He wore a white suit with a dark hand-kerchief in his breast pocket, as if trying to copy Camilla's father. The whiskers had disappeared from his cheeks.

"Let's go," Camilla said to Senger. "You know, I stood somebody up."

An incredulous smile appeared on Senger's face. Then he took her arm and led her away.

After they passed the lighthouse, the crowds dwindled. Only some couples ambled by, people who had wandered away from the festivi-ties as they had, and nursemaids who were taking their charges home after they had been allowed to watch the brightly lit ships. Finally they were alone, accompanied only by the sounds of their own steps and the murmur of the water, which now, in the dark, sounded dif-ferent than it did by day, more varied and serious, with the measured rhythms of heavy, long swells. They walked down one of the little sets of steps that led from the boardwalk to the beach and continued their walk in the sand, to the right of them the dark strip where the surf unrolled.

"What kind of life is that," she asked suddenly, "when you're traveling, when you're always on the road?"

"I don't know any other kind."

"What sorts of things have you sold?"

"Wooden toys, hobbyhorses, dolls, holy statues, tin soldiers. Once I sold a military band—well, that is, I booked it, up and down the country, a great success. Finally I ended up with washday products, first with another firm, then with your father." His answers were hesitant; he did not seem used to talking about himself.

"And how does one get into this line of work?"

"Yes, how—I think it must be in the blood. My father was on the road all his life too."

"As a salesman?"

"If you want to call it that. He was with the circus. 'On sawdust service,' as he called it. The 'Five Eccentrics'—it was a troop of clowns that also did acrobatics, high-wire acts, that sort of thing."

"Then I bet my father saw him. He never missed a circus pro-gram in Berlin. And when I got old enough, he always took me. We went to the Circus Busch and to Schuman—"

"He was with a small circus, not Busch or Schuman. It was called Sidoli. I never even saw my father perform, I've only seen pictures. He had an accident—a spinal injury after a fall, and he had to stop. But he stayed with the circus as a press agent. He traveled ahead and saw to it that the newspapers printed articles and pictures about the company; he had posters put up, programs printed, balloons distributed. He had marvelous, unusual ideas. For example, he gave talks in schools. Children are a wonderful audience. They don't pay, it's true, but they bring their parents into the big top. So he used to go to the principals and persuade them to let him talk to the classes—animal training, that was one of his best subjects—and that very evening he usually had the same children with their parents at the show. He was a wonderful speaker. . . ."

"You traveled with him?"

"Yes."

"And your mother? Was she—"

"No," he said quickly. "I only knew my father."

For a while they walked on silently. They had already gone far beyond the center of town and had almost reached the coast-guard station, which was roughly on a level with Aunt Lenka's house. At this time there was no guard; next to the hut a boat had been turned over in the sand, and they sat on it. Far out on the water a light slowly crept along.

"And where was your home?" Camilla asked. "Was there a house somewhere that you returned to, in the winter, say?"

"We always lived in hotels, and my father died in one, but there was a house. My father was a little odd on the subject. He had nothing against hotels, he loved them; he always lived in the same ones and he insisted on having the same rooms. He brought his own sheets and towels, even our own table silver, and he would drink his morning coffee only from a particular cup. It started as soon as we reached a new city; within half an hour any hotel room looked like any other, he even lugged along a few pictures that he hung everywhere. And he did have a house. He had a photograph of it, and he often showed it to me. He described the garden, the rooms, the furnishings—one day we would move in. The house was his dream. He bought beautiful things for it and stored them with friends, against the day."

"And he never moved in?"

"No."

"Why not?"

"Because there was no house. The photograph he showed me—he'd picked it up somewhere. After his death I asked around among his friends and fellow workers, but they only grinned and guessed it had been a private obsession of his. At first I didn't want to believe them, and I thought that sooner or later I'd find out about the house, but they were right; it only existed in his imagination."

"Do you still have it?"

"The photograph? Yes, I kept it."

"I'd like to see it sometime."

Without a word he rose and took a few steps toward the water. She watched him standing at the edge and thought that when you came right down to it, he was a perfect stranger, and yet she felt as if she had known him for a long time. She too got to her feet and went to stand next to him, as if she could not bear for him to move away from her.

"Do you come here often?" he asked.

"There's a place farther out where I go, half an hour west of town. It's beautiful there in the summer."

"And during the winter? What do they do here in the winter?"

"Wait for summer."

"You father said you would be going back to Berlin."

"He'd like to, but it's the same thing as the house that exists only in a photograph. My father also believes in nonexistent things."

"And you?"

"Me? I don't know—I think I just want to hold on to the things I love."

"How old are you?" he asked.

"Very old. Ancient." Suddenly she was able to laugh. His presence gave her a feeling of security, although she could not have explained why. Perhaps she did not even want to know, she only wanted it to stay that way. They left the beach, climbed up to the boardwalk, and walked toward Aunt Lenka's house. She remembered that afternoon, when she had seen him for the first time, in front of the veranda, peering in the windows. She had been afraid the visit portended some unpleasantness. Now the memory made her laugh, and when he looked at her inquiringly, she said, "I still don't know how you got into the house, I still don't know exactly. . . ."

5

The parade was already in full swing when a cab passed the barricade at the edge of the parade ground and stopped in the outer courtyard to allow a lone woman to get out. Special deputies patrolled back and forth, and a few doubtful characters sneaked around. The spring and autumn parades were a favored "shopping area" for pickpockets; it was said that they came from far afield to attend these events, which netted them considerable booty.

The observers who did not have reserved seats in the grandstand stood in dense ranks at the edge of the exercise yard, pushing and shoving. Lou von Reden began to fear for the lace inserts of her dress and looked around for someone who could clear a path for her to the reviewing stand.

She would never have dreamed that even once in her life she would arrive late at a parade and that she would not care in the least. The field full of soldiers, a sea of vivid colors, glittering helmets, waving plumes—when she was a young girl a place on the grandstand had been the summit of her ambition. A place on the reviewing stand was official proof that you *belonged*, that your name stood on the court list, that you were among those privileged few who were allowed to bask in the reflection of the Emperor's glory.

But since her marriage she had grown bored with parades. For an entire week before each one her husband became unbearable, tyran-

123

nizing her and the servants with the preparations necessary to make sure his gala uniform was in perfect shape.

One of the footmen from the palace staff finally recognized her, took her ticket—Row 14, Seat 32—and tried to clear a path for her. She closed her parasol, gathered up her skirts, and climbed up the narrow steps at the edge of the stand. Her nose was already beginning to tickle from the dust whirled up on the exercise ground. She pursed her lips as if in this way she could breathe in less of it and consoled herself with the thought of the surprise she had in store for her mother. It was only the special-delivery letter from her father that had made her decide at the last minute to drive out to the parade ground after all.

She smiled and murmured apologies as she forced her way through the row. Her seat was almost at the center, and her passage was difficult, for the ladies' hats had grown even more voluminous this fall; yellow and green were the predominant colors. Finally she spied the empty seat and her mother's huge Florentine straw hat. Taking a deep breath, she sank down, lowered her parasol, and glanced at the large yellow surface below, where the regiments were forming up for the grand march past.

"What's the big idea?" Emmi Hofmann asked. "Either you arrive on time or you stay home. Don't you think you're noticed? Are you determined to harm your husband?" She consulted the program in her lap and raised the opera glasses to her eyes.

"I have great news! About Camilla. Are you going to be surprised!" But the upsurge of music drowned out any further conversation. It was a clear autumn day, sunny and brisk, which made the colors look especially bright. But Lou felt only the dust, irritating her throat more and more. She leaned toward her mother's ear. "Listen, I think I'm pregnant." But even this did not manage to attract her mother's attention, for now the great moment had come when the regiments approached the Emperor's box.

"The bodyguard," Emmi Hofmann said. "I think I can see your husband. I must say, he looks marvelous on a horse. The shoulders of his new coat are a little too padded for my taste. He's looking this way, look. Do you want the binoculars?"

"I know what he looks like, including his red dress coat. His tailor presented me with the bills only this week. If I really do turn out to be pregnant, I'm going to have to do something about it."

Again the sounds became too loud to continue the conversation. The drums, the fanfares, the pounding of horses' hooves, the cheers of the crowd, all flowed together. Impatiently Lou waited for the closing ceremony, when the Emperor would leave his box; her thoughts were on her father's letter, which she had tucked away in her bag. Camilla seemed to have hit the jackpot—Lou still could not believe it. And she was stuck with a husband who let all the bills be paid out of her pocket. It really was an upside-down world.

Finally the moment came when the spectators rose to their feet and remained standing until the Emperor had left the stand. At the edge of the parade ground blue tents had been put up for the guests of honor who were invited to a glass of punch, and the crowd was moving in that direction. The two ladies, wise in such matters, remained in their seats until the stand had pretty well emptied.

Finally Emmi Hofmann tore herself away from the sight of the uniforms. "What did you say? You're pregnant?"

"I may be, yes." It was typical of Mama that she asked about Lou's last remark only and not about her news of Camilla. Camilla and her father—both of them were taboo for Mama. She never mentioned them. At the time of the bankruptcy she had declared the subject closed, and she stuck to her decision with an iron will.

"A baby—maybe it's a good idea. Usually it changes a man for the better. In any case, it gives the wife a chance to expand her rights in the marriage."

"You must be insane! I don't want a baby. I'd hoped you'd help me if my fears turn out to be justified. We're cramped enough in that apartment. And the additional expenses! Have you any idea what it costs to lead the kind of life we do? And everything comes out of my pocket—the household, the rent, the servants—and Cilly is asking for a raise of twenty marks! And don't forget Geerd—the next thing he needs is a new horse! Do you realize that in two years Geerd has gone through half my dowry? By the way, I hear you've sold the house."

Emmi Hofmann replaced the opera glasses in their case and got to her feet. "I could stand a bite to eat. Come along, you have to be seen anyway, or there really will be a scandal."

"Has the house been sold? Yes or no?"

"Who is spreading these rumors?"

"I have it from a reliable source. I've been told the amount, too.

A hundred and eighty thousand. A respectable price! Well, how good is my source? Actually, who is entitled to the money?"

Emmi Hofmann was busy looking for something in her handbag. "The other day you said something about your rent going up. You must tell your mother-in-law, not me. Remind her of her grand promise to make an apartment available to you in one of her buildings. After all, she owns three of them. You'll get nowhere with that fine lady by being patient. You'll have to show your teeth before she develops a sense of family loyalty." She spoke out of the corner of her mouth, softly, while acknowledging acquaintances by smiling to the right and left. Lou was familiar with the frozen smile on Mama's lips and knew that at this moment she would get no further. Since they had moved out of the house in Steglitz and Mama was living alone, an astonishing transformation had set in; she had become stingy. In years gone by she had never asked where the money was coming from, she had spent it with open hands. Now that she was dealing with her own money, however, she thought twice before parting with a penny. When she and Lou met in the city for lunch or tea, as they did once or twice a week, Mama made it a principle that she was always the guest. And if Lou tried to push the bill across to her, Mama regularly turned out to have only just enough change to get home.

They had reached the open ground. "Wait. Where are you going?" Emmi Hofmann protested as Lou headed toward the outer court. "There won't be any carriages for at least half an hour."

"You're acting as if I'd never attended a parade before. I asked the cab to wait for me. I had a letter from Papa today, that's what I wanted to talk to you about. Are you going to be surprised!"

Once more her mother acted as if she had not heard Lou's last remark but only said, "All right then, if you can afford to keep a cab waiting."

Later, in the carriage, she complained about the patched leather upholstery, the loose springs and the crowded streets. They proceeded by fits and starts, stuck in traffic again and again, until they were past the worst of the crush and the horses fell into a gentle trot. Lou held out her father's letter. "You'd best read it yourself."

Emmi Hofmann sat stiffly in her corner and pushed away her daughter's hand, as if even to touch the letter were too much. "How

126

often do I have to tell you I've finished with that, once and for all."

Lou looked at the envelope, her father's handwriting, the stamps and the postmark, and the red postage-due notice. "You're always giving me such good advice—like not letting our emotions rule us. Now you're making the same mistake yourself. Your unforgiving-ness—"

"Leave that to me."

"But aren't you the least bit curious?"

"What can he possibly have to tell us? He needs money. He's always going to need money from someone. Be glad that we're out of it. Or are you going to let yourself get drawn in again? I'm certain that's what it's all about. . . ."

Lou had reached into her pocket for a box of fruit drops and placed one on her tongue to rid herself once and for all of the dust and dryness in her throat. At first she had been in a hurry to blurt out her news, but now she found it amusing to put her mother off a little. "You're right that he talks about money, but not that he's in need of it. I'd say just the opposite. By the way, are you going a little gray? Or am I mistaken? Gray is sure to be becoming to you. They say redheads get the most beautiful white hair."

"I never was a redhead. Well, what about the letter, then?"

Lou remained absorbed in the intricacies of her open-work gloves. But she could not keep up her pretense for long. "Our baby, our Camilla—she's getting married."

"She what? Married?"

"You heard me. No engagement, no waiting period, no preliminary announcement, not even a formal invitation. She's getting married, that's all there is to it, helter-skelter."

"Who's the man?"

"Now you're asking smart questions. I knew it all the time. All right, guess. Who would be able to attract Camilla? A painter? A musician?"

"That would be just like her."

"Or so we thought. We thought butter wouldn't melt in her mouth. She caught herself a rich industrialist. There, now what do you say? Our precious little innocent Camilla. A rich industrialist."

"What exactly does he say?"

"Well, you know Papa's letters, he jumps from one subject to

127

another, and you have to pull out the facts, but this much is certain: if only half of what he says is true, the man has to be a stroke of luck. He owns a large factory in Neustrelitz."

"I wonder how she met him." Emmi Hofmann spoke as if this were the point that concerned her most. "Does he say when the marriage will take place?"

"In two weeks. The letter was posted in Neustrelitz, can you imagine."

The carriage came to a halt with a jerk. Lou looked out the window and saw that they had arrived in front of her house. It was a three-story building in the typical Berlin brown, but the facade should long ago have had a new coat of paint.

"Don't you want to come up for a minute?" But Emmi's expression told Lou what her mother thought of the apartment, and Lou could only agree with her. She had never liked the place, and at this moment it was visible proof of the world's injustice: her mother, who sat on her money; Camilla, who was marrying a rich man; and she, who had to spend her life vegetating in the three rooms of her husband's one-time bachelor flat. Originally this had been meant to be a temporary solution, and so she had not taken the trouble to change the ugly wallpaper even though its murky purple, oxblood red, and bluish green made the small rooms seem even more cramped. "Then let's walk up and down a little."

The two women alit from the carriage. "What about the cab?" Lou asked. "I'll ask the driver to wait. I'm sure you'll want it to go home in."

But Emmi Hofmann knew Lou too well not to see through her intentions—which were to make her mother pay for the entire day's driving.

"No, no, send him away. I'll enjoy the short walk back."

Gritting her teeth, Lou paid off the cabbie. Then the two women walked in the direction of the square. One side of the street was torn up; cobblestones were piled high on the narrowed sidewalk. Emmi Hofmann shook her head. "How often are they going to pull up the pavement?"

"This is for the central telephone office."

"In the old days they at least used to dig only in the summer, when people were away on vacation." This thought seemed to bring her back to their earlier track. "How can one meet someone like that in Warnemünde?"

"One of us should go there, I think."

"What's his name?"

"Senger."

"No title?"

"Since when do industrialists have titles?"

"What does he make?"

"Soap!"

"Soap? Senger? Never heard of him."

"Papa writes that he's about to control the entire German market."

"I can't get away." Emmi Hofmann was heading toward the booth where they sold soda water "plain" and "with." "With" meant a shot of raspberry syrup. "Aside from the fact that the season begins on October first, I don't want to. . . . A glass 'with,' and two straws, please."

"A young girl needs her mother before her wedding."

"Come on, that's not what's on your mind."

"It seems to me the situation has changed somehow. Papa will profit by it as well. Wouldn't you think a reconciliation is in order?"

"I have to admit, this does change a few things." Her parade smile twitched on her lips. An instinctive understanding prevailed between Lou and her mother. The feeling had never been strong enough to completely overcome their mutual distrust, but sometimes it worked. "Perhaps you can go and spy out the territory. You'll pay for my soda, won't you."

Lou paid and led her mother away from the booth. "Listen, we've got to get one thing straight. I hope you don't think you can keep all the money from the house for yourself."

Emmi Hofmann glanced at the watch she wore on a long chain around her neck. "It's high time I went home."

"Oh no you don't." Lou laid her hand on her mother's arm. "I could tell Camilla about it. Actually the money belongs to her. The house was intended to be her dowry."

"Don't bother. You won't get far with me that way." Outwardly Emmi Hofmann seemed quite composed. The layer of powder on her smooth, rosy face was impeccable; only a few delicate beads of

129

perspiration glistened on her upper lip. "Legally there's not a thing you can do to me."

"Once you said that if you made a good deal on the house, we might be able to talk about it again."

"At least now you're striking a different note."

"I figured it out for you. I can't make ends meet. I keep having to dip into my capital, and if things go on that way, in another two years Geerd will have what's left of my dowry. Do you realize what he makes since his last promotion? He gets a hundred and seventy-five marks a month in pay. That barely covers the expense of his shirts and patent-leather shoes."

"I can only repeat, keep after Geerd's mother. She gives you nothing but fine phrases, and you fall for it. I warned you at the beginning. Such a ridiculous wedding present! What do old family pieces mean if they're worthless? They're very generous with words, mother and son, but there's nothing to back them up. Both of them are one hundred percent selfish. All they want is to use you. That is, if you let them. Dig in your heels."

"That only leads to trouble. I get my own back in my own way." She came to a halt and held her mother back as well. A carriage stopped before the house and a man hurried indoors, clattering his spurs and dragging his saber. Even when he was not in the saddle, he had the slightly stooped posture of a horseman.

The two women exchanged a look. "Now the changing starts all over again," Lou said. "Three times a day. You should see the performance just once. If it turns out that I'm really pregnant, you're just going to have to have a word with Dr. Clevins."

"His fees are outrageous."

"Surely your daughter is worth it to you."

"What have you got against a baby?"

"If you must know, I'm not sure if it's Geerd's." She laughed secretly at the thought of how shocked her mother would be by her confession. Besides, she knew this was the best possible way of pressuring her. "That's what it is, I'm not sure—"

"Please!" Her mother interrupted. "I'll talk to Dr. Clevins."

"It's a hundred and eighty thousand, isn't that right, the amount you got for the house?"

"Oh, but so much of it goes into expenses. And if I give you some of it, then what about Alice and Maxi?"

Lou felt that she had achieved enough for one day. "Think about it when you have time. We can talk about it again. I never meant to pressure you."

"You're planning to visit Camilla?"

"Shouldn't somebody from the family look after her? I'll write you right away. Maybe then you'll change your mind. There's simply nobody better at these things than you, and who knows, maybe this man Senger is a nice, easygoing person."

"It would certainly be something new and different, a son-in-law who isn't after my money." She waved at a passing cab. She had never intended to walk home. "All right, write me as soon as you get there," she said through the cab window. "Perhaps I'll decide to come after all. You're right, we need to look at such matters objectively. And after all, it's for Camilla's sake."

Lou watched the carriage until it turned the corner. It was cool in the vestibule of the house. The red runner on the marble stairs was as much in need of replacement as was the plaster on the outside of the house. Mama was right, she would have to dig in her heels. The best thing would be if she simply refused to pay the rent. Then their lease would be canceled and her mother-in-law would have to look after them.

When she came into her apartment, she took off her hat. She knew the sight that would greet her when she entered the bedroom, but she wanted to tell her husband at once that she was going away for a few days.

She opened the door. The red dress coat lay on the floor, the saber was diagonally across the bed, one pair of pants was thrown over the back of a chair. The boots had been thrown heedlessly at the foot of the bed. The tailcoat for evening wear was hanging against the closet door, and as always he had hauled out half a dozen shirts because none of them was starched enough to suit him. She could hear him in the bathroom.

She shut the door behind her and went into the drawing room. She rang for the maid and was about to give instructions for preparations for her trip when her husband's voice rang through the apartment. "How often do I have to tell you to put lasts into my patent-leather shoes! Why the devil do we have them? No wonder the shoes get creased! Cilly!"

Lou nodded to the girl. "Go. It's all right." In her thoughts she was already installed on the train, in a luxurious first-class compartment. She had always made particularly romantic conquests on trips.

6

The man had handed the last piece of luggage from the train compartment to the porter and now stepped aside to let Lou descend. "It was a real pleasure. If ever something should bring you to Vienna. . . ." He was holding a visiting card. "This is the address of my club." He winked. "Wives not admitted, but they'll get a message to me day or night. It really was a pleasure, such a charming, nameless traveling companion. . . ."

"Never say never. Anything is possible." She gathered up the candy box and the fashion magazines from the red plush seat.

The porter, who was no less concerned with Lou than was the gentleman from Vienna, stood ready to help her get down. "Everything satisfactory? You're being met? Fine. Your luggage is over here." He indicated the cart piled high with suitcases, traveling bags, hat boxes, and the oblong linen sack with umbrellas and parasols. "I wish you a pleasant stay. The rain, that's just a shower. It will soon be over."

A shower in the midst of radiant sunshine was drumming on the glass roof above the platform. Lou remembered the railroad station in Neustrelitz only from having passed through it the previous year, when she and her husband had taken the train to the seashore. There had just been time for a cup of milky coffee from the station restaurant. It was a forbidding structure, but she was in such a good mood today that it looked inviting.

Escorted by conductor and porter, she marched straight toward the barrier, keeping an eye out for her father. She found him a little to one side, in a pale-gray, three-quarter-length overcoat and pale-gray trousers strapped over his low boots, as well as hat and cane—he was as elegant as ever. She hurried toward him and leaned over the barrier to kiss him on the cheek.

"Not so much zeal, my child. Did you have a good trip?"

"Isn't Camilla with you? I'm dying of curiosity! Your letter really was a surprise. How is she? How is she feeling? Will it be a big wedding? It wasn't at all easy for me to get away, but I just had to come. What is he like? You'll have to tell me everything."

"Look, I think that's meant for you. Turn around." The train had started moving; Lou's traveling companion stood at the open window of the compartment, waved, and called out some unintelligible words.

"A conquest?"

"He owns some ships, on the Danube, a whole fleet of them. Have they decided yet where they're going on their honeymoon? Have you heard about the trip around the world sponsored by Wertheim's? They go to India and the Holy Ganges, Rangoon, Honolulu, Ceylon. They are going on a honeymoon, aren't they?"

They had left the concourse but remained standing under the front canopy, waiting for the shower to end. The porter with his cart remained at a respectful distance.

"Is all that luggage yours?"

"Did you think I was only staying overnight?"

"After your telegram, I thought you were coming for just a couple of hours and were going back tonight."

"I couldn't do that to Camilla."

"Well, let's risk it then." He took a step forward and put out his hand. "The rain's stopped." He took his daughter's arm and walked with her to a cab stand. Lou could not help being astonished. "You in a hired cab? Thats a new one. You always said—"

His laugh interrupted her. "As you get older, you worry more about your health. Walking—the doctor prescribed walking for me. And here it isn't like Berlin. No distances to speak of, you can get anywhere on foot, that's one of the advantages of a small town." As he spoke, he was observing the joint efforts of porter and cabman to stow the baggage on the roof and the box.

Cap in hand, the porter approached Fritz Hofmann. He made no move to reach for his purse but without embarrassment turned to his daughter. "You'll take care of it, won't you."

"You're worse than Mama."

"How is she?" he asked in the most natural way.

"Well, you know, the season is about to start, she's in her element. If you expected her to come—don't forget, it was me you wrote to."

"Oh no, I never thought she would. I didn't even expect you to come. But that makes it all the nicer." He helped her into the carriage, and before he closed the door, he called to the cabman: "Hotel de Pologne!"

"You're taking me to a hotel?" she asked as he sat down next to her.

"Look around you, we'll be passing the castle in a minute."

"You mean I won't be a guest in her home?"

"But Lou! Is that the latest Berlin fashion? I live in the hotel myself."

This answer seemed to satisfy her, for she leaned back voluptuously into the corner of the carriage. "Tell me! What is *he* like? Where did she meet him?"

"One thing at a time. Camilla had best tell you herself. First let me have a proper look at you. You grow prettier all the time. No wonder you make easy conquests. And Geerd has been promoted, I read. And your just getting up and hopping on the train—you must admit, it's no distance at all from Berlin, two and a half hours and good connections all day long. It's child's play to go there and come back all in one day."

"But surely they'll take an apartment in Berlin? In addition, I mean."

"Very possibly. I must say, my letter certainly went fast. One day is all it took."

"How did it all happen?"

"Well, it was just as much of a surprise for us."

"I can imagine. Our Camilla! Who would have thought it of her! To jump right into the honeypot. What is he like?"

"He's a winner, if you know what I mean. You see, at the races there are the declared favorites and then there are the long shots. You stand in the paddock and look over the field, and all the people whisper the names of the favorites, but the experts, the real experts, look for something else. Once in a while they come across a horse they just know will make the race. Senger is one of those."

"And he made his money in soap?"

"I know what you're thinking, but you mustn't judge everyone by me. He doesn't make the mistakes I made. He goes about things in a different way; washday products are a mass article. . . ." His pause was as calculated as his words. ". . . let's assume he has only a twenty percent share of the market in household soap and soap flakes, with a per capita use of about fifteen pounds a year, and with a net profit of five pfennig per unit, in Berlin alone, with two million inhabitants . . . are you listening to me?"

For a moment Lou had been sobered by the word "soap," but the way her father juggled figures had given welcome nourishment to her imagination. Not for nothing was she the one daughter who had inherited his irresponsibility.

The carriage slowed its pace and came to a halt. "Here we are then." Fritz Hofmann was the first to get out. Lou's glance wandered up and down the street: residential buildings, stores, but nowhere a hotel in the luxurious style she had expected. There was only one, a narrow building that seemed modest at best, with an iron canopy over the entrance and natural-colored coconut matting into which the words "Hotel de Pologne" were woven in black letters.

"This is where you live?"

Fritz Hofmann's cheerfulness was unshakable. "Wait! The outside isn't what counts. In houses such as this, the service is often much more individual than in a fancy hotel. Today, when anybody can stay at the Grand Hotel, you're nothing but a cipher there."

The coachman set the luggage down at the entrance to the hotel and waited for his fee. Again Lou had no choice but to pull out her purse. Finally they were left at the hotel entrance with the mountain of luggage. Nothing stirred. Before Lou could stop him, her father had grabbed two of the cases. The sight left her speechless. Papa— who used to find it an imposition to carry so much as a travel rug, much less a bag—carrying two cases! The foyer, with two spindly potted palms and a view through to the breakfast room furnished with wicker chairs, did not improve matters. Nor did the day clerk who came around from behind a desk, pulling on a cap and staring helplessly at the luggage that was growing into a small mountain next to the stairs.

Holding the room keys, Fritz Hofmann walked ahead to the second floor, unlocked the room himself, and gestured for Lou to enter. She took only a single step across the threshold. It was a friendly, light, though small chamber. Two windows gave on an inner courtyard—with a "view of nature," as Papa noted while he opened one of them. It was a far cry from Lou's concept of a suitable suite.

The wooden floor painted a rusty red, the narrow runner, the small wardrobe in which she could not stow half her things, the brass bed—where was the door to the bathroom? "Don't trouble yourself. I'm not interested in the view of nature. You don't seriously think I'm staying here?" She gave her father a sharp look, hoping at last to get an explanation for these absurdities. He was, as always, dressed expensively, even extravagantly; there was nothing about his appearance to suggest that he was being frugal—what a word in connection with Papa! Only one other explanation seemed open to her at this moment. "So that's it! Your fine Herr Senger is a cheapskate! No private carriage. A slum. They skimp when it comes to family—that's how they get their money, these fine gentlemen! Poor Camilla! So that's the kind she's come by! And you play right along. Mama would never have stood for it. A cheapskate. That means you have to dig in your heels, and I mean now, right away, not when it's too late! They've got to be cured before the wedding!"

As if to gain strength for her argument, she briefly rested on the edge of the mattress. "Seaweed! I thought as much!"

Most of her luggage was in the hall outside the room, and the clerk was just dragging up the last pieces. Lou flounced past him, indicating with a short motion that all of it should be taken downstairs again. Fritz Hofmann followed her out on the street, where Lou announced her decision. "We will drive over to Camilla's house at once. Where can we get a carriage?"

"I'll take you there." He could hardly have been more composed if everything had gone according to plan. And while he walked with her through some small public gardens with green benches and rose beds, Lou's mood also became more peaceful. "I'm sorry, but if there's one thing I cannot tolerate, it's stinginess. Mama for example . . ." but she thought it wiser not to complete the thought. "Can we really get a cab here?"

"I tell you what. It's such a lovely day, the two of us will go for a little walk, I'll show you the town, and then we'll have dinner with Camilla. I've already arranged it with her. She knows you're coming. It was her idea; I've reserved a table for us in a very pleasant restaurant."

"As pleasant as the hotel?"

"I was so looking forward to spending time with the two of you."

"No more evasions, please. What is her address?"

He told her but added, "At the rate you're rushing about, you'll drive right by each other."

"There has to be something you're keeping from me. Did she get dumped at the last minute again?"

"History does not always repeat itself."

"Then what is it?"

"Perhaps my letter wasn't quite clear. Senger is only just beginning, his capital is invested in the plant. He is a man with a future. . . ."

His words were drowned in her laughter, an amused laughter at first, degenerating into an almost hysterical screech. "Aha, now I get it!" But she could not even speak coherently—again and again she shook with laughter. "The industrialist, rich as Croesus—Harry Have-Not. . . . A winner, eh? How could I have been so stupid as to fall for your letter! And drop everything to grab the first train. . . . Don't act as if you were lord of the whole world!"

And in fact Fritz Hofmann stood on the path, one hand lightly poised on his walking stick, his head tilted back in the nape of his neck, like a rich, elegant idler.

"And I'm taking the very next train back!" This time she succeeded in suppressing the rising laughter. The corners of her mouth turned downward, making her doll's face suddenly look hard and old. "I drop everything to jump on that miserable train that stops at every water hole and have to put up with the nattering of that fellow . . . that pushy Viennese. . . . Lies . . . is there anything besides lies you men are capable of?"

"Just keep on talking a little while longer." For the first time Fritz Hofmann was altogether serious.

"What is that supposed to mean?"

"It does me good. It's as if I were hearing your mother. For thirty years she held me in check with that, and I'm beginning to understand that it's finally over." But then the pleasant element in his nature regained the upper hand. "I'll admit, it was a mistake. My imagination ran away with me as usual, but that's surely no reason for us to quarrel. . . ."

He tried to embrace her, but she took a step backward. "When does the next train leave?"

"Trains leave all the time, every hour."

"I'll be on the next one. Please don't trouble yourself; you needn't come with me." She turned on her heel and went back the way they had come, heedless of whether he was following her or not.

Only later, on the way to the station, when her anger had cooled and she was sitting in the carriage with all her luggage, did she realize how little real information she had gained. She still did not know who this Herr Senger was, how he looked, how Camilla had met him. Mama would riddle her with questions—these and more. The drive through the town with the conspicuously broad streets and the rich merchants' homes reawakened her curiosity, and so she poked the tip of her umbrella against the partition and gave the cabbie the address she had extracted from her father.

As she continued to look out the window, she noted that part of her father's letter was true; the town radiated affluence. And when the cab drove through a section of mansions—ample white houses surrounded by spacious grounds—she found her equilibrium wholly restored and was expecting the carriage to stop at any moment. A fresh shower forced her to close the window. The panes became fogged, and by the time she could see out again, the picture had changed completely. Small workers' houses of unpainted brick and long, low factory buildings with pointed glass roofs marched past the window.

The street grew more depressing; the houses gave way to storage sheds, stockyards, discarded railroad cars, and ugly, rusty gas tanks. A brickyard with a smoking chimney marked the end. Thereafter barren land stretched out to the right and left; only in the distance, on the horizon, a row of poplars stretched gaunt and barren into the sky.

Lou leaned out the cab window, trying to tell the driver to stop and turn around, but he paid no attention and continued straight through the gates of a warehouse that had appeared behind the trees.

Lou remained seated until the cabman had opened the door for her. "But where have you taken me?"

"This is where you said you wanted to go."

Hesitantly she placed her foot on the running board. The square yard was lined with sheds and open stalls piled high with barrels. A sign fixed to one of the sheds read "F. X. Paal, Barrels." A boy on a ladder was just about to remove it. The whole place seemed to be a construction site, and the rain had made the turned-up earth still more treacherous.

"Who are you looking for?" the driver asked solicitously.

"Herr Senger."

"I guess that's the new owner. Nobody else here, anyway. Want me to go in and ask?"

They had stopped right by the only solid building, the residential part of the premises, a tall four-story box with a flat roof and small windows. It was made of the same plain brick as the workmen's homes they had seen on the way, except that here the yellow of the bricks seemed even more revolting to her. A head became visible at one of the windows. For a moment Lou could do nothing but stare, unprepared for Camilla's short hair; and yet that was not what left her so stunned. Something else, an indefinable fascination, emanated from the face in the window. The cabbie's reaction confirmed her feeling; he stared upward, open-mouthed, and did not release his breath until the figure disappeared. "Is that his wife?" he said at last. And the open admiration in his voice brought Lou back to reality. She gathered up her dress and balanced her way across the board that formed a walkway over the wet ground to the front door, where Camilla now appeared.

Both had imagined the meeting so differently that they faced each other as strangers, almost as enemies. Lou broke the silence. "I must say, the drive here is an imposition."

"I realized you'd feel that way, that's why I suggested we meet in town. But as long as you've come all this way, won't you come in?"

Lou followed her sister. Camilla was wearing a simple cotton frock with elbow-length sleeves. At a glance Lou saw that Camilla was not wearing a corset and that the neckline of the dress, adorned with a little brooch, was quite low.

Workmen were busy inside the house as well. There was a smell of fresh paint and the sound of banging and hammering. The women had to maneuver around ladders in the corridor.

"Right now everything here is topsy-turvy." Camilla opened a door. "This is the only room that's halfway neat."

It seemed to be an office, plain and unadorned, with furniture that was obviously secondhand. The only personal items in the room were two framed photographs that stood on the desk behind which Camilla sat down. Lou chose one of the uncomfortable wooden chairs. Immediately next to her squatted a strong box whose dark-green enamel was peeling. She could not suppress a remark. "Is that for your scads of money?"

It used to be so easy to embarrass her sister or make her angry, but now Lou had to sit by as her arrow harmlessly glanced off a new Camilla. She sat there with a face—what the devil was it about her face? What was so special about it, why had the coachman stared at her open-mouthed? She was not "fancied up," no powder, no rouge, no plucked eyebrows, nothing; perhaps that was just what made it so perfect.

"Lou, listen to me. I felt no need to keep you informed in any way, whether you understand that or not. It was Papa who thought that a family is, when you come right down to it, still a family. And I left it to him whether to write you or not. To tell you the truth, I never expected any of you to come. Since you're here, though, let's get it over with as pleasantly and politely as possible. How are you and Geerd? How is Mama? Excuse me just a moment. . . ."

There had been a knock at the window that gave on the rear yard. Camilla opened it, and the workman who was standing outside said, "We're down to ten meters, but it doesn't look good. Do you want us to go on digging or should we try someplace else?"

"You better take the spot Haase showed you. Sometimes dowsers understand these things better than anyone else." She shut the window and turned back to her sister. "We have a problem with the water. We do have a well, but it doesn't supply enough for our needs." She smiled for the first time. "Water makes up a quarter part of soap, you know, that's the cheapest part of it."

"So, your intended really does make soap. I can remember when the smell made you sick."

"Is that how it was?"

"Does one get to meet him?"

"I'm sorry, I won't be able to satisfy your curiosity."

"Where is he?"

"Away. In Hamburg."

"Hamburg? Isn't that where Papa always bought up that awful stuff: tallow, palm oil—"

"Don't bother, Lou. I know what I've let myself in for."

"Do you really know?" More out of spite and curiosity than from genuine affection, Lou began to act the concerned older sister. "He goes away and leaves you alone here with all the work?"

"Why don't you just assume that I enjoy it."

"Well then, Camilla, all I can say is, you're very brave and self-sacrificing. And how are you going to live?" She made a gesture that clearly indicated the judgment she had arrived at. "Surely not here, in this terrible house!"

"It's roomier than it looks," Camilla answered, hoping Lou would not guess her real feelings. It was true that the house was anything but inviting. The idea of living in it had frightened her at first, and if she was going to be entirely honest with herself, she had to admit that she had not quite gotten over the shock. Though the house was indeed spacious enough, some of the rooms, which had not been lived in for a long time, had been indescribably neglected. Another disturbing factor was its location—next to the factory, in a weed-choked garden full of thistles and overgrown gooseberry bushes.

And yet she had not had to settle for this house at all. Carl Senger had gone with her to look at another one, near the park, half an hour away, in the "nice" neighborhood. The price and terms were very good. But Camilla had noticed very clearly how worrisome the additional expense was to Senger. She had been the one who had finally insisted that they settle out here instead. "Just wait until I've had it done over."

"You—in a place like this. What kind of man would saddle you with it!" Lou got to her feet, prepared to embrace her sister, but Camilla's cool, remote look stopped her in her tracks. "My god, don't you understand that you're about to make a colossal mistake? No one else seems about to tell you, so it's up to me. Whoever this Herr Senger may be—no man has a right to demand this sort of thing from a woman. You must have been really desperate, stuck away in Warnemünde—"

Again she was interrupted. This time one of the workmen came into the office. He wanted to know where to store a shipment of sodium hydroxide that had just been delivered, twenty sacks' worth. Lou had another chance to watch the matter-of-fact, determined way Camilla made her decisions. It only incited Lou all the more. "So that's your future life. It's a lucky thing I got here in time. Come and stay with me, Camilla. I won't ask any questions. Some things just happen. Quite different, more experienced women have been hoodwinked by men."

"Are you talking about yourself now?"

"I understand what it's like. Nobody wants to admit they've made a mistake, but it's still not too late. You can still get out of it."

"You're inviting me to come to Berlin?"

"Why not? Anything would be better than what you've got here. Don't forget who you are! However did that man manage it?" This was the question that troubled Lou most.

"I think we should put a stop to this conversation." Camilla laughed, a light, free laugh that only made Lou more determined to point out to her sister the sort of hopeless life she was about to embrace. She still could not get it into her head that Camilla had made her decision of her own free will—and especially that she seemed happy and contented with it. It was obvious that was how she felt, and Lou took it almost as a personal insult.

"Maybe you believe all of Papa's talk?" she finally asked. "Are you wasting your time imagining the riches that will be yours one day?"

"Let it be, Lou."

"You do believe it, don't you? The brave little girl who puts her trust in the future. And how does that future really look? Fine, maybe you'll make it, and in twenty years you'll be rich. Twenty years—do you know what you'll be by that time? An old woman whose life is over. You don't know what you're doing. When I look at you— you've grown so pretty! Someone who looks like you—you have every chance to feather your nest . . . but . . . perhaps I'd better leave."

"Are you going to see Papa again or are you taking the next train?"

For a moment it seemed as if Lou would make a last attempt to "save" her sister, but one look at Camilla's face told her that any more words would be wasted. It went against Lou's nature to accept such a setback meekly. She would not leave the room until she had had her revenge. She would have to find something. She looked around the office, at last noticing the two framed photographs on the desk. One was of a house in a garden, the other of a man holding a little boy by the hand, both standing before a circus tent. Lou picked up the second one, for no other reason than that an involuntary gesture of Camilla's betrayed her reluctance to have Lou touch it. Lou stared at the picture, but it gave her no clue; it was old and yellowed and unconnected with Camilla's present situation. She would have liked to find a photograph of Senger. How did this man look who had managed to win Camilla over so completely? What was it about him that had brought about this transformation in her?

"Does your intended enjoy your running around like this, displaying your charms so freely?"

Camilla took the picture from her sister's hand and placed it back on the desk. She opened the door and silently preceded Lou down the hall. The carriage was no longer at the door, having made way for a furniture van. The packers had already removed the tarpaulin, and it was clear that these pieces were also secondhand.

"Lots of luck then," Lou said.

"I wish you the same. It was a short visit."

"Well, you can always learn something."

"If you'd like to come to the wedding. . . ."

"I'm not sure I can find time."

"Give my best to Mama and Alice when you see them."

"Oh, of course."

"All right then, we'll meet soon." Both knew the words were empty.

Camilla remained standing in the doorway. She had meant to ask Lou who had bought the house in Steglitz. Her thoughts continued to turn on the subject; still, she was glad that she had not bared herself to Lou. She watched the carriage leave. The mountain of luggage on the roof wobbled slightly in the straps, and as the coach rolled out of the yard and turned into the road, Lou's head bobbed in the window one last time. Better to forget it all, Lou and the world she represented—but that was easier said than done. Camilla had lived too long in that world to be able to cut her ties to it from one day to the next.

"We're ready to start unloading, miss. Where do you want us to put the stuff?"

She had to pull herself together. "On the second floor. I'll be up in a minute to show you where to put everything."

She walked a few steps away from the house, so that she could get

144

a look at the entire courtyard. The old sign of the barrel works was gone by now and the new one had been put up. Beyond that, at the far end of the storage sheds, workmen were busy cementing the foundations for the soap kettles. At the place where they had dug for water in vain, a pile of dark earth was heaped up.

She had no illusions of what was in store for her during the coming years. Life was not going to be a party. She understood Lou's reaction. She herself had been stunned the first time she had seen the place. And during the two weeks that she had spent here already, there had not been a day when she had not lost her nerve at least once, though always only fleetingly. She had only to listen to the sounds of construction to be reassured that soon everything would look different. As she quickened her steps to return to the house, the sun came out from behind the vanishing clouds and turned the many windows into a glittering mosaic.

Three

1

It had not rained for weeks, and the horses running their training
laps were almost totally concealed in clouds of dust. The track was
a small one, an oval of eight hundred meters. The low hedges at
either side were covered with dust, and the few bushes and trees along
the outside of the track had a green side and a gray side.

Originally built as the private race course of a titled landowner, the
track had subsequently been acquired by the Neustrelitz Racing As-
sociation. New stables boxes had been built as they were needed, as
could be seen by the various stages of weathering of the roofs and
the ochre paint job. Behind them were paddocks for the foals. The
animals had retired to the shade of the trees; the night had not
brought coolness or dew, and even now, in the morning, the heat
pressed down on the flat, bare countryside.

The two men standing at the edge of the track watching the horses
made an odd couple. One was tall and elegant, dressed in pale gray
and wearing white gloves in spite of the heat. The other, almost
dwarflike in his shortness, wore a tight jacket of bright yellow silk,
battered jodhpurs, and saffron-colored boots. He had not said a word
since the horses began their run, but his expression had slowly turned
sour. "A killing track," he said. "Killingly uneven."

"That's just the drought. Normally it's a paradise. Quiet. The best
water for miles around. This is a place where you can make some-

thing of a horse. These babies here have marvelous nerves. And the whole world isn't watching you to see what you're up to."

The jockey's face was impassive as he watched the horses running past. "I've seen enough. Now show me yours."

The men went toward the stables. Anyone seeing them together would have been hard put to say which one was older, the jockey with his face creased by worry or the elegant gentleman at his side. Fritz Hofmann was close to seventy. Of course he had grown older in the last thirteen years, but one had to look carefully to see it. It was really only his walk that revealed his age—the hesitant, cautious placement of his long legs.

The tags on the stall doors bore the names of titled families. Hofmann was the only commoner among them. His stall was further distinguished from the others by being free of any medals or ribbons. It was opened before they had to make themselves noticed, and with a gesture as if he were leading someone into his treasure trove, Hofmann invited the jockey to enter. "There he is, my dear Quittel—a stallion, five years old. What an animal!"

The jockey's eyes wandered. He could judge a horse merely by the stall in which it stood. There had been times when he had turned around and left without giving the horse he was supposed to ride so much as a glance. This habit had made Quittel almost as famous as his victories. But that had been long ago, and he had to be glad for any offers now. He knew it, and anyone who knew anything about racing knew it; only this Hofmann chap, who had called him here to Neustrelitz, did not make him feel it—at least not yet.

Hofmann gestured to the stableboy who had opened the door for them. Leo was a gangly youth with light-blond curly hair, which he tried to tame each morning by means of water and a metal brush—an effort that never lasted longer than half an hour. He had been in Hofmann's service for four years, ever since the old man bought the sorrel yearling at auction in Altstrelitz. Leo's head was stuffed with horse lore; he talked horses, he dreamed horses, and at night, after work, when he sat with the other stableboys and the older ones told tales of great horses and great jockeys as if they were talking of heroes and gods, he could never get enough. Quittel often figured in these tales. Leo could name every one of his wins and all his losses, and he was terribly excited at having the famous man in person before him. But the jockey barely noticed the boy as he stepped into the stall that held Hofmann's horse, a solidly built stallion with surprisingly slender legs. Although his head was barely level with the animal's rump, Quittel pushed the horse aside to make more room for himself.

"How did he feed?" Hofmann never took his eyes off Quittel.

Leo's reply was prompt. "Like a plowhorse. If that was to decide it, he'd never lose a race."

Hofmann opened the lid of the fodder box and picked up a handful. "Not enough oats."

"It's the exact mixture you ordered."

It was hotter in the stables than outside, in spite of the open door. "And what about the hoof?"

"Everything in order. Troy is in top form. The only thing that bothers him is the weather—you know it doesn't agree with him. A dry track is poison for him. It should rain. He needs a muddy track, the heavier the better. Do you remember that time in Doberan—it was a mudfight, that's what he likes. If it doesn't rain, don't even bother sending him to Berlin."

Hofmann pulled a small vial out of his jacket pocket. "Rub his hooves with this. It's an entirely new mixture. Twice a day. Massage it in well, let it work for half an hour, then wash it off."

Leo nodded. Hofmann was always bringing miracle preparations, which he devised himself. It was the same with the fodder, for which he thought up a new combination every few months.

Quittel was still busying himself with the horse, and Hofmann interpreted that as a good sign. The purchase of Troy had been much more than a whim. In all the years he went to the races he had always been envious watching the owners lead their winning horses away from the track. He had resisted his yearning to have a horse of his own for a long time; and even when he finally gave in, he kept his possession of Troy a secret. Not that he was worried about the money he had invested—one of these days Troy would bring it all back, tenfold, a hundredfold. And then he would air his secret, after his first big purse.

He had already entered Troy in several races, though only on smaller tracks. Until now this had brought only one win, in Doberan, at a secondary race. But Hofmann was not discouraged. The fault lay not with Troy but entirely with him. He simply should not have sent the horse to races of a thousand and fifteen hundred meters; Troy's strength was long stretches. It was no accident that his one win was at a steeplechase of four thousand five hundred meters. Besides, until now he had been ridden only by third-raters, glorified stableboys, not by a man like Quittel, who knew how to bring out a horse's qualities.

The jockey had completed his scrutiny. His expressions revealed nothing of his verdict.

"Do you remember Husar the Second and Tannhäuser?" Hofmann asked. "Doesn't he remind you of them both? They were slow at the start, but nobody could beat them the last eight hundred meters. When you ride him, remember that he's a slow starter, but then he really gets going."

"A killing track, hard as stone."

"I'll clock him. You can decide afterward."

Quittel gave a last look at Troy and nodded. The comparison with Tannhäuser had shaken him, for that was a horse on which he had won a number of victories.

Leo had saddled the sorrel—Quittel had brought his own gear—and was leading him out to the track. Along the hedge the other owners' stablehands gathered, and their curiosity flattered Fritz Hofmann greatly.

The track was clear, the dust had settled, and Quittel, already in the saddle, was waiting for the starting signal. Hofmann handed Leo one of the two stop watches he was wearing before pulling a white handkerchief from his breast pocket and releasing horse and rider.

"The horse suits him," Hofmann said after the first lap, although he was puzzled by Quittel's riding style.

Leo threw a glance at the stop watch, noting with some satisfaction that Quittel's time for the initial thousand meters was no better than his own. He dreamed of the day when he himself would be a renowned jockey, hired for major races.

"He's handling him too much. Troy needs to be given a free rein."

"He's won over five hundred races."

"A long time ago. He must be nearly sixty years old."

"Age means nothing in a jockey if he stays in shape."

"But he's lost his luck." Leo slowly shook his head. "Luck is just as important as a good horse."

"He leaves him pretty far on the outside in the turns, doesn't he?"

"That's Troy. He doesn't like the inside track, especially when he's running in a field. He always tries to pass the others on the outside. I can't cure him of it."

152

"And how's the time?"

"Better," Leo grudgingly admitted. "He's warming up."

The sorrel soon grew more relaxed, fiery, his gallop swallowing more space. On the track he seemed even taller and stronger, and the jockey on his back more gnomelike.

"Good so far." Leo seemed to have forgotten that another man was riding the horse. "And without a field, too. In a field I bet he'd be even faster. That's his best trait, he can't stand any horse ahead of him."

"You'll see, in Berlin, that will be his breakthrough. It's as if made for him—four thousand five hundred meters." Hofmann gave the jockey the sign they had agreed on and took his place at the finish line. As Troy crossed the line, Hofmann took the stop watch from the stableboy. "He'll beat them all by several lengths."

He hurried toward Quittel. Leo took Troy by the reins and led him from the track. But only when they reached the stable, only after Leo had taken the sorrel back to his stall to rub him down, did the jockey condescend to say, "Not a bad horse."

"With that time! Four thousand five hundred meters in 5:57:3! That kind of time on this track and without a field!"

Quittel nodded. He did not seem to know the meaning of enthusiasm. His face was bone dry, not a drop of sweat. "Hard to ride. Does what he wants. But not a bad horse. And the time's not bad either. But a killing track, bone-hard."

"You'll ride Troy in Berlin?"

"You've entered him?"

"Yes. I've completed all the formalities, the entry fee has been deposited. All you have to do is ride him."

"And transportation?"

"We have a van. He doesn't like trains."

"Any other problems when he travels? Digestion?"

"First rate, especially when Leo comes along."

"Could train him some more on the track," Quittel mused, as if mustering all the enthusiasm of which he was capable.

"You *are* going to ride him! I knew it all along, my dear Quittel. I would have withdrawn him if I couldn't get you."

"That only leaves my fee."

"Of course, your fee. . . . Well, make me an offer."

"A thousand marks up front, plus ten percent of the purse."

153

It was impossible to tell whether Fritz Hofmann had been prepared for the demand. "Fair," he said. "Absolutely fair. But I don't want to take advantage of you. That's never been my way. No matter how good a horse is, it's the jockey who wins the race. I'm willing to give you twenty percent of the prize money."

"And the front money?"

"Let's say—four hundred."

Quittel lowered his head. "I never rode for four hundred."

"Twenty-five percent of the prize money."

The jockey's eyes wandered across to the stables and then to the track. It had been a long time since anyone had spoken to him of prize money. His last great win had been in 1908, six years ago. And six years was an eternity if your luck had run out. That had been a splendid season, one of his best, with twenty-nine wins. But after that it was as if everything had been cut off. His luck had run out, perhaps his skill as well, his nerve. He lived off his name now and his past. It had been a long time since he had ridden a horse on a track like Berlin. He should have retired; they all made that clear to him. And now here he stood, with a man who talked about winning.

"What was the time again?" Quittel asked.

"Five, fifty-seven, three."

Only now did the jockey ask to see the watch. He glanced at it briefly. He was more encouraged by the lively discussion of the stableboys who had watched him ride.

"All right, I'll do it on your terms." Horse owners had been a horror for Quittel all his life—people who, as far as he was concerned, knew nothing about horses and even less about the sport of kings. But this Hofmann had infected Quittel with his optimism, so that the jockey now added, quite against his habits, "If we really should come in first, you have an option for all the remaining races this season."

"Done." Hofmann took off his right glove, and the two men performed the ritual of two horsetraders ratifying a sale. "We'll meet in Berlin. Leo will take care of everything. You only have to give him your instructions." He called for the stableboy, gave him the good news, and added, "Unfortunately I can't stay. As it is, I'll be late for the closing ceremonies. What about the birthday present for Max? Will it be ready in time?" Max was the oldest of Camilla's three sons.

"It'll be ready by Sunday. They delivered the bridle yesterday—red leather, just like you ordered. It looks great on the white fur. All the stuff is over there in the coachhouse. The two billys look great in their gear."

Hofmann struggled with himself; he would have loved nothing better than to go have a look. At heart it was Hofmann's childhood wish he was now gratifying: to have a pair of snow-white billygoats with red bridles pulling a light cart. At the spa where his parents always spent the summer there had been such a team in the gardens, and no day passed that he had not taken a ride. He looked at his pocket watch. "I've got to get back to town. Well then, you know what to do, on Sunday you drive up with the rig, let's say after breakfast, around nine o'clock. You drive into the courtyard and make one complete turn. But be on time. Nine o'clock, at Senger's."

"I'll be there on the dot. We really are going to the Berlin races?"

Hofmann did not consider it necessary to reply. The race had a total purse of thirty-five thousand marks, of which twenty-two thousand went to the winner. This thought, and the calculations that followed from it, occupied him completely as he walked toward the automobile that was waiting to take him back to town.

2

The two-part madrigal had seemed about to end for several minutes, but instead it went on and on, and Fritz Hofmann grew increasingly impatient. He had arrived late. Struck by the reproachful eyes of the proctor, who was guarding the doors to the auditorium, he had not dared to look for a seat but remained standing in the shadow of the choir loft. A closing ceremony with tickets of admission and a printed program—that was typical of the headmaster of Duke Karl Technical High School. Dr. Minding, professor of mathematics, physics, and chemistry, loved mounting special events. His celebrations of the anniversary of the battle of Sedan, of the Imperial Proclamation, of the Grand Duke's birthday, and of course of the end of the school year were so popular that he had to give out cards of admission. The prices he charged for tickets were such that they could be considered a kind of contribution to the support of the school. To fight his boredom as he waited for the boys' voices to stop, Hofmann counted the close ranks of chairs and calculated that this ceremony alone would bring the school a round thousand. Still, the money was no more than a drop in the bucket for a man like Minding, who had high-flown plans. Only five years ago Dr. Minding had prevailed on the authorities to give his institution equal standing with the high school for humanities. This by no means satisfied his ambition but spurred it on all the more, as was clear from his latest project, the erection of an observatory.

Finally the music stopped. The audience applauded generously, and the glee club left the platform. The students came down the side steps in single file and returned to their seats. Hofmann did not need to look for his grandsons among them, for all three were as totally devoid of musical talent as he was himself—not only Max, the oldest, who would be twelve on Sunday, but also the two younger boys, ten-year-old Konrad and Georg. At nine, Georg was the youngest sixth-former in the entire Grand Duchy of Mecklenburg-Strelitz: he had simply refused to stay home when Konrad started school and so the two of them were in the same class. For all his grandfatherly pride, such zeal made Hofmann uneasy—to this day he thought of his own school years with horror. And nothing seemed to have changed since those days, neither the tight blue Sunday suits nor the freshly cut hair. What nonsense, to say that youth was the best time of one's life! He had felt just the opposite. Only now that he was old could he live as he had always wanted.

"Amelung, Attenhofer, Berkel . . ." Dr. Minding, a pile of report cards before him on the stand swagged and wreathed in green, began to call up the youngest students to hand them their certificates. It was a year of many births, 1904, and there were more than thirty boys in the form Konrad and Georg attended. "Sachtleben, Sandner, Schadow. . . ." Now Hofmann would have to pay attention, and he shifted his position slightly to the right. He did not need to worry about those two. In elementary school they had never brought home anything but A's, and judging by their haggling with him over appropriate rewards for this year's grades, they would not have to hide their first high-school report cards either.

"Senger, Georg; Senger, Konrad." Hofmann watched them as they moved forward, both in blue sailor suits, both blond. The interest they aroused in the audience was not just grandfatherly imagination.

Everyone in Neustrelitz knew the Senger boys. A young, developing town, whose magistrate concentrated all his energies on bringing in as much new industry as possible, always needed models. For years the Senger family had fulfilled that role. Everyone had followed the rise of the business until it became one of the town's major tax-payers—first with skepticism, then with astonishment, and finally with great pride, even if some questions remained unanswered. Given the seclusion in which the family lived, the three boys offered the only clues—as well as Fritz Hofmann, of course. He continued to live downtown and did his utmost to embellish the legend of his son-in-law's rise with new highlights. If Quittel should win the Berlin steeple-chase with Troy, the local paper would have material for a front-page story. He must not forget to engage a photographer in Berlin. . . .

"Senger, Max . . . Senger, Max. . . ."

Hofmann was no longer following the awarding of certificates. Was it really already time for the third form? Once more the headmaster's voice rang through the auditorium, impatiently repeating the name a third time. But no student rose from his seat. The headmaster's calling of the next name stifled the murmurs that were about to break out in the audience.

To escape the curious glances that grazed him, Hofmann moved further back into the shadow of the gallery. There was only one ex-planation for Max's absence from the closing ceremony—and it was by no means pleasant. He knew that the greater part of the blame was his. The brown bow tie he was wearing instead of a four-in-hand began to choke him and reminded him that he had not even had time to change his shirt, usually his first act after visiting the track. Dr. Minding was still reading off names, and he would continue to do so until it was the turn of the graduating class. Hofmann began to retreat; quietly and inconspicuously he edged toward the center door, anticipating the silent protest of the proctor with a pacifying gesture. Finally he was outside, in the hall with the niches that held the plaster busts of German heroes. As was appropriate for a technical high school, scientists and mathematicians predominated. Mathematics—it was cer-tain that a failing mark in the subject had led to Max's downfall. . . .

Hofmann was sorely tempted to imitate his grandson and make his own escape, but he resisted and waited in the schoolyard for the festivities to end. Mathematics, of all subjects! The very one he had helped Max with! How could he possibly justify himself to Camilla? He loved his daughter; more, he admired her; he was fully aware of her part in Senger's success. But on certain matters it was better not to tangle with her. One of them was money. Not that she kept him short—he could hardly accuse her of that. He still lived at the Hotel Pologne, by his own wish. He had a proper little apartment there for himself—three rooms on the top floor, with a view of nature and his own furniture, and if he felt like it, he could have them bring his meals up from the dining room. Camilla paid for all of it. In ad-dition she took care of all his other bills, generously and without much discussion. But she kept him short of cash. Fortunately he had his own secret sources as well as the little sums his son-in-law regularly slipped him. That was the second sore spot with Camilla—his allegedly bad influence on her husband. Camilla feared that Hofmann would seduce Senger into doing something foolish—patronizing hotels that were too expensive, buying presents that were too extravagant. She even suspected that he was trying to lead Senger into gambling. Of course he'd tried, but without success. The third touchy subject was the upbringing of her children, where Camilla also accused him of "undermining" her "principles." There was no help for it; he'd have to face the music one way or another.

When he heard the auditorium doors open and when the first students filed out, he returned to the building. Was it the presence of teachers that discouraged any noisy word or was it the gravity of the occasion? In any case, even this final act of the event proceeded with strict discipline, and Hofmann would not have been surprised if the students had left the auditorium walking in ranks and separated by classes.

Konrad and Georg discovered their grandfather before he found them and without waiting for him to ask, proudly held out their report cards. But he was not interested. He took the boys aside to ask, "Where is Max hiding? What happened?"

"Don't you want to see our report cards? You promised, for every A—"

"I want you to tell me at once where I can find Max."

The brothers exchanged a look. They could have been twins, so strong was the resemblance between them. They had their father's sturdy build as well as his fine blond hair, making both of them look older, almost staid.

"I'm sure you know where he is."

They nodded but stubbornly remained mute.

"Fine. You don't have to tell. But send him here at once."

"I thought you were going to take us out for ice cream."

"Listen to me. He has to come here immediately. I mean it. I want to help him. . . . I'm sure you can imagine what will happen at home otherwise. So go get him. He is to report to the headmaster. Don't worry, I'll be there as well. Tell him he has to come, otherwise there's nothing I can do for him. . . . Afterward we'll go for ice cream."

Surrounded by the graduates in their colorful caps, Headmaster Minding emerged from the auditorium. Hofmann motioned to his grandsons to disappear.

He waited until Minding had made his farewells to his class and to a number of parents. During this time the headmaster, who was taller than most of the others, repeatedly threw Hofmann a look to indicate that he too considered an interview crucial. Finally he exchanged the last handshake and came up to Hofmann, holding a single blue certificate in his hand.

Dr. Minding was a robust, almost athletic man and, though only in his forties, already bald. He was famous for his salty Pomeranian expressions, and Hofmann was prepared for something of the sort by way of a greeting, but the headmaster only said, "The parents were too busy to come, I suppose? Not even to a closing ceremony. . . . Well, enough of that. However that may be—I've never in twenty-four years of teaching had anyone play hooky from the closing ceremonies." He led the way to his office.

Hofmann was familiar with the room. He had visited Dr. Minding for the first time after the midyear report, when the present disaster was already on the horizon. Compared with the headmasters' studies Hofmann had known in his own school days, the room was cheerful and light, without the murky, dusty velvet hangings, black furniture, and gold-framed dignitaries. It was more like a laboratory, with shelves full of visual aids for instruction in physics, chemistry, and biology. Dr. Minding sat down behind the broad desk of natural oak. Hofmann stopped in front of the shelves.

"Everything except a skeleton."

"We have one," Minding assured him. "It's being repaired. A victim of the cleaning woman. She literally broke his neck."

"Perhaps she's Catholic, intent on doing a good deed."

Minding seemed to have some difficulty following Hofmann's train of thought, but finally he laughed. "True, she always crosses herself." He shook his head. "To think that for many people hell begins right under the potato field."

"My mother threatened to take me out of school when she discovered that we had to memorize the bones of the hand. Even though she was a Protestant."

"In Berlin?"

"Neukölln."

160

"Then you studied under old man Kuhn! He was the first bold enough to teach such heresies." Minding opened a drawer of his desk. "Have you seen the latest in the field?" He drew out something that looked like a case for table silver; the blue velvet padding held a hand. "A brand new substance—Bakelite, I believe they call it," Minding explained. "You can assemble it like a puzzle; that leaves an impression in the students' minds! Unfortunately it's as expensive as sin."

Hofmann would have liked to dwell longer on the subject, but all at once Minding was holding the report card again. His brow furrowed. He read it through before handing it to Hofmann. "Not exactly a scroll of honor."

It cost Hofmann an effort to pick up the certificate. The two failing marks almost jumped out at him—one in history and the other, as he had suspected, in mathematics. "He won't be promoted, then?"

"How can he be? And yet in mathematics he could be at the top of the class. One year ago an *A,* and now an unadorned *F.* From pure laziness. The young gentleman thinks he's too good to have to study. If he happens to be in the mood, he'll do it; if not, he won't. And for the last six months he wouldn't. The same thing shows up in the other subjects as well. You can see, compared to last year everything has gone downhill. The patience of teachers is not inexhaustible. . . ."

Hofmann took a deep breath. "Unfortunately a lot of it is my fault. When he brought home his midyear grades, naturally his parents were very upset. I said that I was prepared to study with the boy. He came to my rooms after school, I supervised his homework and heard his lessons. And in fact he did improve somewhat, his grades climbed upward a little in the worst subjects, and I must have loosened the reins somewhat too soon." He could not very well admit that he had given up his "tutoring" altogether after his grandson had assured him that he could manage by himself. Instead he had spent his afternoons with Max at the paddock. Max was the only one privy to his secret. "Therefore I'm just as much to blame as the boy."

"The boy is old enough to know what is required of him. Leniency is quite out of place here. What the boy needs is a firm hand."

"He will be made to feel it, you can rest assured. Not by me, I must admit. But my daughter will not let him get away with it. Max is the oldest; and I don't have to tell you that mothers are always strictest with their firstborn. What I fear is that if he comes home with *this* report . . ." he allowed the sentence to trail off. His glance fell on the

161

plywood model of the observatory that occupied a corner table. He was not certain whether this was the right moment for a diversion, but he tried his luck. "When is the big moment?" And when Minding was slow to follow his gesture, he added, "The paper said you were having difficulty raising the needed funds."

"They've got money for everything, but we have to beg for every instructional aid. A whole folder of correspondence for one globe. It's enough to drive one mad. Yes, the humanistic high school, the nobility has plenty of contributions for them. But none of these gentle-folk cares about us, we're the proletarian foot soldiers." Dr. Minding stared at the model. "The plans have been ready for a year."

"I thought Treibel was sponsoring it."

Minding rose and began to pace the room. "That was his wife. Since her death he's turned off the tap. Private initiative! I've heard enough of that. I keep reading how many rich men live in Neustrelitz, but—" He came to a stop before Hofmann. "Don't take it amiss, but the Senger family unfortunately does not belong among the lavish spenders. Still, according to the stories that go around, business there is excellent. Three hundred workers, full-time."

"That's not it. My daughter has three sons in your school, and she does not want her children to be given preferential treatment just because they have wealthy parents. She is overly sensitive on that point —that is the reason. But perhaps there's a different way to go about it. How much would the observatory cost?"

"Thirty thousand, including the necessary renovations."

"How much of it do you have in hand?"

"Barely a third. As soon as we can put down fifty percent free and clear, the city will guarantee my bank mortgage for the rest. At seven and a half percent interest—just as at the time of the Moroccan crisis. Unhealthy, highly unwholesome. I only hope no other world calamity is breaking."

"Then you're short five thousand marks?" Hofman thought about the purse for the Berlin steeplechase; five thousand was a trifle by comparison. "If you'll give me the account number, I'll guarantee the five thousand. I have only one condition—no names please, the gift must remain anonymous, whatever happens. You might be able to start construction this very summer, during the vacation."

Headmaster Minding examined Hofmann. A remarkable man, and a remarkable family. Just look at their outward habits. One of the richest families in Neustrelitz, and they still lived in the house near the old barrel factory. The man went on the road like any commercial traveler, refusing all titles and honorary posts offered him. And the wife worked in the business, a beautiful woman who sat at her desk day after day from seven-thirty on and who was praised and feared because of her competence. Secretly Minding was impressed. The son of a railroad worker, he had a soft spot for anyone who owed his rise exclusively to his own efforts. His mathematical mind, on the other hand, had some difficulty with the family. The Sengers and Hofmann; that was an equation that did not come out even; it contained an unknown quantity that he could not comprehend.

The headmaster's dogged silence did not unsettle Hofmann, much less the sum he had promised. The first prize for the steeplechase was twenty-two thousand marks, and as if the money were already in his pocket, Hofmann decided to increase the offer if necessary.

There was a knock at the door. Minding excused himself, went outside, and returned a few minutes later. "The sinner. He has a pretty threadbare excuse, but anyway." He pointed to the report card. "And what are we going to do with this?"

Fritz Hofmann raised his hands. His expression seemed to say, whatever decision you make will affect me most.

Minding looked at the report and then at the model of the observatory. "If we do promote him, it will be only on probation. In any case, he must take another exam before he can be allowed to enter the next grade."

"That seems a defensible solution."

The headmaster pulled out his watch. "In a few minutes our staff meeting begins. The F in mathematics cannot be altered; the boy's total laziness has outraged his teacher too much. But we can try Dr. Capobus; perhaps he will reconsider the mark in history." He let the lid of his watch snap shut. "I'll expect the boy in one hour. And one more thing, about the tutoring—it would be better if you stayed out of it this time. Hire old Laue, he knows what's expected."

Hofmann found his grandson outside the school building, absorbed in contemplating an automobile parked at the curb. He did not seem tormented by remorse. He fell on his grandfather immediately with a description of the car, its horsepower, and technical data, which he concluded with a sigh. "And Pops still drives that ancient Opel."

After the unpleasant half hour in the headmaster's office, the blatant irresponsibility of his grandson should have angered Hofmann, but in fact, he too would have liked to pass over the matter without another word. He had to force himself to unleash an obligatory lecture. "That was inexcusable—to cut the closing ceremony! One faces the consequences of one's acts. Did you know you would fail two subjects?"

"It's sort of what I expected, yes." Unlike his brothers, Max did not take after Senger in any way. He was a "real Hofmann," as his grandfather was apt to put it, taller than most boys his age, lanky and small-boned, with dark hair and eyes. He was wearing a brown suit with long trousers; his white shirt fitted superbly, the bow tie was exactly in place, and between the buttonhole of the lapel and his breast pocket swung a gold watch chain. He modeled himself on his grandfather, especially in matters of dress. He would be wearing a hat and cane as well if he had his way.

"Is that all you have to say?"

"I apologized to the headmaster, as you asked."

"And what comes next?"

"I suppose you had a talk with him. . . ."

"And what do you suppose came of it?"

"How would I know—you don't look too unhappy."

"So, you think I don't look. . . ." Why wasn't he able to give the boy a proper scolding? He really ought to; it was important to appeal to the boy's conscience. If Max were to get the idea that his grandfather was also taking the matter lightly. . . .

For a while they walked along silently, until Hofmann finally collected himself. "A failing mark in mathematics. Disastrous. History didn't go so badly. A sufficiency, barely. At the end of the vacation you'll have to take a make-up exam, don't make any mistake about it."

"That means I've been promoted?"

"A reexamination. You'll be tutored by old Laue during your vacation—you've made your own bed."

"But I'm promoted?"

"Being held back—that would have been all we need. To lose a year. Your mother . . . I imagine there'll be hell to pay as it is."

They walked on.

"Wait," the boy said suddenly. He pointed to a bench at the side of the road. "Put your foot up, the left one first." Hofmann did as he was told, and his grandson wiped the dust off his shoe with a handkerchief that obviously served no other purpose, since it was already closer to black than gray.

"Thank you, my boy."

"You were at the track this morning? The dust on your shoes was that color."

Hofmann nodded. "You should have been there!"

"Is Quittel going to ride him?"

"By now both of them are surely on their way to Berlin."

"Troy was that good? In spite of the heat?"

"Four thousand five hundred meters in five, fifty-three, seven."

"You think that's good enough to win?"

"It might be . . . it might. . . . It is, he'll win. Tricolore didn't make that kind of time, nor Gay Paree, and Grand Duchess under Captain Joe had a worse time over the distance."

"And I've really been promoted?"

"Yes."

"Would you do me a favor? Please place a bet for me on Troy. Twenty marks."

"Oh, so now you believe he'll win. Twenty marks, you say. May I ask where the money is coming from? If you think that one is luckier with someone else's money. . . ."

"No, no, it's my money. The twenty marks I'm going to get for my report card."

"Wait a minute—twenty marks for *that* report card? I promised you—"

"—twenty marks if I'm promoted. And I've been promoted, haven't I?"

"Poor Camilla," muttered Hofmann, without rightly knowing what he meant by it. By the time he stopped at the Café Sturm, the fit of responsibility had already evaporated. His two other grandsons were sitting in the garden. A waiter was just clearing away two silver bowls and replacing them with two others piled high with lemon ice.

3

S he had gone to the window, opened it, and was peering down into the yard to see what had happened. Her blue linen frock, adorned only with two rows of white buttons running down the side seams to midcalf, where the material was slit, made her appear even more slender, almost seductively thin. The two men in the office with her could not help but ogle her, though both were ready to concentrate on their work again should she turn around. The woman, however, continued to be preoccupied with the events in the courtyard. One of the foremen was helping the doctor from his car, took his satchel, and then hurried back to the accident victim. Dr. Oesterreicher was wearing a dark frock coat in spite of the heat.

The accident had happened in the shipping dock, on the long ramp where the railroad cars were loaded, and the doctor's arrival attracted still more curious watchers. Women and men came running from every direction, wearing the light-blue smocks and coveralls that were supplied to them by the firm. The foreman's voice, intent on sending them back to work, rang as far as her window, but the employees were not so easily intimidated. They stood in little clumps and conversed, taking advantage of the opportunity to light a cigarette. Camilla could watch no longer; she shut the window. "Why do these things always happen on a Friday? The one day of the week we make shipments."

The two bookkeepers, also clad in the light-blue smocks with the ornate white *H* in a blue circle on the pocket, knew that she did not expect an answer. They remained bent over their papers, and for a while the clatter of the adding machine was the only sound in the room.

"Where did we leave off?"

"Thuringia. Glasbrenner's weekly turnover." The bookkeeper who had spoken pulled a strip of paper out of the machine.

"Is that all?"

"Including the orders that came in the mail this morning."

"And Saxony?"

"You can't really compare it with Saxony. Glasbrenner doesn't have Erfurt and Gotha. Schüler kept those. One of these days we're going to have to straighten out the territories. So Glasbrenner can—"

"What does Saxony look like?" She studied the tabulation the bookkeeper had handed her. "It's a good thirty percent higher."

"Thuringia is harder. More small-town customers. Besides, just recently we took over the Lida Works, and their leftover stock is glutting the market."

"We've doubled the advertising in his district to make up for it. No, Glasbrenner is slowing down. The numbers show it, no matter what other territory you compare them with. Sales increased on the average twelve percent this year and his orders have gone up by only half that. That's right, isn't it?"

"That's right, about six or seven percent. But he'll make it up."

"Do you really believe that?"

"Anyway, he's one of our oldest travelers. He's been with us from the beginning, thirteen years. He—"

"We've both been here thirteen years, you and I. And you, Wagner, you've been here for ten. That's no reason to relax and get slack, is it?" She smiled, only with her eyes really, where an expression of mildness and consideration broke through. The two men did not know where to look. It was strange. She got along smoothly with the simple workers. The drivers, the packers, the boiler operators— all of them swore by their boss and did not conceal their admiration. "Our boss puts all other women in the shade"—the line was well known throughout the town. Her relationship with the office workers was not quite so free of problems. For these people Carl Senger was the sole head of the firm, in spite of his frequent absences. Camilla remained simply his wife. Thirteen years had not been long enough to remove the deep-seated prejudice. Camilla had not only learned to make her peace with it but had also learned to draw certain advantages from it, turning the distance between herself and the employees into a matter of principle.

"When you've finished with the orders," she continued, "please draw up a list of Glasbrenner's orders—let's say for the last two years. And include Erfurt and Gotha. Anything else?"

"If you'd initial these invoices, so I can have the checks made out."

She looked over the papers, marked each with a slanted S, and stopped short at one. "Take this down," she said, read off a set of figures to the bookkeepers, asked for the machine result, and compared it with the invoice she was holding. "This time their mistake was in our favor, but it could just as easily be the other way around." She corrected the bill, initialed it, and left the office.

She was a person who needed warmth, who felt happiest in the summer, and as she stepped outside into the brooding heat of the July day, she suddenly realized how cold she felt—so cold that for a moment she shivered. The factory had extended ever further. One tract after another had been created: the modern three-story administration building from which she had come, the laboratory, new processing installations, new warehouses, a new shipping center, company dwellings. And all of it had long since merged with the city. The travelers who repeatedly drove along the stretch between Neustrelitz and Berlin knew exactly when they would first see the chimney with the illuminated sign, the white *H* in the blue circle. Among all the functional buildings the residence, which she was now approaching, was an anachronism.

It simply did not fit in any more. Of course the house had been extensively modernized on the inside, but the improvements on the outside—the white paint, the new window frames, the shutters, the enlarged entrance, the attached terrace and the garden—though a labor of love, were all in vain. The latest attempt was made two years ago—two stone eagles on the posts of the new garden gate—and was a total failure. The house remained a bastard, almost touching in its smartened-up ugliness.

As she entered the house, the twelve-o'clock siren blared from the factory buildings. She had her private office in the old house, the same ground-floor room where everything had begun, long ago. The only reminder of the original furnishings was one narrow loveseat, and even it had been reupholstered. She went into the small cubby off the room to wash her hands and fix her hair. She had let it grow again and wore it very soft and loosely pinned up into a chignon, which made a particularly flattering frame for her narrow face and slender neck. She could be pleased with her looks; now that she was thirty-one, she liked herself better than she had at eighteen. She had confirmation of her good looks daily, not only from her mirror, but also from the reaction of men. It was hard to explain the nature of what she had gained over the years. Once her father had said that all Berlin women were late bloomers—perhaps that was all there was to it.

A smile played about her lips as she sat at the desk. For the first time this morning she felt relaxed. She picked up some work, but she had difficulty concentrating. On the desk lay various samples of packaging for new products; each of them somehow featured the *H. Hof-mann* had remained the company name. Her husband himself had wanted it that way, because it would not have been smart to change it. Somehow she was proud of that fact, although sometimes she wondered if he might not be regretting the decision. Though he always said—

"Come in."

The housekeeper, Frau Ewers, entered with a tray, self-assuredly cleared a space on the desk, and then, both hands on her hips, stood her ground. "You drink that now. I don't go to all this trouble just so you won't touch it."

"May I at least wait for it to cool down, so I won't burn my tongue?"

"Nobody can live on air alone. Half a hard roll for breakfast, and not a bite since."

"It's the heat."

"The heat, is it! You burn the candle at both ends. A breath of air could blow you over, almost. All you need is for some sickness to come along . . . by the way, what about Sunday, the birthday dinner?"

"I'll leave that to you."

"The boy asked for chocolate soup followed by pickled eel. It's his birthday, and Herr Senger likes it too. But what about you?" Frau Ewers was from Mecklenburg, and she had a high opinion of that

169

province's local cuisine—a preference in which she was supported by the male members of the household.

"If it stays this hot, I'll be happy with a cold plate."

"A cold plate, that's what I thought. And Herr Hofmann, is that the right thing for him too?"

"You're the best judge of what he likes."

Frau Ewers, a woman of fifty, had never married because the objects of her passion had always been beyond her reach. Camilla's father was one of them. She adored him—secretly, of course—and her feelings took various expressions. For his sake she overturned her planned menus. From time to time she inspected his compartment in the wine cellar of the Hotel de Pologne. She took personal care of his shirts, and she saved his discarded scarves and gloves in a special box, as Camilla had accidentally discovered.

"In that case I'll see if I can get some game for Sunday. Though July isn't too good for that. He doesn't like wild boar, it's too early for wild duck. I bet there's some snipe, though—"

"I'm sure you'll find the right thing."

"Is he having dinner here today?"

"He should have been here with the children by now." The housekeeper was beginning to get on Camilla's nerves, nor did she have the least desire for the broth. She did not know where the morning had gone, only that she had not accomplished half of what she had set out to do.

"Why didn't you go to the closing ceremony, by the way? Now that all three boys go to that school. And the pains they went to, a madrigal, a cappella, that's the most beautiful thing in the world. Boys, they sing like angels." Frau Ewers had sung in the church choir for many years, and she never missed the oratorio concerts at Easter and Christmas. "Really, I went to hear one of the rehearsals, they sang like angels."

"We've got to get the boys' things ready and fetch the valises from the attic. If they're to leave on Monday for Warnemünde—good heavens, I almost forgot. Lenka has a birthday coming up." She opened a drawer and leafed through a calendar. "On Tuesday! I'll have to go downtown this afternoon and find her a present." She looked at the appointment book. "No, I can't, this afternoon a new traveler is coming in and. . . . Listen, Frau Ewers, I really can't drink this now, take it away and leave me alone. And if Dr. Oesterreicher comes looking for me, please do me a favor and get rid of him. I don't have time to listen to him. . . .

But the housekeeper refused to budge. "Get up at six in the morning, then sit here all day long. Last night the lamp was still lit at midnight."

"Please, my dear Frau Ewers! How often have we played this little game! With all due respect to your maternal instinct, everything really is fine. I've got rather too much to do, but there's sure to be a quieter period soon."

"I've heard that for thirteen years."

"Have I ever complained?"

"If only you would!"

"What?"

"Think about yourself for a change. The household, the children, your husband, the factory—you worry about everything. You'd do it all yourself if you could. It's simply too much. One of these days you'll have to pay for it."

Camilla tried to put an end to the conversation with a laugh, but Frau Ewers was still going strong. "I take it, then, that the boys will be going alone to Warnemünde again. That makes the third year in a row. You used to take the time for that at least, a few weeks at the shore; you don't even allow yourself that anymore. No—you don't complain. That's true enough. We'd all be astonished, too, if we heard you admit that you're tired, that you want some peace and quiet. My sister is just like you—in control, even-tempered, never shows a thing, but watch out when she stands up for herself. Then everything gets turned upside down, and in the end she's the one who has to apologize."

There was a knock on the door, and before Camilla could stop him, Dr. Oesterreicher had entered. He had been their family physician for thirteen years and felt completely at home. He had delivered her three sons, he had saved Senger's life with an emergency operation after an improperly diagnosed case of blood poisoning, and of course he also took care of the other family members as well as the factory workers. Now and again he paid a call without having been summoned, preferably at dinner time, for he thought highly of Frau Ewer's culinary prowess. After he set down his bag, he cast his first glance at the tray holding the cup of bouillon. "Do you suppose the kitchen might have another cup for me?"

171

"Let me give you this one, I think it's cooled down enough," Camilla said.

The doctor looked after the housekeeper, who was beating a wordless retreat. "She should not gain any more weight, our good Frau Ewers. Why don't you tell her that it's not becoming. . . . Yes, yes, you want to hear about the injured workman. Well, it looked worse than it is. A typical accident in coupling two cars. These fellows seem to believe they can stop a freight car with their chests. Three broken ribs. I've strapped it, that's all that's necessary." Dr. Oesterreicher drank the broth, slurping slightly.

"That's the third accident during coupling, although my husband left strict instructions."

The doctor came closer. Camilla knew what was coming and resigned herself to it. Ever since he found out that she was slightly anemic, he always examined her eyes. "Hold still! Do you take the iron tonic I prescribed for you?"

She said yes to keep him happy, though she had not touched the brown bottle in her medicine cabinet for a long time because every time she took the medication, it made her queasy.

"How do you sleep?" he continued, looking at her critically.

"Listen, there's not a thing wrong with me. You keep nagging at me, and I'm the healthiest person in the whole house."

The doctor unbuttoned his Prince Albert. In a way she was right. Of all the Senger family, she had made the fewest claims on his services. Less complicated pregnancies and deliveries than hers he had not seen in all his twenty-four years of medical practice: a week later he had regularly found her back in her office, surrounded by work. But lately he had detected some worrisome symptoms. "You're working too hard and sleeping too little. Let yourself go—everyone needs that sometimes, even you. I'd be a poor physician if I waited until it's too late. God knows, you could easily take six months—"

"I'm no longer twenty, that's all. Next time you come, I'll wear rouge, and you'll be satisfied."

"You're so sensible about everything else. . . ."

"Please spare me. I just heard it all from Frau Ewers, and you know how she can ride a subject." Her voice sounded calm and friendly, but she was sitting so stiffly in her chair, and her bearing expressed so much resistance, that the doctor decided not to press her further. He buttoned up his Prince Albert, picked up his satchel, and

172

shook her hand. "You know the mansion next door to my house. Your husband once hinted that he might be interested. It's up for sale. Spacious grounds, a stand of old trees, a hothouse. It's a property that should fit your tastes as well. And to the best of my knowledge, the price is well within reason. The neighborhood alone is worth its weight in gold. It's only rarely that any of these houses comes on the market."

"It's the property to the left of yours?"

"That's the one."

"And my husband expressed an interest?"

"That was my impression. Haven't you been looking for something of the sort for years?"

Dr. Oesterreicher was not the only one who repeatedly pointed out available properties to the Sengers. No one understood why they went on living where they did. The townspeople considered it almost an affront, especially since their unparalleled rise, their growing wealth, and the firm's excellent reputation had persuaded local society—which consisted of the Grand Duke's court, the nobility of Mecklenburg, and the court attendants—to make an exception and grant a soap manufacturer entry into their circles. Their astonishment was all the greater to see that the Senger family did not seem to care. No good reason could be found for their behavior. Dr. Oesterreicher did not find one either, and once more he was given a vague, unsatisfying answer.

"You may not believe this, but I've become attached to this house." It was not a lie, though it was not the truth either. But how could she confess to a stranger what she so stubbornly denied to herself?

"Well, how about you and Herr Senger coming to pay me a visit sometime soon? Fortunately I can receive guests again. I'm lucky in my new housekeeper. Come along, see me out. Really, this time I've got hold of a gem. Go ahead, laugh all you want, it's not so easy for a widower. The young ones are always after you, and the old ones keep getting sick. You see, I too have my problems."

She always saw him out, and she did so now, although he had already stolen half an hour of her time. The sky was cloudless, the sun almost white. It was the hottest part of the day, and yet she felt none of the warmth, as if she were sheltered under a clear dome that rendered the sun's rays ineffectual. As she shook hands with the doctor, he noted how cold hers was. But this time Dr. Oesterreicher

173

did not remark on the fact. Instead, he pointed to the zinnias with their reddish-gold blossoms. "They don't grow for me. Must be something about the soil."

"Would you like to take some with you?"

"No thank you, I don't care for flowers in the house. My wife knew that, but to make my housekeepers understand. . . ."

An intense odor rose from the flower beds, not sweet as in spring, but harsh, almost autumnal, Camilla thought. Gazing at the lavish display of blossoms, she felt as if she were standing in an alien garden in a season that was not her own.

". . . except for his eyes. Something must be done. In the long run we won't be able to do without the operation. You know him, even the idea that he'd have to wear glasses is terrible for him."

"You mean my father? Glasses?"

"We tend to forget that he's sixty-nine years old. He needs glasses desperately, but he absolutely refuses. He also ordered me not to mention it to you. It's going to happen sooner or later. The way traffic is, he's going to walk straight into a car one of these days. Otherwise he's in excellent shape. Truly, a man who knows how to live, your father. You could take lessons from him."

"Wait. I'll learn in time. Some things can't be hurried. Perhaps I'll grow into an irresponsible old lady who throws her money around; these things happen. You mentioned an operation?"

Dr. Oesterreicher made a sign to drop the subject as an automobile drove into the courtyard and stopped in front of the house. "We'll talk about it another time."

The chauffeur had stopped only briefly to let Hofmann and the three boys get out; then he drove on, toward the factory site. Having the boys driven to school every day and brought home again might seem a luxury, but for Camilla the errand was justified because every morning the driver also went to the central post office and picked up the mail, while at noon he dropped off the outgoing letters. Her father sometimes availed himself of the opportunity and came in the car to spend a few hours in the laboratory. Some of the chemists claimed that he understood more than all of them together, but to Hofmann it was a pastime, and there was no counting on his being there at any particular time.

Camilla's relationship with her father was ambivalent. On the surface all was well; thanks to the financial arrangements she had made,

174

there remained few points of irritation. But the past was by no means erased. Her father continued to arouse memories which even after all these years still pained her; the fear of losing everything from one day to the next was deeply rooted. It was the dynamo that drove her, that fed her energy, but it also kept her from abandoning herself on the proper occasion, from forgetting about work and giving herself a day off.

The doctor and her father had exchanged greetings, but the boys hung back. Their behavior might have appeared well mannered, but Camilla understood it differently. Presumably they had eaten too much ice cream and were glad that they did not have to go in to dinner at once. Nor did everything seem rosy about the report cards, since they made no move to show them. Only Konrad started to pull his out of his pocket, but he quickly shoved it back when Max poked him. Camilla pretended not to see. She did not want to start—not now, not later; she simply did not want to know anything unpleasant.

"Go inside," she said to the children. "Change your clothes. Dinner will be ready in fifteen minutes."

Fritz Hofmann quickly grasped the opportunity to say, "Hurry! Can't you hear? Do as your mother tells you."

The doctor had taken his leave, and Camilla walked back toward the house with her father. She pointed to a bench set in the dappled shade. "Shall we sit down for a moment?"

Fritz Hofmann took off the white Panama hat with the brown ribbon that matched his tie and laid it at his side. He had expected a scolding—"Must you always stuff them full of ice cream!" immediately followed by questions about the report cards. That neither happened was unusual, as was the fact that she took time out to sit quietly with him on the bench. But that was the way things were; today was one of his lucky days, and everything turned out well. "It was a beautiful closing ceremony," he said. "You've got to hand it to Minding, he knows how to get up a celebration. The way he runs his school, it truly is worthy of support. Something ought to be done to help him realize his plans for an observatory. He showed me the model; all that's missing is five thousand marks."

"I'd rather you'd tell me about your eyes. Dr. Oesterreicher—"

"He exaggerates. Always finds something. There's nothing wrong with me. What do you think—couldn't you find a little something for the observatory?"

"An observatory. That's the most important thing?"

"I can remember a little girl. She was nine years old when I took her to the Berlin observatory for the first time. It was just when you could see that comet, and there was no getting you to leave. I can still see you sitting on your chair, a little girl at the huge telescope, and that night we went outside and I explained the constellations to you."

They fell silent. The boys' voices could be heard at the open windows on the second floor. Suddenly Camilla asked, "Have I changed very much? I don't think back as far as you do. I only think of the last few years."

"You know what the workmen say about you."

"Be serious for once. Have I changed?"

"Of course you've changed."

"Not for the better?"

"Is that what you think?"

"Sometimes."

"That's nonsense. Sometimes you could be a little—how shall I put it—more carefree, a little less strict, especially with yourself." He watched her cross her arms in front of her chest. It was a gesture he was familiar with from her childhood; it had been her way of wordlessly fending off a threat. But now he read weariness in it, and that touched him more than her words.

"Why don't you drop everything and come to Berlin with me? You haven't been there in ages."

She laughed, but it was not the kind of laughter he had wished for. "I can't get away, not today. Carl is coming back from his trip tomorrow night. He told me you'd meet in Berlin."

"Yes. He'll get there around noon. We plan to spend the afternoon and come back by the late train." He was jeopardizing his visit to the track, but he went on regardless. "It's only a day, but all the same. One day, Camilla. Do it for me."

"Sunday is Max's birthday. On Monday the children leave for the shore. Lenka's birthday is coming up, too. And this afternoon . . . I can't. When it comes right down to it, everything depends on me."

He noticed that she moved away from him a little, as if eager to escape from his orbit. "Come along, do. And when Carl calls you tonight, don't tell him about it, just be there. We could even leave tonight—we can be in Berlin in a couple of hours. We'll take rooms at the Bristol, we'll have a wonderful supper. Maybe there's something at the theater you'd like to see. And tomorrow morning you'll sleep as late as you like, you'll have breakfast in bed. Then we'll meet Carl's train—"

"Dinner is served." Frau Ewers was standing in the doorway. "You're here, Herr Hofmann? If I'd only known! As it is, we're only having what the boys asked for their first vacation day—"

"It's all right, Frau Ewers. We're coming. Call the children." Camilla rose. Fritz Hofmann picked up his hat and cane. "Are you staying to eat with us?" she asked.

He knew that the subject of Berlin was closed as far as she was concerned. He followed her into the house. The boys came clattering down the stairs and calmed down under their mother's gaze. They went into the dining room, stood behind their chairs, and waited. A large tureen was already set on the table.

"What have you decided?" Camilla asked her father. "Shall I ask them to set a place for you?"

Fritz Hofmann went to the table, holding his hat and cane in one hand, and lifted the lid of the tureen. A sweetish odor spread, and he stepped away. "Actually, I'm not hungry. The heat, you know. And I haven't much time."

"What are we having? Blueberry soup, by any chance?"

Father and daughter looked at each other, and in sudden harmony both laughed—a loud, liberating laughter that even summoned up Frau Ewers.

"Go ahead, go," Camilla whispered to her father. "And think of me while you're having your gorgeous pickled pig's knuckle. Next time—next time, I promise, I'll come to Berlin with you."

4

It was one of the last major races before the end of the season, and a much larger attendance had been predicted at the Berlin track. Whether the unusual heat had driven many Berliners from the city as soon as their vacation began, or whether the renewed rise of the Reichsbank interest rate was to blame—the two explanations were hotly debated among the spectators.

Fritz Hofmann had never really been able to warm up to this particular race course. His heart belonged to the old track. In his opinion the new one was too sober, completely lacking in style. His verdict on the track regulars was similar; standards weren't what they used to be. Only a few were dressed as befitted the occasion. The traditional gray overcoat with velvet lapels was in the minority, and a Malmaison carnation in the buttonhole, such as he was wearing, had become a rarity. The picture was dominated by a new fashion in men's sporting wear, which struck Hofmann with horror: coarse tweeds, trousers and jackets that were not properly fitted, soft collars, brightly colored pullovers, colorful scarves—and dusters!

Unfortunately Carl Senger was no exception to the rule, and Hofmann could only be grateful that at least his son-in-law had left his duster in the car. If the epidemic were to spread, soon you wouldn't be able to tell the chauffeur from the master. Hofmann was able to forgive the camera and all its attachments slung around Senger's neck because his son-in-law made zealous use of it to capture the important event in pictures.

The twelve horses entered for the principal race were already in the paddock. Compared to Troy, the others seemed slight, edgy; even Fanal, a mare considered the favorite, did not seem to Hofmann to have a chance against his sorrel. Quittel was already in the saddle, dour as ever, in bright green silks with white stars. Leo, who was leading Troy by the reins, honored the day by wearing a black tie with his long coat. Troy had drawn the starting number 11—a bad position, but to compensate, the weather was on his side. There had been thunderstorms and showers in the early morning hours, and though the skies were clear now, the track was still sticky.

Hofmann approached his son-in-law. "Well, what do you say? Is he a glorious animal?"

He was hoping for enthusiastic agreement, but Carl Senger, preoccupied with his camera, grunted drily. "He must have Mecklenburg blood."

Hofmann decided to be satisfied. It was miracle enough that he had been able to persuade Senger to come to the track with him. Besides, his son-in-law had taken it only too calmly when he was informed at the last minute that one of the horses in the race belonged to Hofmann. Senger had asked no questions nor mentioned the money it must cost to keep a horse. Basically this attitude was not surprising; it was characteristic of their relationship. For all their fundamental differences, the two men had developed a genuine friendship in the course of the years.

From the beginning Fritz Hofmann had joined his son-in-law, especially on occasional trips, which served as a welcome distraction. They also proved that year by year the business improved. At first, he remembered, they had gone to Berlin only for the day, in order to save the cost of overnight accommodations. Then they no longer traveled in third-class train compartments but changed over to second, at the same time extending their stay slightly. They had started out in the boarding houses and small hotels near the train station, in such places as the Baltic and the Montevideo. But gradually they had moved farther into town, eventually all the way to the Bristol, on the fashionable street Unter den Linden. There was no doubt that Fritz Hofmann had been the moving force in these forays; if it had been up to Senger, they would still be staying at the Baltic. With missionary

179

zeal Hofmann had tried to impress on the younger man the advantages of good hotels, good restaurants, good tailors. He had succeeded on the hotels by bringing up questions of image and tax advantages. But Senger could not be converted in the matter of a tailor. He continued to buy his suits off the rack. There was another limit to Hofmann's success; all his attempts to get Senger to the more fashionable cafés, theaters, cabarets, or even a gambling club fell on deaf ears. Carl Senger's days and nights in Berlin remained laced with appointments; every hour was reserved for discussions with salesmen, dealings with export and import firms, meetings with bankers. The same fanaticism Hofmann brought to entertainment Senger applied to business. Finally the two men had agreed to abandon any attempts at mutual conversion—which is not to say that Fritz Hofmann did not have an occasional relapse. The fact that his son-in-law had come with him to the races today was such an unexpected victory that Hofmann felt encouraged to go a step further.

"Look at the horse carefully," he said. "You'll have to admit he's in splendid form. I hope you'll put a hundred on him."

"I'll keep my fingers crossed for you."

Hofmann gave his son-in-law a sidelong glance. "Cross your fingers! You're throwing away good money. Come along."

He left the paddock in the direction of the tote board. It had not changed much in the last half hour. Fanal continued to be the favorite, while Troy's odds had increased; the horse was a hopeless outsider.

"A hundred marks on Troy," Hofmann repeated, this time in an imploring tone. "I think you should risk it. The victory would bring you nineteen hundred. Isn't that a good deal?"

"You know I never bet. I've never gambled in my life, and I'm not about to start."

"You've never made money so fast and so easily."

Senger examined the board. "What you're trying to say is that I've never thrown away a hundred marks so fast and so easily."

"But Carl, you can't go by that. It's precisely a novice such as yourself who can win. If you don't trust Troy—put your money on a different horse. Go by your feelings."

"That's what I'm doing. My feelings tell me to leave it be. I can't win anyway."

"Win! Winning isn't all there is to betting."

"I thought it was the whole idea."

"Winning is just one aspect. To place a bet—that means tempting fate. And the slighter your chances, the greater the thrill."

"Fine, I'll place ten marks on Troy. Just for you. And I'll contribute a hundred marks to your pot."

Hofmann shook his head. "Hopeless." He handed Senger his ticket. "Center stand, gate A. I'll be there soon." It was important to him to be alone when he counted his money and especially to be undisturbed when he placed his bets. He had paid Quittel beforehand, and after deducting the cost of sending the horse back home, he had a little more than five hundred marks. It was his entire cash estate; he had cleaned out all his accounts the day before. But he was not worried; even sudden fits of caution, such as he had once experienced in the presence of his son-in-law, were now gone with the wind. He decided to wager the whole five hundred—not on Troy of course. He had only wanted to talk Senger into that. If Troy won, he wouldn't miss a paltry five hundred; if not, he had a second iron in the fire.

In his thoughts he had already eliminated Fanal—he could not get excited over favorites—and he made his choice quite spontaneously, his mind half on the horses, half listening to the hullabaloo around him, the names that were whispered from mouth to mouth. This was the big moment, better and more exciting than anything to come, and he stretched it out until the man behind the wicket became impatient. Then, almost in a trance, he decided on a triple play: 2-8-4— Abbess, Russian Blood, Imperial Crown. With the demeanor of a man for whom such a sum is a trifle he dealt out the bills—brand new ones, such as they always had ready for him at the bank—and made his way to the grandstand. Fanal, of all horses, had balked at the start; now the jockeys were leading their horses to the starting line a second time. The stands were silent, the parasols came to rest, and when the starter's bell rang out, a sound like a long, deep sigh went up from the rows of spectators.

The field was away, and the bright-green spot poised over a brown moving object—Hofmann could make out no more than that—was far to the rear. The situation did not change during the first lap, after the first gate; if anything, the distance between bright green and the other colors increased. Not until the horses passed the spectator stands for the third time did green appear in the center field.

Senger, suddenly seized by a sort of chauvinism, kept his father-in-law informed at the top of his lungs about Troy's position, about falls, about Fanal who was now riderless, galloping ahead of the field. Hofmann listened with composure and even refused the binoculars. He sat very still, eyes half closed, as if the race were being run around him, as if he gathered the news out of the air, from the murmurs, the rising and falling voices and isolated shouts.

"He's ahead!" Senger was shouting. "In the lead . . . would you believe it? He'll make it if he can hold out . . . what's happening? Look!"

But Hofmann did not respond. His face a blank, he listened to everything around him. First the word had sounded once—quietly, timidly, unbelievingly. Abbess? Then he heard it more frequently, it ran on like an echo. Abbess. Abbess. Two other names also began to circulate—Russian Blood, Imperial Crown—but the other one remained more important, and as it was shouted throughout the grandstand, angrily by one faction, with surprise by the other, he closed his eyes in bliss, to enjoy it one more time: Abbess, Abbess, Abbess! He remained seated while around him some spectators were arguing heatedly while others left the stands. Senger was one of those who seemed to feel that he had been cheated. "I still don't understand it—he was in the lead, four hundred meters to the finish line, and then he fell back after all."

"To what position?"

"Fourth! What's the matter with you? You don't seem in the least disappointed."

"Fourth place, in a field like this one! All the horse needs is more experience. Next autumn he'll cut quite another figure. . . ."

"I don't understand. How can you be so calm? You must have lost your money, too."

"Let's have a look." Together they walked back to the betting window. The crowd was considerably thinner than it had been before the race, and the ground in front of the wicket was thick with discarded betting slips.

"How much did you lose?"

Hofmann laid a finger across his lips. "Don't knock it. Wait until the odds are put up." He did not take his eyes off the board while the man chalked in the order of the horses and then began again with the odds.

Senger watched his father-in-law as he compared the ticket he held in his hand with the board, but even when Hofmann went to the wicket, Senger doubted that he could really have won. Only when he became aware of the excitement Hofmann caused by handing over his ticket did he became nonplussed. Hofmann was abruptly surrounded by other spectators, strangers who, like Senger, watched in amazement as Hofmann was paid off. The clerk handed over bill after bill, and Hofmann counted them with loving fussiness, then put away his pocketbook, slowly pulled on his gloves, and took up the cane he had hung from the counter. He seemed impressed neither by the attention he had caused nor by the winnings he had made, though they seemed to be considerable; Senger had lost count somewhere around three thousand marks.

"How much did you win?"

"Abbess, Russian Blood, Imperial Crown. That's a surprising order. They paid nineteen to one."

"And how much did you put down?"

"Five hundred."

"So it comes to—"

"Nine thousand five hundred."

Once again Senger could see the bills, the nonchalance with which Hofmann had pocketed them. Camilla's treatment of her father in money matters had always rubbed him the wrong way, but all at once he understood her. "Nine thousand five hundred, you said?"

Hofmann patted his chest on the left side, where his jacket bulged slightly. "Precisely."

"But you were convinced Troy would win the race. So how could you—"

"I could try to explain, Carl, but I'm afraid we'd both be wasting our time. We'd better go and cheer up Quittel."

The jockey was in grievous need of a kind word. He did not blame the horse for one moment but accused only himself. "I should have let him have the outside track, the way he wanted, instead of trying to force him to the inside."

When they left, the jockey was still wrapped in gloom. Hofmann was occupied with more pleasurable thoughts. It was enjoyable to win money, but that was nothing compared to the heightened vitality he experienced when he spent it grandly—and as he walked with Senger to where they had parked the rented car, an idea was already forming in his mind.

Carl Senger was a passionate motorist. In Neustrelitz he had long been content with an old Opel—that was his nature—but when he was in Berlin, he rented the latest models by the day. Cars meant nothing to Hofmann, but as he watched his son-in-law disguising himself in a duster, bright-yellow woolen scarf, and shapeless dust goggles, he said, "A rig like this is a grand vehicle indeed. I hope you won't speed so much. Remember your last ticket. I'm told the traps around Berlin have been reinforced. And after events such as these they're particularly on the lookout."

"I'll be careful. I must say, this Bugatti is a big disappointment. The Benz we drove last time—that's the one I'd pick. Just as fast, much more comfortable, and not so complicated to repair. I liked the Benz, and the new model is said to be even better. And it looked fine, didn't you think? By the way, do you mind if we make a little detour?"

"Drive any way you want, just as long as you don't speed. The Benz, is it?" Just before leaving for the track they had looked at the latest model in the manufacturer's showroom, near the hotel. Hofmann remembered the price, and his idea began to solidify. While it would not leave any winnings for Dr. Minding's observatory, that problem was secondary; he was quite confident that it could be solved eventually. Occupied with his thoughts, he did not pay any attention to the route they were taking. The surroundings seemed to him ever more familiar; finally, when he saw the spire of the Church of Saint Anne in Strelitz, no doubt remained. He maintained his silence. He had never come back, not for thirteen years, not with Camilla and not with Senger. He was not drawn to the place; on the contrary, he avoided the past and all memories of it. On the rare occasions when he thought about the house, he imagined it in a delapidated state, run down by the new owners, perhaps even standing empty, in any case with blank windows, crumbling plaster, leaky roof, and an overgrown garden—as if such a vision could best assuage his guilty conscience. But except for a coat of paint—an odd, dull red instead of the pale gray of the stucco—nothing had changed.

Senger had stopped the car. He seemed too embarrassed to explain, but since Hofmann did not speak either, he said, "That is the one, isn't it? Forgive me if I seem to be taking you by surprise. I . . . I always wanted to see. . . . Shall I drive on?"

Without comment Hofmann opened the car door and got out; Senger followed hesitantly. Hofmann went up to the closed cast-iron gate. There was a small side door, and Hofmann looked for the mechanism he had had installed so that he would not have to ring for someone when he came home late at night, but he could not locate it.

"Don't bother," Senger said. "It was just an idea. We'd better leave, who knows who lives here now."

The sound of barking dogs came from the grounds. The figure of a man appeared in the distance and came closer, white-haired, a large apron tied around his middle. He came to a stop a few yards from the gate.

"Willeke," Hofmann called. "You're still here! Could we take a quick look inside or is it impossible?"

"Herr Hofmann!" The gardener wiped his hands on his apron. "Wait, I'll let you in. They're away, on vacation. Is it possible? Herr Hofmann himself, after all these years! Come ahead, the beasts are in the kennels."

They faced each other, Hofmann in his gray frock coat and a Malmaison carnation in his buttonhole, and the gardener, Willeke, whose hair had turned white. The workman quickly hid his gouty hands behind his back after they had shaken hands, as if he were ashamed to let Hofmann see how much he had aged.

The barking of the dogs grew louder, and now they could see the kennels, the dogs jumping up against the fence. "Hounds!" Willeke shook his head. "Can you imagine the damage in the gardens when they run free? Hounds, such idiocy—but as long as I'm alone here, they're not going to get out, the beasts."

"There don't seem to be many changes otherwise."

"Well, the paint! That awful red, but that's how Italians are. And the espaliered fruit! They want espaliered fruit all over the place, just look, the whole beautiful side of the house covered with espaliers; it looked better before."

"It belongs to Italians?"

"Not belongs, no. It still belongs to the bank, I guess. They rented it to the Italian ambassador. He's the second tenant, he's been living here for seven years, though. I always thought, I wonder when he'll come by, Herr Hofmann. And Fräulein Camilla? To think she never came! I sure counted on her! We really waited, the wife and me. We always thought, one of these days she's just going to be standing there, just like you today." Willeke's eyes alternated inquiringly between Hofmann and Senger. "Is that him? Is that Camilla's husband? He wants to have a look at the house? I can tell you, she was very happy here, she sure was, our young lady. . . . My God, listen to me rattle on. It's the surprise, that's what it is, it's all so unexpected. Suddenly he's standing there, Herr Hofmann. So that's Fräulein Camilla's husband."

Hofmann introduced his son-in-law, and Willeke asked if they would like to look over the grounds while he prepared a little refreshment, something very light, homemade, just right for such a day. They wandered through the grounds, which were unchanged, with the impeccably edged paths and the manicured lawns where not so much as a broken branch littered the smoothly cut expanse of green. Senger asked a few very brief questions, each time breaking a long silence. His questions did not require answers. "Those must be the windows of her room?" "Is that the linden tree?" "And you could really ice skate over there?" His words showed how much he must have brooded about all of this, although that was precisely the impression he wished to avoid. Only once did he give himself away: "I was never really sure if it existed, this house."

"Even I was no longer quite certain." It was the first time Hofmann had spoken.

Slowly they retraced their steps. Most of the windows were shuttered. The sinking sun was at their back, and the facade glowed a fiery red. Willeke had spread a checkered cloth over the table outside the gardener's cottage and set out small glasses. He held the bulging bottle with both hands as he poured.

"I don't know if it's as good as it used to be," he said. "Sometimes I think the wife was the only one who could start the berries properly."

"Frau Willeke isn't here?"

"She passed away."

The silence spread; birds twittered in the grounds as twilight approached. Now and again a bark came from the kennels. The men emptied their glasses, and Hofmann spoke. "The house hasn't changed, but we've grown older."

"Would you like to see the inside?"

"No, better not," Hofmann replied quickly. "We hadn't intended to stay this long."

Willeke nodded. "You wouldn't like what you'd see. Out here I can look after things a little, but inside—Italians have funny tastes. And Fräulein Camilla, she's well? The wife always said, whoever gets her gets the prize. Is she ever going to come here? You should bring her one day, do. I've got something here, you ought to take it to her, I always kept it because I thought, one of these days she'll turn up for sure." He went into the cottage and returned with a broad-brimmed straw hat, yellow with a faded blue silk ribbon.

"It was hers?" Senger held the hat as if it might break.

"Belonged to her, always wore it, even in the rain. Maybe when she sees it, she'll get a yen to look in. Gone all summer, those Italians, left only their dogs behind. You can't imagine what they eat and how many things they break."

He walked them to the gate, still muttering about the Italians. Making Hofmann and Senger promise to return soon with Camilla, he took his leave and walked back slowly, a forlorn figure in a green landscape. The two visitors returned to their car. Senger placed the girlish hat on the back seat; he handled it carefully, almost delicately, with none of his usual brusqueness.

They sat in the car, and Senger made no move to start. The dogs had stopped barking. With no preliminaries Senger said, "What was she like then, as a young girl?"

"Camilla? You don't know? She was a young girl when you married her."

Senger nodded. "I know. But she once said, at the very beginning, that she felt ancient." He sensed that the man sitting next to him was shrinking back from this conversation. Until now they had never touched on these matters, and it was not Senger's way, but now he felt compelled to go on. "Sometimes she really can be very old. Sober good sense is an important part of her nature, and that was what I always wanted, a wife with common sense, one who doesn't hanker after impossible dreams. Without her I never would have made it this far. But sometimes I think the price she's paid is too high. I shouldn't have let myself be deluded."

"You think too much."

"Too little. Is she really happy the way she lives now? I don't know how long it's been since I asked myself that question."

"Didn't you hear what Willeke said? She was a girl who ran around in the garden even in the rain."

"I knew that girl existed. . . ." The men's thoughts seemed to be heading in different directions. "That's why I wanted to come here. I wanted to see the gardens and the house."

"And now that you've seen them?"

"She never once said she wanted to come here with me. And when I suggested it, something always came up. Now I think I understand her. I always wondered why she insisted we stay in the house by the barrel factory, why she rejected every house in Neustrelitz I proposed."

"Yes, why does she?"

"The house near the factory, that was always temporary, something you can leave anytime. We might have gotten attached to another house and that would make it hard to move on. I didn't understand it for a long time, only now that I've seen this house—she wants to come back. That's always been her goal, she never lost sight of it, and she simply wasn't interested in another way station."

"Did she tell you that?"

"No, no, that's not her way."

"She never talked about it?"

"That's just it, and I should have understood much sooner."

"Did you know that it's really hers?" Hofmann asked. "I mean, it was supposed to be hers. She came here with me before the house was ever built, and without her it might never have been built, who knows." He looked at the house. "Perhaps it's the only meaningful thing I've done in my whole life, but I couldn't hold on to it." He pulled out his watch, determined to put an end to such confessions of guilt and gloom. "Let's go. And don't mind me; if you want to drive fast, do. A little wind isn't going to hurt me. I have only one request. Just another little detour. But drive to the hotel first, I'll show you the way from there."

Senger threw a glance at the hat in the back seat. All at once it did not seem safe enough there. He took up a lap robe and wrapped the hat in it. Only then did he begin to start the car.

5

The attic was a part of the house that she usually avoided; perhaps the idea of all the things that had accumulated over the years had something to do with her reluctance. And in fact, when she made an exception now and went up with Frau Ewers, she found the rooms so crammed, in part with objects she had believed long since discarded, that the first thing she said was, "As soon as the boys have left, you'll clean out this place. Take two workmen." As she bumped into a box, colored glass balls fell out and rolled across the floor. "And don't start sorting out. The children have too many toys as it is. Give the things away, do with them what you want, just so you make room here."

"And the children's cribs?"

"The cribs especially."

In spite of the evening hour it was hot under the eaves—a dry heat, as if they were standing in a flameless fire. Frau Ewers busied herself with pulling the boys' luggage out of the pyramid of bags and cases, in preparation for their trip to Warnemünde. Camilla discovered the heavy steamer trunk that had belonged to Senger's father, and then her eyes fell on the bag of woven straw with the scuffed leather corners and the leather strap around the middle; as a young girl she had always traveled with that bag—to the seashore, with her father to Paris. A few stickers from places and hotels still clung to it, even the round, light-blue emblem of Geneva. That, too, was a place she had visited with her father; he had shown her the German church of Clarens on Lake Geneva, where he and her mother had been married. How long ago that was, and how unreal it seemed now; in the church, before the altar, she had made a vow to be married in the same place one day. . . .

"It's too hot for me here," she said. "I'm going back downstairs." She threw a glance at the pieces of luggage Frau Ewers had put aside. "That's enough."

"Only three cases for all the boys?"

"Max is staying here."

"But why? Surely not just because of a couple of bad marks?"

"He's staying here. If he settles down and studies, he can come later."

"He'll study better if he's spent some time at the beach first."

"Let's stop this discussion. You'll pack for the two boys. Enough so they'll have plenty of clothes, but not as much as last year. Listen, was that the car?" All this time she had kept her ears open so as not to miss its arrival.

"You still have plenty of time."

Time—that was exactly what she felt she did not have. She hurried down from the attic to change her clothes and do her hair and face. She had hardly finished when she really did hear the car, and she ran downstairs to meet it.

The chauffeur stood in the hall alone, in the bluish-gray cloth uniform with the leather puttees. He was turning his cap between his hands, seemingly embarrassed. "Nobody came on the train. I was on time, but nobody was there, neither Herr Senger nor Herr Hofmann. Do you want me to stay on call?"

"But surely that was the last train? Or have they put on a later one?"

"No, it's the last one from Berlin. Nothing's changed there. So, if you need me again—"

"No, Franz, thanks."

"I don't see how I could have missed them."

"It's all right. Good night." She remained in the doorway for a moment. The car started, and in a few minutes she heard the chauffeur closing the metal garage doors. She saw his tall figure cross the yard, which was illuminated by a number of lanterns. The door to

190

one of the on-site houses opened; light fanned out, and a woman stood in the doorway, embraced him, and pulled him inside.

Camilla closed the door behind her, went to the telephone, and asked to be connected with the hotel in Berlin. She was told that her husband and her father had left the hotel an hour before. Not until then? Were they sure? Quite sure. And left no message? No message. An hour—in that case they could not have made the train. And she had hurried so. . . .

"What happened? He didn't come?" Frau Ewers was calling from the landing, but Camilla did not answer. She opened the door to the living room. Everything was in readiness for Max's birthday. The table had been laid festively, and the wrapped presents were piled in their usual place on the sideboard—far too many as usual, and there would be more with those that Senger was bringing home. There was nothing here for her to do. As she left the room, she was momentarily tempted to lie down, to rest, but she went to her office instead. She pulled the telephone toward her, convinced that a call would come soon, and waited. At first she still listened for outside noises, then she turned off all the lights except for a lamp on the desk and, picking up the latest contracts, she began to look them over and make some notes.

Could that be a car? She went on working. Her world at this moment was no larger than the circle of light cast by the lamp; white paper, letters, numbers. Everything else was an intrusion— noises, steps, voices calling her name, an opening door.

The ceiling light flashed on, so that she was compelled to close her eyes. Then she looked up: the long, pale duster with the tightly knotted belt, the hair pressed tight into the scalp by the driving cap, and in the dusty face the light circles around the eyes made by the driving goggles.

He stood there, laughing. "Well, here I am. A little late. I'll just take off my coat and wash up. I'll be right back. Everything's all right, I hope." Then he was gone; the house became noisy, the children stirred.

She was still sitting at her desk when he returned. He was carrying something loosely wrapped in paper. He put the parcel aside to embrace her, and when he noticed how stiff she remained, he loosened his hold on her to give her time.

"It's nice of you to wait up for me, but did you have to work?"

"Would you like something to eat?"

It was typical of her that this was her first concern; not why he was so late or how he could have gotten here at all at this hour. He laughed. "No, please, nothing to eat. All I want is to spend an hour with you. I've got so much to tell you. And tomorrow, for Max's birthday, I thought we'd go on an outing. Remind me, I've got some more presents for him; this—this is for you. . . ." He was about to remove the wrapping paper, but the expression on her face deterred him. "Everything is all right? Something bothering you?"

"Look at Max's report card."

He knew there was no point in postponing the matter or trying to defuse it with a joke. He had passed a happy day, and in her life not everything seemed to have been joyful. "Very bad?"

"Look at it. He barely managed to get promoted."

"What do you want me to say? I wasn't exactly a scholar either. Anything else?"

"Another accident. We had to call Dr. Oesterreicher. But most of all—I had them give me Glasbrenner's sales figures. If you'll look at them—"

"But Camilla! Not now. . . . All right, I'll look them over."

He sat down on the edge of the desk, studied the accounting, picked up the second sheet she handed him, and said, "I know the figures."

"You know them?"

"I know the problem, and I have a rough idea of the figures. Though I included Gotha and Erfurt with the rest. Glasbrenner presents a problem, I know that. I had a talk with him on this trip. He has personal reasons—a divorce after thirty years of marriage. It shook him up. But he'll pull himself together, I'm certain of it. At least he deserves a chance. Remember, he used to be our best man. You see, I had the same idea as you. I just wasn't sure if I'd have enough time, otherwise I'd have told you. Satisfied?"

She need only say yes. She need only look at him to recognize him again as the person he really was. She almost hated herself because she could not do it but continued to stare at the desk, paralyzed by weariness and a strange kind of sorrow. Her head was brimming with a million questions, and she asked the first one. "Is there any truth to the rumors from Berlin that they've secretly been print-

192

ing soap coupons in the government printing office, because of the political situation?"

"I've heard those stories. There's a lot of talk. I don't believe there's any foundation for it. All the same, it would be a good idea to increase our store of raw materials. I know it means a capital investment, but . . . now I'm right in it too. You've managed it. But that's enough now, all right?"

She felt a loosening of the hard armor encasing her. She looked up. "All right. Just one more thing. The advertising presentation for the coupon campaign that you were going to bring back from Berlin —did they have any useful ideas?"

"Splendid ones. They're a smart lot; they've already finished mats and a distribution schedule for the ads. I'll have to pay you a bonus for the idea."

"Pay me in time," she said.

He gave her a stricken look and remained silent until he finally said, "Yes, that's our problem, isn't it? But I think I made a start today. I went to see the house in Steglitz." He tried to unwrap the object he had brought, and finally he tore the paper off impatiently. He held out the straw hat; in the artificial light the blue ribbon was almost white. "Go ahead, put it on. Don't you recognize it?"

He had expected a spontaneous response, a joyful sparkle in her eyes, but she stood still, her face expressionless. It had always been that way: the house was a part of her past, and she granted admittance to no one. "The old gardener is still there, what's his name? Anyway, he's been keeping the hat, all these years, for you. I thought I'd be making you happy."

He placed the straw hat on the desk. Her silence made him unsure of himself. Afraid of using the wrong words, he stuck to facts. "Your mother sold the house to a bank. Though they've rented it out on a long-term lease, they're perfectly willing to discuss a sale. I know I'm not familiar with the house as it used to be, but it seems to be in good condition."

"You were . . . you were there?"

"It's a plan I've had for a long time."

"You went there without me?"

"Camilla. Every time you came to Berlin, I suggested we drive out there."

"What good would it have done? Do you think the years here would have been easier if I'd kept thinking about the house?" Her hands reached for the hat and then fell to her sides. "Why didn't you leave it where it was." She turned away, perhaps to hide tears. "That silly old hat. What do I want with it? Shall I put it on and look at myself in the mirror and realize that I've grown too old for it?"

"Too old! When will you learn how young you are? You'll wear it tomorrow, on our outing. The way things look now, it's going to be a beautiful day; we'll all drive out to the country, look for a spot on the lake. We'll take dinner and spend the day. And then, after the children have gone to Warnemünde, we'll take a vacation, a proper long vacation, a trip to Italy or Greece—I've had them plan out some routes. All right, and now we'll lock up the office, and I won't give you back the key before Monday. Come. I have to show you something else anyway. You never asked how I got here."

He really did lock the door and pocket the key. Camilla grabbed a shawl from the cloakroom before following him outdoors. But it had not grown appreciably cooler. Holding the shawl, she walked beside him along the path that led from the house to the works. The large yard lay deserted, and at the center of the broad paved surface, in the light of the lanterns, stood the car with its hood thrown back and its sharply protruding steering wheel.

She stopped, nonplussed, reluctant to go on. He pulled her along toward the svelte machine with its large, circular floodlights at the front of the hood and a second pair at the side, its bristling sheaf of gears, the large black bulb that served as a horn, the fenders that spread like wings over the white pneumatic tires, and the ivory-colored body.

"Are you insane?"

"A Benz. The latest model. It took us less than three hours to get here from Berlin." He tried to persuade her to get in. "Shall we take it for a spin?"

"Did you rent it?"

"No. It's ours."

"And how much did you have to pay for something like this?"

"That's the wrong question. Instead you should say, Isn't it a beauty? Look at it standing there. Shouldn't we try it out?"

She saw his pleasure, his enthusiasm, and yet she said, "Was it your idea? Or is Papa behind it? Of course it was Papa, he talked you into it; you always fall for his wild ideas."

"The car is a present from him."

"It is, is it. And how did he pay for this present? He has no such amounts in his account. It's a miracle that he's not in debt."

"He won at the races."

"Thats what he always says."

"But I saw it for myself."

"You went to the races with him? And placed a bet or two yourself? What did the car cost?"

"A little over nine thousand."

The sum reduced her to silence. After a pause she protested, "Won't he ever stop involving others! And I always thought you were immune to his persuasiveness." She laid the shawl across her shoulders and crossed her arms across her chest. "Sometimes I hate him. Everything started with him. . . ."

"The good things too, didn't they? The thing is to live so that you're happy. That's what your father does, and he'd like to see others happy too. I don't know what there is to hate about that."

He got into the car and gathered up the packages scattered over the back seat. Even before he had piled them all up in his arms, he heard her walking away, back to the house.

6

"You have a bite! You have a bite! Haul it in!"

The shouts came from somewhere along the banks, from a distance. Camilla lay in the stern of the rowboat, her face half hidden by the straw hat, and as she dozed, it was as if she were floating, now in the undulating water, now high in the sky. She opened her eyes slightly. Through the delicate weave of the hat the sun appeared very yellow. She was sleepy from the heat, sated by the fresh air near the water—and happy.

Slowly she sat up and slipped her hat to the back of her head. They were far out on the lake. Her husband had taken up the oars and was steering the heavy boat, almost a fisherman's barge, back to the shore. He had his back to her, and she did not speak at once. His blue-striped white shirt was sticking to his back. At each pull on the oars his shoulder blades and rippling muscles were clearly demarcated. It was a broad, muscular back, and the suntanned neck also testified to his strength. He was forty-two years old now, but she thought he looked much younger. "Take your time."

He stopped the oars and turned around to face her. "Back with us?"

"Was I really asleep?"

"For over an hour."

She looked at the sky; although the sun had long since passed the zenith, it was still a flaming yellow mass. "Then it must be nearly five."

"According to my stomach it has to be. I hope they leave us some of the fish." He reached for the oars again.

At the shore, where the boys were, smoke was rising in clouds, wholly transparent in the bright sunlight. They had bought the plot at the western shore of the lake years ago, but they had left everything as it was, with the sparse cover of pines and firs and the reed-lined banks; they had not even fenced it in. All they had done was make a path to the water and acquire a boat because sometimes Senger came out here at dawn, before work, to fish.

He helped her out of the boat after tying it up at the dock. They heard the boys' voices, no longer quite so jubilant after a long day in the sun. The boys were at the fireplace Leo had built; some fish were hung to broil over the grate. The Benz was standing somewhat to one side—the tires covered against the sun—as was the goat cart his grandfather had given Max for his birthday. As Camilla caught sight of it, she was reminded again how her father had appeared with it. They had still been at breakfast when they suddenly heard the crack of a whip and the clanging of the little bells on the bridle outside the windows. She had not believed her eyes. Hofmann himself had taken over the driving, and he was smartly handling the two snow-white billy goats, with their horns and pointed beards, trotting in the red harness. The rig expressed all her father's foolishness, his thoughtless way of indulging every whim, and for a moment she feared the whole day was spoiled. Now she no longer understood her earlier feeling. Her behavior of the previous evening, when Senger had returned, seemed to her equally incomprehensible.

Hofmann had made himself comfortable at the picnic site. Sitting on a blanket under a large umbrella of sand-colored canvas, he fanned himself with his Panama hat. The ground around him was cluttered with blankets, butterfly nets, and the special boxes used to collect plant specimens. Camilla sat down beside him while Senger went back to the water to fetch the bottles he had put there to cool. Camilla took glasses, plates, napkins, and silver from the picnic basket, but her father said, "I'll just have a drink with you, then I'll start back with the children. Our rig isn't as fast as yours."

"Wouldn't you rather drive with us? There's lots of room in the car."

"I promised the boys a ride on the carousel. They say there's a fair in Jechow. Perhaps we'll catch up with each other there." His eyes twinkled in the sun. "You don't have to hurry, though."

She laughed. "I'm listening," she replied. "From now on I'm going to listen to you a lot more."

"Would you like to tell me what you're laughing about?" Senger had returned. He had rolled up his shirt sleeves; his arms were paler than his tanned hands, and the fine blond hairs were shining wet. Camilla watched him as he uncorked the bottles, and once again she was overcome by a feeling of safety, as she had been in the boat, watching him row.

"Well, what is there to laugh about?"

"I've made a discovery."

"A discovery?" He filled the glasses and passed them.

"Yes, and you're all going to be surprised. You always held Papa up as an example to me, and yet I may be much more like him than you suspect. You'll see, from now on. . . ." She leaned back against one of the pines. She sipped at her glass and laughed, a laugh that was duskier than her speaking voice.

The boys brought the broiled fish; the family sat together and ate and drank, and later everyone helped to pack up the used crockery. Leo harnessed the white goats, and Hofmann took the reins. With a crack of the whip and clanging bridle they drove off, disappearing in a cloud of dust.

Camilla spoke. "He really is to be envied, my father. Maybe he does the only right thing. He takes the nice things in life where he can find them. Most people walk past them blindly until it's too late. That's almost what happened to us, isn't it?"

"No," he said, "that wasn't what I was afraid of. But—"

"But what?"

"I don't think we need to talk about it."

"Maybe we do. What are my faults?"

"Perhaps you don't have enough of them. You demand a great deal of yourself, and that's hard on others at times."

"Hard on you too."

"No. I never wanted you any other way. I know what you're really like. I never forgot."

She put down her glass. She did not feel like drinking any more. This hour was one of those she wanted to experience very consciously.

She leaned against her husband, and he put his arm around her.

"Tell me where you want to go."

"There's one trip I'd be most fascinated by, to Egypt. To Venice by train, then an Adriatic cruiser to Cairo. There you rent a Nile boat; you sail to Luxor and Aswan and view the rock temples of Abu Simbel and Dendur."

"It sounds wonderful."

"But it's more a trip for the winter—I mean, when it's winter here. Do we want to wait so long?"

"Do you want to?"

"No. With a different tour, we can leave in two weeks, on August seventh. That one goes first to Venice, too. From Venice we take a boat to Greece, and from there a trip around the islands—Corfu, Aegina, Depidauros, Delos."

"Let's leave as soon as possible. Two weeks. I'll worry every day that something will happen to stop us at the last minute."

"Nothing will stop us."

"I'll have to buy new luggage. Do you realize that I own only one valise?"

"We'll order a dozen."

"And we'll be traveling on a real ship?"

"Yes. On this trip it will be the *Proserpina*. I've brought home all the forms."

"A real ocean liner? With a swimming pool, a dining salon, entertainment, a dance band?"

"I think two dance bands, even."

"You'll have to dance with me! Do you realize that we haven't danced together since our wedding? Not for thirteen years. And we've gone to Berlin to the theater only eight times."

"You kept count?"

"Oh yes, because each time it was really torture for you."

"You know, the theater—"

"As long as you dance with me, all is forgiven."

"Just so long as it isn't that new dance."

"You mean the tango?"

"Yes, I think that's what it's called. That would be a sight to see—me trying to tango."

"Come here, I'll show you. Come."

She held him and tried to show him the steps and movements.

The ground was uneven; he shook his head, laughed, then stumbled. He let himself fall, still laughing, and pulled her down to the ground with him.

"You did that on purpose, you did, you did. You'll never learn that way."

But he laughed and turned her around so that his face was over hers, and then he kissed her.

At first it seemed that he would go on laughing even as he kissed her, and she too felt laughter rising in her, pervading her whole body, a careless joy. . . .

They put the rugs and the two picnic baskets in the car; after a last look to check that they had not forgotten anything, she climbed in. The sun was still beating down, and she put on the straw hat. Sensing him watching her from the side, she said, "I don't know what was the matter with me last night, that I couldn't feel happy."

"All that matters is that I know."

"You know?"

"We are going to buy the house." And because she did not answer, he went on. "You never forgot it. It was always your destination, I've realized that."

"It was my dream, but I always told myself that the present is more important than a dream. Perhaps it was a mistake to remain so attached to it. It's only a house, nothing more. Did you mean it, that we should buy it?"

"Yes. I spoke with the bank. The price seems reasonable. We'll clinch the deal right after our vacation. Of course we wouldn't be able to move right away. The lease is for ten years. That will give us time to plan. A move to Berlin will bring some problems. The factory for one thing; it can be moved only in stages. First the executive offices, and only after that's running smoothly, the plant. That's how I see it. And then the children, changing schools, that ought to be arranged so it doesn't happen in the middle of the school year. We have to think about the details carefully, but we can talk about it later, at leisure."

She laid her hand on his arm. "You're doing it for me?"

"That wouldn't be a bad reason now, would it? But it's not the only one. After I saw the house—do you remember what I told you about my father? When I was in Steglitz, walking through the

200

grounds, I thought, so that's what my father dreamed about all his life. That's what he was thinking about when he was sleeping in hotel rooms. And suddenly I knew that I wanted the same thing. A home, a place you never want to leave. And then I understood, too, what it meant to you then, when you had to leave it." He busied himself with starting the car before she could reply.

The roads were sandy, and wherever they drove, they left behind a high flag of dust. Camilla had been here a few times with Senger, but today she lost all sense of direction, until the pines and firs grew sparser and she could see the first few farms and a church spire. Cornflowers and poppies grew at the side of the road. The wheat was very full for the time of year, the kernels already clearly visible in the spikes.

Suddenly an alien sound mingled with the noise of the motor— a bright, tinny barrel organ. At the edge of the village they saw the merry-go-round, the booths and stands of the fair, and over to one side the rig with the two white goats. The carousel was just beginning to turn again, and the barrel organ was blaring forth the triumphal march from *Aida*.

After they left the car, Camilla hooked her arm through her husband's. "Will you ride with me?"

"If they'll let us." The air smelled of Turkish honey and roasted almonds. Guns banged at the shooting gallery. From the "strong man" booth came the dull thud of hammer on anvil, and the hoarse voice of the shill rang out. Camilla's father was dickering with the balloon seller. When he joined them, he was holding a sheaf of brightly colored balloons.

"I'm glad you got here," he said. "I can't get the boys to leave the merry-go-round, and I'm beginning to run out of change." He broke a red balloon from the stick which held them together, and Camilla tied the cord around her wrist as she had done as a child, to keep it from slipping and floating away.

Senger had gone ahead to the carousel to look after the boys, and Hofmann immediately seized his opportunity. "Another thing I meant to tell you, about Max. Have you thought it over? Are you really going to keep him from going to Warnemünde with the others? Even if it's the right thing to do on principle, surely on a day like today—"

"I can't refuse you anything, you mean?"

"Something like that. And you really should think some more

201

about whether you can't scrape up a contribution for Dr. Minding, for his observatory."

"You're very tricky. You're counting on my being unable to say no to anything today. But first I want to ride the merry-go-round."

She hurried to catch up with Senger at the carousel with the pointed red-and-white roof. A stocky bald man in worn black dress trousers and a striped vest balanced among the glitteringly arrayed horses, pink pigs, and various vehicles, collecting the fares.

"What do you want to ride?" Camilla asked.

"The fire truck was always my favorite, but we can't both fit in."

She pressed her way through to a round bench that turned during the ride. "Aren't you coming?"

"He doesn't seem to want to let me." And it was true; the owner threw a worried glance at Senger and then said to Camilla, "That's just for children."

"Can't you see I'm a child?"

The owner collected the fares wearing a sullen expression, looked around, grabbed the clapper of his bell, and rang in the next turn. Then he disappeared behind the motor housing. The barrel organ began its tune, but the crowded carousel seemed to make little progress at first. From somewhere Camilla heard the voices of her sons, who had caught sight of her, and she saw her husband running alongside to keep up with her. Gradually the merry-go-round began to gather speed. She closed her eyes, and suddenly the ride seemed to fly at an incredible pace. The drone of the motor, the tune of the organ, car horns, bicycle bells, the clang of a fire truck—everything mingled, and when she opened her eyes, she saw that the carousel was really turning so quickly that Senger was having trouble keeping up. As always, it stopped too soon.

"Pay him for three rides," she called to Senger. "Without stops!"

The merry-go-round started up again, and once more she was wrapped in sounds. This time it seemed even louder and faster. Senger's face bobbed up only for a second at a time, sun-tanned, with laughing eyes. She called his name, and when he began again to run alongside, she shouted, "When did I last tell you I love you?"

"What did you say?" Constantly impeded by the spectators, he could no longer keep up with the merry-go-round.

"I love you!" But around her she saw only the faces of strangers, and she closed her eyes.

When the carousel finally came to a stop, she could not see him at once. When she stood on firm ground again, she looked around, searching, moving a few steps in one direction, still dizzy, the ground seeming to give beneath her feet. She waited a moment, hoping that he would appear, but the crowd around the carousel only grew more dense. She elbowed her way through. And then she saw him.

He was standing with Hofmann and a third man at the edge of the meadow where they had parked the Benz. The third man was wearing a gray-blue chauffeur's uniform and dark leather putties, but she did not at once recognize him as their own factory driver because his dark clothing seemed so strange among the bright summer clothes of the fairgoers.

The three men fell silent when Camilla joined them; they lowered their eyes, and no one spoke. She did not understand what had happened until she noticed the telegram in her husband's hands. "What's wrong?"

The men exchanged a look, and then the chauffeur spoke. "I'm very sorry, but I thought it important enough to come and find you. I was on my way to the lake when I accidentally saw the car here."

Camilla took the telegram from Senger's hand. She read the text, and at first the words seemed to lack all meaning. She heard the voices around her, laughter, barrel-organ music, the bangs from the shooting gallery. The boys came running, but Hofmann took them aside, spoke to them in a low voice, and led them away.

"When did it happen?" she asked.

"Probably early in the afternoon. The telegram was dispatched two hours ago. We'd better return at once."

She looked at the telegram, the strips pasted on the paper, looked for the dateline—14:30 hours, Warnemünde—and stared at the sender's name: Dr. Hermann Witte.

"But how can it be? I talked to her on the telephone only yesterday, and it would have been her birthday day after tomorrow."

Her husband took her arm, and they walked to the car. Only after they had both gotten in did she notice that she was still wearing the red balloon on her wrist. She loosened the knot and released the cord. The balloon floated upward, at first very straight, and then slowly climbed to the west.

7

The house was silent, and she wished that the children would come back from the beach and fill the rooms with their voices.

She sat at the desk in Aunt Lenka's bedroom. On the green felt surface lay the many keys, already arranged by rooms. The smallest group consisted of only two, for the drawers of the desk where Lenka had spent so many hours. A week ago Aunt Lenka had been buried in Berlin, and since then day after day Camilla had put off the necessary trip to Warnemünde—and with it the decision of what to do with the house and the sorting out of Lenka's personal effects.

She had arrived early in the morning, and she was already entertaining the idea of returning to Neustrelitz the same evening, just so as not to have to spend the night in her aunt's house. And yet everything was as it had been during Aunt Lenka's lifetime; one would have thought she had gone out for a walk and would be coming through the door at any moment.

In the hall stood the shoes Lenka usually changed into as she entered, in order not to track sand into the rooms. In the living room her crocheted stole hung over a chair, and even her tarot cards were spread out on a table near the window. The children had not shown the least uneasiness. They had not stepped more lightly or spoken more softly than usual. They had rushed upstairs to look for the toys they had left behind the previous year. Neither the news of Aunt

Lenka's death nor the burial had made a deep impression on the boys, and that was why Camilla had brought them with her to Warnemünde. In the first couple of hours their presence had helped her, but not now, as she sat alone at her aunt's desk.

The daily calendar—each day's detachable sheet printed with a Bible verse—stopped at the day of her aunt's death. Just to finally get things started, she tore off the leaves until she came to July 31. Or was it already August 1? In a week they would be starting on their trip to Greece. On the drive home from the fair she had thought that now the trip would certainly come to naught, but Senger had insisted on going ahead. She was only too happy to agree, and the day after the internment in Berlin they had gone together to buy luggage—a dozen cases, in fact, as he had promised.

Lenka's death—at heart she still did not grasp it properly, and oddly enough, it seemed even less real in this house. Her aunt had been sixty-four, but that did not seem so old, especially when you were thinking about a person who was the picture of perfect health.

Once, years ago, when Camilla's whole family had fallen ill during an influenza epidemic—even Frau Ewers and the hired nurses—Aunt Lenka had remained the only unafflicted person. She had run the household unaided, taken care of the patients cheerfully and indefatigably, on her feet from early morning to late at night. "Heart failure," the physician had entered on the death certificate, but he answered all other questions with raised hands and a shrug of the shoulders, until he finally admitted that he too thought it somewhat of a mystery. Lenka had always wanted to be buried at her husband's side; at the time of his death she had bought a double plot—for a period of ninety-nine years—and as they learned after her death, she had left precise instructions for her own burial and the wording of the tombstone. Camilla had only to take care of the necessary formalities, the conveyance of the body from Warnemünde to Berlin, the selection of a casket, the death announcements, and the arrangements for the funeral repast.

When she thought back on it, she felt that none of it had anything to do with Lenka. The day of the funeral had been hot, with a cloudless sky and a dry wind from the east. The family had to leave their cars some distance from the cemetery because repairs to the sewer system had riddled the whole width of the street with excavations. Along the cemetery wall the wind had been especially strong. She could still visualize her mother and sisters on the narrow walkway struggling with their hats and veils, which the wind threatened to tear from their heads; the men, who held down their top hats with the curved handles of their canes, their patent leather shoes gray with dust; and the children, bothered by neither heat nor wind, wholly absorbed in making up for the long time they had not seen each other by telling each other all their news.

This was the first time in years that the family had met all together. Everyone had arrived for the dinner in the Blue Salon of the Bristol Hotel—her mother and father, though seated far apart, her sisters with their husbands and children.

The conversation had dealt with inheritances and with the will, the contents of which had not yet been made known. They debated the value of the house in Warnemünde, gave their various opinions about the worth of their aunt's stock holdings, and were already busy dividing among themselves Aunt Lenka's jewelry, her china, her furs. Alice was determined to have the china service, and Maxi overcame her inhibitions enough to remind them all that Auntie had promised the sable set to her. Nevertheless, all of them were far more interested in Carl Senger, Camilla's husband, who until this day had been known to most family members only by name and by the rumors of his riches that circulated throughout the family. On this occasion he was more or less the guest of honor.

The drawn-out wail of a ship's siren howled across the water, reminding Camilla of where she was. She listened, hoping for the children and for Frau Kleinhans, whom she had sent on some errands. But the house remained silent. No matter how long she waited, Lenka would never again walk in the door, scraping her shoes to rid them of sand in the summer, of snow in the winter. Never again would she sit in the window laying out her cards or with an impatient gesture throw in a hand that did not come out.

Camilla ordered herself to get busy. She tossed the old calendar sheets into the wastebasket and unlocked the two desk drawers. The will had been read in Berlin, in the lawyer's office where it had been deposited. Mama and her sisters were outraged to learn that Camilla would inherit the house and Hofmann most of the stocks. Mementoes had been set aside for the other family members. A list three pages long had been compiled many years before, like the will itself.

Camilla pulled out the first drawer and found it filled with little

206

boxes. They lay next to and on top of each other, in different sizes, each tied with red grosgrain ribbon and labeled in red ink. The packets must have been here a long time, for the ink had faded.

Camilla picked up one of the boxes. "For Emmi," the inscription read, and there was a number in the upper right-hand corner. Camilla compared it with the list and found there the notation "Cameo ring for Emmi." When had Lenka made up the little packages? How many years ago? Camilla opened the other drawer and was greeted by the same sight: packages, red grosgrain ribbons, faded red ink. Who would behave like this? Someone who was always thinking about death?

She was confronted with a mystery. Her aunt had been very important in her life; she had been Camilla's great model. Hadn't she once said that she wanted to be like her aunt? She had not seen Aunt Lenka in death—she had refused the offer to have the coffin opened. She could read the passage of the years well enough in everyone she knew. Papa had aged in spite of everything; his movements were becoming more cautious, his eyesight was failing. Her sisters had changed, and Mama frightened her each time she saw her by her pink, breathless shapelessness. She herself had aged. The only one whom time seemed to pass by without leaving any scars had been Lenka. She had always remained the same: not young, not old.

So many questions, but where was she to find answers? She pulled all the boxes out of the drawers in the hope of perhaps running across something more, something that would provide some clues, and in fact at the bottom of one of the drawers she found a thin blue notebook. She opened it and recognized her aunt's handwriting, even smaller and more cramped than usual. It was clear that she had made some diary notations but had abandoned the project long ago, for most of the pages were blank.

Camilla leafed through the notebook, but something kept her from actually reading until she came to the page where the entries stopped. They ended in mid-sentence, as Lenka's life had ended: *There is no justice in the world*

Those were the final words, halfway down the page, no period, no comma following them. Camilla stared at the sentence, at the embittered words. There is no justice in the world—and with that Lenka had shut her life off, some time many years ago.

Camilla stood up so quickly that the chair fell over. The crash was almost a blessing in the enveloping silence. As she righted the chair, her eyes fell on the wall mirror. She stepped closer, observing herself, searching carefully for signs that would tell her that she was no longer seventeen but over thirty. Sometimes during the last few years she had been afraid of growing older, but now she experienced a feeling of calm and relief as her fingers traced the fine lines at the corners of her eyes. Growing older was natural. A face without age—surely that could only mean that the person was not truly alive.

Outside, in the garden, shouts erupted. There was some childish crying, then the voice of Frau Kleinhans. A glance at the clock told her that she had spent almost an hour doing nothing at the desk.

Suddenly she was in a hurry to finish, and she thought also of the other rooms, of the bureaus and wardrobes full of things that had to be sorted and given away. She emptied out the other drawer and laid out all the boxes ready for mailing. She took away only the notebook, resolved to burn it unread.

The boys had already started back to the shore, and she found Frau Kleinhans alone in the kitchen, busy unpacking a big string bag. There was a smell of iodine, and bandaging materials were lying on the kitchen table.

"What happened?"

"Nothing to worry about. Konrad cut himself on a shell. That happens more than once at the beginning. City children aren't used to running around barefoot. Wait until they've been here a couple of weeks. . . . You're staying the summer, aren't you?"

"The children are, anyhow. My plans aren't certain yet. Perhaps Frau Ewers will come—or my older sister."

"But it's your house. She left it to you. You'll keep it, won't you? I could look after the children. I could move in for as long as they're here, then they wouldn't have a thing to worry about. We'd get along, believe you me. They're good as gold with me, and they've always liked my cooking. My, how they've grown this last year! It just goes to show how time passes. Remember when *we* were that age? I can remember the first time you came! Do you remember? The gulls' eggs we went looking for?"

Camilla looked at Frau Kleinhans. Was it the dark, plain cotton dress and the severe, unbecoming hairdo that made her look so much older? Whatever it was, for years Camilla had not felt that she was dealing with a woman of her own age.

"One year, then another, time does fly," Frau Kleinhans said as she continued to put away the groceries in the pantry. "Who would have thought that your aunt—that very morning the druggist came to pick her up to go to the concert." She lowered her voice. "They say Witte asked for her hand—seriously you know. And I think there was something to it. Witte worshiped your aunt, anybody could see that. How often he came to see her, and never without flowers or some other kind of present. But I guess she wasn't interested anymore. She was dressed all in white that Sunday morning, so elegant, nobody would have believed she'd made the dress with her own hands."

"She left her clothes to you. A little money for your husband, and for you any of the dresses you'd like. I'm sure they'd all fit you."

"You mean her clothes? I never saw anybody who could sew like her. She never used a pattern when she cut out the material, she only marked it out with pins and tailor's chalk. And what good taste she had! If only I could have done something like that! She could have opened a shop any time she wanted, anywhere, in any city. And Witte—believe me, he really meant it. He wasn't her only suitor either. She could have married lots of times . . . oh, I'm sorry, I didn't mean to get started on that. She really left her dresses to me?"

"Yes. Pick out whatever you like."

"And you're really going to keep the house?" A fearful undertone crept into her voice. "You're not going to sell it?"

"I promise I won't."

"Don't worry, we'll look after it when it's empty, my husband and me. And I'd be glad to take care of the children. Are you and Herr Senger going away together?"

"Yes."

"I have just one request. If it wouldn't be asking too much." She blushed and had trouble getting out the words. "I always wished that—just once, but your aunt—I just didn't have the nerve to ask her."

"What is it?"

"The new bath, you know. You're going to laugh at me. Always when I cleaned it, well, she used to say, what's taking you so long to clean one bathroom? . . . Well, the new bathroom with the sunken tub and the beautiful tiles and the mirrors—I always thought to myself, just once I'd love to take a bath, at night would be best, with the lights on, and I'd like to use the bath salts in the crystal bottle. . . . Is that an awful thing for me to say?"

209

Camilla could not look at the woman, and she could not laugh either. The woman's request, this simple desire, made her thoughtful and sad. A woman who had no greater wish than that. . . . "Of course you may use the bathroom, anytime you're in the house."

"Really? Oh my God, thank you so much, and I never had the nerve to ask. To have a bath there just once . . . and take a lot of time doing it. But now I'm going to have to see to dinner. Sea air gives you an appetite. I'll take good care of them, the kids, they always ate like horses, anything I cooked for them. We'll have something very simple today, sausages, and hot rice pudding after. It'll be ready in half an hour or so."

Camilla suddenly yearned for sun and air. She went outside. The day had turned hot and almost perfectly calm. The sky was a glowing sheet, making it impossible to tell where the ocean began. The voices from the beach sounded muted, as if heard through a veil.

While she stood in the doorway and looked down the garden, her thoughts returned to the day when the stranger had first appeared here, holding his white straw hat—the man she had not wanted to let in the house. And then the evening on the beach near the coast guard station, when they sat side by side on the boat upturned in the sand. . . . The pressure that had lain on her in the last few hours began to lift. She changed her shoes and left the garden.

She walked along the beach for a long time, away from the town, through the sun-drenched landscape. Her feet sank into the warm, dry sand, and she grew hot. In the afternoon, when the temperature fell, she would take her bicycle as in the old days and ride to her place, spend an hour or two alone there, sorting out her thoughts. But even as she made plans, she became eager to return to Neustrelitz that very night. Never before had she found the separation from her husband so difficult; even half a day seemed an eternity.

She started on the way back. The locust trees along the boardwalk had grown, and the vegetation in the gardens was more dense, so that all she could see of some of the houses were their roofs. She walked along the water's edge; indolently and almost noiselessly the waves rolled in, bringing no relief from the heat. Behind them the ocean stretched out, mirror-smooth and motionless. The whole day seemed to stand still.

The children were no longer on the beach across from the house. The whole shore was empty of human figures. The sand castles and beach chairs stood abandoned, and some forgotten beach balls lay in the sand. The only crowds were further in the distance, toward the lighthouse, along the vendors' stands.

Frau Kleinhans met her at the garden gate. "Everything's ready. The children are waiting for you. They're well brought up, I must say—they even washed their hands without having to be told. I'm leaving now, my husband will be home soon. What a day! Not a breeze."

The shrill ring of a bicycle bell broke the silence. Both women looked down the street. The cyclist was still at a considerable distance, but the uniform and the cap made him immediately recognizable as the postman.

"He seems to be heading for your house," Camilla said.

"My house?" A deep, vertical wrinkle formed between her dark eyebrows. "We get a few notes at Christmas time, that's all."

The postman had indeed stopped before the neighboring house. He leaned his bicycle against the fence, took off his cap, and wiped the sweat from his forehead with his handkerchief.

"He really does seem to want to see me. I'm very curious." Her voice expressed fear, and the haste with which she now ran toward her house was proof of her anxiety.

Camilla remained standing at her garden gate, held fast by a strange feeling of enervation.

The postman had taken a letter from the black leather satchel attached to the front of his bicycle. Frau Kleinhans shook her head when he held the letter out to her. The man said something and then pressed the letter into her hand despite her resistance, while she was still shaking her head vehemently.

Everything then seemed to happen simultaneously: the postman swinging onto his bike, the woman tearing open the envelope, and the scream. The piercing scream of Frau Kleinhans tore the silence like an explosion. Only gradually did single words become comprehensible: "No! No! No! Never! I'll never let him go. No!"

Camilla wanted to run to her but remained where she was as if paralyzed. But when the screaming continued, she pulled herself together and hurried to Frau Kleinhans. The postman flew away on his bike. Frau Kleinhans stood still, ashen-faced, clutching the envelope.

"What is it, for God's sake?"

Frau Kleinhans stared at Camilla as if she were a stranger, almost with hostility, and then she continued to shout. "I'll never give him up! Never! Nobody can take my man from me! No! No! No!" It was an alien voice and an alien woman. . . .

Everything else that happened in the course of the day—the first more precise news about mobilization, the extra editions of the newspaper that were torn from the sellers' hands, the posters around which crowds gathered, and even what happened to Camilla on the following day, on her trip back to Neustrelitz in the overcrowded train— none of it meant a thing compared to Frau Kleinhans' screams.

Even years later it remained the most vivid of all the impressions connected with the outbreak of the war. Not the precipitate return to Neustrelitz, not the boys' many questions which she did not know how to answer, not her husband's grave face when he came to meet her at the train station, not the long lines of volunteers standing before the recruiting office, not the band playing marches in the town square— the first day of war was, for her, one woman's scream. And something more: the new suitcases, piled up by size in their bedroom, in gray dust covers with the black monogram C. S., ready for the trip they would not be taking now. . . .

Four

1

Once the train entered the magic circle of Berlin, it was as if they had happened into the forcefield of a strong magnet. It doubled its speed and made no further stops. A station rushed past, a brick building, a sign with unreadable words, then they were once more enveloped in a dense fall of snow.

The train was late, and it was not likely that it would make up the time. Everyone had gotten used to it. In this third winter of the war train schedules existed only on paper, and no one thought it worthwhile to discuss delays.

They had left Neustrelitz twenty minutes late because they had to give way to a troop transport. Perhaps the weather was to blame as well. That morning, in Neustrelitz, there had been no sign of snow, the air was frosty and clear. But then, halfway to Berlin, they drove into a dark-blue wall of weather, and for the last hour the snowstorm had been raging.

Once again the outlines of a station emerged; a few muffled-up figures were standing on an open platform. Camilla edged away from the window because of the draft coming through its cracks, tucked her hands deeper into her muff, and looked at her father, who was sitting across from her.

"We're almost there. I bet that was one of the suburban stations."

Hofmann did not reply. The first-class compartment was overcrowded, the luggage nets piled high; everything that would not fit there stood on the floor, between the travelers' legs. This, too, was something she had become used to during her trips to Berlin. Mecklenburg was still a good region for hoarding, and anyone who could afford it traveled first class because, for mysterious reasons, they carried out controls more superficially there—though this was no longer such a marked advantage now that the controls at the Berlin railroad stations had become more thorough.

The compartment showed signs of the war years. The red velvet upholstery was worn through, the floor runner was ragged at the edges, and at the windows the straps had been cut off, so that there was no way to let in air. The travelers, too, gave evidence of the war—not only in their careworn, thin faces, but also in the shabby cloth of their coats, their patched shoes, their mittens knitted from wool remnants, and the women's kerchiefs. Camilla was aware that her father with his beaver collar and she in her sable coat appeared like beings from an alien world. The looks that showered down on them made it very clear.

Hofmann loosened his scarf, opened his coat, and pulled out his watch. The silent resentment in the compartment grew even stronger at the sight of the massive gold watch chain. That someone should still possess such an object might be tolerated, but that he dared display it publicly after the recent appeals to turn in every form of gold provoked extreme disapproval.

Hofmann pretended not to hear the whispered remarks. Slowly and carefully he pushed the lid open. He held the dial at arm's length, but Camilla knew that he could not see it even then; it was simply his vanity that made him keep up the fiction. He took care not to ask her for the time but shook his head and inquired, "I don't know if my watch is slow or not. What time do you have?"

She pushed back the sleeve of her fur coat. "Almost eleven." They had left Neustrelitz at eight; that meant they were a full hour late.

"Just in time for brunch in the Palm Court. What do you think? A piece of Prague ham, fresh from the oven."

He was referring to the buffet in the Wertheim department store, near the fountain, where they had sometimes arranged to meet in years past. But it had been a long time since Prague ham had been on the menu, and he knew it; it was another of the fictions to which

216

he clung so tenaciously. For Camilla anything that had happened before 1914 was in the far-distant past.

"We'll drive to the hospital at once."

Hofmann snapped the watch shut and tucked it back into his pocket just as ceremoniously as he had extracted it earlier. "Is that necessary? Can't I go to the hotel for at least one night? Now that it's January, the puppet theater should be open; we could go see a performance tonight. What difference will one day more or less make?"

She refused to be drawn into an argument. He had succeeded for too long in keeping his true condition a secret from her and even from Dr. Oesterreicher—until two weeks ago, when he had walked straight into a car. Fortunately he had gotten away with a couple of bumps and scratches. Only then had he confessed that for a considerable time he had been seeing the world only through a thick veil; objects and people were recognizable only as outlines. A specialist had diagnosed cataracts and had declared that only an immediate operation on both eyes could restore Hofmann's vision.

"Fine, fine," he said. "We'll drop it. But I'll tell you now, I won't put up with just anything. The sisters can get on your nerves something awful. They are sisters, aren't they? And if they think they can convert me. . . . I know perfectly well they always try to convert a person just as soon as he's helpless."

Camilla considered it best not to respond. The train gradually slowed as it came into the station yard. A network of tracks and switches traced its way through the snow, and red and green signal lights glowed through the whirling whiteness.

Years ago, before the war, when she rarely came to Berlin, she had always looked forward eagerly to this moment of steaming into the station. Now, when business brought her to the city so often, it signified only the beginning of a long day packed full of unpleasant events: pilgrimages from agency to agency to obtain licenses; conferences in the Procurement Division of the War Ministry; appointments at the customs office to clear shipments from abroad.

The train shuddered once or twice before it came to a stop with screeching brakes and whistling valves. Hofmann was one of the first to rise from his seat. As if every minute counted, he reached up to the luggage rack, managed to take hold of his own suitcase among the many pieces of luggage, swung it over the heads of the other travelers,

217

and placed it on the seat. With growing impatience he watched the efforts of a man to free the door from ice. When it finally sprang open with a bang, he vigorously pushed ahead—that is, he pushed Camilla ahead, for he was sensible enough to let her go first, so that she could help him get down the snow-covered steps. But once on the platform he immediately resumed the initiative. "Porter!" he called loudly. "Are there any porters here?"

People turned around to stare at him and rushed on. Camilla picked up both cases. "We can count ourselves lucky if we get a cab. Come on now, keep right in back of me."

"What kind of times are we living in?" He followed her, banging his cane angrily at every step. "No porters, no cabs. Give me my valise. Give it to me—I want to carry it myself. I'm not an invalid." He insisted on carrying his case; he had even packed it himself, indignantly rejecting Frau Ewers' offer of help.

Outside the gates, officials at tables inspected the travelers' luggage, and long queues had already formed. The lines moved slowly; the officials were thorough. Finally they were left with only one woman, wearing black earmuffs across an old cap and an old man's overcoat that had been clumsily altered to fit her. Suddenly potatoes rolled across the table and fell to the ground. Camilla bent down to help pick them up, but the gesture only earned her a suspicious glare.

That was another thing that had changed. At the beginning of the war people took the controls calmly. They had joked about the nuisance, and the officials joined in the laughter. A feeling of camaraderie had filled everyone, but there was no trace of it left now. Indifference, coldness, and animosity were the prevailing moods.

The woman had grabbed her bag and was leaving. Camilla was about to raise her valise to the table when the official looked at her and then at her father. "You're together?"

"Yes. This gentleman is my father."

"You may pass." His nod was close to a bow. "You there, make way for the young lady."

But they remained jammed in among the people who were pushing their way through the gate and had no intention whatever of letting anyone get ahead. When they finally reached the spacious concourse, where the crowd rapidly dispersed, Fritz Hofmann was grinning to himself. "If he'd suspected what I have in my suitcase! But that's how it is, clothes make the man, just as they always have."

218

"It could just as easily have blown up in your face."

"Surely one is still allowed to carry a few pieces of soap! Who knows what the food in the hospital is like. You can get anything you want for soap."

She was about to give a sharp answer when she heard her name called. She looked around inquiringly. Her face grew a shade more sober when she recognized Dr. Kautsky, the firm's attorney, but then she thought: he's sure to have a cab waiting.

She had some reservations about Kautsky. He was a shade too smooth and cunning for her taste, but of course that had its good side too, especially in times such as these, where you had to go through all kinds of maneuvers to get your rights.

He came closer, a short man, slightly dragging his left leg—the consequence of infantile paralysis. His disability had exempted the relatively young man from military service.

"It beats me how you can get along with such a person," Hofmann whispered.

"He's competent, that's the only thing that counts, not whether I like him. So please don't start up with him right away like last time, I beg of you."

Dr. Kautsky briefly raised his hat, revealing his dark, very curly hair. For a moment he seemed to be considering whether to remark on the weather or the lateness of the train, but then, as always, he came right to the point. "They've moved up the appointment. I only learned about it an hour ago, too late to reach you in Neustrelitz."

"What's the new time?"

"Two o'clock in the Naval Procurement Office, second floor, room four. I was not certain that you would check in with me before the conference, that's why I came to meet you. There are a couple of things we have to talk about."

"Do you have a cab?"

"Yes. May I take you to your hotel?" He pointed to the suitcases. "Is that all the luggage you brought?"

"Do you mind going out of your way just a little? We can talk during the drive."

"Not in the least. Where would you like me to take you?"

"To the Wallbaum Clinic. It's close by; if you'll have the driver start, I'll give directions."

"Fine, I'll tell the driver."

Dr. Kautsky took the suitcase from Camilla and walked ahead. When they came out of the concourse into the open air, the snow flurries had stopped. Camilla was almost sorry, for the snow might have served to soften the dour aspect of the square: the queues of people in front of the stores on the other side of the square, often extending along two or three housefronts; the rusty carts of the snow-clearing crew, consisting of women and boys; the advertising columns, no longer plastered with colorful posters but covered only with public notices. Currently it was the announcement of the fifth war loan.

The arrival in Berlin, which used to be a celebration, was always a shock to Camilla now. Each time the gradual disintegration of the city became more visible. Sometimes it seemed to her as if the city she loved so much—her Berlin—had ceased to exist. . . .

They had bought the house in Steglitz from the bank in 1914, in August still, at a favorable price. When Italy joined the enemy in May 1915 and the Italian embassy in Berlin folded its tents, it had suddenly become vacant. But they could not bring themselves to move in and had postponed the move to the end of the war. The decision turned out to be a wise one, since conditions, from the avail-ability of labor to the quantity of food, were better in Neustrelitz. The deserted house had later been requisitioned and transformed into a military hospital. . . .

Once in the cab, Camilla would have liked to pull down the blinds to spare herself further depressing sights. Her father had involved the attorney in an argument about the latest war loans.

"As my daughter's attorney, you really ought to be advising her against further subscriptions."

"We already didn't subscribe to the one before this one."

"Then you should sell the old ones. Get rid of everything you have. The rejection of our peace offer—any idiot can figure out what that means if America really enters the war. Material assets, those might come through, but that's all. It's a good thing you bought the house when you did."

Dr. Kautsky seized the opportunity to interrupt Hofmann's tirade. He looked at Camilla, who was sitting across from him. "I meant to tell you. There's trouble about the house."

"What kind of trouble? Did they refuse to accept the rent raise?"

"No, not that. They swallowed it without a murmur—everything's getting more expensive, after all. No, it's the sewers. The old ones are no longer sufficient for the current occupancy. A hundred patients. On their own initiative they started to lay new pipes, and the gardener is protesting. Willeke comes storming into my office, claims the whole garden is being ruined. I haven't had time yet to drive out there and see for myself. Somehow or other the complaint seems justified. I know the soil out there is difficult, water won't run off—"

"I'll look into it."

"I'm sorry that all I ever seem to have for you is unpleasant news."

"I had intended driving out there anyway."

"Really? I could send an expert—"

"I want to see for myself, for a start. And what about the negotiations? Why the change in the time of the appointment?"

"I think it's going badly. It's best for you to face the facts."

The claim was four weeks old. It had been lodged as the result of an anonymous denunciation. The firm had furnished the Hotel Bristol with soap and laundry products, items subject to general rationing and of the higher quality that was permitted only for supplying the troops. Profit had not been the motivating factor but rather an old loyalty, for the Bristol had been one of the first major Berlin hotels to become one of their steady customers. Of course Camilla did gain certain advantages by the deal. A room was at her disposal any time she wanted it, and if she brought dinner guests to the Bristol, they were served dishes that remained a memory to others.

"I get the feeling that they're trying to set an example," Kautsky began again. "Morale among the general populace is low, and they feel that a quick verdict will soothe feelings for a while. I must urge you to compromise."

"How can I do that if they intend to make an example of me?"

"Compromise is always possible."

"And on what terms?"

Dr. Kautsky was not sure how she would take his suggestions. In years past he had dealt only with Carl Senger. He had not met Camilla until the beginning of the war, when it became clear that her husband could no longer expect to be exempted from service and that she would have to carry on the business by herself for the duration of the war. He still remembered their first meeting. Female clients— in his experience it had generally meant a string of problems. Therefore he approached her with a fair amount of prejudice. But her appearance had taken him by surprise, and even more her clear reason-

221

ing and ability to use common sense, unmuddied by emotions. He handled similar cases in his practice, but none of the other women had managed the new situation as well as Camilla Senger.

Not only had she carried on the existing business, she had further expanded it with troop supplies and with substitute products for the home market. Granted, this had only been possible through unremitting efforts that often came perilously close to the edge of legality, especially in the obtaining of raw materials. She had been astonishingly resourceful in making her way through the jungle of regulations and statutes, and more than once he had been present when even the most unpleasant types in government agencies were suddenly transformed into quite polite persons as they sat across from this woman. This time, however, the case was different.

"It's a delicate matter. I had counted on a fine. In that case I would have told you, don't hesitate to pay it. But they've sharpened the law in this area. This kind of black market is now punishable by a jail term, and as I said before, it looks as if they're planning to hand the case over to the courts."

"Listen, what are you talking about?" Hofmann broke in.

Camilla laid her hand on her father's arm. It was almost a gesture one would use to calm a troubled child. "What is it they're proposing, then?"

"I had an opportunity to speak with the chairman in private. I know that for his part there is a . . . certain readiness to quash the matter. For one thing, there are personal relations with the owner of the Bristol, and for another, well, as far as you're concerned, he expects an appropriate renumeration."

She caught the lawyer's searching glance and responded to it with a sudden smile. "Bribery, in other words."

"I would not use the word myself. If you think he is asking for money, you are underestimating him. He has a brother. He wants you to offer him a job in your factory with a ten-year contract at a good salary. By the way, the man is a trained chemist and highly qualified."

She lowered her head, so that the edge of her sable cap threw her eyes into shadow. "And you're recommending that I agree?"

"I consider this way of resolving the case worth considering—at least given the circumstances."

"What is his name?"

222

"Blessing. We can have dinner with him."

She took her time before answering. She looked out the window to check their whereabouts and told Kautsky where the driver should turn. Then she said, "I think I'll assume the risk and attend the meeting. If he'd asked for money, I would have agreed. But to be forced to take someone into the firm, a stranger—never."

The lawyer knew her well enough to realize that any attempt to make her change her mind would be futile. "Shall we meet there?"

"Let me go alone—given the circumstances. But perhaps you'll be good enough to see me right afterward." She smiled. "In case we have to appeal the decision after all."

"There's a café just across the street. I'll be waiting there for you." There was silence until Dr. Kautsky asked, "How long are you staying in Berlin?"

"A few days at least. It depends on how the operation turns out. Now, the first cross street to the left, then we're there. I don't know the number, but you can't miss it."

Hofmann, who found it hard not to be the center of attention, for so long, leaned forward. "I only hope this Professor Klier is as good as his fee is high. Do you know him?"

Kautsky was a cautious man when it came to this sort of information. "I can tell you who the good lawyers in Berlin are, but physicians. . . ."

"Beware of doctors. They're worse even than lawyers. Cutthroats every one of them. Operate until the scalpel drops from their fingers. How old did you say this Klier is, Camilla?"

"There it is, we've passed it."

When the cab came to a stop, Camilla started to get out first, but the lawyer was quicker, asked her to wait, opened an umbrella—it had started to snow again—and stretched out his hand to help her out.

She thanked him, almost confused. She had become quite unused to such courtesies.

The hospital was set far back in a garden, a mansion in the gothic style with a modern addition. She rang the bell at the iron gate while Dr. Kautsky lifted Hofmann's suitcase from the cab.

"Shall I take your luggage to the hotel? You're staying at the Bristol, I'm sure. I'll be passing it in any case."

"That's nice of you. And don't waste any more of your time. Someone's coming now."

A manservant with a large black umbrella appeared, and Hofmann made one last attempt. "Couldn't we postpone it by at least a day? Surely you won't begrudge me one day at the hotel."

The servant reached for the suitcase, held the umbrella over Hofmann, and walked the old man to the house. The entrance was in the old building, and the hall they now entered smelled more of a church than a hospital. The colored glass windows created a subdued light; a niche held a statue of the Virgin Mary, an eternal light burning before it.

"You're sure we're in the right place?" Hofmann, who could barely make out details, noisily drew the air in through his nostrils. "Tell me, is that incense?"

A woman in a habit appeared. Her bright, shiny face looked as if it had been cut out from the edge of the dark, close-fitting wimple. She nodded at Camilla and then turned to Hofmann. "So there's our patient. You don't like hospitals, your daughter tells me."

"I've never been in a hospital in all my life," Hofmann insisted stubbornly.

"Well, it really doesn't look like a hospital here, does it? Someone will take you to your room now. I'm sure we'll get along splendidly."

"May I see the room too?" Camilla asked.

"Of course, but let's get the formalities out of the way first." She summoned a second sister, who took Hofmann by the arm and led him away.

"It's always best if we leave them alone at first," the sister said when the elevator door had closed behind the two. "Now I understand what you meant when you told me that your father is difficult. But don't worry. Sister Regina has a way with elderly gentlemen." She led the way through a door, and again, as at her first visit, Camilla was struck by the starkness of the room, the simple desk, the telephone on it, the metal cabinets along the wall.

"Please sit down."

"You'll take a check for the deposit?"

"Of course."

"Will five hundred be enough?"

"Quite enough for patient care. Of course if you'd like, you can also make a down payment on the surgeon's fee. Professor Klier is never displeased by such a move."

Camilla wrote out a check, then a second one; only when she

handed both across the table did the sister's hands emerge from the wide sleeves of her habit—slender, well groomed hands, the nails cut to the quick.

"I'll write you out a receipt." She reached for the colorfully patterned pen, dipped it into the inkwell, and finally blotted the paper. "There. We filled out the personal-information forms last time. Anything else—I mean, any special character traits we ought to know about, any special likes. . . ?"

"You heard him yourself, he's never been in a hospital. You won't have an easy time with him."

"How does he sleep? Does he need medication?"

"He never takes anything."

"And how about foods? Does he require any special diet?"

"Just be prepared for him to ask for whatever you don't have."

"I see. Well, we'll try our best."

"Has the operation been scheduled?"

The sister glanced at a bulletin board hanging next to the desk. It was covered with many slips of paper. "He'll be the first one tomorrow morning. Promptly at seven o'clock."

"And the second operation?"

"That will depend on how well he recovers from the first one. Normally, four or five days later. If there is hemorrhaging, there will be some delay. But don't worry. With Professor Klier he's in the best hands. If I may mention it at the outset—as few visitors as possible during the first few days."

Camilla thought of her mother, of Alice, of Lou—such admonitions were entirely unnecessary as far as they were concerned. They were unlikely to find their way to the hospital even once. As always, she would be left to bear the brunt of it all, and for a moment she almost wished she too could lie down safely in one of the hospital beds. To let others take care of her and wait on her, to go under where no one could reach her—to sleep for an eternity. . . .

"No, there won't be any other visitors."

"You are his only daughter?"

Camilla nodded. What was the point of long explanations?

"Your husband is in the army?"

"Yes." She met the sister's glance, and something in the nun's eyes gave her courage to put the question she had been carrying around inside herself for so long. When she had tried to approach Dr. Oesterreicher, her preliminary hints had met with an unmistakable rebuff. "What kind of man is Professor Klier?"

"How do you mean?"

"I'm thinking of my oldest son. He'll soon be sixteen, he'll get his school-leaving certificate this year. He has already received his induction notice, and I—" She came to a halt, afraid of using the wrong words and spoiling everything right at the outset. "I'll go to my father now."

"Does your son have eye trouble?" The sister had understood her very clearly and was trying to give her an opening.

She need only say yes, but she could not manage it. Why was it necessary to lie about something so natural as trying to keep a sixteen-year-old boy from becoming a soldier? "What room did you say my father is in?"

The sister, behind the desk, got to her feet. "I can't say how the Professor would respond," she said. "Actually he should have some understanding. He has lost two sons in the war. You can certainly try it, but I can't promise you anything. This war . . . sometimes I think it's less bad out there than here. There at least you can tell friend from foe, but here it's getting harder to know. . . . Your father's room is on the second floor. Room thirty-four, at the back."

While Camilla walked along the quiet halls, she was again overcome by the desire for sleep. She met no one. One of the radiators was knocking, and heavy snow fell outside the windows.

When she entered her father's room, the first thing she saw was the suitcase, unpacked. Hofmann stood in a recess, still wearing his coat. He turned around at once and narrowed his eyes in order to recognize the person who had come in.

"You haven't taken off your coat?"

"I won't stay here. This is supposed to be a first-class room? Did you see, the dumb waiter is right across the hall. And the sister's impertinent tone when I remarked that the place was too hot."

"Then take off your coat."

"Look, Camilla, are you sure the operation is necessary—I mean, that it's the right thing to do?"

"You have cataracts. Do you know another way to cure them? You've waited too long already."

"I heard about a man, somewhere in the mountains. They say he can cure cataracts without surgery—he's very successful, to the point

226

of the miraculous. It seems to me it wouldn't hurt to give him a try."

"We've discussed it a hundred times."

"And the wallpaper in this room. It drives me crazy to think I'm going to have to stare at it for a week."

There was no wallpaper; the walls were painted a pale green. Camilla came close to losing her temper, but she remained silent and began to unpack her father's bag. He did not object, and finally he let her help him out of his coat.

"I'm going to have to leave you now," Camilla said at last. "I'll stop by again tonight. Is there anyone else you'd like to see?"

"Could you have someone come in to shave me?"

"Surely they'll be able to see to that here for you. I meant someone in the family. Lou or Alice?"

"Please—no."

"They both have telephones; you can call them anytime."

"I don't understand you—all of them, they only come when they want something from you. Your mother, Lou, Alice, Maxi. Have they ever lifted a finger for you? Never once."

"You don't understand."

"But I see it! Even Maxi, and I always thought she wasn't as bad as the others. What has she been doing ever since she moved to Neustrelitz? Use you!"

"She lost her husband, the war took her home, and there she stood with her children and no roof over her head. I had plenty of room. After all, she is my sister."

As early as August 1914 Maxi and her children had fled from the advancing Russian army, leaving the estate in East Prussia. The very same month her husband, Otto von Donath, fell at Allenstein. The following year, in April 1915, Lou lost her husband at the second battle of Ypres.

"Is that any reason for her to behave as if she were mistress of the house—folding her hands, letting herself be waited on, emptying out your clothes closets, going around complaining that you're not doing enough for her children? And the house in Warnemünde—she's commandeered it as if it were her own. All I see is the way they all smother you. Don't talk to me about the family."

"A family has to stay together, and in times like these that person has to help who can, that's all, and that happens to be me. If we start being calculating about our families and weighing everything as if

227

it were gold. . . . No! I'm a family sort of person. It hurt me very much when everything fell apart, in the old days. Who else do we have in the world besides the handful of people who belong to us? You should be glad that's the way I'm made. After all, you owe your pleasant life to me. I'm sorry that I've had to say it just this once. So please don't make things harder for me, please."

He lowered his head. "Stay in Berlin," he said. "Have a couple of wonderful days, buy yourself something pretty, go to the theater or a concert, forget everything for a change. . . ."

She had gone to the window and gazed at the garden with its old trees that could only be seen in outline through the thick snow flurry. His complaints and his egotism—she could deal with those more easily than with his reminders of all she was missing. She was not thinking of clothes, or evenings at the theater—she missed her whole life, and not only since the war but also during the years before that. . . . She did not usually allow such thoughts to come to the surface; she kept them from entering her mind. They were there all the same, just like the dozen new suitcases in the attic at Neustrelitz that they had bought once upon a time for the grand tour and that were never packed after all.

She turned around. He would not have been able to see the tears in her eyes, but the bond between them was so strong that he knew what she felt.

"Are you worried about the negotiations? Do you really have to fight it out by yourself? What do you have a lawyer for?"

His effort to put himself in her place, to think for a moment of someone else for once, was deeply touching. "Don't worry, it will work out."

"And you'll surely come back?"

"I promise."

He walked with her to the door. "Maybe you'll have a word with the Professor after all. I mean, those doctors have to be made to feel that we're watching them every inch of the way."

"I'll try."

"In the end, a fellow like that doesn't even perform the operation himself. He pockets the money and lets his assistant do the work."

She looked at him. No, he would never change, he'd always remain the same. But at this moment it was almost a comforting thought in a world that seemed to be altogether topsy-turvy.

2

"Is there anything else?" The waiter cleared the small marble table and took away the newspapers.

"Something, yes. Perhaps a cup of coffee." Dr. Kautsky sat near the window; he had pushed aside the curtain and looked out on the square in front of the Ministry of Finance and the Academy of Vocal Music.

"I wouldn't recommend the coffee, sir. Perhaps a cup of tea? It's only German tea, but—"

"Bring me anything. And the bill at the same time, please."

The Café Otero was almost empty at this hour; a little later, when the offices closed, a few clerks would be coming in to read the evening papers. A skimpy Christmas tree, shedding its needles, stood in a corner. The snow had stopped, and Dr. Kautsky was watching the wide portal of the Academy of Vocal Music, where the Naval Procurement Office was housed. He had kept on his coat, for the café was barely heated. Besides, he wanted to be ready, and he arose at once as soon as he saw the woman dressed in the long fur coat and the fur cap come out of the building. A swarm of pigeons flew across the square and came to rest among the gargoyles on the gable. It was growing dark.

Dr. Kautsky rushed across the square to meet her, but when he caught up with her, he was shy of putting a direct question. The

229

session had lasted almost two hours, and he was hard put to decide whether that was a good or bad sign. He pointed to the café. "You cannot get anything there, only German tea—whatever that may be— and the place is not adequately heated. Shall I take you to your hotel?"

She was grateful to him for not asking questions, but of course he was expecting her report. "I'd like to walk a little."

"I don't want to rush you but—how did it go?"

"Well."

They were going toward the center of town, with the river in sight ahead of them.

"Does that mean you were successful?"

"Yes . . . they're dropping the investigation."

"How can they do that?"

"They overlooked one aspect, and luckily I happened to think of it. There is a special law according to which soap in the A category may still be supplied to military officers."

"But you supplied the Hotel Bristol."

"Ninety percent of the hotel guests are officers. The hotel provided the soap exclusively for their use—at least there's no way to prove otherwise. I must say, the members of the commission were on my side from the first. This time you were the one who was too pessimistic."

"To be frank, I did not think you could get away with it."

She should have been relieved, pleased with what she had achieved, but she only felt exhausted. She could still see the conference room, a rehearsal hall that had been turned to other uses. The closed grand piano in one corner, the saddle cloths of gray felt that reached halfway up the windows to keep out the cold, the lamps hanging low over the table where the commission members sat, the glasses of water for which a hand reached now and again. She could remember none of the faces, only voices, especially Blessing's clipped speech, increasingly more impatient and irritated as the conference continued.

"I congratulate you." She felt his hand on her shoulder—not a gesture of sudden intimacy but an expression of comradely male recognition. But she was not flattered, only pained. What she needed right now was some admission that she was admired purely as a woman, not for what she had done or achieved.

230

Dr. Kautsky, still unable to grasp the happy outcome of the conference, said, "No man could have done a better job."

It was the worst thing he could have said, but perhaps for that very reason it helped her. She laughed. "My father always says, if I'd studied law too, I'd be unbeatable. Anyway, thank you for waiting for me."

"You really intend to walk?"

"Yes. It will be good for me." To walk without a purpose, without wondering about the time, that was the only thing she longed for at the moment. After Dr. Kautsky had left her, she continued along the avenue, past the arsenal. During the recent severe frost the water had frozen over, and she watched the children who were sweeping a strip clear of snow so that they could go ice skating. But she was unable to stop thinking about the point touched on by Kautsky.

To be in charge of her own life—that had been her major purpose after her father's bankruptcy and the break-up of the family. She had succeeded. She had learned to assert herself, to get her way. But she had had to develop qualities that had changed her, so that sometimes she scared herself. When she thought of her mother and sisters, she knew that she had taken the right road. But at times like this the price she had had to pay seemed almost too high, and she wondered if she could ever again be the person she used to be.

Among the passing pedestrians, a man scrutinized her thoroughly, walked on a few paces and stopped, turning around to watch her some more. Not to think about anything! To take a rest from all of it for just one hour—even from her longings.

Longings—that word, too, had taken on a very different meaning. The only thing she still dared hope for was that the next day would not bring anything bad. It was almost dark when she reached the square at the arsenal, with its view of the city's most fashionable avenue. She turned toward it. Only every third street lamp was lit, and many of the stores that used to do their principal business in the early evening hours were already closed. The shop windows were only dimly lit, and the meager decorations spoke of the scarcity prevailing everywhere. A men's tailor, renowned for his English cloth, was displaying only a single uniform coat; the window of a china shop contained nothing but a row of ceramic vases and decorative plates with the inscription *God Punish England*. And the watchmaker where her father had been a client for years had put in his window only a blue velvet pillow holding some medals. She heard the peal of a church bell, four high notes and six low ones; it could only be coming from the Hedwigskirche. It was not much farther to the Hotel Bristol. She had been on the go continuously for twelve hours, and the thought of getting out of her clothes and into a warm bath was tempting, but one more hour for a visit to her mother would not make much difference now. Her father might be right when he called Mama and her sisters selfish, but Camilla saw only that, with the war, the connection had become closer again and, in spite of some reservations that would probably never be entirely resolved, more cordial. She met with her mother almost every time she had business in Berlin. They went shopping together, shared a meal, or if there was not enough time, she made at least a telephone call; nevertheless, she seldom came to the house where her mother lived.

It was one of those typical town houses of the aristocracy that circled the court like satellites—in this case the palace of the Empress and of the Crown Prince. Few windows were aglow on this particular evening, and the steep staircase leading to the parlor floor was only dimly lit, the gas lights turned low. The red runners had disappeared from the marble steps, and the large Chinese vases had been removed from the wall niches.

On the second floor she rang the bell at the door with the opaque glass panes etched with flowery garlands. For a long time nothing stirred inside. When the door finally opened, it was not the maid, as in years gone by, but Frau von Schack herself who stood there. She seemed so surprised by Camilla's visit that she could not find a word of greeting and forgot to invite Camilla inside.

"My mother isn't in?"

"Oh yes," Frau von Schack replied. "Of course she's in but. . . . Oh, but do come inside." Mama's friend was a short, dainty woman with powdery white hair. They were standing in the vestibule with the huge mirror and the coat rack hung with many coats.

"You have company?" Camilla asked. "Am I disturbing you?"

"Only a few ladies from the Red Cross." Frau von Schack had the clear, overly precise enunciation of a teacher, and a teacher's glance that missed nothing. She examined Camilla and then pulled her over toward the étagère; in years gone by it used to support vases of fresh flowers, but now it held only a dried-up asparagus fern and a sickly

African violet. "As long as you're here—may I have a word with you about your mother?"

"But of course, what's the matter?" Camilla had her suspicions, for occasional remarks her mother had let fall had made her realize that the home life shared by the two women was largely at the expense of the good-natured Frau von Schack. Nevertheless she was surprised at what she heard.

"It's to do with the marriage brokering."

"With what?"

"Oh, perhaps you can talk to her. You know that the court is very liberal, but there are limits—and professional marriage brokering, that just happens to be one of the things they won't tolerate. If it were to get out, I'd have to quit on the spot, after forty years at court. I'd be fired and would have to leave, just like that. I keep begging her to drop it, but she does the opposite, she keeps expanding. She's even thinking of advertising, using *this address*. And yet it's already like a pigeon coop here, constant comings and goings. There's a gentleman with her right now. Maybe you can have a word with her. Come on in, don't you want to take off your coat?"

Camilla hung her coat with the others but kept on her cap. Frau von Schack preceded her into the parlor. Only a few of the bulbs were lit on the twenty-four-branched chandelier, throwing a dim light over the circle of eight ladies rolling bandages. They raised their heads only briefly before turning back to their work. Their laps were filled with the linen and cotton stuff, and the threads to be worked into wrappings lay in little white heaps on the floor at their feet.

Frau von Schack pointed to a sliding door. "I don't know, do you want to go in right away? Sometimes her visitors stay a while." Again the ladies raised their heads in a synchronous gesture that looked almost rehearsed, and Frau von Schack gave Camilla such a beseeching look that she was compelled to nod.

The room behind the sliding door was larger than the parlor and suffused with dazzling brightness. Emmi Hofmann was enthroned in all her fullness behind an ornate desk fitted out with gilded utensils. The man sitting on the other side of the desk was wearing his coat, holding his hat and cane on his crossed legs.

He was clearly on the point of leaving, for he rose and said goodbye to Emmi Hofmann. On the way to the door—not the sliding door but a second one, leading to the corridor—he came to a stop and looked at

233

Camilla with great interest, seemingly on the point of making a remark. But Emmi Hofmann forestalled him. She gave a loud laugh
that shook her whole heavy body. "Oh no. Oh no, my dear Herr
Carow, that one's already spoken for. We'll just stick to our agreement. What would you want with such a young girl at your age
anyhow!" She waited until the door had closed behind him, then in
a serious, almost disgusted tone she said, "The older they get, the
more revolting they are."

Emmi Hofmann leaned back in her armchair, but even in this position her body remained an amorphous mass, long past the point where
a corset could lend it shape. She had always been stout, but in the
three war years she had—there was no other word for it—come apart
at the seams. Camilla sometimes thought it was a matter of pride for
Mama, to keep gaining weight while almost everyone else grew
gaunter. At any rate, when they dined together at the Bristol, she
gorged herself as if she were not going to get another bite for a week:
not one appetizer but two, and she followed a meal of several entrées
and a rich dessert with a liqueur and a piece of cake. Her conversation turned by preference to food, and according to her letters which
arrived in Neustrelitz regularly, one might have thought that it had
been years since she had been genuinely sated. As far as clothing
went, she was worse than slovenly, although she tolerated no material
except pure silk, with the rationalization that wool and cotton gave her
a rash. On the other hand she lavished the greatest care on her hair
and face, and looked at from the neck up, she was still a remarkably
pretty woman, with a smooth, rosy complexion, hair bleached a pale
blonde and freshly waved twice a week. Piled on the desk in front
of her was a bundle of banknotes, obviously a fee from the visitor.
When she saw Camilla's look, Emmi Hofmann hastily raked in the
bills and managed to make the money disappear in a drawer. Then
she opened the desk's lower cupboard, pulled out a glass and a bottle
of Danziger Goldwasser, and helped herself.

"Tell me, why are you doing this?" As she came closer, Camilla
discovered the photographs spread out on the desk—pictures of poten-
tial brides.

"Doing what?"

"Marriage brokering. You can't be serious."

"You turn up out of the blue and start lecturing—what manners!
First of all, hello. When did you get to town?"

"Frau von Schack is worried. She asked me—"

"Well, well, so my dear friend is worried. But offering my coffee to her ladies—that doesn't worry her. Rolling bandages! They think they're so patriotic, but the stuff is just as unhygienic as can be."

"She's afraid of losing her job at court. Really, why are you doing it? Surely you don't need it. You have enough money, and whenever you've needed anything, I've been there."

"Is that a fact? Enough money! Only you could say a thing like that. You have everything, all of you in Neustrelitz. You're sitting pretty, while we here in Berlin! What can you know about how everything gets more expensive, day after day? Are you trying to blame me because I have to make money? Make money in my old age, just because it was my luck to come by a no-good husband and have daughters who think of nobody but themselves. Do you know what a pound of coffee costs today?"

Complaints, reproaches, demands—should she have expected anything else? "I wanted to look in because I was in the neighborhood. I had to take Papa to the hospital."

There was a pause; Mama seemed to be struggling with herself whether or not to acknowledge Camilla's remark. "To the hospital? Then it has to be serious."

"He's in the Wallbaum Clinic, Professor Klier's patient. His eyes are worsening, cataracts. Professor Klier is going to operate."

"Oh, I see. That's all. . . ." She seemed disappointed. She had a fixed idea, perhaps connected with her immoderate eating; she wanted to survive her husband any way she could. "Well, he's going to have to wear glasses afterward. Him and his vanity."

"Is that all you have to say?"

"What do you expect? After all he did to me. Forgive and forget. . . ." She shook her head. "I'm not like that. And he wasn't even punished for it. He lives like a king, he has everything. You take him to the hospital . . . when I begged you to take me to Bad Neuenahr last fall, you made excuses."

"Because you were determined to go in a chauffeured car."

"Well? Don't you have a car? Don't you have a chauffeur?"

"Not for that purpose, no. I take the train to Berlin myself."

"Who's got any gasoline left except manufacturers? You get everything thrown at you. Didn't you get my letter? I've been waiting for two weeks. . . ."

"I'm sorry, but cocoa and chocolate have been confiscated since December. I can't do anything about it."

Emmi Hofmann pulled out a box of candy, took out two pieces, and put it away. "That's the end of my stores." She chewed luxuriously, raised her hands to press in the combs holding her hairdo, and got to her feet. She went to one of the high windows. "What a month it's been." She sighed deeply. "January! What do you think, will he come to Berlin for his birthday at least?"

"Who are you talking about?"

"Who am I talking about! My God—what times we live in! In three days it will be January twenty-seventh. *His* birthday. The birthday of our Emperor. But no one wants to have anything to do with that anymore. What a comedown." She stood still, serious, almost ceremonious, as if a huge birthday parade were passing down below, coming from the Brandenburg Gate, filing toward the palace. She undid the hooks that held the lined silk drapes and let them fall over the windows. "There were times when I was offered a hundred marks for a seat at the window."

Camilla could not stop herself from saying, "And now you take five hundred from your gentlemen."

"Don't think it's all that easy. Normally they don't pay at all. The ladies pay. Don't forget, there are far more women than men, and the surplus gets worse every day, because of all the widows. . . . What about Maxi, by the way? I wrote you about her, too. Did you speak with her?"

"You know her opinion on the matter very well, and it hasn't changed. She does not want to marry. Not as long as there's a war on."

"The suitor I had for her, he's past being endangered by the war— all he can do is get a little richer."

"Does everybody have to marry for you? Can't you believe that a woman like Maxi expects a little more out of life than just being taken care of?"

"More out of life! That's all I need to hear. What more can she have than a husband with money? A shoe manufacturer with army contracts—perhaps a little crude, not an aristocrat, but what does that matter if he's got the money? And almost sixty-three. She'd have no trouble outliving him."

Camilla could overlook everything in her mother's behavior—the groundless complaints, the unfair reproaches—except her cynicism. At

236

such moments they had nothing in common, and Mama seemed no more than a thick, soft mass surrounding a hard heart. "I'd better go." She got to her feet. "I don't know how long I'll be staying. I'll call you." Her eyes fell on the family photographs arrayed on the grand piano: there they were, all of them assembled, the daughters, the sons-in-law, the grandchildren; only her father's picture was missing.

"Are you going to be seeing Lou?"

"Possibly. I told you, I don't know how long I'm staying." She wanted to be alone. To close the door of the hotel room behind her, turn the key, see no one, speak to no one. She would tell the desk not to put any calls through to her room.

"I'm worried about Lou too. Plays away the nights and sleeps away the days, and every week a new beau. Wasting the best years of her life with chance acquaintances. Right now it's an air force officer, and can you imagine—"

"Please! Spare me. . . ."

"You've been lucky in life, that's all!" It was a sentence that recurred over and over. Depending on Mama's mood, it expressed admiration or envy or, as it did now, a hostile accusation. Then she changed her tone again. "Wait just a minute. I've got a good deal to propose to you. I won't even ask for a commission. It's in your best interest. I've got someone who's willing to pay in Dutch gulden for paintings. I've told him about some of the pictures from the house in Steglitz. You've put them in storage anyway. And gulden! Are you interested? I could arrange something. I really don't want to make a profit from it myself—unless you'd want to share with me."

"Given your enormous number of acquaintances, I'm sure there are several who'd like to sell some pictures." Camilla had to exert a good deal of self-control to remain calm.

"Gulden," her mother began again, "at a time like this. I'd like to steer the business your way." She had returned to the desk and again poured out some Danziger Goldwasser.

"Think about it some more," Camilla said. "Whether you couldn't really give up the marriage brokerage. It would be a disaster for Frau von Schack if she had to resign. Once it meant a lot to you too that she's employed at the court. If it's a matter of money, I'd be glad to contribute."

Emmi Hofmann set down her glass and dropped into the chair, and once again her whole body shook as she laughed. "Oh, don't think

237

I'm doing it just for the money." She poured out another drink. "I enjoy it! All those hard-working gentlemen who can't wait to catch a wife. And the things they want, the illusions they have, though they're all old enough so they should have learned from experience . . . those old donkeys. . . . And the way I describe it in such glowing terms—all the time imagining what's really ahead of them. The money—pah! I could never make your father pay for everything he did to me. Everything always turned out well for him. But I can get my own back on these gentlemen. . . ."

Even in the hall Camilla could still hear her laughter.

3

He was fully aware that some guests thought of the night clerk as a very lowly rung in the hierarchy of hotel service. He did not care; Makowsky loved the night shift, and in the twenty years he had spent behind the reception desk in the Hotel Bristol—he had been hired for the job in 1897—his position had lost none of its charms for him, except that now, at sixty, he had the necessary distance to smile about it all.

True, the day man pocketed better tips, but in compensation Makowsky was spared the hectic pace of arrivals and departures. By the time he came to work, the guests had other concerns than misplaced luggage, lost tickets, and complaints about expensive telephone charges.

The hotel was full to the rafters, and as evening approached, the atmosphere he loved so much set in. The war had not changed this, except to make things even more interesting than before.

One reason was the officers who made up the bulk of the guests—men who seldom stayed more than twenty-four or forty-eight hours and who intended to live as fully as possible in that short span of time. All of them could count on Makowsky. He still had access to a few tickets for theaters, night clubs, revues; and of course he happened to have some special addresses. In peacetime his notebook had contained a few appropriate names, but since the beginning of the war it had turned into an awesome list.

That was not to say that all the action took place away from the hotel; even from his porter's lodge he saw a thing or two. Around nine, ten o'clock of an evening, when the officers, freshly bathed, left their rooms—not using the elevator but walking down the broad central staircase because that way they could make a preliminary survey—the hall was already filled with waiting ladies. Night after night the scene was repeated, as if butterflies were hatching out of their cocoons.

Not all these ladies would have been admitted to the Bristol in years gone by, and even now some of them still slipped in by the side entrance. But even a person as experienced as Makowsky did not always find it easy to draw a clear line. The crowd included too many genuine ladies, members of the highest society, such as the widowed Baroness von Reden, at this moment sweeping in through the revolving door, punctual to the minute as always. On the dot of ten—you could set your watch by her. She seldom stayed longer than an hour, always came alone and usually left escorted, but never went upstairs to one of the rooms. With all her irresponsibility and vitality, she was a woman who knew what she owed her name and her family. Makowsky had known them all for many years—her father, her sisters, and her sisters' husbands.

She made straight for his station, quite indifferent, it seemed, to the attention she aroused.

"Good evening, Baroness."

"Good evening, Makowsky. And let's forget about the 'Baroness.'"

"You're looking splendid again—may I say that?"

It was a rehearsed dialogue, and yet there was nothing false about it. They had known each other for so long, and they knew so much about one another, that they were almost like father and daughter.

"War paint. Sometimes I ask myself what I do it for. The worst is the food. I gain weight if I so much as look at a piece of cake. I must take after my mother. To stick to my hundred and ten pounds is a constant struggle. But if I gain so much as five pounds, I can't bear to look at myself. If at least I could drink with impunity. But so much as a glass of orange liqueur—and I have to forget about supper."

A page had taken her coat, and she leaned against the counter, her purse at her side. "How is your wife's fever?"

"Much better. I guess it isn't going to turn into pneumonia after

240

all. She sends her most heartfelt thanks for the coat. But you mustn't do that again. You give away everything. By the way, I have something for you." He reached under the counter and handed her one of the hotel's envelopes. "Three hundred—I hope you're not disappointed."

"Three hundred strikes me as a very good price."

"Not bad. After all, the case was only vermeil. And that's the way it is, engraved inscriptions always bring down the value."

Makowsky had assumed the job of selling the presents Lou was given by her male acquaintances as farewell souvenirs—mostly cigarette cases, occasionally a ring, a bracelet, a pin. She was embarrassed to sell these trifles herself, and so she had taken Makowsky into her confidence. She did not care about the money so much, although she could always use a supplement to her meager pension and shrunken capital. She simply did not wish to be constantly surrounded by these objects. They only served to remind her that, while it was child's play for her to latch on to a man and to inflame his passions, she could not hold on to any of them.

"Don't you want to count it?"

But she had already picked up the envelope and shoved it deep into her pocket. "Anything special?"

Makowsky understood the question at once; it was part of the nightly ritual. "A few air force officers," he informed her. "Arrived this morning. They spent the day testing new airplanes. Now they are in the ballroom on the second floor, by themselves, no ladies. They ordered their rooms for two nights."

"The usual, then." Lou looked over toward the bar. Sometimes, when the velvet curtain at the doorway was raised, the band could be heard. The three hundred marks would be just enough for two bottles of champagne.

"A few Turks in mufti, probably armament dealers, and one American. He arrived late last night from Hamburg. And your sister. But I'm sure you already know that."

"Camilla! When did she get in?"

"This morning. She went to her room an hour ago. Asked not to be disturbed."

Lou smiled. "You're right—the usual. Nobody would believe that we're sisters, would they?"

"Oh, I wouldn't say that."

"Can you picture her sitting in a bar? Selling jewelry?"

"That doesn't mean anything. Perhaps she'd like to change places with you sometimes."

"Makowsky, my darling—never. Not Camilla. And I wouldn't like to be in her shoes, either."

"Perhaps you would."

Lou shook her head. "The conversation is getting too deep for me," she said. "At this time of night I don't feel like serious talk. Give my regards to Frau Makowsky. Tell her to take care and not get out of bed too soon, so she won't have a relapse."

She walked through the lobby toward the bar, and suddenly two pages were at her side, holding the velvet drape open for her. She loved the moment when, flanked by the pages, she entered the bar and came to a stop at the entrance, abruptly enveloped by the dusk, smoke, warmth and music, to look over the room. It was the same every night and yet always marvelously exciting: the glances turned toward her, the guests who recognized her, the band leader who raised his hand to wave to her and sometimes, if the band had just finished playing a piece, directed them to strike up a particular tune especially for her. Then she forgot the whole long, idle day just past, the empty apartment that was too big for her, too quiet and neat since her husband's death. The pages cleared her way to the bar, and did not withdraw until she had taken her place at the corner seat, the only one still unoccupied. The barman interrupted a conversation with a customer, came to her, took away the "Reserved" sign, and set out a champagne glass and a bowl containing three cigarettes.

"Good evening, Baroness." He could not be weaned away from this form of address either. He poured a sip into the glass, waiting until she had tasted it. "Chilled enough?" And not until she had nodded her approval did he fill the glass. Then he pulled a lighter from his vest pocket and lit her cigarette.

He too had information for her and gave it in a subdued voice. "You should talk to Albert, we've had a shipment of caviar today. And over there, about halfway down the bar, that's the American. White jacket, with his back to you."

"Alone?"

"He's been sitting there for an hour. Doesn't dance, drinks his own whiskey. I guess he doesn't trust ours." He pushed the ashtray a bit closer. "Is it really chilled enough, the champagne?"

242

As always, the bar was crowded, and he had to repeatedly wait on the other customers, but she could always count on his attention. Of course his and everyone else's interest had something to do with her name, her connection to nobility, as well as with the tips she handed out. But there was a deeper cause; quite simply, everyone liked her because wherever she turned up, things got loud and cheerful.

She sat still, her head leaning against the paneled wall, taking an occasional sip of champagne, humming along with the band, her eyes wandering. She wore her hair far down into her forehead, parted in the middle, and so heavily pomaded that it gleamed like the silk ribbon stretched across it. She watched the American, his back, his dark hair, a little longer than everyone else's. She was in no hurry to attract his attention. That was not her way. She let things come to her. It was better than everything that came later, this hour of waiting to see what was going to happen.

Three young officers were sitting next to her. They were drinking a lot and throwing dice on the bar to see who would pay for the next round. The bar phone rang. The bartender picked up the receiver, nodded, and approached the three officers. Lou could not hear what he said, but when they paid at once and left, she knew that in an hour they would probably be sitting in a darkened train, heading toward the front.

In the confusion she had not noticed that the American had also risen and was about to leave the bar. He freed himself from two girls who were about to take his arms. He passed her, looked surprised, stopped, spread his arms wide. "Lou! Would you believe it!"

She looked in his eyes, heard his voice, smiled automatically, and was still not sure where she had met him. He kissed her on both cheeks, then stepped back to get a better look at her.

"Don't tell me that you don't recognize me. How long has it been? Sixteen years?"

She still did not know who this man standing before her was. Sixteen years . . . that meant she had been twenty at the time. Now she was thirty-six. "Just as long as you recognize me."

Sixteen years. . . . The man's face was deeply tanned, and when a strand of hair fell over his forehead, it began to dawn on her: New Year's Eve, the dinner, the ball, the laundry room. . . . Still uncertain, she said, "Keith, isn't it?"

243

"It took you a long time."

"It's been a long time."

He sat down next to her and made a gesture that took in the whole room. "I don't know, my picture of Germany was different. I didn't think anything like this was possible. I brought my own whiskey, and a wool blanket. I was sure the hotels would not be heated. From what I read in the papers at home, all of Germany is hungry and cold."

"What you see here is another country."

"I noticed that."

"When did you get here?"

"Last night."

"Oh, then you're *that* American." She laughed at his expression. "We don't see many of you here, not any more. What are you doing here? Besides seeking out an old love. We *are* an old love, aren't we?"

She was still unable to recall exactly what had happened between them, how far it had gone. She remembered a very, very young man in comparison to whom she felt incredibly grown-up, while now she had the feeling that he was older than she was. With a dreamy smile she hummed the tune "Long Ago But Not Forgotten," and when she realized that he did not understand, she asked again, "Why are you really here?"

"A very boring job. I'm buying up patents. As long as it's possible."

"You own breweries, is that right?"

"Right. But let's talk about something else. Is there someplace that's not so noisy?"

She beckoned to the bartender, and after a few whispered words she said, "They'll give us a quiet corner." She walked ahead, one hand gathering up her long gown. A man in uniform made a sign to her as he danced past, and she answered it by raising her hand slightly.

In the semicircular recess, upholstered in red and far away from the band and the dance floor, the "Reserved" sign disappeared as soon as they took their seats. She whispered with the maitre d', and when he had left, she said, "You'll allow me to play host to you, won't you? Or is that indecent?"

"It's unusual."

The waiter brought a silver bucket with ice, the neck of a champagne bottle sticking out over the edge. Lou felt happy here; she knew that in the reddish dusk that permeated the niche she looked younger. She picked up her glass, laid her other hand on Keith's arm, and proposed a toast: "To you, to chance, and to everything chance brings."

He set down his glass. "Do you come here often?"

"Every night."

"Alone?"

"No one stays alone here for long."

"I understand."

"Maybe. Maybe not. It isn't important. Are you staying long?"

"It's hard to tell, the way things are right now. If possible, I'll stay a while. I'd like to see them all again, your family. How is Camilla?"

"Is the champagne cold enough for you?"

"I tried to call her, but they said she was in Berlin."

"You telephoned her?"

"It was the only number I was given."

"I'm in the directory."

"I didn't think of that. And your father?"

"Just the same. Papa always knew how to live."

"How old is he now?"

"Let's see—he'll be seventy-two this year."

"And your mother? While Aunt Lenka was alive, I used to be kept up to date. She was the only one who wrote me long letters. Your parents are still living apart?"

"That's not about to change."

"And you lost your husband?"

Yes, but I don't brood about it. It was horrible because it was so senseless, but not because I lost him. Please let's not talk about it. I'd rather you told me about yourself. You're married?" He was not wearing a wedding ring, but that meant nothing.

"Not any more."

"Oh, I didn't know. Is it all right to ask why?"

"If only I knew. Perhaps you were one of the reasons. Once Aunt Lenka sent me a picture of you. You wore a dress like this one, low-cut. My wife got very angry about it. She treated me to a full-scale jealousy scene—she was very good at making scenes. By the end there was only one subject left we could talk sensibly about, and that was the brewery. She was an extremely capable business-woman."

245

"That sounds like Camilla." She could have bitten her tongue for having brought the conversation back to Camilla, and she quickly rose to her feet. "Will you dance with me?"

He was a good dancer. Her head nestled comfortably on his shoulder, and her fingers toyed with the hair at the nape of his neck. "All day I've had a good feeling," she said softly. He did not answer, but she felt him pulling her closer.

"It really is a miracle," she said. "How did you get here in the middle of a war?"

"By boat."

"And you're going back by boat too?"

"Of course."

"A big boat?"

"Pretty big."

She closed her eyes. The idea that there were still boats, luxury liners that crossed the ocean with their bright lights, fascinated her. She pictured New York, the ships entering the harbor. Her thoughts went on to other things—not the brewery; she was content to dream about all the money it earned. "You're an excellent dancer."

"It's the first time in years. My wife thought the new dances were scandalous."

"You used to say that you would only consider a wife from Germany."

"Is that what I said? I guess it would have been the smart thing to do." And without a pause he added, "Do you know where Camilla stays when she's in Berlin?"

"Didn't they tell you that when you telephoned Neustrelitz?"

"No. They had instructions not to tell."

"That's so typical of her. She wouldn't want anyone to think that she'd allow herself any luxury."

Fortunately the dance came to an end, but when they were back at their table, he continued the conversation. "Are you on the outs with Camilla?"

"Did you ever hear of anyone fighting with a saint? Camilla is our family saint. We all know she exists, but we only catch rare glimpses of her. She bestows her gifts across the land and disappears in a cloud of incense."

"That doesn't sound very much like affection."

"We never had much between us. We're like fire and water."

"You're the fire? She's the water?"

"Something like that. Every time I run into her, I'm not myself for a couple of days. I keep thinking I ought to make myself useful in some way. She doesn't have to say anything, it just happens. All she knows is work. Do you think I've ever once seen her here in the bar, in all the years she's been staying here—"

It slipped out against her will, and Keith was on top of it at once. "She's staying here, at the Bristol?"

"Yes."

"You mean here in the hotel? Do you know if she's in? Maybe the two of us could—"

"You can try. Yes, she's staying here, and I know she's in her room. I told you, sometimes she's here for days and I don't get to see her. When I try to fix a meeting with her, she always fusses around with her appointment calendar. She's meeting her lawyer, she has to run from office to office, what do I know. A woman with an appointment calendar! And every other word out of her mouth has to do with soap."

"It's hard to imagine."

"The dreamy girl of long ago? You'll be surprised. Her head is full of business, that's all. She's one hundred percent materialist—and I'm not exaggerating."

"The man she married—"

"Oh, that was a pure stroke of luck. A real nobody. When I heard about it, when it first happened, I felt sorry for her. But all of us were wrong. Papa would say only a dark horse can bring high odds. Anyway, she bet on him. . . ."

She felt they had talked quite enough about Camilla. She asked him to dance again, but she noticed that his mind was not really on it. From time to time he turned his head, looking toward the door to the bar as if Camilla might appear. How stupid of her to have let it slip about the hotel! It would be best to take Keith away from here, take him somewhere else, where he would no longer be able to think that he and Camilla were under the same roof.

"I'm beginning to get hungry," Lou said. "It always happens around this time. I know a restaurant near here. What do you think? A little walk and a nice supper. And then . . ." she did not complete the sentence. There were some men who didn't like you to make sug-

247

gestions too directly; they preferred to think of it themselves and for the woman to be slightly reluctant. "Well, we'll see what we do then. In any case, a reunion like ours calls for a celebration."

They did not return to their table but left the bar at once. The page brought her coat, and while she waited for Keith to come back from his room, she still had visions of the boat, the large luxury liner, gleaming white in a dark-blue sea. This really could turn out to be a lucky day if she played her cards right. And in addition he was good-looking. A vision of a man as he came down the broad staircase, tall, dark, a tanned, slightly melancholy face. With satisfaction she noted that he was making an impression on others as well; she had never been frightened of competition.

He handed his key to the night clerk and asked a question. Lou could not hear Makowsky's answer, but she saw him shake his head. Keith asked for some paper, wrote a few lines, and Makowsky placed the folded sheet into one of the pigeonholes at his back.

It was snowing outside. Isolated flakes floated straight to the ground, glittering in the brightly lit courtyard of the hotel. Lou put her hand in the crook of Keith's arm. He had his hands in his coat pockets; when Lou sneaked her hand in with his, he hesitated a moment. Then his hand closed over hers, and slowly the feeling grew in her which might not be love but which Lou preferred to all others: he didn't have a chance of getting away.

4

As soon as the Steglitz water tower became visible from the train window, there was no holding the children in their seats.

Heavily wrapped, their ice skates slung across their shoulders, they pushed their way to the windows. Their voices filled the compartment, and their shouts and gaiety increased when, in the station, other boys and girls from other compartments also rushed out.

It had snowed all night, but now the sky was cloudless and sunny. In the city neither snow nor sun could soften the picture of the dark lines of people in front of the grocery stores and shelters, but out here the extravagant whiteness and the blue sky created the illusion of a world at peace, and Camilla was glad that she had decided to come out so early.

The station was just as it was in her memories. Even the old advertising boards were still there, the Sarotti Moor, the Senoussi caravan, the hot-air balloon filled with bottles of Burgeff champagne. And next to the gate she even discovered the old automat with the horoscopes. Rust had destroyed the bright paint, but it seemed to work still; she had no trouble turning the pointer to November—Camilla was a Scorpio—and the apparatus swallowed her coin. But nothing further happened; it neither spewed out the horoscope card nor returned her money. Camilla took this failure almost as if it were a human reaction, as though the machine were expressing its disapproval of her sentimental gesture.

She looked for the old path, a shortcut running along the brook, but the watercourse must have been leveled or filled in. In any case she could not find it, and she returned to the road. When they had bought the house from the bank in 1914 and returned to Steglitz for the first time in thirteen years, she had found many changes, and even now there were things that were new to her: houses that had been built in the meantime, building sites where the work had had to be stopped because of the war, and of course gardens that had been transformed into fields of turnips and potatoes. And everywhere along the houses the disfiguring black pipes of the iron stoves, run through the windows into the open as a makeshift measure.

As the gable of the house rose up in the distance, she began to walk faster, half impatient, half fearful of the changes she might find. The gate to the drive stood open, and a Red Cross ambulance was just pulling out.

Except for the vehicle, one might have thought that the house was empty. Though the shutters were open, the lack of curtains behind the windows created the impression of empty rooms. She looked along the front of the house—her house. In Neustrelitz, the thought of the house was always something from which she could draw strength, but now she felt only that it belonged to her and yet did not belong to her. Suddenly the war seemed like a rising flood: run as fast as she might, it rose inexorably higher and higher and would one day engulf the whole world.

She was startled by a noise, a rushing and clattering in the air, followed by a muffled thud as the snow, loosened from the roof, hit the ground. The almost flat roof had often caused trouble in the winter. When it was very cold, the icicles had to be knocked off the eaves, and after every heavy snowfall the roof had to be cleared to keep the weight from becoming too great.

A man wielding a broad snow shovel stood on the roof just beneath a chimney. As he stepped to one side, Camilla thought she heard the slates cracking under his heavy boots.

Another avalanche came rushing down. Once more a white powdery column stood in the air for seconds, then sank into a little heap. The cleared place revealed the red cross that had been painted on the roof. Would they be able to remove the paint later on, or would it be necessary to install new slates? She smiled at herself and thought, it really is *my house*!

The three shallow steps to the front door had been swept and strewn with reddish salt. The stone flags were deeply cracked. The door lacked both the name plate and the bell pull. Leather padding on the jamb kept the door from ever closing tightly.

She entered hesitantly but stopped after a few steps, disturbed by the smell that greeted her. The very special odor of the house—the scent of the wood paneling mixed with that of flowers brought to the house on a large tray and divided among the many vases in all the rooms—had always remained so vivid to her that it had never occurred to her that it might change. But now the house was suffused with a penetrating odor, a mixture of foods and medication, so that for an instant she thought she would be sick.

Still other changes struck her, and each one gave her as much pain as if they had been carried out on her own body: the nails that had been hammered into the wood panels in the lounge because the cloakroom was no longer adequate; the dented, scuffed door frames; the iron knobs that replaced the brass handles on the doors; and the broken dowels in the banister that lined the broad staircase leading upstairs from the lounge.

The folding doors to the dining room opened. A Red Cross nurse was pushing a cart holding bandages and instruments. Through the open door Camilla saw a straight row of iron bedsteads, and in them figures lying flat on their backs, most of them with thickly bandaged heads.

The nurse did not seem to see her in the gloom of the hall. Without looking to the right or left, she pushed her cart toward another room—it was the parlor—and as she opened the door, Camilla was greeted with the same picture as before, except that this time she thought she could hear moans, and the antiseptic odor that filled the lounge mingled with the stench of rot.

After the nurse had disappeared there was silence. Suddenly the house seemed deserted, and Camilla felt as if she had seen things that did not really exist. This feeling was so strong that she mistrusted the sound that now assailed her ears: single notes struck on an out-of-tune piano. It came from the conservatory, and she followed it. The plants were all gone, with the exception of an overgrown rubber plant. Some of the old wicker chairs stood along the glass wall, and newspapers were spread out on a table. The man at the piano, dressed in pajamas of washed-out blue flannel, was picking out broken

251

chords, thirds, fourths, fifths, with his left hand. She waited for him to use his right hand as well, until she noticed that the right sleeve was dangling empty from the shoulder.

He stopped playing abruptly. He raised his shoulders and turned his head. For an instant his face seemed gray and old, but when he smiled, it turned very young. He had the mouth of a child and probably was not much older than Max. "Are you looking for someone? One of the patients here? Visiting hours won't start for a while. They're very strict about that."

"I heard you play," Camilla said.

"It's too bad that there are more compositions for four hands than for one." He did not sound bitter, but rather as if he wished to help her over her embarrassment.

"I'm looking for the gardener. Don't let me disturb you." She had only one desire: to get outside, to breathe fresh air. With difficulty she pushed open the outer door, which was stuck. The young man had begun to play again. She inhaled deeply and looked out at the grounds, across the broad expanse of snow glittering in the sun, the trees, the blue sky.

She could not see anyone at the gardener's cottage, but smoke was rising from the chimney. She went in that direction, certain that Willeke would soon turn up. The hothouses seemed to be in use, since the panes of glass were not frozen over but covered with steam. She heard laughter, the dusky sound of a man's voice and the bright trill of a woman's, and then through the misty glass she saw the outlines of a couple, closely entwined, standing among the plants and kissing.

She went on, past a mound of earth covered with snow. She had almost reached the cottage when she heard Willeke's voice, loud and threatening: "How often do I have to tell you! Find someplace else!"

When Camilla turned around, she saw the couple come out of the hothouse, Willeke in hot pursuit. He was brandishing his fists in the air, uttering oaths, but the nurse only laughed and fastened her cap as she ran.

Willeke had always been a man who took as much care with his appearance as with his paths, but as he approached Camilla, she saw that an unkempt beard, rusty brown flecked with white, covered his face, and one of the pockets of his three-quarter-length jacket was

252

torn. He was hatless; a black-and-green scarf was twisted twice about his throat.

He came toward her, his eyes slitted with suspicion, until he recognized her and stopped in midstep, staring at her in consternation. Not quite certain, he stretched out his hand tentatively "Excuse my language, but it's the only way to talk to riffraff like that. In my hothouse, of all places. . . . Those nurses certainly carry on. If I didn't lock it up every night. . . . Fräulein Camilla . . . you don't mind if I go on calling you that, it's hard for me to get used to anything else. Nobody told me you were coming. If I'd known, I'd have spruced myself up a little." He stared at the big house, and the hostile expression returned to his face. "Have you been inside?"

"Yes, but—"

"Oh, I keep track of everything, you can rest assured. I report it all to your lawyer, every brass fitting they take down, every sink they tear out. I can't stop any of it, not in the house, but I keep after all of it, and I make him sign everything in my notebook, the administrator, with the date. He's scared of me, believe me. They've got to make it all good one of these days."

Camilla thought about the odor in the house and wondered whether it would be possible ever to get rid of it. She said, "It's good that you're here."

"Sometimes there are more than a hundred of them. They cram it as full as they can. And the staff on top of that. Sometimes I think it would have been better after all if you'd moved in at the time."

A silence ensued, then Willeke continued. "All I know is, I want to live long enough to see you live here again. I do what I can. I've already stopped leaving for any reason. I can't stop much of what they do in the house, but out here, I keep them in check, believe me, at gunpoint if I have to. Guess what, they were going to cut down the walnut tree the other day, when they ran out of wood. The walnut tree your father planted! And how we all waited for it to bear fruit for the first time! Six years without a single nut, and then it started—remember, twelve nuts the seventh year, isn't that right?"

His whole appearance seemed to change as he spoke. His bearing was more erect, his eyes began to glow, and then he made a broad gesture with his hands. "Nothing will happen to the grounds, you

253

can depend on that. What a day this is, eh? You really picked the best one. And you look good. A little pale. Years ago, I remember, you used to have your summer color even in winter. But it'll come back to you, you'll see, just as soon as you live here. And your husband? Good news? I'll never forget the first time he came here, with your father, and wandered through the grounds. How he looked around! He fell in love with the place right away; he didn't have to tell me, I could see for myself. You do have good news of him?"

"Yes." The last letter had come ten days ago. A long time during a war, and a lot could have happened. . . . The gardener's presence had dimmed her anxiety for a moment, but now it came back to life and with it the image of the rising flood.

"That's what I live for, that day, I want to be here to see it, when everything here is as it used to be."

"What about the sewer installation? Dr. Kautsky said there was trouble."

"Does that surprise you? More than a hundred people—and suddenly they say the fault is with the pipes, that they're too small, and with the runoff. And how there's trouble! The water was rising in the cellar, but where do they expect it to run off to, the way they use it? The ground here is six feet of clay, you can't expect the water to sink in."

"What is to be done?"

"They wanted to drain the whole area, dig up all of it, though it wouldn't have helped a bit. I made a deal with 'em, they could lay new pipes down to the main sewer, that has to be enough. We're doing it now, and by spring I can reseed the place."

He turned away, toward the drive, like someone catching a scent. Then Camilla also heard the noise of the motor.

"They're bringing coke," Willeke explained. "If you'll excuse me, I have to be there. If I don't watch them, they'll throw the whole load on the flowerbeds at the side of the house. You'll stay a little longer, won't you? I harvested the nuts in the fall, you'll have to take some with you."

"I'll walk around a little."

"That's a good idea. I've cleared some of the paths. Look—didn't I tell you, he's heading straight for the beds." And the gardener rushed off.

The grounds had not changed, and the paths were shoveled as

before, their edges neatly trimmed. The sun was stronger than it had been in the morning, and occasionally a little clump of snow fell from a branch. When she stopped and looked back at the house, she was reminded of what she had seen there, but the longer she walked, the more the house receded from her thoughts. In the silence that surrounded her, in the expanse of the grounds, another feeling gradually arose: hope of survival. She would live through the war. She need only believe in it, just as she had believed that one day this house would belong to her again. It did belong to her, and one day she would live in it again, too. . . .

"Camilla! Camilla!"

She did not stop; she did not think the voice was real. It belonged to her image of the future: someone was calling her because a particular plant had flowered in the hothouse, or someone wanted to show her the spoor of a wild animal.

"Camilla . . . Camilla. . . ."

She turned her head and was convinced that her eyes, blinded by the bright sunlight on the snow, were playing a trick on her. The man came through the thick snow, first only a narrow silhouette in the prevailing whiteness. Then she could make out the half-boots, the sand-colored jacket, the dark hair. The sun was blinding her to such an extent that she still could not recognize his face, but then she remembered the note that morning in her hotel pigeonhole.

He had caught up with her. Out of breath after running through the high snow, he stood before her. He did not take his hands out of his jacket pockets. "What a beautiful day," he said, still out of breath.

He had changed hardly at all; the passage of time showed only in the lines around his eyes and on his forehead. Somehow she was sorry that he had brought her back into the present from her dream of the future.

"Why are you running from me?"

"Running *away*—in German we use an adverb for this phrase."

"At least now I'm sure it's you. All right then, why are you running away from me?"

"Did I do that?"

"Didn't you get my note?"

"Of course I did. But I had to leave very early. How did you know I was here?"

"When they told me you'd already left and hadn't left a message, I asked the desk clerk. He thought you must have gone to the hospital."

"I had to be there at seven o'clock."

"Yes, I know. I drove there, but you'd already gone."

"You saw my father in the hospital?"

"Yes, he was the one who told me you planned to come out here." He unbuttoned his jacket and looked around. "Everything's just as it used to be. Your father said you'd bought the house again."

She nodded and started on the path to the gardener's cottage.

"Do you remember my last day? I wanted it to snow, and in the last night the snow came."

"When did you get to Germany?"

"Day before yesterday."

"Is it really so easy to come over from America?"

"Not so easy, but if you have connections at the embassy, it can be done."

"Will you be staying a long time?"

"If you promise never to run away from me again, yes." But then he grew serious. "I can't say, really. We're not at war yet, but it looks as if we can't avoid it. This morning I had an interview at the embassy. It doesn't look good."

His words had finally brought her all the way back to reality. The penetrating medicinal odor in the house, the young man with the empty right sleeve sitting at the piano in the conservatory—it all returned. She looked at Keith, and this time she found him completely changed, another person entirely from the one she remembered.

They had reached the gardener's cottage, overgrown with ivy. On the side of the house that got the morning sun, a bench had been set out. She sat down to wait for Willeke. Keith remained standing before her.

"What are we going to do today?" he asked.

"What do you mean?"

"I thought we could do something together that would be fun for you. It's such a beautiful day."

"I can't. I've got to go back tonight. I have to see my father once more at the hospital, and then I have a couple of meetings. I've stayed here too long as it is."

256

"Then Lou was right."

"Lou? You saw Lou?"

"I ran into her. Last night at the hotel."

"And the two of you had nothing better to do than talk about me."

"It just happened. Are you as hard-working as she says you are?"

"Is that really the word she used? Or did she say that I've become dreadfully materialistic, a person with no other thought in her head than business?"

"Something like that, sure."

"Then you were prepared for what you'd find."

He did not get a chance to answer, for Willeke appeared. First he was surprised to find another visitor with Camilla, but when his memory nudged him, he was beside himself with joy. As if a well had suddenly been tapped, reminiscences came pouring out—anecdotes and events from long ago that even Camilla had long forgotten. There was no end to it, something more always occurred to him, until she could not stand it any longer and said she must leave. He walked with them to the gate, still talking, happy to forget the present that would catch up with him again soon enough.

"That was almost rude, the way you suddenly wanted to get away," Keith said.

"What's the sense of it! So many memories. We can't live on memories!" Surprised, she stared at the motor and driver parked at the gate, where Keith was leading her. "Is that your automobile?"

"We have the use of it. All day if we like. The embassy put it at my disposal."

"An embassy car? Are you such an important person?"

"Well, how about it?"

"No," she answered. "I don't have time."

"But Camilla! One day! By rights I should be on the way to Oranienburg and Neu-Ruppin—urgent business, very important conferences. I'll postpone them, just for you."

She shook her head.

"Then at least let me drive you back to town? And we'll plan something for tonight. Surely you don't *have* to go back home."

"Thank you. But I like the walk to the railroad station. Really I do. And it was nice to have seen you again. Perhaps I'll be back in Berlin in a few days, and if you're still here, and if you have the time, perhaps we could have dinner together at the hotel."

He made no further attempt to detain her, and as she walked along the road, she could hear the motor starting. Why did you treat him like that, she asked herself. Why don't you ever allow yourself a little time off? Turn around and call him back. But she did not do it.

At the railroad station two green-and-white cars stood in readiness; there was still time before the departure, and the few people who were going into the city at this time of day were walking up and down on the platform, presumably because it was warmer in the sun than in the compartments.

Camilla had just bought her ticket when a motorcar stopped at the curb and Keith jumped out. He raised his hands. "Don't worry! I'm not trying to talk you into anything. But we didn't say a proper goodbye to each other."

He discovered the horoscope automat. Perhaps he remembered; in any case, he pulled a coin out of his pocket and was about to insert it.

"It doesn't work any more," Camilla said. "I tried earlier, when I got here. It swallows the money and doesn't give anything back."

"No?" Keith's fist hit the side of the machine once, twice, and abruptly the machine gave forth a rattle, a card fell out, and shortly afterward, with a clatter, it returned the coin as well. Keith held up both, the horoscope card and the coin. His eyes were dancing. "Scorpio—is that you?"

"Yes."

"Shall I read it to you?"

"But hurry." A woman conductor had appeared, clad in a long coat that blew about her legs and sporting a tin whistle on a chain around her neck. She walked by the cars, hoarsely urging the travelers to get on board. Keith looked at the horoscope card: "You expect too much of yourself. Your strength is not inexhaustible. Think of yourself for once. You are not responsible for the whole world."

"It doesn't say that! Show me!" She heard the conductress slamming the first door. "I have to get on."

"Of course," he said. "Otherwise you'll miss your train."

She went to one of the open doors. "Is that really what it says on the card?"

"Get in," he said. "Or they'll leave you behind." He leaned forward, took her in his arms, and kissed her without haste or clumsy

258

ardor, as if there were unlimited time. It had come so unexpectedly and yet seemed so natural that she put up no resistance. Only afterward she said, "What are you doing?"

"Isn't it done?" he asked. "Surely everybody kisses when they say goodbye at railroad stations, don't they?"

Not exactly like this, she thought, but she did not say it. Somehow she expected him to get on with her, but he only shook her hand. She went up the steps, and then someone slammed the door.

She wanted to open the window, but it was stuck. She saw him standing on the platform. His lips were moving, but she could not understand what he was saying through the closed window, and then the train started.

For a while she could still see him as he stood on the platform and waved. But when the train sped up, he faded from her line of vision.

Camilla took a window seat and looked back. Coming through the panes of glass, the sun was stronger and warmer than outside.

She tried to remember why it was so essential that she return to Neustrelitz this very day. She closed her eyes, enjoying the warmth that gradually penetrated and suffused her body. A great calm came over her, nothing seemed important any longer, there was no hurry about anything. To remain like this for a while—it was all she wanted.

5

Makowsky came on duty at eight o'clock each evening. There were routine chores he had to attend to before he could make himself comfortable and settle down. In his case that meant to lay out the crossword puzzle books in readiness for the quiet night hours and to ask a page to take into the kitchen the tea he had brought from home—he had to be careful of his gallbladder. Then he picked up the freshly written list of arrivals and departures. He was about to begin looking it over, when Frau Senger, the wife of the industrialist, entered the lobby.

A look at the check-out list told him that her name was not entered. He took her key from the hook—Room 308—as well as the envelope waiting for her in the pigeonhole. He could not keep himself from expressing his astonishment. "I thought you were leaving today. Are you staying longer?"

"Yes, I may be."

He searched for an explanation, and only one occurred to him. "The operation—did it go well? I hope there are no complications?"

"No, no, everything is fine. I went to the hospital this afternoon. Herr Hoffmann asked me to thank you for your good wishes."

"Then everything went well. And you're staying until after the second operation."

They had discussed it thoroughly that morning. With all the personal interest he displayed, Makowsky was someone who never made you feel that he was intruding. Even so, Camilla now thought: Is that the only reason he can understand, that I'm staying because of my father? She was tempted to say something, but she suppressed it. "I can't say yet how long I'll be staying."

"You know, for me your father, if I may be allowed to say so, embodies all the good old days. Everyone here in the hotel was glad when he came. Everybody liked waiting on him. I always say it's also up to the guests to create the atmosphere in a hotel. Bad guests, bad service. How about it? Would you let me reserve a nice table for you?"

She took the key and the envelope. The latter, stamped with the address of the Naval Procurement Office, presumably contained the written notice that the case against her had been dropped. "No other messages for me?"

The clerk checked the pigeonhole again and actually pulled out a slip of paper. "Excuse me, I overlooked it. A message from the switchboard. You are to telephone to Neustrelitz."

"Oh, that. I took care of it."

"And now how about a nice table?"

"I'll have supper in my room."

"I'll send Albert up."

"Thanks, that won't be necessary. I'll have the usual."

"Really. Let's see: tea, double portion with cold milk, white bread, butter, a little ham, some cheese. Sent up in one hour."

"That's right."

Makowsky pulled out the wake-up schedule. "And a call for six-thirty in the morning."

"I didn't say that. Tomorrow, for a change, I don't want a wake-up call." He nodded, but the way his pencil dropped betrayed his consternation. A natural reaction, and he surely thought nothing of it. A desk clerk, after all, was there to remember the habits of regular guests, and six-thirty in the morning was her normal time. But she remained lost in thought as she walked through the lobby and walked up the stairs because too many people were waiting for the elevator. Her mother had never gotten out of bed before ten in the morning, and her sisters kept the same habits. You never saw Maxi emerge from her rooms before noon, and ever since she had moved in with the Sengers, Frau Ewers had had to bring her breakfast in bed. What

261

if she, Camilla, were suddenly to expect the same treatment—the astonishment that it would cause throughout the house could not be imagined.

The sliding doors to the Blue Salon on the second floor stood open. Two waiters were busy setting the long table; twelve silver plates were already laid, along with glasses, flowers, and right in the middle a many-layered cake topped with a chocolate airplane. The Blue Salon was something like an established institution for Berlin family celebrations, and Camilla would have been hard put to say how many times her own family had occupied it. This is where they had celebrated her sisters' engagements, the christening of Maxi's first baby, the promotion of Lou's husband to first lieutenant—or had it been captain? And the last time they had gathered here had been on the occasion of Aunt Lenka's funeral. Would the time ever come when all of them would be sitting around this table again? Surely not. Lou's and Maxi's husbands were dead, and who knew what else would happen before the war came to an end. . . .

"Excuse me."

She stepped aside for a waiter pushing a cart holding the polished silver place settings.

What more would happen? Years ago, before the war, such a thought had been full of pleasurable anticipation, full of curiosity and unformed wishes for the future. Now it was nothing more than an expression of anxiety and worry, and one had to rejoice if nothing happened, if time stood still.

Rapidly she walked on. The idea that any moment now she would be in her room, able to close the door behind her, calmed her.

She liked the room. It was not the double she had always shared with her husband; 308 was a single on the top floor, at the end of the corridor. It faced north, with a view of the sandstone facade of a ministry on the other side of the street, and when she stood in the small alcove, she could watch the guard in front of the closed Russian embassy.

There were rooms that were more quiet, facing the garden, but she liked the street noises, especially in the early morning hours. The room was small, cozy because it was in a corner, its walls covered with gray silk. The marble bathroom was almost larger than the room itself. As always when she returned after a long day, the first thing she did after taking off her coat was to go into the bathroom and turn on the taps to fill the tub. Catching sight of the mauve toilet soap in the porcelain holders at the sink and the tub, Camilla felt herself smiling.

On her bed, still wrapped, lay the box with the housecoat she had bought and had delivered to the hotel that morning. The telephone on the nightstand reminded her momentarily of the conversation she had had with her household in Neustrelitz when she had called from the hospital.

"You're not coming home tonight?" At first it was Frau Ewers on the wire, then Maxi, and finally she had spoken with the boys. They had all responded as if the world were coming to an end. "But surely you're coming on the early train tomorrow. You're not? For heaven's sake what has happened?" As if something had to have happened! Did she always have to behave like clockwork? Didn't she have the right to grant herself a respite? Did she have to get permission first? Be accountable, why and how? Had it come to that?

She put out the "Do Not Disturb" sign, undressed, and climbed into the tub. She liked hotels; she felt at ease in them, perhaps because a hotel was the exact opposite of a home. Only a hotel was full of so many different noises—and the bathroom, with its marble tub and its many pipes and faucets, was like a big ear that heard everything. That too was something she liked: the image of all the rooms and all the people, hundreds of strangers under a single roof and busy with something, mostly very simple things and thoughts— what to wear, where to go, what to have for dinner. These rooms were genuine sanctuaries. Whatever occurred in them they kept to themselves, always ready to shelter the next guest and grant him the same protection.

She stayed in the tub longer than usual. Then, the large heated towel across her shoulders, she undid the string on the package. She was usually frugal and conservative in matters of dress, but when it came to housecoats she was lavish, almost extravagant. She already owned more than a dozen, but this morning when she had noticed the kimono of black and purple quilted silk in the store window, she had been determined at once to acquire it. As she pulled it on and looked at herself in the mirror, she had already forgotten the insanely high price she had paid for it.

She took in the "Do Not Disturb" sign, did not lock the door again, lowered the lights, and sat down in the alcove. The street was quiet. It would not come to life again until the theaters emptied. She did not rise to her feet when there was a knock on the door; the floor waiter opened the door and wheeled in the serving cart.

"Good evening, madam. I have your order."

She had never asked his name, and she was just about to when she noticed that there were two place settings on the cart, two bowls under silver covers, and an ice bucket with the neck of a bottle peering out.

"There must be some mistake. Room three hundred and eight. I ordered the same as always."

He pushed the cart a little closer. "This is the order for three o' eight." He pulled the bill out from under a napkin. "Three o' eight. Precisely. If you'd be so good as to sign here?"

"But I told you, there's a mistake." She leaned forward and raised the lid of a round tureen. "Potato soup . . . never."

"I'll check it out."

"Take the cart with you when you go."

The waiter glanced at the bill and then at her, undecided as to how to proceed.

Neither of them could have heard the knock, or perhaps there was no knock. Whatever the case, Keith was already standing in the center of the room when they became aware of his presence. His bearing and step were slightly hesitant. Obviously he had heard some of the discussion, for he said, "There's no mistake about the order. I changed it. I thought, after such a long day we've earned a proper meal." And turning to the waiter, he added, "It's all right. It's not your fault. You may go now."

The waiter bowed and backed out of the room. When he was gone Keith said, "If you ask me what the word 'European' means, I'd have to answer: a waiter in the Bristol. You don't mind that I changed your order, do you? No, don't get up, I'll push the table closer. And I really mean it, both of us have spent a long, hard day."

He pushed the cart—really a table on wheels—into the alcove, locked the wheels, took a chair for himself, and sat down across from her.

All his actions had the same matter-of-factness with which he had kissed her at the train station, and suddenly she burst into laughter. "Do you have much practice in such sudden attacks?"

"I'm going against my real nature, that's all."

"Were you really in Oranienburg and Neu-Ruppin today?"

"Of course. Duty before pleasure. You reminded me just in time. But now we've done our duty."

He took up a napkin and unfolded it. "So you stayed after all."

"I thought why not."

"You went against your nature too. And nobody complained?"

"Everybody complained. I think that only made me more determined. So often I've said to myself, one day, sometime or other, you'll simply go out on strike."

"You're learning."

"Oh, I could be a good pupil. But how did you know that I was here?"

"I spied on you. The old traditional tactic. Wait in the lobby, hidden behind a newspaper."

"You were in the lobby?"

"Yes, and when I saw you I thought to myself, give her an hour. Then I called room service and changed the order."

"Then let's see what you have to offer."

"I didn't want to go too far. No champagne. Only some wine for you and beer for me. And a very simple meal. Potato soup—they say it's particularly good here—and quenelles of fish with dill sauce. As I remember, you used to—"

"Please," she interrupted. "Do me a favor. It's everybody's topic today. Do you remember. . . . I don't want to hear about it anymore, about the old days, about the past, about yesterday, about what used to be. And nothing about tomorrow and what will be someday. Today—that's what I want, this hour. Nothing but today and this moment. All right, let's eat. I think I really am hungry."

This was something he could not know. As a child she had eaten a lot and passionately, even though "none of it stuck to her ribs," as her nanny had always complained. Nowadays Camilla did not care for food. It had become an obligation, and when she left the table she had generally already forgotten what she had been served. But tonight she was hungry and ate with zest; it was as if she were rediscovering a skill she had lost. Perhaps it was only that for once she did not have to think of others—as in Neustrelitz, where there were always at least nine at table—but that, instead, someone was thinking of her, taking care of her, concerned at every moment to anticipate her wishes, handing her the salt before she stretched out her hand.

They did not speak again of the old times, and they also avoided anything that might be too personal. Even so, enough remained. She told him about buying the kimono; he told her about the deal he had negotiated in Neu-Ruppin. Camilla tried to prolong the meal, and when there was a knock and the waiter appeared to clear the dishes, she had the feeling that everything else would also come to an end if the table were rolled away, and so she said, "Leave everything and bring us some dessert . . . perhaps some ice cream—yes, a double portion of vanilla." When he returned with it, she asked for tea, but only to be brought in later, shortly before the floor kitchen closed. But this extension of time also passed, the tray with the tea stood before her, and she was left with silence. And when Keith rose, she knew what he was going to say, and he used the precise words. "It was a lovely evening."

She still did not want the evening to end, but what could she do to prolong it? From the beginning she had known that there would be only this short hour, only today, no tomorrow.

She stepped to the window in the alcove. Snow-covered roofs over dark buildings; only in the ministry across the way one window was lit up, and she remembered that it had been the same on earlier nights. "The horoscope," she said. "This morning. You made it up, didn't you?"

"Didn't it sound genuine?"

"Who would think up anything like that? Someone who knows people very well?"

"I don't know, I'm afraid not."

Who might the person be who sat over there in the ministry, night after night? Someone working late? Someone afraid to go home? Someone who at this very moment was standing at the window as she was?

"When will you be leaving?" she asked.

He put his arm around her shoulders. "You're breaking your own rule. No yesterday, no tomorrow."

"Can there be such a thing—no yesterday, no tomorrow? Isn't everything connected? And don't we always want things to last?"

"But they don't last."

"I'm glad you said that."

"To say the opposite would be easier. It really was a lovely evening."

266

She had no right to hold him, and still she did not want him to go. Something had arrived with him that made her happy, and she wanted it to last—if only for today.

She was certain that he felt the same way. Then why was he waiting, why didn't he relieve her of making the decision?

He stood beside her, mute and motionless, and finally he said the words they had both been afraid to hear all this time. "I think I'd better go now."

I can only say it if I don't look at him, she thought. But then she turned toward him and looked into his eyes. "Stay," she said.

Time passed before he answered. "I should have been the one to say it."

"Perhaps it's better this way. I wanted you to stay. I wanted it. You can always remind me." She had not believed that her lips could say the words, but now she felt immeasurable relief.

He took her in his arms, and he moved with a caution that reminded her of how he had entered the room several hours ago. And when he kissed her, it was like the morning in Steglitz, without haste, making her feel that they had all the time in the world.

6

S he was in the habit of waking at an early hour, and even after all
these days there was always a first brief moment of amazement
that she was not in her room.

He lay next to her; he slept on his left side, his face buried deep
in the pillow, as if he did not need to breathe in the night. One of
his arms was stretched out toward her. He always awoke when she
released herself from him—that is, he came to the surface of his deep
sleep, was able to speak as if he were wide awake, but later he had
no memory of it. "Is it that time again?"

In the dark she reached across to the nightstand, fingering the surface until she touched the watch. She held it close to her eyes and
then laid it back down. "Go back to sleep."

"No, no, I'll get up with you."

She snuggled up to him.

"Must you leave today?"

"Yes."

"Tonight? The same train?"

"The same train. Go back to sleep."

She allowed him to pull her closer. She need only keep still for a
few minutes before she would be able to hear his calm breathing
again, at some moment a deep sigh, and then his breathing would
grow gradually softer, his embrace looser. Then it was easy to get up

without his noticing, so deep was the morning sleep into which he fell, and as she observed him now, she experienced something like envy. She rose from the bed. At six o'clock the hotel was still quiet, a very different quiet from the kind that prevailed in the late evening. Now, in the morning, it was possible to think that the two of them were the only beings alive in the building.

She did not turn on the light; the pale sheen of the winter morning in the window was enough. Anyway, there was nothing in his room that was hers except the watch, the kimono, her slippers, and her room key. Before she left, she went to the bed once more. He was sleeping very deeply, his head buried in the pillow, and all she could see was his dark hair and the stretched-out arm on which she had lain. She bent down and kissed him lightly. Then she picked up the watch and the key from the nightstand and left the room. In the doorway she stood still a moment longer, looking along the corridor. His room was on the second floor; to reach her own room she had to go along the hall, up the stairs, and then the full length of another corridor.

Actually it should have been otherwise. It should have been he who left her in the morning, but this was the way it was. Even the first night they had spent not in her room but in his. Why? The suggestion had come from her, and at the time she could not have given a reason, but then, the following morning, when she returned to her room, she was glad it had turned out that way. Everything was still as she had left it—the curtains drawn, the table where they had eaten —and she was glad that the memory of the night could remain separate from the rest.

In the corridors the night lights were still burning. Sometimes the polished shoes had already been put back in front of the room doors, sometimes not yet. She had never yet run into the valet who took care of this work, nor had she figured out his timing and his system. Sometimes he started on the top floor, sometimes downstairs. As she hurried up the stairs now, she heard him, this time coming from below.

It was certainly strange, this . . . affair—what else could she call it? The inconveniences it brought were all on her side. The first two days after that supper in her room she had remained in Berlin, but since then she went to Neustrelitz every morning and returned to Berlin at night. Every morning she hurried to her room as she did now, dressed, breakfasted on the run, and was driven to the railroad station to catch the early train to Neustrelitz. It was fairly empty, and so she was generally able to have a compartment to herself and to take a nap. The evening train was so crowded that often she had to stand for the whole trip. Keith met her at the station, and they drove to the hotel at once.

Only one other time had she remained in Berlin for two whole days —at the end of the first week, when her father's other eye was operated on.

In effect, she led two lives. The nights she spent here in Berlin, the days in Neustrelitz. She was genuinely needed at home, for there were always business decisions to be made that could not be settled by telephone. Besides, she was driven by conscience; in this situation especially she did not want to become guilty of negligence.

She had reached the top floor. The shoes had already been put back at the doors; why had the valet skipped a floor? Hers was the last room at the end of the long corridor, and 308 was the highest number. That was all the rooms there were in the Bristol. These were her thoughts, she later recalled, as she neared her door, along with a feeling of leaden weariness and of the struggle she had to go through every morning as she walked upstairs—the wish not to take the train to Neustrelitz, but to lock herself in her room and to sleep, to sleep. . . .

The red message slip together with the "Do Not Disturb" sign hung from the doorknob. She took down both and unlocked the door. The little night light that she always kept burning left the room in semidarkness; its shade cast a shadow on the wall behind the bed. This, too, was something that became engraved on her mind's eye for ever and ever.

Usually her first act was to muss up the untouched bed, as if she had slept in it, but now she picked up the telephone receiver. It took longer than usual for the night clerk to answer. "I just found the message," she said. "When did the telegram arrive?"

"An hour ago," Makowsky answered and added, "You must have been sleeping very soundly."

"Send it up, please. Do you know where it came from?"

"No. But it seems to have been sent on from Neustrelitz. I hope—"

She replaced the receiver quickly. She did not want to hear anything more. She looked at the telephone as if it were to blame for everything. And there was something else—the singular sensation as if she had experienced the present moment once before, in just the same way. Or was what happened only what she had felt coming all this time—the end? Whatever the telegram might contain, she knew one thing for certain; it meant the end.

She stood still, next to the phone, unable to move. Last night, too, they had had supper in her room before going to his. The table was still in the alcove. They did not take as long as they did the first night, but that short respite meant a lot to her, allowing her to detach herself from the cares of the day and to find her way back to herself and to him. The shared meals at the table in the alcove were always the same as the first except for their conversation. He had been the one who had violated the rule, who one evening began to speak of the future, of joint plans. . . . She had listened, silent, but she had never forgotten that every hour might be their last; she had always been prepared.

There was a knock. She opened the door and took the telegram. The page held it out on a silver tray, his hands in white gloves, his little round hat pulled deep onto his forehead.

And this image, too, would remain: the silver tray and on it the telegram on gray wartime paper. She did not open it. She laid it on the night table next to the telephone. Then she went into the bathroom, washed her face and did her hair, no more slowly than usual, but no faster. When she was fully dressed, and when her breakfast had been brought, she began to pack. Then that too was done, and she gave one last look at the closet and the drawers. Finally she mussed up the sheets.

She sat down on the edge of the bed, picked the telegram up from the night table, and examined the postmark. She had difficulty opening the envelope and unfolding the paper. She read the text and let her hands drop, staring at the suitcase already standing near the door. She read the telegram a second time, and only now did she feel the pain, quite suddenly, as if something inside her were tearing.

She folded the gray paper, picked up the phone, and asked to be connected with the switchboard.

"May I help you?"

She had to talk to someone; but she could see him now, lying in bed, his head deep in the pillows, saw him start up when the telephone rang, reaching for the receiver. . . . "May I help you, please?"

And then—what could she say? She replaced the receiver. When she picked it up again, Makowsky answered at once, as if he had been waiting for her.

"Send someone up for my luggage, please," she said. "And have my bill ready. I'll be leaving."

She dropped the telegram into her purse, picked up her hat and coat, and went to the door. She longed to turn around once more, to look back at the room, at the alcove with the table still standing there from last night. But she did not turn back.

7

"Douai," a voice was saying in her ear. "The next station. You wanted to get off in Douai. This is Douai."

She had not known that there was a place with that name until the moment she opened the telegram. And even later, when she held the train ticket in her hand, it had remained an imaginary place, one that had no existence in reality. She did not immediately react to the voice, as if in that way she could expunge the place from the map. She would have played dead if she could, but a hand took her by the shoulder and shook her awake.

She had not been sleeping, and yet the deepest sleep would have been easier to shake off than this deadly exhaustion. Forty hours—a day, a night, another day, and now already half another night on the train—had left her paralyzed and apathetic. She no longer felt the cold or hunger or thirst; she no longer responded to the occasional detonations or the signal flares that sometimes lit up the sky.

Sleep was out of the question anyway in this darkened train that crept through the night, slowly, as if it had to feel its way, stopping over and over without anyone's knowing when it would start again. For forty hours she had not slept properly, and toward the end she had stopped trying.

"This is Douai here, Nurse."

She had become used to it and no longer contradicted those who

273

addressed her as "Nurse." Presumably they could not imagine what else a woman would be doing in these trains crammed full of men.

Camilla peeled herself out of the blanket she had wound around her legs and returned it. It was pitch dark, and she could not make out the faces of the men in her compartment. She could not even have said whether they were the same soldiers who had gotten on the train with her in Aachen. Everyone who had sat across from her during this long trip had the same face and the same smell of earth and sweat, so sharp that not even the cigarette smoke could smother it.

And there was one more thing they all had in common: a reproachful solicitude. Whatever they did—whether they gave her a blanket, offered her rum from their canteens, or, as now, handed down her suitcase from the luggage rack—it was done in a manner that made her aware that they were irritated by her presence, almost as if she had thrown their world into disorder.

When the train came to a sudden stop, she lost her balance and bumped into several bodies. "Watch it!" Someone kicked open the ice-encrusted door.

For a moment the fierce cold threatened to take her breath away. The night was pitch black and the platform without any kind of illumination. Now and then a flashlight flared up, somewhat like the occasional matches that had glowed in the train compartment behind the cupped hands of a soldier. Otherwise there was no light to be seen, nor any sign that on the other side of the platform there was a town. The compartments emptied out with a confusion of muffled voices, the clatter of tinware against the field packs, and finally the sound of nailed boots as the men, arrayed in columns, walked away.

Camilla had set the case down at her side. The cold night air was better than the sticky air inside the compartment, and she felt her spirits gradually reviving. The train doors were already being slammed closed again, and suddenly she was overtaken by doubt—had she gotten out too soon? Alarmed, she picked up her valise and began to run, straight into the arms of two men.

"Is this really Douai? Tell me! Is it Douai?"

The men were wearing steel helmets, pistols in dark leather holsters, high boots, and mufflers covering their coats. "It's Douai all right, Nurse. Where are you headed? May we see your papers?"

She was familiar with the question. In the course of the journey

274

she had lost track of all the controls she had been subjected to. It had begun in Berlin. She had had to spend an entire morning to obtain the necessary documents, and it had required all her powers of persuasion. New documents had been added ever since—more papers, additional passes. Each military policeman seemed to ask for still different ones.

"Your papers, Nurse." The shine of a dimmed flashlight was directed at her face.

She reached inside her coat for the leather satchel she wore around her neck. The flashlight was lowered, the two men put their heads together. "Come along, then." Their voices sounded neither friendly nor hostile, but she was used to that, and it did upset her now that the men held on to her papers.

She picked up her case. It was small and contained only essentials. The platform had emptied completely. The two military policemen headed toward a wooden barracks. There was still no sight or sound of the town itself.

The man holding the papers entered the barracks, the other one stayed with her. No word was spoken, and when the first man returned, he only gave her a silent sign to enter.

The room was small and even colder than outside—at least that was what she felt. Her papers had been placed on a crude wooden table. A woman sat behind it, typing. She wore a heavy coat with a Red Cross band around the sleeve and roughly knitted gray gloves, cut off to expose her fingertips, bluish with cold. In the bright light of the tin lamp hanging from the ceiling Camilla could not tell whether the woman's hair was blonde or white, whether she was young or old.

She was copying from a list—obviously names followed by dates. Camilla was reminded that during her entire journey she had not gone near a newspaper, for fear of running across the casualty lists— she who otherwise always sought certainty in all things. . . .

With a jerk the woman pulled the paper out of the machine and placed it in a blue folder. After she had raised the lamp, which hung from an adjustable chain, she leaned back. "So you are not a nurse," she said. Camilla pointed to her papers.

"I've seen them. Usually we deal only with nurses, not with ladies who arrive from Berlin for a visit." She scrutinized Camilla, and perhaps she noticed that her coat was made of sable; in any case, her tone became even sharper. "I'd never have granted you the permission.

275

We're twenty kilometers from the front here, we're not set up for visitors. I don't know if I can help you; I'm certainly none too happy about it."

The woman had spoken with more hostility than any of the men until now, or perhaps it only seemed so to Camilla because she had expected more understanding from another woman.

"To turn up here, all the way from Berlin. We'd certainly have a fine howdedo if all the ladies began to go in for it."

"Please help me." Camilla pulled the telegram from her purse. The creases were beginning to wear through from repeated unfolding.

The woman took it and shook her head. "It's over two days old, and it doesn't mention the unit."

"He's a reserve lieutenant. Twelfth Transportation Corps. And it says Douai."

"There are half a dozen field hospitals here, inside the city and on the outskirts."

"But you have his name—and the name of his doctor. Dr. Kraussneck. He sent the telegram. My husband is seriously wounded."

"And maybe he's been moved by now. Didn't you think about that, or. . . ."

During the journey Camilla had seen many transports of the wounded, ambulances marked with the red cross, and each time she had been tempted to run to them and ask about her husband.

". . . that he might be dead?"

Camilla avoided the woman's eyes. What did she get out of torturing her? Next to the typewriter stood a small frame. Camilla could not see the photograph it contained, but perhaps that was the reason this woman had become as she was.

"Help me," Camilla said. "I beg of you."

The woman glanced again at the telegram, wrote a few words on a memo pad, and handed the note along with the other papers across the table to Camilla. She pushed back her chair and stood up. She was neither as tall nor as stocky as Camilla had assumed; it was only the heavy coat that made her look that way.

"First I'll see that you get a room for the rest of the night."

"I don't need a room. Can't I stay here? I couldn't sleep anyway."

"I told you, I have to make some inquiries first to find out where they've put your husband. It's after midnight now. What do you expect of me? I have other things to do."

"Please. . . ." She had reached her destination, and yet she was further away from it than ever, and she felt the strength draining from her abruptly. Black spots danced before her eyes; it was as if all the blood were running out of her body. She fought the feeling, groped for the back of a chair to grasp until gradually the ground under her feet felt firm again.

"Now don't you keel over," she could hear the woman saying. "I'll find out where your husband is, don't you worry about that. But it takes time, and even then I have to find somebody who'll take you there. All right, I'll take care of everything, but you can't stay here, there's no room. Drink this." She poured a red beverage from a thermos bottle into a paper cup.

"Thanks." Camilla grasped the cup with both hands. The scent of cinnamon and cloves arose from it, and only then did she understand that it was mulled wine—genuine, properly made mulled wine.

"Go ahead, drink it."

She obeyed.

"It's been a long time since you've had anything warm, am I right?"

"Yes."

"And not a lot of sleep."

"Yes."

"All right then, go straight to the hotel across from the railroad. When you leave the station, just across the square. You can't miss it. Hotel is a grandiose name for it, but it's the best we can do around here. I'll let you know when we have anything. And if he doesn't come to the door right away, just keep on knocking. It's the owner himself."

"I—"

"All right, all right. Just as soon as I know anything, I'll get a message to you. I'll do my best. Here, don't forget your papers."

A sleepy man, fully dressed in a black suit and white shirt, opened the hotel door. He had answered her knock at once, and in the lobby she saw a leather couch where he had established a temporary bed. His greeting had been an incomprehensible mumble ending in a dry cough. He let her carry her own case and climbed the stairs ahead of her, shuffling in his felt slippers. In the room, he began by checking the blackout covering at the windows before he turned on a light. "Don't mess with the windows," he said. "Otherwise the fines come pouring in, and I'm the one who has to pay up." His tone was as

277

harsh as everyone's here near the front, except that his voice had a French accent.

The room was furnished with a chair, a table, a cupboard, and a brass bed. A couple of brown blankets were folded at its bottom end.

"Can't give you any sheets. Nobody to launder 'em. If you're tired enough, you can sleep without."

Camilla could not have said whether the room was heated or not. The hot wine she had drunk in the Red Cross nurse's shack was beginning to have an effect, and she felt almost too warm in her coat.

"I'm expecting a message," she said. "Call me at once, please."

"I'm used to that, nights." He went to the door. "Anything else?" He must have become aware of the absurdity of his question, for he ran his fingers through his graying hair, which stood up like a brush from his narrow, bony skull, and gave an embarrassed smile. "Not that there's a lot I can do. Maybe a little hot water in the morning. I could do that." He was still holding on to the doorknob. "Try to sleep. It's the best thing we can do these days."

"There is one thing."

"What?"

"I noticed you have a telephone."

"Sure. We had one of the first ones in town. Four-three-nine, one of the lowest numbers."

"Could you try to put a call through for me?"

"A call now, in the middle of the night? Where to, for heaven's sake?"

"Berlin."

"Berlin, you said?" He stared at her, and then the idea seemed to give him pleasure, for he came back into the room. "So you want to telephone to Berlin? And you think that can be done?" He was shorter than she was, and he looked up at her expectantly. "Once we had a guest who telephoned to London, can you imagine, London. But that was before the war. Berlin, now. . . ."

"I'll write down the number for you." She searched in her purse for paper and pencil. She did not need to look up the number—she knew it by heart.

He took the slip of paper and stared at it, still doubtful. "I don't know how long it'll take. London that time, they came through at once, I mean it went pretty fast. You better come along, there's no extension in this room. Berlin, what do you know."

278

"I'll follow in a minute. You get started."

He left.

For a while she heard the shuffling of the felt slippers, interspersed with coughing; then there was silence. She lifted her case up on a chair and took out her few things. She took off her coat and fur cap and wrapped a woolen stole around her shoulders. She had left Berlin without leaving a message for Keith. By the time she had collected the necessary papers for the journey, she only had two hours before her train departure, and she had spent them visiting her father in the hospital and speaking to Neustrelitz by phone. She could not bear to telephone the Bristol, and then something very odd had happened—the farther away from Berlin she traveled, the less frequently she had thought about it. And even when she tried to remember, she could summon up only vague, blurred pictures. There was that one moment she could visualize sharply: herself in the corridor, in front of her room, and the red message slip hanging from the doorknob. Everything that had gone before seemed as remote to her as if it were part of her distant past.

All the same, she did not want to avoid the call altogether. Presumably Keith had long since learned from her father everything that had happened, but she had to talk to him herself. She owed it to him and to herself. Perhaps all she needed had been this little space of time.

Even on the stairs she could hear the owner's voice, excited and with a strong accent. He had taken off his jacket and hung it from the back of a chair, and he sat at the telephone installation in the reception desk, his white shirtsleeves caught up by an elastic above the elbow. The telephone was old, antedeluvian; a speaker you had to hold and a separate earpiece on a long black cord. He was just replacing it when Camilla joined him, and he looked at her and shrugged his shoulders. "Now it's a matter of waiting and crossing your fingers."

He did not take his eyes off the phone. "That call to London," he said. "What do you think, have they got a cable running under the water?"

"I guess so."

"I'd make you a cup of coffee, but if I leave the phone, that's when the call is sure to come through." He did not offer her a chair, and she stood next to him in the narrow space between the reception desk and the cabinet with the pigeonholes for the room keys. She counted eighteen boxes, three rows of six, but only two keys were hanging from their hooks, and she wondered whether all the other rooms were really occupied. They waited. When the bell rang, the man was more startled than she was. For a moment he sat frozen, then he grabbed the earpiece, the speaker. "Hello, Berlin!" He nodded and stood up so she could take his chair. He pressed the earpiece against her ear, handed her the speaker, but he did not leave to let her carry on her conversation in private. He remained standing next to her, bent over, as if the connection meant as much to him as it did to her.

Camilla listened into the instrument: a rustling, and then now and again the voices of the central operators when they completed other connections, until finally a voice said, "You may speak now."

"Hello, Makowsky, is that you?"

"One moment, please. I'll connect you."

"Hotel Bristol, night clerk."

"Makowsky?"

"Hello, who is this?"

"Can you hear me? I'd like you to—"

"Hello! Yes, now I can hear. . . . Frau Senger?"

"Yes. Tell me, is room two-two-one in? Can you connect me?" She did not know why she hesitated to speak his name. She had forgotten that someone was standing by her side. It took all the concentration she could muster to hear the faraway voice.

"Hello, did you hear me?"

"I can hear you very clearly. You want room two-two-one."

"Yes, and please let it ring, let it ring a long time. . . ."

All she could hear now was the rustling until suddenly the voice was crystal clear. "I'm sorry but—"

"Did two-two-one check out?" She had heard the soldiers on the train talk about it over and over again: America's entry into the war seemed imminent. Some thought they knew that the American ambassador had already been handed his papers.

"No, not checked out, but he's not in the hotel. His key is here, in his compartment. But I can give you the number. He left a telephone number with me, in case anyone needs to reach him. Everybody in Berlin is talking about how the Americans. . . . Hello, can you still hear me? Do you want me to give you the number?"

"Yes please."

"Do you have something to write it down with?"

On the table in front of her, near the phone, lay pencils, and even as he gave her the number and she wrote the figures down on the edge of the green blotter, she knew where Keith was.

"Do you want me to repeat it?"

"No, thank you, I got it."

"I'm sorry I can't do more for you. I hope everything is all right?"

"Yes, and please excuse my calling so late. Good night."

She put down the speaker and the earpiece and looked at Lou's telephone number. She became aware once more of the man standing next to her and realized that he was jumping up and down.

"Did you really talk to Berlin? And how fast they made the connection! Not even a half-hour waiting time. Berlin—they've got a whole other spirit there than we do. You want to make another call? Want me to put it through right now?" He actually crowded her off the chair.

Camilla stared at the wall clock, which showed a few minutes before one. She shook her head. "No, I don't think so."

"Less than half an hour! And I thought they wouldn't even let me make the call."

"I'm very grateful to you. I'll try to get some sleep. And you'll wake me immediately if a message comes for me."

She had just set her foot on the lowest step of the stairs when the phone rang again. For a moment she thought that it could only be Keith, that he had returned to the hotel and now. . . . But then she realized what nonsense such a thought was.

The man put back the earpiece and his voice rang with disappointment when he said, "Just the charges. It isn't even expensive if you think that it was all the way to Berlin. I'll add it to your bill. Good night, then."

She fell into a deep sleep at once, and did not wake up at six as she did every other morning.

She had even forgotten to lock the door, and she awoke only when the hotel proprietor was already in the room. He raised the blackout curtains halfway, poured a jug of hot water into the large china bowl on the table, and then, holding the empty jug, stepped to the side of the bed.

"You must excuse me. I knocked and knocked, but I couldn't wake you."

"What time is it?"

"A little after eight. A motorcar has come for you."

"A car for me?"

"Yes. It will take you to Château Vernou. My God, that used to be such a fine estate, famous for its roses, you know."

"Château Vernou?"

"The most beautiful roses far and wide. I guess you want to go to the hospital they've got there now."

"And the automobile is here now?"

"Yes, but take your time. I'll fix some breakfast for you now. I hope you weren't cold. If you're going to stay a while I'll give you another blanket, and maybe I can find a set of sheets."

He had prepared breakfast for her in a long, narrow room with ivy-patterned wallpaper. The high arched windows looked out on the square in front of the railroad station. So there really was a town by the name of Douai. Houses, shops, a monument at the center, and at the rear, the railroad station. The car the proprietor had mentioned was parked in front of the hotel gate. An ambulance car. Its driver was walking up and down on the sidewalk, beating his arms across his chest to ward off the cold.

She ate her breakfast, paid her bill, and asked permission to leave her case for the time being. The proprietor assured her that it could not be safer anywhere and that he would keep the room in reserve for her, should she want to stay on after all. He accompanied her to the gate, and he remained standing there until she had taken her seat in the automobile.

It was an open car, loaded with wooden crates of medicine. She sat in front with the driver. In spite of the gray wool cap that left only his eyes, nose, and mouth exposed, it was clear that he had no need to shave yet. His skin was smooth and soft, and not even his upper lip gave any sign of down.

He had acknowledged her presence silently, and during the drive he also remained taciturn. He concentrated on the road, which grew very bad as soon as they left the town. There was less snow here than in Berlin, only a thin layer, frozen solid, but a ringing cold prevailed. The potholes were filled in with ice that splintered under the weight of the wheels, and in the meadows to either side of the road great patches were iced over.

"How far is it?" she finally asked.

282

"Not much farther. A quarter of an hour. The little woods over there. Once we're through that, you can see it."

She recalled the hotel proprietor's words. "It used to be a château?"

He nodded silently, as if it were important to block any further questions at the outset. She had no intention of asking about her husband anyway. Now, when she was almost there, she was glad for every minute's delay she was granted.

"It's supposed to be famous for its roses."

For the first time he turned his head and looked at her. "You know about the roses?" The car bumped over a pothole that he had not avoided in time, and he turned his attention back to the road, but his reticence was gone. "I never saw roses like that before. And nobody's looked after them for years. They haven't been fertilized, they haven't been pruned, nobody's done a thing, and the hothouses. . . . You'll see for yourself. . . . This here was part of the front for a long time and kept changing hands. Sometimes us, sometimes the French, sometimes the English, then us again. Nobody has time for roses."

"Are you interested especially in roses?"

"I've studied landscape gardening, you know. Last fall I pruned them, especially those close to the house. Climbers, a dark red kind. And blossoms so full, like I never saw on climbers before. I dug up one plant and sent it home, but I can't be sure it will take, of course."

They had reached the copse, and he fell back into his silence. When the trees receded he turned right, toward a large gate of which only one post remained standing. The other one had been shot away and lay in the snow together with the fencing. At the end of the long poplar drive stood the château—a central structure with two slightly recessed wings. The red cross had been painted on all three roofs. The castle itself was undamaged, but that made the traces of war around it all the clearer: the broken hothouses, the collapsed well, the garden beds turned up by shell holes, the boxwood hedges gone to seed.

Another car was already standing at the main entrance. Camilla's driver parked behind it. "Just go on in. The nurse at the door will tell you where you can find Dr. Kraussneck."

She was surprised and startled to find that he knew the name of the doctor who had sent her the telegram. Abruptly the fear that had gripped her throughout the journey returned in full force—the fear of coming too late. She got out of the car. Her eyes traveled along

283

the house, and she noted that the espaliers of roses along the wings had been protected with pine branches and hopsacking. She wanted to turn around to ask the driver whether that was his handiwork, but he had already started the car. The turnaround in front of the entrance was free of snow and covered with fine white gravel; although her shoes were thick-soled, she thought she could feel the pointed stones.

Four shallow steps, taking up the whole width of the central facade, led up to the entrance. She had just reached it when the door was opened from inside. A nurse came out and stood at the door while the chaplain and his assistant went past her. The priest was a tall, sturdy man, and the stone flags clattered under his boots. The heavy military footwear contrasted oddly with his clerical robes, and Camilla wondered how he could step silently to a dying man's bed. The white surplice his companion wore over his uniform was too tight and too short. His hands held the gear for the extreme unction.

The priest looked at Camilla and then at the nurse. He seemed relieved when the latter shook her head, and he quickly walked to the waiting car.

The nurse came to meet Camilla. "You're the lady from Berlin?"

"Yes." She tried to read the nurse's face, but all she could see was weariness. The chaplain's car started. Again Camilla's eyes strayed over the front of the house. Somewhere, behind one of the many windows, a man lay dying. What did a dying man care whether the priest wore heavy boots as he approached his bed? The car noise faded into the distance. There was a drip from one of the eaves.

"If you'll be so good as to follow me," said the nurse.

The stone flags near the door were loose and clattered under her feet as well. As she entered the hospital behind the nurse, she had only one thought. "Let him live," she thought. "Please, let him live."

284

Five

1

He listened to the noises coming from the bathroom. He even closed his eyes so as to concentrate on them completely. He loved these sounds, when Schütte honed the razor against the strap. None of the barbers he had had to make do with all those years had done it with such loving care. Sometimes the noise was light, like a stretching saddle girth during a light trot, at other times heavy, like someone walking through damp autumn foliage. *Rosh . . . rosh . . .* Fritz Hofmann was absolutely crazy about the sound. Counting back, it was twenty years that he had had to forego Schütte's services. They had not returned to Steglitz until 1921. Even now, after living there for three years, Hofmann rejoiced daily.

"Just a second more," the voice called from the bathroom. "Why don't you get ready?"

But Hofmann was in no hurry. He looked at the calendar. For a moment he was uncertain—had he torn off yesterday's page or not? It was one of his unalterable habits to close each day with this ritual, and it irritated him that he could not remember.

"I'm getting old," he said.

Razor in hand, Schütte came through the door. "What did you say?"

"I'm getting old, Schütte."

"We're all getting old. But to get old like you, that I wouldn't mind, I tell you. You really haven't got a thing to complain about, have you?"

No, Hofmann had nothing to complain about. But he'd made sure of that in advance! Schütte, for instance: long ago, the first time he'd asked him to come to the house, thirty-five years ago, Schütte had been a boy of nineteen, just finished with his apprenticeship. At that time nobody could understand Hofmann's choice. A barber should be a man of a certain age. But now he had his reward. Schütte was fifty-four, and it was certain that he'd be able to shave Hofmann until the day he died. How important that was! What use was your own good health if the friends your own age started to die off? Suddenly the poker group was no longer complete and you could not find a replacement, then another bunch of card-playing buddies fell apart, and you were left behind, depressed, asking yourself who would be next. At such times it was comforting to have chosen a young barber and a young tailor at least, so that one would not lose them too soon. Every morning when Schütte appeared at the house with his black bag, Hofmann praised himself for the wisdom he had shown in planning ahead.

He took off his glasses, shed his coat, and loosened his collar; then he sat down in the leather chair with the adjustable back placed near the window. The chair was a new acquisition, as were several objects in the room. The house had been in bad shape, and many things—such as the built-in glass cases for his collections—could not be fixed. But the most important thing was that he was once again living in the house he had built with so many hopes, that he even occupied the same rooms—the den with adjacent bedroom and bath, on the ground floor. How wise of him this was, too, for though at seventy-nine he was still spry, he hated climbing stairs. "I'm ready now."

By the time Schütte arrived each day, Hofmann had already been up for an hour. Another sign that he was aging: he required less sleep. In the summer he also usually took a half hour's walk, especially now, in August, when he often felt too hot outdoors later in the day.

The barber wheeled the table with his tools closer to Hofmann. He always used the same razor for him; by now the blade was very narrow, and the brass handle had once been gilded. He owned a matching scissors, and on it, too, the gold plate had worn off. He had won both pieces in a contest, and it had been a question of whether to put them away or use them even though the gold would wear off in time.

Schütte tied the white bib around Hofmann's neck. "A marvelous day, isn't it?"

"But hot."

"The dog days. That's how it has to be. Maybe it's just my imagination, but now that the times are getting better, the weather's getting better too."

"What's today's date, do you know? Is it the twenty-first or the twenty-second?"

"Friday of course, the twenty-second."

"You're sure?"

"Absolutely. Haven't you seen the paper yet? Solemn reception of the Mexican President. That's going to be some to-do! The first foreign head of state to honor us again. Things are looking up. And the financial section reports the first bond issue by a foreign creditor. Should a person invest in something like that?"

"I'd wait if I were you. I think we can trust the government currency. And you're quite certain that it's Friday? Then give me a special shave, thorough enough to last until tonight."

"Why, is it a special day?"

Hofmann, completely covered with lather, only nodded. They had developed a very precise schedule for their conversations. During the preparations and even while Schütte was lathering Hofmann's face, it was simple; they both talked. But during the shaving process itself Schütte did all the talking, with a little gossip about his other clients, with weather forecasts and politics, or he restricted himself to such questions as could be answered with a nod or a shake of the head.

"Will you be going out tonight?"

A shake of the head.

"Have the young gentlemen returned from their vacation?"

A nod.

"I hear tell Warnemünde has become a real mass enterprise."

A nod.

"Anyway, frying in the sun for hours—can that really be healthy?"

A shake.

"A sound heart, that's the important thing."

A nod.

"And a good digestion. Eating enough. The organs need work, otherwise the juices dry up. The machine has to be kept oiled."

He patted away the rest of the lather, laid the prepared hot towel across Hofmann's face, replacing it with a cold one. The scent of camphor spread as he uncapped the bottle; he poured a little of the

289

fluid into his hands and used it to massage Hofmann's cheeks. "Okay, you're done. That should last you until tonight, or I could drop by again later."

"It will last. The young ladies don't come that close to me anymore."

The barber wheeled the table back into the bathroom, and after he had packed up his gear, Hofmann wanted to accompany him from the room, for it was time for his breakfast. But Schütte held back. There seemed to be something on his mind. Finally he blurted out, "Could you give me a tip on tomorrow's race?"

"You know I no longer play the horses."

"Of course. It isn't for me, either. My friend keeps begging me."

It was a fact that Hofmann no longer put money on the ponies. During the war there had been no races; besides, he had lost Troy. He had managed to keep the horse until the middle of 1917· but then it had been taken from him, officially drafted, just as other people's cars were requisitioned. He had tried to keep track of Troy; after the war he had even placed classified ads in every sort of magazine and paper with a description of the horse, its brand, its bloodlines—but all in vain. No one had ever heard him utter a word of regret about anything else he had lost—his business, his clock collection—but to this day he spoke about Troy, and whenever he saw a sorrel that bore even the slightest resemblance to Troy, he was likely to importune the owner with a storm of questions.

Perhaps that was the reason why he no longer attended the races and placed no more bets, although he continued to subscribe to racing journals. He did keep up his card parties, though he wagered only small amounts. And he held on to innumerable lottery tickets, always playing the numbers 1-1 in every possible drawing. The family smiled at this trait of his, but no one ever suspected that he won regularly, now and again even astonishing amounts.

"Tell your friend to trust his instincts."

"But you still understand a lot about it. Couldn't you make an exception? He swears by your tips. He refuses to believe that you've given up betting."

"Just tell him any one of the horses' names. If he loses, he won't bother you again."

He pulled out his pocket purse and paid the barber. In the old days he had settled his accounts at the end of the month, but during the inflation period such a procedure had become unworkable, and stability was still so novel that he kept up the habit.

He walked ahead to the door. It stuck a little. Everything had been done to remedy the damage, but no one could fix it entirely. In the hall there was a scent of roses, and in the morning room, where the door stood open, a young man was just changing the flowers in the vases.

Hofmann and Schütte stepped outside. The house had been restored to its original pale gray finish, but the front gardens were changed. In place of the rhododendron bushes, three round rosebeds had been planted, edged with boxwood, and along the paths covered with white gravel ran narrow rose borders.

"I keep wondering," Schütte remarked, "what kind of roses these are."

"Tea hybrids, I think—I don't remember exactly."

"Imagine them blooming here—and so well. They say our soil is all wrong for roses."

"It's the new gardener," Hofmann replied. "He has a way with them."

"What a sad thing about Willeke. He held out here for such a long time. He watched over the place like a Cerberus, and then, just after you moved back in. Six months . . . he wasn't even granted one final summer." Schütte bent over a rose. "But I'd sure like to know the name. You don't see that kind anywhere else around here. And the climbers, fantastic."

"You're right in fashion, aren't you! The words people use nowadays! Fantastic—how about that."

Schütte smiled. "I'll have to ask the gardener where he got those roses. Did your daughter hire him?"

"Yes. She takes care of all that, I stay out of it. It's going to be hot today."

"It sure will. The dog days. We may be in for a siege. All right then, see you tomorrow."

"Tomorrow."

Hofmann started back to the house. Not a cloud was in the sky, only a thin haze that caught the heat like a glass bell. He must not forget to close the shutters on his windows before the sun came around the side of the house.

Only on Sundays, did the family appear in a body at breakfast, and then not even regularly, for the young gentlemen preferred to stay in bed when they had the chance. For Konrad and Georg it depended on their classes at the university during the week. As for Max, it was a matter of whether he had gone to bed before or after midnight.

The only certain thing was that Camilla, Senger, and Hofmann gathered every morning at seven at the breakfast table, but today there was no sign of Senger, and Camilla's place setting had already been used. Fritz Hofmann took his seat, not at all unhappy about being deserted, since this made the newspapers exclusively his. The short-stemmed roses in the round vase had a strong scent. Other bouquets were placed on the sideboard and the cabinet. Hofmann thought once again that the new gardener overdid it a little keeping the whole house in flowers, but he was probably only following Camilla's instructions. From time to time she claimed that the house still had the odor of a field hospital, and then for the length of the morning she made them open all the windows wide. No one else agreed with her, and Hofmann had requested that his rooms be spared these drastic airings.

His punctuality was known to the servants, and he had barely pulled the large white linen napkin out of its silver ring and tucked it into the V of his vest when the maid came in.

"Has my daughter finished her breakfast already?"

"Yes, sir. Madam has already gone out, she had some things to do in the city."

The maid was new, thus the "Madam." There had been something between her predecessor and Max. Hofmann had been only vaguely aware of it. Whenever possible he stayed out of these things. Satisfied with himself and his world, he watched the girl as she put breakfast in front of him, the basket with fresh rolls, the egg that had been boiled precisely four and a half minutes, three kinds of jam, warm milk, a pot of coffee—the kind that was easy on the stomach, filtered for him according to a special recipe.

"Very good, my child. You're doing very nicely. There's only one thing missing, the cod liver oil, probably no one has told you yet. Lecithin, my child, essential to the body."

After she had left, he laid out his pills—one for digestion and one for strengthening the heart, made up according to his own recipe by a friend of his who was a druggist—and moved closer to the table.

He was already so content with the idea of breakfasting alone that it seemed to him almost an intrusion when Max came in.

"Morning."

"Good morning," Hofmann said. "So, cat got your tongue again? And you're going to the office looking like that?"

Max was a favorite grandson, in some ways the son he had never had. Hofmann saw his own reflection in him, not only outwardly but also in his way of moving—for example, how he took his jacket, which he had carried over his arm, and hung it across the back of the chair before sitting down. But for this very reason he was particularly critical of him. He especially objected to Max's way of dressing. The trousers he was wearing today—the material was too light and the cut too loose; the white shirt, open at the neck; the canary yellow sleeveless pullover; and with all that, a checkered jacket!

"Young men today! No tie! Do you really think that looks well? And your baggy trousers! If that's supposed to be elegant! I'll repeat my offer, you may go to my tailor."

"Oh no, not your tailor, anything but that. He's hopelessly old-fashioned. Will you pass me the coffee, please?"

"Have things come to such a pass? I suggest that you get up and first pour me a cup."

Max did so, without objecting, and as he moved, he noticed the used place setting. "Has Mother already had breakfast, then?"

"Stop! Not so much coffee. More milk. You ought to know by now. Good, that's fine."

"Mother has already gone out?"

"It seems that way. I didn't hear her. But the girl said she just left, errands in the city. What's wrong with that?"

On his way back to his place Max stopped at his mother's chair, which was pushed away from the table a little. He gave an angry laugh. "And I thought to myself, do her a favor, make yourself do it for a change, she hates it when you come too late. She can't stand it, her son ought to be a paragon. So I set the alarm. Two alarms! And what happens—she's gone!" He was talking to the empty chair as if his mother were sitting there. "One of these days I'm going to get up at four in the morning. But probably I'll be too late then, too. And I deliberately set two alarm clocks."

"Hurry up and sit down." Hofmann was knocking apathetically at his egg. He avoided such confrontations as much as he could. He had had more than enough of them in the old days; now he wanted his peace and quiet. But Max succeeded time and again in involving him. It had begun when the boy was still in school; he had had to take up the cudgels for him so that he would be allowed to quit after earning a school-leaving certificate and begin training in a bank. Next had been the business with the army; it had not exactly been easy to arrange for a deferment. And even now it did not stop; the most frequent source of trouble was the great number of girls. He had never been bothered with such problems as far as Konrad and Georg were concerned; their lives always ran smoothly. They had graduated with honors, both were at the university, as Camilla had wished. One of them would become a chemist, and the other was studying law. Only Max had remained the family troublemaker. "I guess you got out on the wrong side of the bed?"

"I did, that's for sure. But does she always have to be first? And the last, too, of course! She can never stop trying to prove how competent she is and how much work is waiting for her. She gets on my nerves, can't you understand that? She wants to do everything herself. Here and in the business. But she favors the business, that's her real family. I really wonder why I bother going to the office at all. She doesn't need me. She doesn't need any of us. If you ask me, not even Father—"

Fritz Hofmann raised his hand in protest. "Now you're going too far. What would we have without her? Certainly not this house."

"All right."

"No, it's not all right. Can't you get it into your head that she might have preferred to live a different kind of life?" Against his will, his temper and his sense of justice had run away with him, but now, he thought, there must be an end to talk or he would be robbing himself of his breakfast.

Unfortunately Max did not understand his viewpoint at all. "That's the way she wanted it," he said. "She could have had a different life."

"Oh, do you really think so?"

"Okay, calm down—"

But Hofmann tore his napkin from his vest and threw it on the table. He was not certain that he would be able to find the right words. Whenever he was forced to play Camilla's advocate, he invariably felt a little inhibited, almost guilt-ridden. "Now I want you to tell me, when could she do as she wanted? The first thirteen years in Neustrelitz perhaps? Oh yes, I remember, she wanted to go abroad with your father, take a vacation after all the years of work. That's what she wanted. Only, it didn't happen. And the war? Those years without your father. And then? When she brought him back, and nobody would believe that he would ever be able to walk again. And the time after the war, the inflation and a helpless man in the house. Add it up. You're supposed to be good at arithmetic. Count up the years, nothing else. She was eighteen when she married—not even eighteen. In three months she will be forty-one. More than twenty years—and they say those are the best years in a woman's life. I'm almost finished. When your father came back, there wasn't a single doctor who held out any hope for him. And usually they're quick with the pretty words. But not in his case. Absolutely hopeless. I think even he himself gave up. Not your mother. She believed that some day he would not need the wheelchair anymore—not even crutches. She was the only one. If you've forgotten, go outside and look in the tool shed. Look at the wheelchair. That's where it's still kept. It was she who was sure that your father would get well. All right. Do you really believe that anyone would choose such a life?"

He fell silent, exhausted. He picked up his cup, intending to drink from it, but he set it down again when he realized the coffee had grown cold. He pushed the egg away and put the pills back in a little silver box. These were calculated gestures, intended to underscore his words, but he dimly felt that he was really devaluing his defense of Camilla. He knew very well that he had persuaded Max only to a degree; this grandson had the ability to let things he did not wish to hear go in one ear and out the other. Hofmann saw through and understood that, for in this too Max resembled him. Why ever had he let himself be carried away? What concerned him even more, how could he come by a fresh cup of coffee without losing status?

"I'm sorry." Max, sitting across the table, bent forward slightly. "Would you like a fresh cup of coffee?"

"If it's still hot."

"I'll ask them to make some more hot milk."

"In that case they can bring me a clean cup, too. Wait. And maybe another egg. This one is cold."

Max rang the little bell, the maid came in, Hofmann's wishes were met, and grandfather and grandson breakfasted in silence for a time.

"What's happening tonight anyway?" Max asked.

"What do you mean?"

"The garden party Mother is giving."

"Just a garden party. The weather is just right for that sort of thing. Who knows how long it will last."

"No special occasion?"

Hofmann looked at his plate. "None that I know of."

"All right, can I talk to you a minute? I seem to have a problem."

"Something to do with the office?"

"Personal. Female."

"Do you ever have any other kind?"

"This time it's serious."

"That too sounds familiar. Let me count, this year alone. The tournament rider, the medical student, the girl from the post office. All of them serious. I'm sure I left out a few."

"I want to get married."

Hofmann sighed. "You know what I think about that. Marriage—that's the beginning of the end. It's bad enough if you make yourself unhappy ten years from now. For all I care, you can have as many 'serious' affairs as you like, just don't get married."

"But this time it's the right one."

"The right one—that's even worse than I thought. With me it was the right one too; I was prepared to put a bullet through my head if I couldn't have her. I got her, and I paid dearly for it. I still get the shakes when I think that there isn't ten miles' distance between her and me. Sometimes I dream that she appears and takes possession of the lot. . . . Does she have money at least?"

"That would affect your attitude?"

"Money is important. Very important."

"Not a penny. Her parents lost everything they had. But you know I'm not dependent on money. I earn twice as much on the side as the salary Mother pays me."

He was not exaggerating, Hofmann knew, for he was the only one who was privy to Max's private business. In this too the boy was *his* grandson. Max constantly had some "irons in the fire," just as he had had, except that the younger man proceeded cautiously and at the age of twenty-two was already in possession of a personal fortune. There was no doubt that Max was a financial genius, though perhaps not all his deals were of the kind that one could boast of. He had speculated in real estate; during the inflationary period he had helped arrange the smuggling abroad of valuable paintings, on which there was an export embargo, in return for gulden or dollars. More recently, since the mark had become stable again, he was financing spectacular night club revues. These private affairs of her son's had always been a thorn in Camilla's side, and Hofmann, who saw nothing morally reprehensible in the transactions, but rather a legitimate gamble, had defended Max more than once. Remembering that, he spoke more mildly. "Do I know the girl?"

"No."

"And you really mean to marry her in earnest? Does your mother know what's going on?"

"That's just it—she doesn't. That's why I wanted to talk to you. I'm counting on you. Maybe you could break it to her gently."

"I don't foresee any problem there. After all, she has always encouraged you to bring your girls home. And she's always very nice to them."

"Oh yes. She's very nice to the girls—always. Nice, courteous, and attentive; and almost every time, after a couple of weeks, it's all over between the girl and me. I can't figure out how she does it. It's a mystery to me. And the girls always agree that she's a lovely person —remarkably lovely—'Your mother is fantastic!' I think that's the reason. Unconsciously the girls always compare themselves with her and find they can't compete. The same thing happens to *me*. I tell myself, your mother is a woman of forty, but when I see her standing there with the girls and make a comparison, I don't like any of them any more."

"Are you reproaching your mother with that?"

Max had risen to his feet. He took the jacket from the back of the chair and tossed it across his arm. "If you want to put in a good word for me, swell; if not—I'll marry her anyway."

Hofmann had risen as well, and he left the morning room together with Max. They were in the lounge when a door opened and Carl Senger appeared, wearing a white terry-cloth robe, a towel across his shoulders, his face gleaming with perspiration. The basement held a room with medical training equipment, wall ladders, rings, dumbbells, weights, and balls, and every morning Senger spent half an hour there. Three times a week a masseur came to the house, and on the other days he worked out by himself. He would not allow any member of the family to enter the room, but if one were nearby, one could hear the doggedness with which he went about his exercises.

"Morning, Father," Max said.

"Did you have a good night?" Hofmann asked.

"I think we're in for a change in the weather." Senger wiped his face with the towel. His pale hair had thinned a little, but his face, slightly flushed from his exertions, radiated strength and good health. To look at him, it was hard to believe that he had spent two years flat on his back and another two years in a wheelchair. He pointed to the open door of the breakfast room. "She's finished already?" Turning to his son, he asked, "Can you drive me into town?"

"Of course."

"Fine, I'll hurry. A quarter of an hour, I won't need any longer than that."

"Don't you want to have breakfast first?" Hofmann asked, but Senger was already going up the stairs. He rested one hand on the banister, but he seemed to be acting more from habit than because he required the additional support.

"You can wait in my rooms," Hofmann said to Max. "I've got something to show you." He fetched the newspapers from the morning room, now that they were no longer needed by anyone else, and placed them on the table where he kept the weeklies and specialized journals. The fact that for once he had the papers all to himself, before anyone else had read them, cheered him considerably. Papers that had already been paged through lost half their value for him, no matter how carefully they had been folded again.

He had settled at his desk, and from a drawer he took an envelope gaudy with foreign stamps.

"He has to ask me to drive him," Max was saying. "Mother has her car, I have mine, but he's dependent on one of us to give him a ride."

"You know he's not supposed to drive by himself," Hofmann said absently, for his thoughts were on the letter he was holding. It had arrived well over a week ago, and it had been bothering him ever since. At first the deadline had seemed far away, but now the day had come, and he had to do something. He looked up. "This is the twenty-second, isn't it?"

298

"Sure."

Hofmann pulled the letter from the envelope. "There's only one woman who can use so many words to say nothing. She uses three pages when half a page would do." He cleared his throat. "Your aunt, Lou, is arriving in Berlin today."

"Aunt Lou from America?"

"The very one. That's all we need. And if we don't put a damper on it at once. . . . She was so nicely out of harm's way!"

"What does she say exactly?" Suddenly Max was interested. His sense of family was not highly developed. He managed to be absent most of the time when any of his aunts came to visit, no matter how rarely that occurred. And Hofmann had succeeded in inoculating him with a thorough aversion to his grandmother. Though he occasionally volunteered to drive his mother to the Retirement Home for Ladies in Potsdam where Emmi Hofmann had lived since the death of Frau von Schack, he himself waited in the car. But in Aunt Lou's case it was a little different.

"She is arriving today, at eleven, by train. And she expects me to meet her. She never cared what happened to me, and now she expects me to meet her and to listen. . . .'"

Aunt Lou. At the dinner in the Bristol's Blue Salon after Aunt Lenka's funeral Max had been seated next to her, and he often recalled the scent of her perfume, and especially her rustling taffeta dress. He had been wearing short pants, and the material rubbed his ankles, stirring him strangely, in a way that it took him years to interpret correctly. That was the last time he had seen Aunt Lou except in photographs, but that event, and the fact that at home she was spoken of only in whispers, had kept his curiosity alive.

"A totally mixed-up letter."

"May I see it?" Max thought he could smell her perfume. "Is she traveling alone or is her husband with her?"

"All alone, my boy, there's the rub." He put the letter back and made no move to hand it over. "I don't know how she managed to catch such a nice man, but now she seems to be finished with him."

"What's your problem?"

Hofmann looked up. "I don't want her here. My God—Lou in this house! I'd never have another quiet moment. It wouldn't take her more than a day to turn everything upside down."

"Didn't you talk to Mother about it?"

Hofmann raised his hands in supplication. "Oh no, no, the two of them are like fire and water. Would you meet her train?"

"Me? Sure, why not. I always thought she was swell, as a matter of fact."

"That just shows what an innocent you are when it comes to women. Please, I'll talk to your mother. I'll do everything to make sure that tonight works out, but do this one thing for me. And listen —take her to a hotel. She must have gotten quite enough money out of him—yes, I'm sure of that. Only, whatever you do, don't bring her here. Promise me. Don't let her talk you into it! No way. Be prepared for anything."

"You make her sound like the devil incarnate."

"A devil with the tongue of an angel. My boy, I can only hope that you will be spared anything like that. And please, let me say it again, don't let her involve you. And you might as well take two porters along. I can imagine the mountains of luggage. Go on now, don't keep your father waiting. And remember, just don't bring her here, or my peace and quiet will be done for."

A little later, alone, he became aware of the enormity of the things he had already been asked to handle that morning. He decided to ring for the maid and ask for fresh, really hot coffee. He prepared his morning cigar, cutting it with a small damascened pocket knife—he hated cigar cutters—and carefully removed the wrapper. He still collected the bands for Kleinhans, although in his opinion the designs had long ago stopped showing any imagination.

His coffee was brought, almost boiling hot. He lit his cigar, the first and only one of the day, and picked up a racing journal.

Today's event? Two horses in the first race. Scheherezade—a seven-year-old mare—Scheherezade would not have been a bad tip. But then, what had Schütte said, a sound heart, that was what mattered. He had had enough excitement in his life. Now he had to think about his heart.

2

"Stretch out your hands, close your eyes, walk normally." The doctor watched the muscles move along the man's scarred back. "Perfect. Now back again. Stay on the line. Fine. You may get dressed now."

Carl Senger stepped behind the screen in the corner of the examination room. He heard the sound of running water as the doctor washed his hands, then the screech of a chair moving as he sat down, and shortly afterward the scratch of a pen on the cardboard of the medical chart—not easy and smooth, as if guided by a hand for which writing was an infrequent and disagreeable chore.

The doctor was a giant of a man; Senger's back still smarted from the surgeon's touches during the examination. It was not a pain that he could locate precisely; radiating downward from the nape of his neck, it extended across his back, more a sensation of annoying leadenness than a directly concentrated point.

For years he had lived with these aches; they had become a matter of course, something he had come to terms with. Then, after the fifth operation, after his recovery, there had been a time when the memory of pain had been almost blotted out. But in the last few weeks the aches had suddenly reappeared, as strong as ever, especially during the night, so that they woke him and he felt as if he were lying on a fiery grate.

Looking in the wall mirror before he buttoned his shirt, he encountered the image of a healthy, strong man. In a way that had been the worst—the injury that had kept him confined to his sickbed for so long was hidden from his sight. The same was true for the scars of his operations. All he knew was the pain, and it had sometimes seemed to him as if everything existed only in his imagination or as if he had been put under an evil spell. Perhaps, too, this feeling was connected with the way he had been injured; he had been wounded not in action but in a traffic mishap. In his two and a half years at the front not the least thing had befallen him, and then, in January 1917, he was riding in a car—he was not even the driver—that had skidded on an icy road at high speed.

The memory of the cause and course of the accident had dimmed. All the more precise was his recollection of how he regained consciousness, to find himself in a bed in a darkened room. He had not noticed any bandages on his body, had felt nothing beyond a heaviness in his legs. He had thought he could get up. He was surprised when his arms and legs would not obey him. The only way he could explain it to himself was that he had been tied down to the bed.

And then, when he gathered all his strength to try to raise the upper part of his body, someone in the room had cried out very loudly. Then he realized that he was alone, that he was the one who was screaming, and that the only thing tying him to the bed was his own inability to move. And that was when the pain had come, this feeling as if he were lying on a fiery grate.

"Come over here." Professor Hahn pointed to the chair across from his desk. "I must say, your call disturbed me. There was no reason to expect any change for the worse. Sit down, sit down. Is the sun bothering you? I can close the curtains. No? I must say, this weather —almost twenty-five degrees in the shade—makes me feel marvelous. Reminds me of the time I spent in Nkongsamba. What a paradise! They grow the best coffee in the world there. May I offer you a cup?"

"Thank you."

"Thank you yes or thank you no?"

"No."

When Carl Senger entered the examination room for the first time, he immediately noticed the African masks that adorned the walls. Until the September 1914 occupation by the French and English, Hahn

302

had been a physician in the Cameroons, where his father had built the so-called coffee and banana railroad from Bonaber to Nkongsamba.

The doctor pushed aside the sheaf of charts, as if he could not find any help there. "Exactly now, when did the deterioration start?"

"A few weeks ago."

"And just how does it manifest itself? A leaden feeling in the legs?"

"No."

"In your hands? Move your hand."

"It isn't anything specific. More a general lack of strength. Some discomfort if I sit still for a long time, as if I could collapse any minute. But none of that is very bad. It's the old problem, anxiety during the night. I wake up and feel that I'm paralyzed again. And sometimes it happens even during the day. I sit at my desk, convinced that I won't be able to get up from my chair. . . ."

"Fricke still comes regularly to massage you?"

"Yes."

"And you do the exercises I prescribed?"

"Of course."

"No experimenting? Tennis or horseback riding?"

"No."

"No long automobile trips?" The doctor asked his questions not to get answers but to gain time, to observe the man, to see through him. A particularly sturdy, exceptionally handsome man for someone of fifty-one, sun-bronzed, in superb physical shape—a true athlete, someone you would expect to breeze through hours on the tennis court. "You do understand that some discomforts can reappear from time to time, along with a kind of neurological sensitivity, especially when there are abrupt changes in the weather? But probably that's not what you mean when you speak of deterioration."

"No. That isn't what I mean."

"Fine." Professor Hahn rose. "Then let's look at the x-rays together."

The doctor turned on the light in the screen where the three pictures were hung. "This one was taken two years ago, this is last year's, and this is the one we took this morning. Here is where it starts, and these places on the seventh cervical vertebra, that's the pains you sometimes feel down to your wrist. But I don't want to go into detail. I mean, the picture isn't altogether normal—after all, you've been through five operations. What I want to show you is this. Compare

303

the new picture with the old ones. Can you see anything different?"

The two men stood together before the pictures, the doctor towering over his patient by almost a head.

"How could I, as a layman."

"No, no, I won't let you get away with that. All right, one more time. Here . . . here . . . here. Where is the difference?"

"I can't really see any."

"Quite right. You can't see any. Because there isn't any. Not a single indication of deterioration. Quite the opposite, in fact. Scars well healed, the tissue has regenerated excellently. There, do you see this particular incision? Three years ago the scarred area was still this wide, now it's only a thin seam. The scars continue to heal—that means that the pain ought to diminish more and more." He pointed to another spot. "It's the same all over. The destroyed tissue is returning to normal, visibly."

"Then why do I have this trouble?"

The doctor turned off the light and returned to his place behind the desk. He waited until Senger, too, was seated. He sensed that Senger was not reassured by the x-rays. He himself was in the same position. Though the evidence of the pictures was useful, the symptoms Senger complained of indicated that the evil had other roots.

Nevertheless the physician said, "Everything is in perfect order. Really, what more can I say. You can be satisfied. All in all, you're in splendid physical shape. Many a man of your age would envy your vitality." He knew that he was exaggerating slightly, but he had a purpose.

"To you I may seem that way."

The doctor picked up the totem fragment lying on the desk. It was only a sliver of a larger figure, dark, polished wood with remnants of white and red paint. He enclosed it in his huge hands, almost as if he wished to draw strength from it.

"Don't give me any trouble, Senger. Sitting there across from me, you're a medical miracle. Try to remember. How was it five years ago? Your wife wheeled you in here. You were a cripple, forgive me, a helpless cripple. You'd been given up by a dozen of my colleagues. You were stuffed full of narcotics, that's all they did for you. Can you remember?" He pointed the fragment of the totem at a stack of Senger's records. He did not have to check; the date was engraved on his mind. "On March sixteenth, nineteen nineteen, you came to see me for the first time." He waited until Senger met his eyes, and then he spoke of a matter that he had never before touched upon in all the years Senger had been his patient. "Just before that you tried to take your own life, didn't you?"

Senger's instinctive reaction was defensive, but Hahn was speaking the truth. A dozen doctors had treated him. They had all given him to understand, with greater or lesser directness, that his case was hopeless. They could keep him alive, they could give him medication to alleviate his pain, but he would remain paralyzed. At the very beginning he had been grateful simply to live, but when he began to understand that from now on he would vegetate, life had lost all value and meaning for him, and he became determined to end it.

"I had my reasons at the time," he said.

"I know. Or let's say I have an idea."

"She was a young woman, and I—well, as you put it, I was a cripple."

"It's a good thing that you remember. You really were a hopeless case. I had no reason to make you promises. My surgical method was new, and in a few cases it had failed. You were taking more of a risk than I was. But you took it."

"There was no risk in it for me. On the contrary, I hoped—"

"You hoped that you would die on the table . . . that wasn't hard to guess either. But afterward you helped. The operation alone could not have restored you. The crucial factor was your will, your newly awakened will to become a healthy human being again. Do you want me to tell you the truth? I think a similar situation exists now."

"It's possible. Yes, maybe I'm thinking that it would have been better if I had never consulted you. My wife—"

"Now you're merely saying that you would have preferred it if your wife had left you to your fate. You should be thankful she got on the train and went to the front to bring you back. That she never gave up. That more than any of the rest of us she always believed that you could be restored to health. Excuse me, but if there's one thing I can't stand it's self-pity. I'm ready to bring a corpse back to life, but I'm the wrong doctor for a healthy man who gives up on himself. As I told you, you've reached another point where you're the only one who can help you."

There was silence, and it almost seemed as if the conversation were at an end, yet Senger felt the urge to confide in the doctor. He had really come only for the talk. It was absurd—normally he did not suffer from such inhibitions. He could express everything in words, it was an innate gift; only when the subject was himself was he overcome by an almost insurmountable shyness. At such times he depended on someone coming to his aid, approaching him and giving him an opening. The doctor's expression remained impassive. He had stretched out his hands as if to say, that's what I could help you with, you can't expect more from me. Nevertheless it was these hands that allowed Senger to speak.

"You see, I was always someone who . . . how shall I put it—a man who had mobility. I needed it, I only felt right when I was moving. Perhaps you don't know, but I used to be a commercial traveler, and basically I haven't changed. To be on the road, here today, there tomorrow, recruiting and training a new group of salesmen, opening a new, tricky territory, driving the competition from the arena. As long as I could do that, I was in my element. That's how I built up the business in the first place. I was nobody and I had nothing. That was my capital. And then. . . . I was never able to travel again."

"You wouldn't have done it anyway, would you? With the size of your business now, you would hardly have gone on the road yourself? Perhaps now and then, but surely it would not have been your primary activity. I don't understand your business, but I assume that it's not so different from my hospital. The larger it grows, the more I have to steal the time to do my surgery. Administrative junk. I'm sure your experience is the same. And now, I've heard, you're building a new plant and a new office building here in Berlin?"

"Yes, we're building. I'm going to get a beautiful office. And I'll be sitting there and asking myself what business I have being there. What can I do that she can't do better?"

"Now listen to me. Are you blaming your wife for the situation? What choice did she have but to take it on herself? When you come right down to it, she had to do it alone because you—"

"Because I was good for nothing. Now you've said it yourself. Yes, I know what I owe her. It's marvelous to have such a competent wife, but not always easy when you feel like a wreck yourself."

"I'm afraid we're getting into an area where I cannot help you. There have been several such hurdles before, black days when you talked the same way. I thought that was all over. Really, Senger, there's nothing more I can tell you. You'll have to find the solution to your problem yourself. Do something. Sell the firm if you like!"

"I was thinking along those lines."

"Well then." Professor Hahn got to his feet. "Where there's a will, there's a way. You just got bogged down in a fixed idea. Self-torture, pure and simple. And most important, talk it over with your wife. You haven't, have you?"

"No."

"Do it. And next time, I hope, you'll have a cup of coffee with me. I have it roasted specially—West African coffee, you can't get such a bean in the whole city. My God, Senger, what do you expect from life! Look at me—I'm what they call a big gun. They pass me around at congresses. I make more money than you'd believe. I can afford anything, and what is it that gives me pleasure? A cup of coffee after I've performed surgery. Nothing more. And I'm not blessed with a wife like yours!"

He accompanied his patient to the upholstered door. He came to a stop once more. "You've told me something that isn't said easily. Now I'll confess something to you, too. And please, don't misunderstand me. I'm a confirmed bachelor, you know that. But your wife— sometimes I think, what would I do if she were available? She always stayed with you—think about why."

3

At the left of her field of vision was the canal, almost an idyll. The heavily loaded barge rode low in the water, the wash was hung out behind the wheelhouse, and a dog ran back and forth along the rail. A few fishermen were standing on the far shore. She had never seen anyone catch anything, but of course she never spent much time at the window. Far to the right she could see the elevated railroad, an iron cobweb of rails, but this too was not of great interest at the moment. Her attention was fixed on the area directly in front of her—the building site, the excavations in the foreground and the rubble and planks strewn where the old factory and the dwelling had once stood. Only one wall was still standing, the one with the large advertising picture of the laughing laundress. A yellow crane was stationed there, a powerful iron ball dangling from its flexible arm and now brought to swing.

Camilla was overcome with a kind of impatience as she watched. The ball hit the wall once, twice, without any effect, as if it were made of rubber. But then, when the ball struck a third time, a tremor ran through the brickwork and the whole facade collapsed. When the cloud of dust had settled, all that met the eye was a mountain of bricks.

The scene of destruction did not depress Camilla. On the contrary, it put her in an almost euphoric mood, for she saw in it not

308

the end of something, but the beginning of something new. Where once her father's first soap vats had stood, the walls of the new factory would soon be rising. The thought that she had once hated this area and everything connected with soap never entered her mind. The moment signified simply that the circle had closed; she was back in Berlin.

She turned away from the window. Her office was furnished simply, almost provisionally, and was located on the fifth floor of a one-time cardboard factory. During the inflationary period she had been able to acquire the building together with the real estate from the original Hofmann property; after their move to Steglitz they had housed their offices here. The manufacturing plant had remained in Neustrelitz, but from the outset they had planned to rebuild. The plan was to proceed in two stages, first a new factory on the old Hofmann grounds, and then an office building.

The model had been in her office for several days. She came to a stop in front of it. The location was ideal, with direct access to waterways and railroads and, as a bonus, cheap cooling water from the canal.

She went back to her desk. The room was warm, but if she opened the windows, the room would be filled with the dust of the demolition work and the noise of the machines. She picked up the papers dealing with the forthcoming bank negotiations, began to go through them, made some notes, then pressed the buzzer that summoned a fifty-year-old woman with bobbed and marcelled hair from the next room.

Palleck, as she was called, had been working for Camilla for many years. At one time she had been employed at the revenue office in Neustrelitz; Camilla had lured her away from there after she demonstrated her skills in a way that was most unpleasant for the Senger business. Palleck took care of all tax matters, but she called herself Camilla's secretary because she also looked after Camilla's appointments and supervised the clerical staff. As always, she rushed in, clasping two thick folders. Because of a hip injury she was forced to wear orthopedic shoes, and she compensated for her debility with a particularly brisk manner.

Camilla pointed to the stack of papers on her desk. "Didn't my son go through these? I can't find his initials anywhere."

"He worked on them yesterday. Look on the bottom sheet. I must say, he found a couple of things that even I hadn't noticed; we'll easily be able to bring in a hundred thousand on the taxes. He's a genius in the field, that one." She put down both her folders.

"I'll sign the mail later."

But Palleck shook her head. "It won't go out in time, not on Friday. And a half-hour from now the inspectors from the water resources commission are due, to talk about the rates. And at twelve-thirty you have to leave for the meeting with the bankers. I've ordered the table. By the way, your mother called twice; she wouldn't tell me what it was about. She'll call again, but I don't know if I can put her off a third time. . . . You know how stubborn she can be."

Camilla made a gesture as if to ward off what was coming. "If there's any way to avoid it, please, not today." She had begun to put her signature on the originals and the copies Palleck was handing her one by one. Camilla was not in the habit of paying much attention to her own signature, but suddenly she noticed that in the course of the years it had changed and had become almost identical to her husband's, *CamillaSenger,* condensed into one word, just as he wrote *CarlSenger.* The fact that their first names began with the same letter was not the only reason; the resemblance went further, all the way to the upward curve into which the final *r* flowed.

She interrupted herself and listened. "Isn't that my husband?"

"It might be, yes."

She finished the first folder and pushed the second one aside. "I'll sign these later. Tell me, has the ventilator been installed in Herr Senger's office?"

"It was done last night, just as you asked."

Camilla rose. "Tell the girls to make some tea. Cold, with lots of lemon and a little sugar, in a thermos. I'll be in Herr Senger's office."

After Palleck left, Camilla gathered up the notes for the meeting with the bankers and went out into the corridor. The passageway had been narrowed by the file cabinets lining the walls between the doors and windows. Similar temporary arrangements prevailed throughout the building. The hand-me-down furniture, small rooms, long walks were simply an expedient until the new office building was ready for occupancy. The only room Camilla had furnished from scratch was Senger's, located at the end of the hall. That had been done before the fifth, the final, operation, as if by this action she were imploring the gods to allow him to resume his place and carry the responsibility that had been on her shoulders for so long. Outside the door she hesitated for a moment. It was quiet inside, and she knew the picture that would greet her eyes when she entered: her husband behind his massive desk, which was just as neat at this hour as it was at the close of the work day. She knocked—a habit she had retained from the years of his illness.

It was as she had expected. He was sitting at his desk. The top was bare except for the calendar, the telephone, and a few newspapers. The desk set still looked as new as the day it had been unwrapped and put in place.

He was on his feet at once, coming to greet her. "You were in a hurry this morning."

"You know, Fridays. And then there are some errands I have to run this afternoon, for tonight." She put down the file she had brought. "Here are the papers we need for the bank meeting, the estimate of building costs, financing plans. I'd like you to have a look at them. But first tell me what happened at the doctor's."

"I could have saved myself the trip." The room, with its two outside walls, was even warmer than her office. He went to a window and opened it, but closed it at once when a generator began to rattle.

"I had them install a fan for you."

"I saw. Thanks."

He was speaking formally, almost as if she were a stranger. She was used to this; whenever he returned from a visit to the doctor, he was in the same mood. She watched him as he stood at the window, looking out, one shoulder slightly hunched and his arms held close to his body. How well she knew this defensive posture! She had always respected his desire to avoid discussing anything connected with his disability, but recently she had been questioning the wisdom of it.

"What did he say?"

"You know how he is."

He walked away from the window and returned to the desk as if he felt safer there. "He gave me a lecture on the advantages of particular sorts of coffee."

"Surely that isn't all he said."

"Please. The x-rays showed nothing. The complaints are all in my imagination. Satisfied? In his eyes I'm a completely healthy man, maybe a little healthier than most men my age."

311

She knew this aggressive note in his voice as well; he sought refuge in it in order to hide his feelings, to close himself off. This too was something she had always allowed him. A man who had been chained to a wheelchair for so long and who had never complained must sometimes react in this way, to air his feelings. But in this, too, she now asked herself whether she might not have been silent too long. "Maybe Doctor Hahn is right," she said.

"Then you agree, the two of you."

She noticed that he withdrew into himself even more, becoming even more remote from her. From outside, the noises of the construction site penetrated the room with greater strength, helping her to get through the moment. The new factory—that was the magic word that until now had always worked its spell during all difficult times. Looking ahead, starting on the next task—but for some time she had been noticing that she was reaching the limit of her strength.

She walked up to him and placed her hand on his shoulder. "What are we doing wrong, Carl? There's something we're doing wrong lately."

He looked up, thinking of the doctor's parting words. Yes, why had she stayed with him? He could not shake off the question. Why didn't he put it to her? But instead he said, "It would never occur to me that you could do anything wrong."

She stepped back. "You demand a great deal from me."

"I'm sorry. Let's not talk about it any more."

"There's something we're doing wrong."

"I said I'm sorry. I shouldn't have gone to see Professor Hahn. Let's go over the notes."

The telephone on his desk shrilled. He made no move to pick up the receiver; instead he said, "It's sure to be for you."

But then he answered the phone, listened, and with an almost apologetic smile said, "It is for you."

The connection had already been made, and her mother's words flooded her until she was finally able to interrupt. "Yes, I have two tickets for. . . . Of course. Why do you always think you'll be forgotten. . . . Two. . . . No, orchestra seats, fifth row. . . . Listen to me for a change. . . . They were sold out. . . . I'm sorry, but to get these two tickets I had to. . . . If you don't let me finish, I can't explain it to you. The play is sold out! Besides, fifth row of the orchestra, you'll be able to see even better. . . . No. No box seats. . . . I'll repeat it one more time. The play is sold out, for weeks and months. . . . No. . . . Make up your mind, do you want the tickets or not? Fine then, why must you always carry on so first? . . . No, the chauffeur cannot call for you. Even a chauffeur has Sundays off. . . . Yes of course I'll pay for the taxi. . . . I'm sorry, what did you say? I'll have to think about it. And now you must excuse me. I'll call you tonight. . . . What? What else is there? . . . No, I don't believe that. Palleck would never talk nonsense at you. She had strict instructions from me not to put any calls through. . . . No, not even you." For an instant she held the receiver away from her ear, and the sound of a high voice could be heard, weepy, almost sobbing, though it degenerated quickly into a harsh, nagging tone.

"Talk to you later," Camilla said in conclusion. "Yes, of course I'll think about it." When she had replaced the receiver, she realized that during her talk with her mother she had begun to perspire. She moved a chair and sat down. "Complaints, reproaches, demands—she never changes her methods."

"What did she want?"

"It was all about two ridiculous theater tickets."

"No, I mean at the end."

"She said that it was absolutely essential for her to spend four weeks in Bad Neuenahr, otherwise she wouldn't be able to survive the year. And last time she came to see me, she was absolutely blooming. Where she is she has everything—and a hundred pounds over."

"You could just as easily have told her that in the first place. Afterward you always give in anyway and pay for all her extras and trips and cures."

"What choice do I have? She lost all her money." She looked at her husband. Couldn't he feel how all this was devouring her energies? Why wouldn't he get up, put his arm around her—just that, nothing more, only a sign that he understood?

There was a knock and one of the girls brought in the iced tea. When they were alone again, Camilla said, "Fine, let's talk about the financing plan. If you'll turn to the first page, you'll find the essential figures. By the way, we're meeting the bankers at twelve-thirty."

"Do I have to be there?"

This too was something she was prepared for. They had always discussed everything, arrived at decisions together, but as soon as it came to the new buildings, he had always arranged things so that he was absent from crucial conferences. Even acquiring the site had been like that, when he did not show up for the closing. Every time they were to meet with the architect he had just spent a bad night; and he walked past the model in her office as if it did not exist.

"I really do think you should be there. We're applying for a four-million-marks loan—in installments, admittedly. We've got to get it. We need the new factory. The encumbrances in the next few years are going to be high, though."

"It's all settled, isn't it? The bank has as good as agreed." He riffled through the papers.

She was still holding the glass of tea. Her hands felt hot, her face felt hot, but inside she was freezing. "You thought our turnover projections were realistic. If that's true, we have no choice but to expand."

He looked up from the papers. "Expand—that's what it always comes down to, doesn't it. Did you ever ask yourself what for?"

"No. That's never been a question for me. Do you think I could have done any of it if I'd asked myself why? I always counted on you—and on the children too, of course."

"Leave me out of it for the moment. And our sons? What makes you so sure that one day they really will take over the business? You never know with children. Perhaps they have different plans. Max, for example, he goes his own way even now. Can you read their minds?"

"Right now we're the ones that are important—you and me. I can't carry all the responsibility alone. I don't even want to. You'll have to get used to having it back again. We've talked about it so many times."

"Yes—too many times. That's why I'd like to suggest something different."

"Yes?" She put down her glass and looked at him expectantly. It was the first time in a long time that he volunteered a suggestion.

"This bank loan—fine. We can swing it. Three, four lean years, depending on the overall economic situation. I can see a couple of uncertain factors. Perhaps unemployment will rise even more. But what is certain is that our competition will increase."

"You never worried about that in the past."

He lowered his head and lightly twisted the pencil between his fingers. "In the past I was a different person."

"Why do you say something like that?"

"Because it's true. But let's drop it. You know we no longer control the market. We've gained competitors from abroad, the English first, and now the Dutch. They're buying up factories wherever they can get them, and they can pick them up for a song."

"That was one of the reasons for building a second manufacturing plant here in Berlin."

"But that's only the beginning. Those are international corporations, Camilla. They'll keep on buying and taking over a larger share of the market. They're not the kind of competition we've had in the past. They work with our methods, but they're more cunning than we are. They won't be satisfied with small shares of the market. They want the whole thing. They'll try to push us against the wall, and they have everything going for them: capital, ingenious advertising, sound products. It won't be easy to stand up to them. That takes— and I'm sorry I have to say it—someone in possession of all his powers."

"You were going to make a suggestion."

"Yes. I believe we ought to take in a partner. Whether I owe money to the bank or have to share the business, I don't see any difference. On the contrary, it seems to me it would have certain advantages, given the present situation. Well, I've been talking to a few people recently."

"You never said a word." She forced herself to remain calm; the most important part was his reawakened concern. "A silent partner? Why not. But how come you only mention it now, at the last moment?"

"I wasn't certain that you wouldn't oppose the idea right from the beginning. And besides, I wanted to have a concrete offer before I spoke to you."

"And you have one?"

"Yes. From the Dutch. Quite generous, in fact. We can build the factory without a penny from the bank. That way we'd avoid all the burden of interest payments. We'd have more room—"

"What's the catch?"

"I don't see any, but you may feel differently. I beg you to keep

315

one thing in mind, though—in all my dealings, I've kept you upper-most in my mind."

She had gotten to her feet. "What's the catch?"

He unlocked the desk drawer and pulled out a sheaf of stapled typed pages. "Don't you want to see the details of the offer first?"

"What do they want?"

"Well, they do set one condition: they'll only come in with us if they can take fifty-one percent of the voting stock."

After a moment's silence she said, "Never. I'll never agree to that, never."

He had expected some such reaction—just as unequivocal, just as vehement—and as he saw her standing there, an image from the past rose in his mind. His sickroom in the field hospital near Douai. She had been with him for two weeks. She spent all her days with him. The doctor had admitted that there was nothing they could do for him, but at the same time he refused her request that she be al-lowed to take him home. The conversation had taken place in his presence. The doctor had accidentally dropped the fact that he con-sidered it senseless to transport the patient, since no one at home would be able to help him either, and besides, it would be impossible to obtain a car to send him home in.

"You'll never be able to stop me!" It was as if he were hearing her voice again, the same vehemence. She had actually managed to dig up a car and even a male nurse to go with them: it had taken them four days to travel from Douai to Neustrelitz. He had only a hazy memory of the trip. The inside of a half-darkened car, the con-trols, flashlights flickering in the dark, delays when they ran out of gasoline. What had remained of the trip was not the memory of pain; that was blotted out. One thing only stayed with him—the feeling of her presence, sitting next to his litter in the narrow car, and combined with it an intense happiness such as he had never before experienced. Now he asked himself, what had become of it? What had they done wrong?

"Never," she repeated. "And I cannot believe that you're seriously considering it." She made a gesture that took in the whole room and much more. "You expect strangers to decide what happens here in the future?"

"I was thinking of you."

"And did you think that I gave half a lifetime for this?"

"Half a lifetime is enough. Do you want it to be your whole life? Look at the proposal. Not much will change. You or I, one of us, can remain on the board, and a director's seat is reserved for each of our sons—"

"I don't want to discuss it any further." She had never before ended a conversation in this maner. She turned away. Where was the door? She could not feel the floor under her feet. And she did not hear what he said next. She was unable to think clearly; she only knew that now she would need every ounce of energy to get to the door.

4

The sports car came from the direction of the bridge. It crossed the canal, turned in at the gate of the factory without slowing down, barely managed to sail safely past the piles of empty oil barrels, and came to a stop in front of the Senger Company's private gas pump.

It was an open two-seater with leather straps across the hood. The car was familiar, and so was the owner's manner of driving. The only reaction of old Pölzig, who took care of the company cars, was a shake of his head, for he had sensitive ears, and squealing brakes and loud honking set his teeth on edge. Hoping at least to prevent young Senger from tooting his horn, he quickly left the hoist and rushed outside in his blue smock, an old scarf slung around his neck, his ears stuffed with cotton.

Max Senger swung himself over the side. To get out by the small door would have been even more cumbersome, given his height. He turned the keys hanging from a ring bearing the seal of an elegant Berlin sailing club and tossed them at the car supervisor, whose hands were already cupped to receive them.

"Wash it, fill it up, change the oil, and a new set of tires on the rear wheels wouldn't hurt."

"Boy oh boy." Pölzig examined the treads. "I'm not surprised, the way you drive." He stood up. "But you better have a word with the boss first."

Max Senger was already halfway to the porter's lodge. Handing his car over to old Pölzig, to get it back freshly polished and with a full gas tank, had become such a matter of course that he gave the old man a look of surprise. "What's happened now?"

Pölzig toyed with the keys. "Frau Senger has been checking your monthly chits. There was a lot of fuel this month, and then the repairs, two new headlights—a lot for just one month. She was just checking, all the cars, and I've got orders to hold back some. I'll fill it up and do all the other stuff, just so you tell her. . . ."

"I'll speak with her." He had to shout the last few words to be heard above a steam shovel that was starting up. The *boss*—that's all he needed to hear! The rage he had felt that morning rekindled as he marched toward the porter's glass cage, his jacket over his arm. Presumably the man did nothing but give him a friendly nod, but he interpreted it differently and said, "All right, call the *boss*. You must have kept a record of how long I was away from my desk. Go ahead, call her."

He knew that he was behaving childishly, and it made him even angrier to think that he had let himself be carried away. What he really wanted to do was turn on his heels. To drive out to the country, to the lake, to work off his rage behind the oars—that would be far better than sitting in his office. His office—the very thought made him seethe. What it was was a hell hole, stifling hot in summer, an ice pit in the winter. It was not even his alone any more since they'd put the raw-materials buyer in with him. Orders from the *boss*. Two people work better than one, they can keep an eye on each other. At least during August he was on vacation. . . .

The office was on the third floor, which also housed a large room full of machinery that had been converted to package one kind of soap flakes. He could have reached his room by a different route, but he deliberately chose the way that led through the hot hall and the roar of the machines, which sometimes could be heard all the way in his office. The country! He could still leave.

He tore open the door to his office. He had let the blinds down in the morning, so that now the room was dusky. He saw her at once and yet he did not trust his eyes, it was so unusual for his mother to seek him out. In all these years it had happened at most once or twice.

She was sitting in one of the plain wooden chairs, and her hands

—this struck him as equally unusual—were empty, holding no papers, no documents. Quite clearly, too, she had done nothing in his absence, looked for nothing. She simply sat there and looked at him, as if she had been waiting for him. And something in her bearing, in her manner of looking at him, caused him to close the door very quietly.

"Good morning, Max. Your yellow sweater—is it new? I must admit the color suits you."

His jacket still across his arm, he stood there and realized that she was taking the wind out of his sails. "Grandfather thought it was hideous."

"No, it's becoming to you."

He stared at her. As always when he was furious at her, determined somehow to escape her influence, he was more than ever aware of her beauty: the full dark hair with the first gray strands which she did not color, the dark eyes, the lips, the narrow, supple neck, the delicate skin. It was always like this when he looked at her as a stranger. But this time there was another element. Lou, whom he had just left, had dropped certain hints. He was not even certain that he had understood them correctly, but they were enough to make him look at the woman in his office even more carefully.

He knew how hard all these years had been for her. How had she endured it all and still remained the woman sitting there? From where did she draw her strength? And her calm? Where was the source? Did she have secret affairs? He asked the question for the first time. The thought was so out of place, so inconceivable, and yet it brought her closer. Abruptly he wished to put his arms around her, without explanation, but then his warning system sounded the alarm. She's tricking me again, he thought.

He hung his jacket on a hanger and took the case from his pocket. He placed it on a desk in such a way that she would have to notice it. When she did not comment, he opened the lid and held it out to her. The gray velvet pillow clasped a narrow platinum ring with a star sapphire surrounded by small diamonds. "Don't you want to know who it's for?"

"For a girl, I assume."

"Yes, for a girl. You'll meet her tonight. I'm going to marry her." He waited for a mocking remark, for opposition; he almost wished for it so as to gain another issue for controversy. But she only sat still, silent. "If it wouldn't be too much trouble, be nice to her. Did you hear me? I'm going to marry her."

"I heard you."

"Well? No objections? Doubts? You're not even going to ask whether she has money?"

As if to do him the favor she said, "And does she have money?"

"Ah, that's beginning to sound better. At least now we're back on familiar ground." He tore open the blinds, so that the room was abruptly bright. His mother raised her arm to her eyes; it was a gesture of helplessness, and her voice held the same note.

"What is it you all hold against me?"

"Do you want me to tell you? I can tell you. Because you take everything for granted."

"Please, can't you lower the blinds?"

He went on as if he had not heard her plea. "Because everything always has to go as you want. Take the three of us, Konrad, Georg, and me. We're nothing more to you than a good capital investment. Portfolios. How well you thought it all out. What do you need in the business? A good chemist. A good lawyer. And one who knows all about money. And what happens? Konrad studies chemistry, Georg studies law. And even the third of the allies, the black sheep, dutifully learns the banking business and turns out to be exactly what you expected him to be. All three sons dutifully do whatever Mama always wanted them to do. And what's more, they do it of their own free will. Everything is done by everybody's free will. No one is coerced into anything. The whole loving family obeys voluntarily. That's how it is in a marvelous family like ours. And one of these days the three sons, of their own free will, will share the firm, each in his own post—"

"Yes, that was my plan. Is it so evil? I had no way of knowing what would happen to Father. And even aside from that, I always knew that one day the three of you would take over the responsibility."

"Take over responsibility! And you checking my gasoline chits!" The narrow room, the heat, the woman who did not argue with him —the idea came to him spontaneously. "I will take over nothing. Not junior, son of the lady boss. Please, may I have some gas? I'm sorry I'm late. I can stand on my own two feet. I'll prove it to you, but not here. Perhaps I'll emigrate. America. Yes! Europe has had it anyway. America, that's where the future lies. . . ." Beads of perspiration

321

dotted his forehead, his throat felt dry, and now that he had aired his feelings, his anger, too, seemed spent. He pulled down the blinds, sat down, and made another start. "All right, let's talk about my gasoline consumption. I assume that's why you're here."

"No, that's not really the reason."

Once again, as when he had first come in, something in her voice confused him. She had placed one of her arms on the desk for support, as if the chair were no longer enough. He felt an urge to put his hand on her arm, but he restrained himself. "Then why did you come?"

"Do I always have to have a reason? Perhaps I only wanted to sit here and have a little quiet. Perhaps I wanted to talk with you. But perhaps I just wanted to sit here."

He looked around the room, with the used office furniture, the shabby files, the world map showing markets for raw materials, the whitewashed walls. And he thought, this is where she has to come for quiet?

"I didn't really mean it," he said, "all that stuff about America."

"No? Are you sure? Even that wouldn't surprise me today. Perhaps you're right in your accusations. One can't really plan anyone's life but one's own. Not that of other people. You've got to understand me. It was simply an idea I clung to—three more years, then at least Max will be ready. A lot of times I felt as you do now—I can't go on! I've had enough! Day after day, get out of bed. Day after day, rush over here. No matter how I might be feeling. Did it never occur to you that I might wish for something different?"

Though there was no real connection, he was suddenly reminded of the scene at the railway station. He had been a few minutes late, and Lou was already standing on the platform, next to a mountain of luggage, dressed all in violet, from her pointed and buttoned shoes to her hat the size of a wheel. Not alone, to be sure, not helpless, but surrounded by the gentlemen she had met in the course of her journey and by porters who fought for the privilege of transporting her baggage to the taxi. She had needed two of them, and the whole game was played all over again in the hotel. Pages and bellhops crowded around her as if her perfume had a special power to attract. He was almost surprised that he did not reek of it.

This time he did place his hand on his mother's arm. "Yes, I think I understand you. I have an idea. I'll take you out. To the country!

322

We'll rent a boat and I'll row way out. It's crowded there Friday afternoons, but not our lake—it's still deserted. I wonder if the old beach house is still there? And the old boat? Do you remember that time, my birthday, when Grandfather gave me the rig with the two white goats? He always thought of unusual gifts." He looked at his wrist watch. "Listen—it's twelve-thirty. Weren't you supposed to meet with the men from the bank?"

She looked at him and thought, all he remembers is the goat cart, the two white animals. That meant birthday to him, not the telegram with the news of Lenka's dying. And I'm the same way, I can think only about the way he just put his hand on my arm, just that, and everything else is forgotten.

"The lunch meeting? It's been canceled."

"But why? I thought it was all settled. Did a problem come up? Aren't they satisfied with our collateral? You worked out such a good deal, four and a half percent interest and as a second mortgage."

"Father has another plan. He wants to sell."

Max Senger jumped up from his chair. "What? Sell? But to whom? What a crazy idea—selling! You didn't agree, did you?"

She tried to be as objective as possible, telling him his father's plan, giving no sign of her own reaction, but she felt better already just talking about it and because of his immediate response. "He thinks it would be best to take in a partner," she concluded. "He says the competition in our markets will get rougher, and he doesn't feel up to it."

"Fifty-one percent—he must be crazy."

"You could realize all your plans if we sell. You could get your share in cash. And then we have to think about Konrad and Georg. They might like the idea. It's a decision all of us have to make together. And if all of you are in favor of it, I've decided I won't object."

"But Mother! You can't give any weight to what I said before. All of us are committed to the business. And Father—did you ever stop to think that there may be something else behind it?"

"He's been negotiating with those people! He has a firm offer." Once more her outrage came to the surface. "All of it behind my back, without a word to me."

"He's jealous, plain and simple."

"Jealous?"

"Yes. Didn't it ever occur to you? He feels you can get along without him. He's a fifth wheel."

She tried to recall their earlier discussion. Until now she had only been aware of the pain Senger had caused her. But now she said, "When he told me about his idea, I realized how attached I am to all of it. Too attached, don't you see? It just happened that way. It means too much to me, I depend on it far too much. After all, I'm only a woman!"

Once more he looked at her, and once more he could not help but compare her with the woman at the railroad station. "You are who you are. And I'm proud of you. I mean, Aunt Lou . . . is striking, but you're beautiful."

"Lou. What makes you think of Lou right now?"

It did not happen to him often, but now he blushed. "I . . . I've just come back from the railroad station. I met her train."

"Lou?"

"Yes. I wasn't sure whether I should tell you. She wrote to Grandfather. She wanted him to meet her, and he delegated me. You should have seen it! Grandfather prepared me for a lot of things—huge amounts of luggage, a big scene—but she exceeded my expectations. Maybe I shouldn't have told you. . . ."

"Where is she?"

"I took her to the Bristol. She got rooms there."

"Rooms? She's not alone?"

"Oh yes. . . . When I say rooms, I mean a suite. A single room wouldn't have been enough for her. . . . May I ask you something?"

"Go ahead."

"And you'll give me an honest answer?"

"I'll try. Or not answer at all, which is a kind of answer too. Well?"

She forced herself to look at her son, but the question he put to her was not the one she had expected.

"Tell me, why did you stay with Father? It can't have been pity. If that had been all, you wouldn't have done it, would you?"

"What strange questions you ask." She had still not recovered from the shock.

"Can you answer it?"

"Oh yes. The answer is simple: I love him." And she added, "Maybe in a different way from what you think the word means. I don't know. I'd have to think about it." She had risen to her feet.

324

"About tonight," he said. "Please be nice to this girl. It's not at all simple to find one you won't put in the shade. So be nice to her. It's serious this time. I mean, I love her. What kind of party are you giving, anyway?"

"The party? I thought when the weather is so beautiful there ought to be a party. Just for us. And we'll have the first woodruff punch of the season."

"I have a feeling that somehow it's some kind of special day."

She did not reply. She came to a stop at the door. She wanted to say something more, but he anticipated her.

"I know, my car expenses are too high. That's what you were going to say, isn't it?"

She laughed. "I'm afraid that's exactly what I was going to say."

5

The shouts and cheers of the crowd jamming the sidewalks could be heard all the way into the watchmaker's shop. The old jeweler placed the gold hunter on the velvet cloth and took off his old-fashioned pince-nez for a moment. "They'll end up smashing my plate-glass windows."

"What's going on? What is the crowd all about?" Camilla looked through the window, which was dark with people, and she wondered how she had managed to make her way through.

"Some official function. A state visit. Some South American president or other. But that's how Berliners are—just so they can gather in a crowd. Wherever they think they'll witness a spectacle, that's where you'll find them, that's what they have time for."

"They haven't exactly been showered with diversions lately."

But the jeweler stuck to his guns. "You won't find any people more addicted to pleasure than your Berliners." He clamped on his pince-nez, set the watch, and wound it. "Nobody left around to appreciate it, either, a watch like that! Wrist watches, that's all I can sell anymore. Men like your father, they understood something about watches. How is the old gentleman, anyway?"

"Fine, as always."

"We're the same age, did you know that? A good year, durable like the old watches. Too bad he had to sell his collection. I was able to

buy back a few of the pieces. Wrist watches—what times we live in."
He pressed open the lid of the hunter. His knuckles were gnarled
from arthritis, but his hands were quite steady as he held the watch
out toward her. "Is the inscription right this way . . . eighteen
ninety-four. . . . Is it really thirty years ago? Your father was forty-
nine then, and you were a little girl of ten. You often came along
when he brought me his watches to check them over. Do you remember? Eighteen ninety-four . . . in August, in the year—"

"Will you wrap the watch for me?" She did not want him to rummage around in his memories any further. She had remained peculiar
in this; the house was something that she would share with no one.
"Only a box. . . ."

"No gift wrapping? It's no trouble. And you don't want to look at
the mechanism? Precision, that's what counts."

She pulled her checkbook from her purse and wrote out the amount.
The jeweler walked her to the door. It was clear that he would have
loved to prolong the conversation. "If Herr Hofmann would like to
have a look at his old pieces, just ask him to come in anytime. He
might want to buy back one or two of them. Tell him I'll give him a
good price. Though I don't know what will happen to the shop once
I'm gone. It's been in the family for more than three hundred
years. . . ."

Camilla knew that he had lost both his sons in the war. "I'll tell
my father. I'm sure he'll come."

He held the door for her. The noise from the street grew. "Make
way for the lady." He pushed aside some adolescents. "You'd best
go that way, you're more likely to find a taxi. I wonder where all the
old cabs went. . . ."

The people pressed up against the walls of the houses. Some of
the shopkeepers stood on chairs and boxes so as to be able to see
above the heads of the crowd. The windows were hung with German
and Mexican banners and pennants.

She made slow progress against the stream of spectators. It was
several blocks before it thinned, and by that time she was within
sight of the hotel.

Several luxury limousines were standing at the entrance, their
chauffeurs standing beside them. A red carpet led to the main entrance, which was surrounded by pages. A delivery boy was just carrying a large bouquet of flowers into the hotel.

It was difficult to get by, and she had already been half thinking of looking up her sister. It was not quite five o'clock, and she would get home in plenty of time to have a rest before the garden party that evening.

It still cost her considerable effort to enter the Hotel Bristol. She avoided the place as much as she could, but some of the firm's clients always stopped there, and then there was no getting around it.

Hesitantly she entered the lobby. It was quiet and pleasantly cool after the brooding heat of the streets. She was about to go to the reception desk when she noticed a woman dressed in white speaking to a man near the fireplace. She could not see her face, only a white hat lavishly decorated with white tulle, and two hands in white lace gloves twirling a parasol.

Hesitantly Camilla approached the figure. "Lou. . . ."

The hat straightened. Camilla stared at a face the color of porcelain, with a full red mouth and deep-set eyes with heavily darkened lashes. As in a doll's face, the lids blinked up and down a couple of times. Then Lou put down her parasol, stretched out her arms so that the loose sleeves of the blouse flickered like wings, and came toward Camilla. "Camilla. My darling little sister!"

Strangely, the arms never touched Camilla. Lou held them out wide, and the whole embrace shrank to a fleeting touch of cheeks.

"Well, that's what I call a surprise! Where shall we sit? How about the garden? Truly, I never dared hope for this. My oh my. Just a minute."

She returned to the table by the fireplace, picked up her parasol, whispered a few words with the man who was still sitting there, and then joined Camilla. "Berlin men." She took Camilla's arm. "They haven't changed. Can't leave a woman alone."

Camilla had anticipated the meeting with mixed feelings, but now she could not help but laugh freely. "Is that a very terrible thing for you to find out?"

"Not necessarily. Though I'm dead tired from the trip. I went to bed at once, and I stayed asleep until an hour ago. It must be the air. Shall we sit here?" She pointed to one of the tables underneath a red umbrella. "Of course I was going to telephone you. But I did not want to take you by storm the minute I got here. You're looking well. Can I order something for you? Some ice cream?"

"All right, ice cream. Only vanilla."

She gave the order to the waiter, and Camilla said, "This was so sudden. Are you planning to stay a while?"

"Stay a while? I'm staying for good! I can't quite believe it myself. Back in Berlin! And for good. You know that your son met my train? What a young man he's grown into! How about girls? I bet they run after him! If I were twenty years younger. . . ." The tip of her shoe poked around in the gravel. "Have I aged very much?"

Camilla tried to find the right words, but Lou spared her having to answer by continuing her questions. "And your other two sons?"

"They've become young men too."

"I hear they're at the university?"

"Yes."

"And Papa? You know, I thought he'd take it better than any of you, that's why I wrote to him. Is he still the same? And Mama? And Maxi and Alice? You'll have to tell me everything."

As Camilla answered Lou's questions, she could not avoid examining her sister more closely. And yet she really did not want to look too closely, for there was something in Lou's face that she did not like or, to put it more exactly, that pained her. Yes, Lou had changed. It was not noticeable at first. In the lobby, at the fireplace, she was the same as always, and even out here she was the same as soon as a man came into view, passed them, looked for a table. But at other times it was there, in the bright sunlight: the lines across her forehead and around her eyes; the nose, which had grown more pointed and more imperious; the contemptuous curve that pulled the corners of her mouth a little downward. It was not good to see. It did not even have so much to do with Lou, at least not solely with Lou. Rather, it was the fact that something that had once been beautiful could be destroyed.

". . . and Mama wrote that they boss her around at the Home."

"Visit her. You'll find out soon enough who bosses whom."

"As soon as I have time. First I have to get my bearings a little."

"What are your plans? Will you get an apartment?"

"I don't know. Really, I have no idea what I'll do. I feel good at the Bristol. Even though I never lived here. . . . Were you awfully surprised that time?"

"At what?"

"Well, that time, when we got married, Keith and I. Surely you can't have expected that."

329

"None of us expected it. Suddenly the two of you had disappeared."

"It happened just like that. In the morning we were married in the embassy, and that same night we were on the boat. We had to travel by way of Sweden because of America's entering the war. My God, the time it took us to get a boat then. And what a rotten tub it was! Everything went wrong from the beginning. You know, all I wanted was to get away from here, that time, and he was the only way. I stuck to him like a leech, but for a while it looked as if he weren't going to bite. I was about ready to give up."

She spooned up the ice cream, which was beginning to melt. She had ordered raspberry ice, and it was exactly the color of her polished fingernails. "Did you see him that time he was here, by the way?"

"Just briefly." As Camilla answered, it did not even seem like a lie to her.

"And I thought. . . ."

"What did you think?"

"Not at the time. Actually, not until later, over there. Sometimes I couldn't help thinking, he only took me because he couldn't get you." She looked at Camilla. "I do believe the two of you would have suited one another. But that's all ancient history. Gone and forgotten. Well, that's how it is. I can't live any other way."

"You're divorced?"

"Uncontested. I had a good lawyer, he has to pay. So you see, I won't be a burden on anyone. I can live very nicely in the future. But of course. . . . What is it, Camilla, what am I doing wrong?"

"You don't regret anything do you?"

"No, not that. All the same, it bothers me. What is it? It just isn't working. First every man is crazy about me. Until he gets me. Then the jig is up. That's how it is, I can't hold a man. At forty-three, one should have learned how. But I'll never learn. And one of these days the other won't work any more either. I used to tell myself, I've just had bad luck. But now I know; it's something about me, I can't hold on. That's the thing, everything depends on it. You have your family, a husband, three sons, and you're living in the house in Steglitz again. . . ."

More and more she had adopted a sentimental, lachrymose tone. This, too, was a new trait for Lou. Camilla would not have been

330

surprised if, to heighten the effectiveness of her words, Lou had squeezed out a few tears.

"I'm afraid I've got to be leaving," Camilla said. "We're giving a little party tonight. There are always a few last-minute preparations to attend to. If you think it would amuse you, you're welcome to join us." The reunion with her sister had gone off more smoothly than she had expected. All the same, she was relieved to have gotten it over with.

"So you're back in the old house."

"Yes, for more than three years now."

"Is it just as it used to be?"

"More or less. Well, how about tonight?"

Lou examined her polished nails. "How will I get there? It's pretty far, isn't it?"

"You take a taxi, that's the simplest way."

"A party, you said. Will there be a lot of people? Interesting people?"

Camilla smiled. The same old Lou was back again. "Oh no, just the family more or less, and of course a lot of young people, my sons' friends."

Lou began to pull on her lace gloves, carefully smoothing one finger after another. "I'd like to come, but. . . ." The man who had been talking to her earlier, near the fireplace, had just come out into the garden. He looked around, caught sight of her, and picked the table farthest away. But the moment of passing had been enough for him and Lou to exchange a look of understanding.

Camilla rose to her feet. "Think about it. I'd be pleased to see you, anyway. Or you can come later on. Usually it goes on quite late. The best part is when it gets dark and the Japanese lanterns are lit."

"I don't know . . . my very first night, after the long trip. Perhaps it would be too much for me."

Camilla was about to beckon the waiter, to pay him, but Lou stopped her. "My treat. It was nice of you to come so quickly. Perhaps I'll come see you over the weekend. I'll be in touch in any case. Would you like me to walk out with you?"

"You don't have to."

"I think I'll stay out here a little longer. This air! I've missed it for so long!"

"Let us hear from you." At the door to the lobby Camilla looked back once more. The man had already arisen, ready to move. Lou, all in white, sat at the table in the flimsy garden chair, under the red umbrella, and from this distance she looked like a young girl.

6

It took her a moment to remember where she was and what time of day it was. Though her nap had been brief, she had slept deeply, all the while confused by dreams: Lou—all in white, in a witness box—accused of adultery by Keith; Max at the railing of an ocean liner that was just pulling out; herself down below, on the pier, jammed in the crowd, waving; strange men walking through the house, estimating objects and slapping the auctioneer's seal on them; and her husband, outside in the garden, back in his wheelchair, hands on the wheels, driving straight through one of the rosebeds.

She had not meant to fall asleep, only to rest a little after her bath, before doing her hair and dressing. Now voices from the garden came through the half-open window, and the room, which was almost the same as it had been when she was a girl, once more took on its familiar shapes: the desk, Grandmama's portrait, the curtains of yellow cretonne, the walnut armoire against which was already hung her dress for tonight—blue chiffon, low-cut, with long, narrow sleeves and a wide, twisted silk belt as its only decoration.

She had not yet spoken to any member of the family since her return from the city. Max had already driven off to pick up his girl. Konrad and Georg busied themselves in the gardens hanging the Japanese lanterns. And Senger had retired to his room, she was told.

She had gone to the kitchen, where the platters for the cold buffet had already been set out. She had tasted the punch and given her final instructions. She could not have been asleep for more than twenty minutes. Her watch said eight-thirty. She went to the bathroom to fix her hair and her face, then she put on the blue chiffon. The room was gradually growing dusky, but she did not turn on the light.

Outside, in the garden, it would not be dark for a long time. On days such as this the sky remained bright long after the sun had set behind the grounds. And even when this light faded, the house, with its many brightly lit windows and open doors, continued to spread brightness, as did the lanterns hung around the terrace in the trees. And later still the moon would be high in the sky, brightening the paths and turning the yellow roses in the rondels before the house a snowy white.

She heard footsteps coming along the hall, toward her room. There was a knock. Even before the door opened, she knew that it was her father—she recognized his footstep.

"We're waiting for you." He was wearing one of his natural-color linen suits.

"I'm ready. Is everyone here?"

"I don't know who all has been invited. A lot of young people."

"Is Max here? With his girl? What's she like?"

"I'm supposed to put in a good word for her, but I don't think I need to. You'll like her anyway. A very nice girl. And imagine, with long braids. Ready?"

"In a minute." She picked up the box lying on the desk. She had not wrapped it, for all his life her father had been made nervous by gift paper and ribbons. "I've got something for you."

"For me?" He smiled. "Is this a special day?" He took the case. "Let me guess. A watch."

"That wasn't hard to guess."

"Shall I go on guessing?" He took out the watch. "I bet there's an inscription." He took the watch to the window, where there was more light. He snapped open the lid and peered at the writing. "So it is a special day," he said, "and you didn't forget."

"Did you think I could?"

"Thirty years—no age at all for a house, come to think of it. Do the others know?"

"No."

334

"You know, I was not at all sure whether the day meant the same thing to you that it does to me. My life is over—I mean, I can no longer hope to have any more to show for it than this house. It's the only thing I've accomplished, perhaps because it's the only thing I did with love." He let the lid of the watch snap shut. "Do you remember, the day was a total disaster really. You and I, we were the only ones who knew what was going on, none of the others. We drove out here, I wanted to surprise them, and your mother had a fit. The house stood empty all that fall and winter, we didn't move in until spring. The day was a disaster—the scene she made once we were back home, the tears, not to mention the rest. . . ."

Camilla was thinking, and this day—how will it end? But what she said was, "I'd almost forgotten all that. I only know that this is where I belong, this is my home. It's a good feeling to know that nothing can hurt me here."

He shook his head. "I don't like you when you're so serious. How can you, on such a day. Go on, put a smile on your face. All right, that's better. . . ." He faced her squarely. "Have I ever told you how pretty you are? Is a father supposed to tell his daughter such things?"

"When she's young."

"I'm telling you now. Do you know what I've sometimes thought? If I'd had a wife like you, my life might have been quite different."

"This is my day for compliments," she said, but she did not sound pleased. "First Max and now you. Only. . . ." She did not complete the sentence. "I think we really must join our guests."

"One moment." He unbuttoned his jacket, took his watch from the vest pocket, detached it from the chain, and hooked on the new one. Then he gave her his arm.

The house had been cooler than the garden, and quieter. The grounds were humming with voices and laughter, intermittently broken by the short, dull thud of a wooden mallet hitting a croquet ball. The rings were set up on the lawn on the other side of the long rosebed.

It's an especially good year for roses, Camilla was thinking as she walked across the terrace on her father's arm. In the house, in the vases, they had a different scent, and now at night they gave off an odor that was different from their perfume in the morning or the heat of noon. It was rapidly growing dark. The moon had not yet

335

risen. Someone began to light the candles in the bright Japanese lanterns.

She had caught sight of her husband at the edge of the terrace: alone, holding a glass, he stood staring out at the grounds.

"I'll leave you now," Fritz Hofmann said.

"No, stay with me."

But he withdrew his arm and moved away while she continued to stare across at her husband, standing there like a stranger, a guest who had never before been invited to the house. Perhaps it was only the dinner jacket that created this impression. He was not comfortable in formal clothes, and he could not have worn it more than half a dozen times. She could not remember when she had last seen him in it.

She joined him. Even up close the strangeness remained. The dark material, tautly encasing his body, robbed his appearance of all that was familiar.

"May I get you a glass of punch?" he asked. "It's excellent. When did you start it?"

"This morning. Some people say that you have to let the woodruff ripen in a glass container in the sun, but I think that gives it a bitter aftertaste. Of course the wine you use has something to do with it as well."

At some point during the afternoon she had imagined that their first words would make everything all right, requiring no further explanations, but that was not how it was. He handed her a full glass, and the gesture made the memory of their encounter in his office even more real—of how she had held the glass of iced tea in her hand and been unable to drink.

"I see you're wearing the pearls," he said stiffly.

"Yes." In the afternoon, on her way to the jeweler's, she had stopped at the bank and taken the necklace from the safe. "They lose their luster if you don't wear them now and then." The pearls were dark, almost black, of different size. Originally it had been three necklaces; he had given her one after the birth of each son, and later she had had them worked into one.

"I was hoping that you'd wear them."

Voices came from the lawn. The lanterns were all lit now. "Don't you want to drink your punch? It really is good."

336

"It's Aunt Lenka's recipe." The one word—why couldn't she find it now? "How are you feeling tonight?"

"Better. I . . . we had a talk, the boys and I, this afternoon—"

"Wait," she interrupted.

"Don't you want to hear about it?"

"Yes. But whatever you talked about, and whatever you decided—it isn't very important. The thing between us is much more important." The words were on the tip of her tongue; why was it so difficult to voice them? "I need you."

He looked up from his glass, and it seemed to her that some part of the strangeness was fading. "You need me? Surely it's been just the reverse in the last few years, I'm sorry to say."

She shook her head. "That time when I went to Douai, when I was standing outside the field hospital and the chaplain came out and looked at me as if I were the wife of the man to whom he had just given the last rites—right then I thought, *Let him live.* That was all I wanted. And later—later I was so thankful, so happy. You survived, and nothing else mattered but that."

It was not what she had meant to say. There were too many words. But she went on. "The years that followed, they were very hard for you, and for me too. Not just because of the work in the business that I had to go on doing. There you were—and yet you weren't there, for me. But that was just how it was. I managed somehow. The main thing was that you were alive. But now—now it's no longer enough." She heard Max's voice, calling her. She would never be able to find the right words for what she meant to say, and so she simply contented herself with "I need you. I need all of you."

"Why are you hiding?" Max came toward them, leading a girl by the hand. "There she is," he said, out of breath.

The girl wore a light, high-necked dress with a little pin, and her hair really was wound into long brown braids.

"This is Christina. This is my mother."

The girl leaned forward, in a gesture simulating a curtsey, and her braids fell across her chest.

"I thought they were all gone," Camilla said, "girls with braids."

The girl looked at Max. "First he thought it awfully old-fashioned. Now he's used to it. But I guess I'll be cutting them off soon."

"Tell her not to do it," Max said.

She'll cut her braids off, Camilla thought. She will cut them and save them, as I did for so long, and one day she'll come across them again and ask herself, where did my youth go and what did I get in its stead?

"Don't be in a rush about it," she said.

"You see, my mother says so too." He turned to his mother. "Did Father speak with you? Did he tell you he's dropping his plans and that we've made another appointment with the bank, for Monday?"

"We were just going to talk about it."

"That's all right then. You'll excuse us?" He took the girl's hand. "Come, I've got to show you something—something special."

She curtseyed again, smiled, and allowed him to pull her along. This time, as she ran down the steps of the terrace and across the lawn, the braids flew out behind her.

"A nice girl," Senger said.

"Yes, remarkably nice. And so young."

"You'd like to be young again?"

"No, that's not what I meant."

They stood still and watched the two bright creatures running across the night-darkened grass, coming to a stop under the linden tree.

"Do you think he'll tell her the story of the tree?"

"Oh, yes. He will."

"And you think she'll believe it?"

"Absolutely. When you're that young, it's easy to believe that all wishes will come true."

"And later on?"

"Later on you know that nothing in life is certain. You know that today you get something and tomorrow you lose it again. But some things you can hold on to. Not everything. But love is one of the things you can hold on to."

The young couple was almost invisible now, only two light shades at the trunk of the tree. To Camilla it appeared taller and more majestic than ever.